PRAISE FOR THE BOOKS OF NANCY HERRIMAN

"Intriguing mystery . . . will keep readers turning the pages."
—Anna Lee Huber, National Bestselling Author of the
Lady Darby Mysteries on *No Comfort for the Lost*

"Highly recommended!"
—Historical Novel Society, Editors' Choice on *Searcher of the Dead*

"Well-written and absorbing . . ."
—Historical Novel Society on *No Comfort for the Lost*

"You'll love the intrepid heroine, nurse Celia Davies."
—Victoria Thompson, bestselling author of the
Gaslight Mysteries, on *No Pity for the Dead*

"A tremendously riveting read . . ."
—*Newport Plain Talk* on *Searcher of the Dead*

"Skillful storytelling . . . a standout historical mystery."
—*Publishers Weekly* starred review of *A Fall of Shadows*

D0987653

NO DARKNESS
as like
DEATH

NANCY HERRIMAN

BEYOND THE PAGE
PUBLISHING

No Darkness as like Death
Nancy Herriman
Copyright © 2021 by Nancy Herriman

Beyond the Page Books
are published by
Beyond the Page Publishing
www.beyondthepagepub.com

ISBN: 978-1-954717-03-9

To my fellow Sleuths in Time authors,
because no writer is an island.
You ladies are the best.

✂ CHAPTER 1 ☞

"Is he dead or alive, Mr. Griffin?" Celia Davies asked the man standing across from her, anxious for the answer that might allow her to breathe freely again.

After two months of not.

"My husband—is he dead or alive?" she repeated.

Mr. Griffin grinned, the breeze along the street wafting the rose water scent he wore. He had, she'd come to discover, an interesting smile, his mouth full of white teeth, unlike other men like him. Men who were scoundrels. Gamblers. Thieves.

"Ah, Mrs. Davies. What a question." He winked and held out his hand, wiggled his fingers.

She understood what he wanted, and she reached into her reticule, but not before taking a look around to see who might be watching. On a sidewalk near the wharves and the warehouses, however, folks knew to pay no one any mind. Unless they were shouting *fire*, and even then she doubted anyone would heed the warning.

"Here." She handed him the seventy-five dollars she owed him . . . the money *Patrick* owed him. A small loan from her dearest friend, Jane, because Celia's husband was not here to pay his debt, and Caleb Griffin had been patient enough in waiting for remuneration. He'd made plain to her that he had no intention of continuing to be patient.

"Thank you kindly, ma'am."

He hefted the bag of coins, hesitated—likely wondering if he should count the money out right then and there—before deciding to trust her and hastily tuck it inside his coat, snug against the cardinal red waistcoat he wore. His trademark. His bit of vanity.

"My husband," she repeated once again, a trifle more irritably. Mr.

1

Griffin would know what had happened to Patrick in the months since he'd been reported alive. Mr. Griffin made it his business to know all he could about those he had dealings with. "Please tell me if he is dead or truly alive."

"Oh, he's alive, Mrs. Davies," he answered. "Your husband has gone to the Colorado Territory in search of placer gold."

"Colorado . . ." She thought she'd feel relief to know Patrick was now many miles away. But the tension in her shoulders, in her chest, did not ease. She believed Mr. Griffin. Patrick had brought her to America in search of gold. He was not someone who'd permit his initial lack of success to prevent him from continuing his pursuit. "More gold."

"He's got the itch."

"As I am well aware," she replied and thanked him.

He grinned again, because *he* should have been the one thanking her for finally handing over the sum of money he was due. Not the other way round.

"I pray we never meet again, Mr. Griffin," she said, perking her chin, as she did when she wished to be more in control of a situation than she often was.

"You never know, ma'am, do you? What's gonna happen. You never know."

"I suppose not."

He tipped his hat and rushed off. She stood on the pavement, getting jostled by passing pedestrians who grumbled at her to get out of the way, and stared, long after Mr. Griffin was lost to view.

You never know.

• • •

Nicholas Greaves squinted into the sunlight, which sliced through gaps in the buildings packed tight the length of Pacific Street. Another ordinary late afternoon in this part of San Francisco, sidewalks crowded with longshoremen and warehouse laborers and sailors. Ducking into oyster bars and restaurants. Or turning south, down the lanes that would take them into the Barbary, where more than a meal could be purchased, even at this hour of the day.

He scrubbed fingers through his hair and reseated his hat. A coal wagon rumbled past, and he strode across the street once the path was clear. Bauman's wood sign squeaked in the wind. Three men in dark cotton duck trousers and sack coats ignored his approach and dashed down the steps to the basement saloon, more interested in the sausages Bauman's wife was frying up than in a detective wandering along the plank walkway.

The brothel that used to be located next door had closed, the sign removed, the window shuttered. Nick wondered, idly, when that had happened. Its closure wasn't due to any excessive vigilance on the part of the police, that was certain. So long as folks didn't cause trouble—and that included the ladies who'd once plied their trade in the depths of the brothel's dusky parlors—the cops didn't go looking for it. There was more than enough crime to occupy their time. Once the sun set, crooks and sharpers would ooze through half-open doors, like blobs of tar escaping their bucket, to settle onto the road. They'd stick themselves to every unlit, secluded spot and lie in wait for a greenhorn to wander along. Greenhorns who'd be lucky if the worst result was losing some money.

With a sweep of his hand, Nick wiped dust from his coat and descended the steps. The gas lamps suspended from the ceiling had already been lit, the glow of their flames reflecting yellow off the pressed tin overhead. A fire had been set in the cast-iron stove to heat the room, and the tables were crowded with workers having a meal and a beer. A haze of cigar smoke hung over the room, and the smell of frying meat made Nick's mouth water.

Bauman looked over from where he stood behind the saloon's long walnut bar, drawing a beer. "Mr. Greaves!" His German accent was as round and thick as his chest.

His customers gave Nick cursory glances before returning to their food. He wore nothing that indicated he was a policeman, no uniform, no badge. And if any of them were aware of his occupation, they were convincingly pretending not to care.

"Bauman," said Nick in reply.

The saloonkeeper slid the glass of lager beer across the bar toward a waiting customer. "You return at last, Mr. Greaves."

It had been weeks . . . no, months. It had been months since he'd been inside this saloon. "Miss me?"

The other man laughed. "Do *I* miss you? Or does she? What is it you want to know?"

"Is she in?" Nick asked, squinting at the hallway that led to the quarters at the rear of the building. It would be early for her to be at the saloon, but sometimes she came in to help serve the customers and prepare for the evening's entertainment.

Bauman shook his head before replying. "Ah, Mr. Greaves."

The saloonkeeper had been witness to Nick's drawn-out history with Mina Cascarino. A history that had only in the briefest of moments been what any sane person would call happy.

"She is here," he replied. "Be kind."

"When aren't I?"

Bauman didn't laugh that time.

Nick tapped fingertips to the brim of his hat and wove his way through the tangle of tables and chairs. Mrs. Bauman was bent over her cooking stove and didn't notice him passing in the hallway outside the kitchen. Mina, on the other hand . . .

"Go away," she announced from the doorway to the room she and the musicians used when they weren't out in the saloon performing. A bandana tied over her head secured her glossy black hair, and around her shoulders she clasped a fringed shawl, its color an iridescent blue that altered its shade with her every movement. The checked tan gown she wore was the plainest dress he'd ever seen on her. She looked tired.

Maybe she was simply tired of him. She had every right to be.

"Can we talk, Mina?"

"I don't have anything to say to you, Nick." She spun on her heel and stomped back into the room. "And I don't have time to talk. I need to get to work. Adolph is already unhappy that I asked to leave early tonight. I don't want to anger him more. So, goodbye."

His hand stopped the door before she could slam it shut. "My father's dead."

Of all the places to first go after landing at the dock, he'd chosen to come to Bauman's. To a cramped, musty room with a wobbly dressing table and some chairs shoved into the only corner not occupied by crates and casks of beer. Standing near enough to Mina to see the flush on her smooth cheeks and inhale the aroma of her tuberose perfume. Near enough to take her in his arms if he reached out. But he didn't take her in his arms.

"Why are you here?" she asked, her voice weary.

"My father—"

"Is dead." Her gaze studied his face; he loathed the pity he detected in her eyes. "Condolences on your loss, but what else do you want me to say? What do you want me to do? Tell you that nothing was your fault? Well, I can't say that, Nick, because I don't know that it's true."

"You're probably right."

She dropped onto a chair set before the dressing table, her back to him. "If you're looking for comforting, you should be talking to Celia Davies, not me."

Celia . . . "How do you know about her?"

Mina examined his reflection in the cracked mirror, propped up on the table, the gold paint on its frame worn away in spots from handling. "She lives next door to my family, Nick. And as much time as she spends tending to my siblings' sicknesses and injuries, why wouldn't I know about her?" she asked. "About her and *you*."

"There is not a 'her' and 'me.'" Two months ago, it had become clear there wasn't ever going to be. Celia's husband had returned from the grave. "Her husband's not dead. He's back from Mexico."

"Oh, so that's why you're here. Because her husband's alive. Just get out. Please." In her haste to stand, she bumped against the table, knocking a ribbon-tied box that had been on its surface to the floor.

Nick picked it up. "Candies from Roesler's. With a note attached . . ." He narrowed his gaze to read the handwriting in the dull lantern light. "'From A.S. with affection.' Who's A.S.?"

She snatched the candies from his grasp. Her hands were shaking. "Just leave before I say something stupid or you say something stupid."

"I hope you don't think this is stupid to say, Mina, but I'm sorry." The weight he'd been carrying since his sister had summoned him to their father's funeral became a boulder. A boulder heavy enough to force him to his knees. "Sorry for how I've always treated you."

Her gaze softened, but she kept her distance. "That's nice, Nick, but it's too late. Way too late to fix."

• • •

"Are you positive you can spare the time to get a portrait taken, Cousin? You were gone most of the afternoon," said Barbara. "Maybe we can do this later."

Celia looked over at her cousin and ward. "I can afford the time away from the clinic, Barbara."

"Oh," she replied, frowning.

Barbara resumed staring at the shopfront window they'd stopped in front of, at its sign painted in large block letters on the shopfront window glass. *REBECCA SHAW: PHOTOGRAPHIC GALLERY.* Examples of her craft were on display—tintypes and cartes de visite and sepia-toned salted paper prints. Impressive work. The display was intended, perhaps, to prove her abilities as a photographer. She was, after all, the lone female in San Francisco pursuing such a career.

"Your patient with the milk sickness won't be back today?" her cousin asked.

"I suspect she did not actually have the milk sickness." All the cases Celia had read about in the newspapers had occurred in farm country back East, and were usually fatal. "I sent her home with an ipecacuanha emetic, which, if she takes it, will do a thorough job of purging her of any toxin. She is not likely to return, meaning my calendar is clear."

"Oh."

"You will like Miss Shaw, I promise," said Celia, reaching over to squeeze her cousin's arm. "And I have already given her a deposit, so we cannot back out now."

The window's blinds were pulled up, admitting as much of the light coming in from Montgomery as possible. Inside the shop, Miss Shaw moved about. She was a tall woman in a dark gown, her hair a thick wave of upswept auburn, occupied with rearranging a painted screen that would create their portrait's backdrop. Miss Shaw had yet to note their presence.

"You could probably get the deposit back," said Barbara.

Celia had to applaud her cousin's persistence. The idea to commission a photographic portrait had seemed so sensible when she'd thought of it. Barbara was missing her only friend, who'd gone to Benicia at the end of July to attend the Young Ladies' Seminary there, and Celia had hoped to provide a pleasant distraction.

Clearly, her idea was not working.

"Barbara, what is bothering you?"

Her cousin was eyeing the contents of the window. "I don't want my portrait on display like a . . . like I'm some traveling circus oddity. Or a weird disfigured limb like what they show at the Anatomical Museum."

"I will specifically ask Miss Shaw to not display a copy," said Celia. "We can trust her to be sensitive and discreet. I promise you."

Barbara shifted her attention from the window to the people on the street. The photographic gallery was located in the business district of the city, where well-dressed men marched past and wealthy women strolled in and out of shops, their skirts swishing. Wagons clattered across the macadam road, and the Omnibus Railroad bell clanged as the driver reined in the horses and brought the car to a halt. Newspaper boys sang out the headlines—mostly comments on the shocking victory for the Copperheads in the recent election—and street vendors peddled their wares.

Her cousin wasn't distracted by the commotion, though. She was watching for the pedestrians' reactions to a half-Chinese girl wearing a stylish purple gown, a soberly attired Englishwoman at her side. Waiting for the insults, the sneers that often occurred when she visited an area of the city most Chinese never dared venture into. For once, none came. At least, not as yet.

"If we go inside, Barbara, we can escape the scrutiny," whispered Celia.

Barbara looked up at her. The brim of her bonnet shadowed her face, darkened her eyes. "They're not staring at you. They're staring at me."

"If we go inside, then *you* can escape the scrutiny."

"Okay," said Barbara, her resistance dissipating on an exhalation. "If we're going through with the sitting, I want a carte de visite made so I can send it to Grace in Benicia. I don't want her to forget me while she's away at college."

"You are her dearest friend, Barbara," said Celia gently. "Grace is not going to forget you."

Barbara nodded and reached for the door, pushing it open with a tinkling of the shop bell. It was a happy sound. Insufficiently merry, however, to lift the disquiet that had descended. Celia glanced around, uncertain of what or who she searched for.

"Cousin, what is it?" called Barbara from just inside the doorway. "What's the matter?"

Celia collected herself. "Nothing, Barbara. Nothing at all," she replied and swept inside, letting the door close behind her.

CHAPTER 2

"Sit very quietly, if you will, Miss Walford." Rebecca Shaw cradled Barbara's jaws in her hands, adjusting the tilt of her head.

"I am trying as best I can, Miss Shaw," she answered, her voice taut with misery. "But the support is jabbing into my neck."

"Forgive my cousin, Miss Shaw," said Celia, standing at Barbara's side. She altered her stance to relieve the twinge that had developed in her lower back while waiting for Barbara to settle down. "This is our first experience of sitting for a portrait and we are both a trifle impatient. I offer my apologies."

"There's no need to apologize, Mrs. Davies. And you're definitely not the most impatient subjects I've attempted to photograph." She reached behind Barbara and raised the half circle of iron meant to hold the subject's head still while the photograph was being taken. "Is that better, Miss Walford?"

"Yes, thank you." She gazed up at the woman standing over her. "Who's been more impatient, Miss Shaw? Anybody famous?"

"Barbara, we cannot ask Miss Shaw to gossip about her clients."

Miss Shaw smiled. Celia judged the woman to be near to her own age—twenty-eight or twenty-nine, perhaps younger. She had an earnest appearance that might disquiet some people, but not Celia, and eyes that were the most riveting shade of blue-green. They were presently fixed on Barbara with even-tempered good humor.

"Your cousin is right, Miss Walford. It really isn't wise of me to talk about my clients' foibles." She stepped back and examined the tableau she'd created. Celia would prefer to pose with her medical bag and stethoscope rather than an artificial Roman column and massive potted palm. Too formal an image when Celia's life was anything but formal. "I have my business to consider."

"Maybe it was Mr. Hearst," Barbara persisted. "Isn't that a portrait of him and his family on that easel over there?"

"Yes, that is Mr. Hearst and his family. He and my father are acquaintances." Miss Shaw glanced over at the photograph, a large albumen print nearly two feet high. "I'd hoped to do a portrait of Mr. Twain before he departed the city last December, but I never had the opportunity."

"A portrait of Mr. Twain would have been quite a coup," observed Celia. "As it is, you must be proud to have had Mr. Hearst as a customer."

Miss Shaw's face hardened for a moment before resuming its formerly calm expression.

What an intriguing reaction.

"The portrait was a favor to my father. They know each other because of their mutual involvement in politics." Miss Shaw's words revealed less about her opinion of that acquaintance than the momentary change in her expression had done.

"I believe I have read about your father in the newspaper, Miss Shaw," said Celia. A man whose opposition to universal suffrage Celia did not agree with.

"I'm sure you have, Mrs. Davies." Tersely stated. Miss Shaw leaned forward to straighten a fold in the shawl she'd draped over Celia's shoulders. It had come from the woman's stash of props—bottles of black hair dye and various hats, chairs and tables and drapery, painted scenery to hang if a blank wall proved too boring—the shawl's violet color apparently lending "energy" to the portrait even if the hue would simply become another shade of gray. The material itched against Celia's neck and smelled of photographic chemicals. "I am grateful to him for recommending my photographic services to his colleagues, even though he . . ." She did not complete her sentence.

Barbara finished it for her. "Even though he thinks his daughter shouldn't be operating a photographic gallery and doesn't approve?"

"Barbara, please be polite," chided Celia. Her cousin was being particularly bold that afternoon.

"You don't need to scold your cousin, Mrs. Davies. She's correct about my father's attitude toward my business venture." Miss Shaw turned her attention to the silk ribbon tied around Celia's hair. "However, as I said, he occasionally recommends my studio to his acquaintances, and I'm grateful. My family tolerates me, which is better than what other women with my sort of occupation experience. So long as my progressive ways do not interfere with my father's political ambitions or the smooth running of his bank, our relationship is sufficiently amicable."

If Celia's family were here, rather than in distant England, would they approve of the women's clinic she operated? Doubtful.

"I'm glad he accepts your work, Miss Shaw," said Barbara. "Because your photographs are so fascinating and so . . . genuine."

Rebecca Shaw scanned the interior of her gallery. "I feel as though I am capturing my subjects for all eternity, Miss Walford. Preserving the essence of who they are. A life beyond death." She smiled an apology. "I'm sorry. That's rather morbid."

"But truthful, Miss Shaw," said Celia. "Is your father's portrait among those hanging here?"

Finished with fussing over Celia's attire, Miss Shaw stood back. "He'd been meaning to sit for me, but he's been unwell lately and was forced to postpone."

"Is there anything I might do to help?" asked Celia. "I am a nurse, and I would be happy to lend my assistance."

Miss Shaw flashed a wry smile, as though the idea of Celia providing medical aid to Mr. Shaw was a comical idea. "My father has been experiencing some troubles with his heart lately, which gives him chest pains. He hasn't been able to sleep well as a result, so he's partaking of the water cure at the Hygienic Institute."

"Ah. Of course," Celia replied.

Miss Shaw retreated to her camera, built of mahogany and mounted on a sturdy tripod, a few paces away. "What is your husband's line of work, Mrs. Davies?" she asked, glancing at the wedding band Celia had taken to wearing again. Ever since she'd learned Patrick was alive.

"He pursues gold, Miss Shaw. Elsewhere," she replied. "Due to his absence, I am free to engage in my occupation without interference. I operate a free clinic for females who cannot afford a doctor's care."

Barbara shifted slightly, the shoulder beneath Celia's resting hand tensing. "My cousin does more than simply operate a women's clinic, Miss Shaw."

Oh, no.

"Really?" Miss Shaw asked, her voice muffled by the length of black velvet, firmly attached to the rear of the camera, that she'd draped over her head.

"My cousin means the charity work I do," said Celia.

"No, I don't. I'm talking about your involvement in murder investigations with that police detective, Mr. Greaves."

Miss Shaw lifted the rectangle of velvet cloth and peered around its edge. "Murder investigations?"

"My cousin exaggerates my involvement, Miss Shaw. There is no need to be alarmed." For she *did* appear unsettled by Barbara's comment. To be frank, who'd not?

"I'm not exaggerating," insisted Barbara.

Celia tightened her fingers around her cousin's shoulder, silencing her comments. "Contrary to my cousin's claims, I am not in the business of investigating murders, Miss Shaw." Not intentionally, at least.

"It would be rather daring if you were, Mrs. Davies," said Miss Shaw. "Far more daring than my job as a female photographer."

Far more dangerous. "I am simply a nurse, Miss Shaw, and I regret that my cousin brought up this topic at all," said Celia, relaxing her grip on Barbara's shoulder.

"It's only natural she would," she said, smiling. "It's very intriguing."

Miss Shaw ducked back behind her camera and set about focusing the image, moving the body of the instrument backward and forward. "Ah, I believe that should work." She tightened a screw set in the body of the camera and came out from behind the cloth. "Let me fetch the photographic glass plate and then we can proceed. I'll only be a moment. Don't move."

She strode past and into a room behind them.

Barbara fidgeted.

"Do not move, Barbara. We do not want to have to start all over again."

"I'm sorry about mentioning your investigations, Cousin," whispered Barbara, surprising Celia with the apology.

"I know how concerned you are about my safety." She feared the risks Celia took, the dangers she'd brought to them. "But I believe you alarmed Miss Shaw."

The woman returned with a processed plate of glass held in a frame, a whiff of the chemicals spread upon its surface trailing in her wake, sharp and eye-watering. She hastily slid it into the body of the camera. "Good. Think on what you're most passionate about but do not move an inch. This only requires a few seconds."

She removed the cap from the front of the camera, counted slowly to five, replaced the cap, and drew out the glass plate. "Now to develop the photograph. It'll take a few minutes, but I want to be certain I'm satisfied with the result before I let you leave."

Celia nodded, and Miss Shaw hurried into a tiny dark room nearby. She firmly shut the door behind her, rattling the heavy yellow glass of its small window.

"Furthermore, Barbara, I no longer have any reason to interact with Mr. Greaves," said Celia. Not since early July, the last time she'd had cause to work alongside him. And when they'd been forced to bid each other goodbye. "I expect my days of investigating are past."

• • •

"Sir! You're back from Sacramento!" announced Nick's assistant, J. E. Taylor. Loud enough that everyone else in the basement police station could hear, too.

"Hurray. Detective Greaves is back," smirked the booking officer from behind his corner standing desk, situated near the barred door leading to the holding cells beyond.

Taylor scowled at the fellow and got to his feet. "How was your trip, Mr. Greaves?"

Nick strode through the station, his assistant falling into step behind him. "The stern-wheeler didn't sink. So there's that."

"I was worried, 'cause I thought the boat was supposed to get back a couple of hours ago."

Worried. Taylor worried about him. "I made the mistake of stopping by Bauman's first."

"Oh," said Taylor, a plain short word that expressed a great deal more than simply acknowledging Nick had gone to the tavern. "How was, you know, the—"

"What's been going on here while I've been away?" Nick interrupted. He didn't want to talk about his father's funeral. Didn't want to talk about his family or Sacramento at all.

"Detective Briggs is back."

"Briggs." Nick glanced over at the other desk in the detectives' office. Empty, for now, of the other man he shared the space with. "Back from his leave."

Just when Nick had come to the conclusion Briggs had actually been fired and not sent off to recover from some mysterious illness, which had been the official story. He'd never seemed sickly, though. Irritating, yes. Sickly, not so much. Unless all those fried doughnuts he liked to eat had finally caught up to him.

Nick tossed his hat onto his desk and slid open the street-level window behind it. The musky scent of the cab horses waiting for customers near the square drifted in, along with the sharp smell of coal fires and something rotting in the sewer beneath Kearny Street. The breeze was damp and cool. Not at all like his family's property outside Sacramento, where the air could be dry and hot and fresh.

"Sir?" Taylor sounded concerned.

"The trip from Sacramento was long and boring," said Nick, dropping onto his chair. "Guess I'm tired."

"'Course you are, sir." Taylor retrieved a cigar and a friction match from his inner coat pocket. "As I was saying, Mr. Briggs is back, but he hasn't been in the office much. Maybe he's still sick."

Nick, only partly paying attention, listlessly sorted through the paperwork on his desk. "Maybe."

"You missed the hubbub we had in here a couple of days ago. A local Copperhead politician came in to tell us that he's being followed. Called it 'threatening behavior.' I didn't talk to the fellow myself, but he caused quite a ruckus." Taylor struck his match across a rough section of the wood floor and lit his cigar, the tip flaring red as he puffed. "He's had run-ins with one of his political opponents recently, I heard. Maybe the same person is trying to scare him. But that's all I know."

Emotions had run high all summer and spilled over into the fall, resulting in the anti-Reconstruction Copperheads winning the state elections. So much anger and fear that former slaves—and by extension, the Chinese—might become equals. The burning-hot hatred left over from the war had cast a long shadow, helped along by those willing to continue to stoke the fire. The old healed wound in Nick's arm took to throbbing, and he reached up to massage it. Why couldn't people leave well enough alone?

"Sorry, sir." His assistant shot a glance at Nick's arm. "I didn't mean to remind you of the war."

"Stop calling me 'sir,' Taylor. And I think of the war whether you remind me or not." Nick lowered his hand. "Is the captain expecting us to do anything about this politician's complaints?"

"No, because the fellow spoke with Mr. Briggs," said Taylor. "But I thought you'd like to know."

"Thank you."

"You also missed out on that Mr. Higgins and his hand organ marching down Montgomery last week because of that bet he lost over the election results, sir. Never seen so many folks lining the street to see the spectacle, outside of the Independence Day parade. Just to watch Mr. Higgins grind his organ, a friend of his carrying a tame monkey as they walked." Taylor paused to blow a stream of cigar smoke toward the ceiling. "Quite a sight. Heard he collected nearly six thousand dollars for the orphan asylums, though. A good cause."

An organ grinder and a tame monkey sounded way more enjoyable than a guilt-laden funeral in a dusty Sacramento graveyard.

"Is that it, then? A complaining politician?" asked Nick. "No suspicious deaths to look into? No arsonists to interrogate? No robbers to track down and arrest?"

Taylor peered at him. "You weren't hoping there'd be more problems, were you, sir?"

"Of course not, Taylor." Nick shoved aside his paperwork. "Of course not."

• • •

The front door closed, and Celia looked up from the book she'd been reading since they had finished dinner. Her housekeeper, humming, glided into the parlor.

"Good evening, ma'am, Miss Barbara," said Addie Ferguson, untying the small flower-trimmed hat perched atop her curling brown hair, her eyes gleaming.

"Home already?" asked Celia. "You could have stayed for the entire concert. Barbara and I are perfectly fine here. Unless it was disappointing."

"She doesn't look like the concert was disappointing," said Barbara, reclined on the parlor settee beneath the painting of her father, a novel—The Woman in White by Wilkie Collins—resting atop her lap.

"I've never heard such a lovely rendition of 'The Blind Boy,' ma'am," said Addie. "Oh, the singing made me blubber in front of Mr. Taylor."

When might Mr. Greaves's assistant ask Addie to marry him? Celia wondered, and not for the first time. When might Celia lose the woman who'd been her bulwark against the rough tides of life? As much a dear friend as a servant.

"I am certain Mr. Taylor found your tears most endearing, Addie," said Celia.

"Aye, ma'am, perhaps he did," she mused. She resumed humming and wandered out of the parlor and into the dining room.

Barbara exhaled loudly.

"At least Addie is happy," said Celia. "Have you changed your opinion about this afternoon's session at Miss Shaw's gallery? I thought you'd enjoyed yourself, after all."

"It's not that." Above her head, the painted grin on Uncle Walford's face was the precise antithesis to the frown upon his daughter's. "Is the tutor you hired still planning on coming tomorrow?"

"Now I understand what has been bothering you all day." Celia set aside her book. "Barbara, we've discussed this matter before, and I intend for Miss Campbell to provide you lessons. Beginning tomorrow."

"We aren't going to Sacramento later this week to attend the state fair?"

"We did not ever make plans to go to the fair," said Celia. "And you cannot convince me you are suddenly interested in displays of floral arrangements or farm produce."

"But I don't want to learn French, or improve my singing or my ability to compose essays," she replied. "What's the point?"

"Your father wanted you to continue your education, and I intend to abide by his wishes."

Barbara sighed. "It would be nice to be like Miss Shaw," she said. "Independent and free-thinking. Running a successful business on her own, without answering to anybody. Even if I'd have to pay that completely unfair Chinese police-tax."

Celia seized on her cousin's comment. "Any venture will require more education, Barbara."

"Who'd come to a business I'd run, though? The Chinese do not trust me and the others . . ."

17

Do not either. "You are always welcome to continue to work with me in the clinic," she said. "Perhaps you could even operate it yourself one day."

"I suppose." Barbara grabbed one of the satin cushions and hugged it to her waist. "Why did you ever marry, Cousin? You're just as independent as Miss Shaw, and you love your clinic more than anything."

"Barbara, I love you and Addie. You know I do," she replied fervently. "But when my brother died in the Crimea, I was heartbroken and married impulsively." Ready to fall into the arms of a charming Irish soldier who'd promised to make her forget her pain.

"I never did much like Cousin Patrick."

"I know." He'd never been kind to her cousin; his charm only went so far.

Barbara stared at her, the flames of the overhead gas chandelier washing light across her pale skin, deepening the shadows in her dark eyes. "Cousin Patrick isn't dead, is he? And don't look startled that I know. I've heard Addie talking to you about him. She's loud when she's upset."

"No, he is not dead."

"Which is why you stopped wearing mourning and put your wedding ring back on," she said. "And stopped seeing Mr. Greaves."

Yes. Indeed, yes.

"Will Cousin Patrick move in here?" asked Barbara, when Celia didn't respond. "Or will he take you someplace else?"

"According to someone who should know, Patrick has gone to Colorado and I would be utterly staggered if he ever returned to San Francisco," she said.

"But he might."

"Patrick Davies's existence is neither here nor there, Barbara," she said. "And all I ask is that you give Miss Campbell a chance."

The doorbell chimed, the person outside giving the knob a vigorous twist, startling Barbara. "Were you expecting a patient this late?"

"No."

Addie, muttering, rushed past the parlor doorway on her way to answer. Celia hurriedly followed her into the entryway.

One of the neighbor's children—the eldest of the Cascarino boys, if Celia recalled correctly—stood on the doorstep.

"Come now, Signora Davies. Mina. She is . . . sick." He waved his hand for her to follow. "Come now!"

"I must collect my supplies first," said Celia. "Tell your mother I shall be right there. You understand, yes?"

"Sì," he said and ran back down the steps to the street.

"Addie, I'll need your help changing out of these things and into my working dress," she said. "Barbara, please gather up my medical supplies. Quickly!"

• • •

"Mr. Greaves, you should be resting after your tiring journey." His landlady looked at Nick with a pity so deep that if the emotion were a hole in the ground, the depth of it would reach the center of the earth. Mrs. Jewett wrapped her patterned Oriental robe around her stout frame. "It's after eight and dark as pitch outside. What were you doing out there?"

Nick reached down to pat his dog's head. Riley sat obediently at his feet, his brown-and-white tail wagging, sweeping across the floor in the entry hall. "You didn't need to check on me, Mrs. Jewett. I took Riley out for a stroll around the neighborhood. That's all."

"That dog of yours." She clucked her tongue against her teeth. "He has missed you."

"I was only gone for six days." Six miserable days.

"It was *seven* days, Mr. Greaves, and I missed you, too. There. I've said it."

Nick. The replacement for the son she'd lost in the war. A pitiful replacement, frankly.

"I'm glad somebody beside my dog did." Mina didn't, but why

19

should she? Their relationship was well in the past, and it needed to be left there.

"Bah, don't be saying foolish things like only your dog misses you." Mrs. Jewett peered at him. "I'd guess that lady friend of yours also missed you. Although she hasn't come around here in months."

She didn't mean Mina. And Nick didn't want to discuss Mrs. Davies with her any more than he'd wanted to talk about his father's funeral with Taylor.

"I'll be heading upstairs now," he said, evading the topic. "Good night. Come on, Riley." The dog got to his feet, his tail wagging happily.

"It's not right for you to always be alone, Mr. Greaves," said Mrs. Jewett, stopping Nick.

"I'm not alone. I've got you and Riley."

"Bah." She swatted him on the arm, her smile dimpling her cheek. She must have been a handsome woman in her youth. She was a handsome woman still. "I'll be turning the lamp off here, then. Will you be wanting breakfast in the morning?"

"Yes. Thank you."

A fist pounded on the front door. Riley took to barking.

"Whoever is that at this hour?" asked Mrs. Jewett. "Hush, there, Riley."

"Let me answer it," said Nick.

A street cop waited on the top step, the star sewn to the left breast of his dark gray coat eerily bright in the flare of the gas lamp at Nick's back.

"Sorry to disturb you, sir, but we got a message at the station for you." He tipped his cloth cap at Mrs. Jewett, who'd come to stand behind Nick.

"Can't it wait until the morning, Officer?" she asked. "Mr. Greaves returned today from his father's funeral. He needs to rest."

"Can't wait, ma'am. Sorry," he replied. "There's been a body found, sir. A Mr. Ambrose Shaw. Found in his room at the Hygienic Institute. Could be suspicious."

✍ CHAPTER 3 ☙

The lamps lit in the ground-floor parlor of the Cascarinos' house spilled light onto their barren fragment of a front yard. Mrs. Cascarino waited for Celia in the doorway, a frayed dressing robe tossed over her thin nightgown, strands of her graying dark hair peeking from beneath the scarf tied over it.

"Thank you, Signora Davies," she said, her normally deep and powerful voice muted.

"There is no need to thank me, Mrs. Cascarino." Celia stepped inside, her medical bag swinging at her side. "How is Mina?"

"Bad. So bad. Her face white. Her head hurts her, and her stomach . . ." She made a gesture indicating nausea. "She is so tired she cannot stand. I send for you as soon as I see how sick she is."

The Cascarino children—there were five in total, including Mina, who was the eldest—huddled in the entry and in the front room, their expressions grim, the younger ones clinging to their older siblings. Usually boisterous and happy, they scuffed bare feet against the oilcloth-covered floor, twisted anxious fingers in the fabric of their hand-me-down nightclothes.

Angelo, the youngest boy, stepped forward. "Mina will be okay, si?"

Celia ruffled his dark hair. "I shall do my best, Angelo. You and your brothers and sisters should find something to occupy yourselves with. I will let you know if I need you to fetch Barbara or Addie to help me."

"Si, signora."

"Come, Signora Davies." Mrs. Cascarino climbed the steps, the treads creaking. "Mina is in our room. Away from the children. The noise."

Celia entered the bedroom. Mr. Cascarino, whom she rarely saw because of the long hours he worked, sat next to the bed.

Mina heard her footsteps and looked over, her eyes struggling to focus. "Mama?"

"I am here. Shh, *piccola*. Shh." Mrs. Cascarino hurried to her daughter's side, taking the stool her husband vacated.

"Signora Davies," he said with a polite nod of his head.

Celia greeted him, wishing she had comforting words to smooth the concern on his face. He and Mina had come to America together, years before the rest of the family had been sent for, and his attachment to his eldest child was fiercely strong.

"You make Mina well again, signora," he said.

"I shall do all I can." The room smelled of sickness. Celia went to open the window before going to Mina's bedside. "What has she told you?"

Mr. Cascarino brought a chair for Celia and she sat. "She makes no sense. She came home—she never comes home—she came home, sick. Her mind . . . she remembers nothing. And she looks like this." He gazed down at his daughter. Mina, normally so vibrant, lay wan beneath the embroidered coverlet.

Celia lowered her medical bag to the floor and drew the bedside lamp closer. "Mina? It is Mrs. Davies. I've come to help you."

Her eyelids fluttered open. She squinted in the lamplight. "Mrs. Davies. I feel awful." She drew in a shuddering breath. "I am so tired. So tired . . ."

"Are you in pain?" Celia ran a hand along the girl's bare arm, rousing her before she dozed off again. "Do you have an injury to your head?"

"My head hurts, and I'm . . . I'm so dizzy."

Celia eased her hands beneath Mina's head to feel for any lumps or contusions. Her fingers found what she sought.

"There is a substantial swelling on the back of her head," she replied to Mrs. Cascarino's questioning look. She examined Mina's arms and palms. Her skin was scraped in spots. "Do you recall falling and hitting your head, Mina?"

"I don't. I . . . what has she . . . ? She didn't . . ." She shook her head. "Terrible. It's terrible."

"What's terrible, Mina?" asked Celia. "What do you mean?"

"I don't know. I don't." She peered at her mother, who gripped Mina's hand. "I'm sorry, Mama. Sorry."

"You must not be sorry, *piccola*. Shh. Shh."

Suddenly, Mina blanched and curled into a ball on her side. Celia grabbed the bucket someone had helpfully placed nearby, but the young woman's bout of nausea passed.

"What has happened to my Mina?" asked Mr. Cascarino.

Celia looked over at him, noticing that one of Mina's sisters stood outside the open door at his back, her face blotched with tears.

"She has suffered a concussion, it appears," replied Celia, gesturing at her own head by means of explanation. "Your daughter needs rest. Maybe tomorrow we will learn more about how it occurred."

But would they like what they discovered?

• • •

"Thank you for coming so quickly, Detective." The fellow who'd met Nick at the front door of the Hygienic Institute waved him and the street cop inside. "This is quite alarming."

"I'm sure."

Nick looked around. Glass-shaded gas jets lit the entryway and curving staircase. A patterned runner—clean of the ever-present city dust and grime—covered the checkerboard marble floor. The banister of the oak staircase gleamed, and the air was thick with the scent of roses, an overflowing vase of the flowers in the adjacent parlor. An establishment working as hard as possible to look refined and respectable.

From somewhere nearby—possibly the passageway that crossed the far end of the hall at a T—came the sound of whispers, folks trying to simultaneously gossip and hush one another.

Nick looked over at the man. He must have hastily thrown on his clothes, the buttons of his black frock coat misaligned with their respective holes. "The officer here tells me you've had a resident die, Mr. . . ."

"Ross. Milton Ross. The Hygienic Institute is my facility." Short and thickset, his wide face was bracketed by heavy black whiskers and equally lush eyebrows that moved as he spoke. A pair of wire-rim spectacles perched on his nose, and he blinked at Nick over the top of them. "Yes, one of my patients has passed away unexpectedly. Suicide, I fear."

"A Mr. Shaw, I've been told."

Mr. Ross shuddered. "Yes."

"Have you sent for the coroner?"

"I have," he replied. "I didn't mean to disturb the police, given the nature of the death, but my assistant thought it best."

"Ah." Maybe his assistant wasn't as convinced that Mr. Shaw's death had been a suicide.

"I've sent for Mr. Taylor, Mr. Greaves," said the police officer, dawdling near the front door.

"Thank you." Nick nodded in the direction of the staircase. "Since I'm here, I'd like to see the body, Mr. Ross."

"Yes, certainly, Detective. Mr. Shaw's room is on the first floor above this one, in our largest accommodation and apart from most of our other patients, which are on the upper floors. As he'd requested," he said. "Mr. Shaw is a prominent banker and politician, as I'm sure you're aware. For his peace of mind—very important to his recovery—he wanted our most private and spacious room. I had no idea how fragile he was. I should have recognized the extent of his melancholy, his weakness, but . . . this is dreadful. Truly."

"Yes," said Nick. "Can we go upstairs now?"

"Of course. Please follow me, Detective Greaves." Ross padded up the stairs, light on his feet.

"What exactly goes on here, Mr. Ross?" asked Nick, climbing the steps past the walls covered in flocked paper, the gas lights flickering.

He glanced back over his shoulder. "You are not familiar with the water cure, Detective?"

"Can't say that I am. Is the treatment like what they do at the Turkish-Roman Baths over on Pacific Street?"

"In some ways they are similar. However, we primarily believe in the healthful benefits of perfectly pure, cold water. Although steaming can be salubrious," he replied. "Cold baths, wet bandages and sheets, and drinking plenty of good, fresh water are most beneficial. A plain diet, vigorous exercise, and absolutely no alcohol. Those, Detective Greaves, are the elements of a therapy guaranteed to cure the most stubborn malady. We have treated chronic nervous conditions, headaches, piles, rheumatism, stomach disorders, palpitations of the heart—"

"And what malady was Mr. Shaw hoping to cure?" asked Nick, cutting off the man's litany. "Besides his peace of mind?"

Ross paused at the landing and frowned over the question. "I'm not at liberty to say, Detective."

"A patient has unexpectedly died on your premises, Mr. Ross. I imagine we'd both like to resolve the manner of his death as quickly as possible."

"Our patients are treated in the utmost confidence, Detective. I can't break that trust. No matter the consequences."

"The coroner is going to ask, so you may as well answer now."

The fellow considered Nick over his glasses, using the tip of his forefinger to adjust where they sat on his nose. "A heart condition among other, more sensitive, issues," said Ross. "I see now that he'd become agitated these past few days, rather than refreshed by his treatments. If I'd suspected—"

"How long had Mr. Shaw been a resident at the Institute?" interrupted Nick.

"Since Monday morning."

Three days. "Any explanation for what had caused his recent agitation, Mr. Ross?"

"None."

A door to their left opened and a matron, clutching her emerald silk robe around her small-boned frame, poked her head into the hall. Shaw

25

had clearly not been the sole patient on his floor. "I thought that was your voice, Mr. Ross. Something *has* happened to Mr. Shaw, hasn't it? I knew it. I knew it!"

"Now, now, Mrs. Wynn, there's no need for you to be alarmed," he responded in the soothing voice of a doctor. Or a quack. "Please return to your room."

"No need to be alarmed?" She narrowed her eyes to slits. "We could've all died from gas poisoning, Mr. Ross. Why shouldn't I be alarmed?"

"Gas poisoning?" asked Nick.

"Coming from Mr. Shaw's room," said Ross. "It was . . . ahem . . . the means by which he . . ." He shot a glance at Mrs. Wynn. "You know."

"How he supposedly killed himself," said Nick.

Mrs. Wynn gasped. "Killed himself? Oh, no! Not at all! There was an intruder!"

Ross's face drained of blood faster than Nick had ever seen a body manage, until his skin turned the same shade as the white collar around his neck. He gaped at the woman. "An intruder? There was *not* an intruder." He turned to Nick. "I operate a very safe establishment, Detective. Mrs. Wynn is merely upset."

"Detective?" she asked. "So you *do* believe Mr. Shaw was murdered."

"Can you describe this intruder, Mrs. Wynn?" asked Nick.

"I only caught a glimpse of the person. There, at the end of the hall. Escaping through that door." She pointed to a closed door, the hallway's gas light flickering over its dark wood.

"Could you tell if it was a man or a woman?" Would be helpful to narrow down who he'd be searching for.

"No, not really," she said. "A man? A female wearing trousers?"

Great. "What's beyond that door, Mr. Ross?"

"The staircase leading down to the private side entrance, which is solely used by the occupants of our suite," he said. "Mr. Shaw currently is . . . was the only one with access to it."

The street cop had followed them upstairs and leaned against the wall a few feet away. "Look around for any clues as to how somebody got into the building, Officer," Nick said to him, and he hustled off. "What time did you see this intruder, Mrs. Wynn?"

"Around a half hour after supper had concluded and I had retired to my room," she said.

"Which would make it . . . when?" asked Nick.

"Seven thirty or so," replied Ross. "We serve the last meal of the day from six fifteen to seven. We encourage our overnight patients to retire at that time and rest. Some choose to briefly socialize before turning in, but most are in their rooms by eight."

"Whenever the precise hour was," said Mrs. Wynn, more interested in telling her story than in worrying about the exact time, "I was readying for bed when I heard a door closing. It was too early for Mr. Platt to be making his rounds—"

"Who is Mr. Platt?"

"My evening assistant," answered Ross.

The fellow who'd told him to send for the police.

"As I was saying," continued Mrs. Wynn, "it was too early for Mr. Platt to be making his rounds and Mr. Shaw had already retired to his room for the evening. The sound of a door shutting was very disconcerting."

"How do you know he'd already retired, Mrs. Wynn?"

"On my way down to supper, I noticed him in the private parlor having his meal. He did not care to eat with the rest of the patients," she said. "I'd returned to my room around six thirty and again observed him in the small private parlor. He'd finished his meal and was preparing to return to his room. I expected he did not mean to join the other men in the main parlor."

"Six thirty?" asked Nick. "An awfully quick dinner, Mrs. Wynn."

"I . . ." She pursed her lips. "I did not care for my supper companions and cut short my meal."

"My sincerest apologies, Mrs. Wynn," said Ross.

"So when you later heard a door closing and, naturally curious, you . . ." Nick prompted.

Mrs. Wynn picked up where she'd left off. "I stepped out into the hall, wondering what was going on. It was then I saw a shadowy figure exiting through the far door and smelled gas coming from Mr. Shaw's room. I was too frightened to check on him. Perhaps I could've saved him if I had." She pressed a hand to her mouth and let out a whimper. "I tried to summon Mr. Platt, but nobody answered the bell. After a few minutes, I rang for him again. When a response never came, I went downstairs to locate him. He went into Mr. Shaw's room and found the poor fellow dead."

"I wish you'd mentioned this intruder to me earlier, Mrs. Wynn," said Ross. The fellow was starting to visibly sweat.

"Did you hear anything else, ma'am? An argument, for instance?" asked Nick.

Mrs. Wynn screwed up her face, her brain chasing a memory. "Possibly, Detective," she said. "What should we do? Should we all leave? How did someone sneak into this building and murder a fellow patient? Are those of us left even safe here?"

The last question was followed by a reproachful glance at Ross.

"I'd say any danger is over, ma'am," answered Nick.

Ross, relieved, smiled. "So you see, Mrs. Wynn? There's no need to worry. We'll get to the bottom of this."

"I hope so." She turned on her heel and swept back into her room, slamming the door.

"This is a disastrous situation, Detective. Mrs. Wynn is a frequent guest and is acquainted with all sorts of folks. If she speaks ill of the Institute, who'll be willing to visit?" he asked. "And how can she claim that a stranger snuck into my establishment and possibly murdered one of my patients?"

Because that was what happened? "Which room is Shaw's?"

"That one." He pointed at a door that stood ajar at the end of the hall. Not far from the door to the stairs. A pair of men's shoes sat just outside, waiting for a polish by whoever took care of such things at this place. "Those are Mr. Shaw's shoes," said Ross, observing the direction of Nick's attention.

"Mrs. Wynn looks to be correct that he'd gone to bed for the evening."

"He did tend to retire earlier than the others." Ross started down the hall toward Shaw's room. A brass plaque labeled *Blue Suite* hung on the door. "If there was an intruder, do you think it's possible he was the one who turned on the gas jet?"

"Maybe."

Shaw's suite consisted of two rooms, the hallway door letting onto a small sitting room, the bedroom immediately off to their right. A cane and black silk plush hat waited near the door. A pamphlet about the water cure had been strategically left on the marble-top table in front of a sofa. The window shade had been pulled down for the night, and if the space had once smelled of coal gas, it didn't anymore. The fixture was next to the door, and Nick turned the stopcock, which moved easily, gas releasing with a hiss.

"When Mr. Platt notified you about Mr. Shaw, he didn't mention that Mrs. Wynn had reported a trespasser?" asked Nick, tightly shutting the valve.

"When I arrived here from my house—I don't live far away—all he told me was that she was hysterical," said Ross.

He glanced toward the bedroom and shuddered. The door was ajar. A man's bare forearm was visible through the gap, the rest of the fellow sprawled out of sight atop his bed.

"Poor Mr. Shaw," breathed Ross.

Nick entered the bedroom. Shaw, dressed only in a nightshirt, sagged into the large four-poster bed's mattress. His slippers were tucked beneath the bed where Shaw had left them. He was a robust fellow, his hair graying, which made the washed-out color of his face look all the more blue. Nick leaned over his body. There weren't any obvious signs of trauma, no cut wounds, no bruises, no blood on the sheet underneath him.

"What do you think, Detective?" asked Ross, standing in the doorway, his gaze fixed on some spot above Nick's head. Queasy, maybe? "Death from gas asphyxiation?"

"The coroner will make the determination, not me," he said, straightening.

Shaw had pulled back the sheets and laid down, his arms at his side. No indication, that Nick could see, that he'd been attacked and had attempted to fight back. A casual glance might make somebody think Shaw was simply asleep, his mouth slack-jawed, a snore due any minute. Peaceful-looking, almost. Aside from the unhealthy color of his skin.

"Anything stolen from the room?" he asked.

"I haven't thought to check, Mr. Greaves," said Ross, his attention apparently now occupied by the floral pattern of the paper on the walls. Looking at dead bodies, even ones without signs of trauma, could be pretty nauseating.

"I'd guess that private entrance at the bottom of those stairs is normally locked," said Nick.

"Yes, and only I, Mr. Platt, and Mr. Shaw had a key."

As if on cue, the street cop bounded into the room. "I found a side door unlocked, Mr. Greaves. Not forced. Plus, look what I discovered outside the door. In the alley."

He held out the item he was carrying. A woman's fringed blue shawl.

An iridescent blue that altered its shade with its wearer's every movement.

• • •

"What's going on, sir?" asked Taylor, his notebook tucked under his arm. Did he keep it with him wherever he went? He had to have come straight from his lodgings—with his notebook. Dressed more nicely than usual, though, his shoes polished, a clean collar and new tie about his neck.

"I didn't mean to interrupt your evening, Taylor."

He blushed; his assistant was prone to blushing. "It's okay, sir. I was back at home when I got the news."

"Well, to answer your question, a local politician is dead. Discovered after an intruder was noticed outside his room," said Nick.

He'd left Ross upstairs, busy calming his various patients. Keeping the bunch of them from stampeding downstairs and getting in Nick's way. From the doorway of Ross's office, Nick eyed the evening attendant. He'd taken up a position near his boss's massive walnut desk and its neat stacks of paperwork.

"No obvious wounds, though," Nick added. "At least not that I noticed."

"So how'd he die?"

"Heart failure? Or maybe coal gas exposure." Nick shrugged. "Who was that politician who'd come into the station complaining about suspicious people stalking him?"

"Mr. Shaw, sir. Ambrose Shaw."

"Well, we won't be hearing from him again."

Taylor glanced up at the ceiling, at the floors overhead he couldn't see. "He's the dead man?"

"Yes," he said. "I need you to locate Mina Cascarino and quickly. Try Bauman's, her lodgings, even her parents' house on Vallejo. I'll question the night attendant on my own."

Taylor's forehead puckered. "Mina Cascarino? What's she got to do with Mr. Shaw's death?"

Why was your shawl outside in the alley, Mina? "I'll explain later, but I need you to hurry."

"Yes, sir," said Taylor. The night attendant watched him leave.

Nick closed the door behind his assistant. "Mr. Platt—that's your name, right?—why not come over here and take a seat." He turned one of the chairs in front of Ross's desk to face the center of the room.

Platt hesitated but sat down. He had stick-straight red hair cut very short, leaving him looking like a smallpox victim whose head had been shaved as part of the treatment and only now was his hair growing back. The man wasn't sickly, though. He had a thick torso and a heavy jaw, making him appear just as robust up close as he had from across the room.

Nick leaned a hip against the edge of the desk and folded his arms. "How long have you been employed at the Hygienic Institute, Mr. Platt?"

"I've been here four years, Detective."

"And what do you do as night attendant?"

"It's my job to help any of our overnight patients, if they need something," he replied. "If a serious problem develops, I'm to send for Mr. Ross."

He stared at Nick down the length of his broad nose, which had been broken once and poorly repaired. Overall, Platt was average and unremarkable-looking. Maybe better-looking before his nose had been rearranged. A face belonging to the sort of man Ross would trust to tend to the Institute in his absence. Not a fellow to mess with.

"You have a room in the building, Mr. Platt?"

"Not much. Just a place to wait between my rounds," he said. "I have lodgings a few blocks away."

"The patients can summon you with some type of bell system, is my understanding," said Nick.

"Yes."

"Did anybody summon you tonight?"

The edge of Platt's right eye twitched. Not much movement, but Nick was used to closely watching the people he was interrogating. *They'll give it away, Nick.* That's what his Uncle Asa would tell him, back when his uncle was around to give advice to a green cop aiming to also become a detective. *They'll give it away with their hands or their feet, or their faces.*

"I didn't hear the bell, because I was down in the parlor helping our cook clean up a mess some of our guests had caused."

"Is the cook still in the building?" Somebody else to question.

32

"No, I told her I'd finish straightening up the parlor, so she left and missed all the fun."

Nick would get Taylor or one of the men to speak with her as soon as possible. "You insisted that Mr. Ross send for the police. Why didn't you believe that Mr. Shaw had killed himself?"

"A man like that, rich and smug?" asked Platt. "He's the type of fellow who has a mighty positive opinion of himself. And is able to convince others to share that opinion, too. Not the sort who wants to end his life by turning on a gas jet."

But the sort who would have enemies. "Mrs. Wynn claims to have glimpsed an intruder around seven thirty. Did you notice any strangers in the building?"

"Is that what she was going on about?" he asked. He shook his head. "I didn't notice a stranger, Detective. But I'd been in here with Mr. Ross—I arrive around seven and we review who's in residence overnight who might need special assistance—then went to help Mary Ann in the parlor."

"The alley door to the private entrance was found unlocked," said Nick. "We're presuming that's how the trespasser got inside."

"I hadn't made my rounds yet to inspect the outer doors," he replied calmly. Not easy to ruffle. "It's usually kept locked, though."

"What time again was it that you helped the cook clean the parlor?"

"After I'd seen Mr. Ross out the front door," he said. "Tonight, a couple of our male patients had stayed up to play cards. Mary Ann heard a crash in the parlor and came running to find me. Must've been . . ." He glanced at the clock ticking on the wall to Nick's left. "Must've been five or ten minutes before seven thirty. They'd broken a crystal pitcher and a couple of glasses, which took a long time to straighten away. Mary Ann had stayed past when she usually left, so I told her I'd finish and was heading for my room when Mrs. Wynn barreled down the main staircase, shrieking about Mr. Shaw."

So far, his story was consistent with hers. "So you went to check on the fellow and found his door ajar . . ."

"Unlocked, not ajar," he corrected. "I smelled the coal gas, knocked, and called out to him. He didn't answer, so I went inside and found him on his bed. It was clear he'd died, so I went to Mr. Ross's place and alerted him."

Nick contemplated Platt, uncertain what to make of the man. "What's your opinion of Mr. Ross and his operation here, Mr. Platt?"

The night attendant paused about the amount of time required to breathe out and in before producing a response. "I think it's all quackery."

Hmm. "Does Mr. Ross know that you doubt the usefulness of the Institute's treatments?"

"Do I look like I want to lose my job, Detective?" he asked. "He's a decent enough man. Even if he doesn't always pay my wages on time."

Nick raised his brows. "Financial problems at the Hygienic Institute?"

"You didn't hear it from me, Detective Greaves."

• • •

"If you do not mind, Mrs. Cascarino, I will stay overnight," said Celia, stretching to ease the ache in her back. Once she was alone, she intended to loosen the ties on her corset.

Mrs. Cascarino glanced over at her daughter. "Her head . . . she get well?" she whispered.

Celia smiled reassurance. "It may take some days. Do not worry."

Feet pounded along the hallway, and Angelo charged into the bedchamber. "A police officer is at the door, Mama."

"Nick?" asked Mina, her eyes fluttering open.

Nick? "Do not try to get up, Mina. You need to rest," said Celia.

"Mr. Taylor is here," said Angelo.

"Why does a police officer come?" asked Mrs. Cascarino. "We do nothing wrong. We do not cause trouble."

"I will speak with the officer and discover what he wants." Celia stood, apprehension clenching her stomach. *Terrible. It's terrible* . . . She opened her medical bag and drew out one of the bottles. "Pour a few grains of this powdered ginger into a glass of water and see if Mina can swallow some. It might help settle her stomach. I shall return once I have finished speaking with the policeman."

Celia hurried from the bedchamber, Angelo speeding down the stairs ahead of her. Raised voices echoed up the staircase. Children chattering and crying. Mr. Cascarino shouting in both English and Italian.

"What has she done?" shouted Mr. Cascarino, waving a finger in Mr. Taylor's face. "Nothing! You no arrest her."

"Mr. Cascarino, I doubt that the police officer is here to arrest your daughter," said Celia.

"Mrs. Davies!" exclaimed Mr. Taylor. "I sure am glad to see you!"

"You know this man?" Mina's father asked Celia, his tone accusing.

"Please, Mr. Cascarino, Mr. Taylor can be trusted. You need not stand so close to him," she said. He backed away. "Mr. Taylor, what brings you here?"

"I'm looking for Miss Mina, ma'am," he said, glancing nervously at Mr. Cascarino. "Is she home? I couldn't tell what this gentleman was saying."

"She is. Why?"

Mr. Cascarino eyed him suspiciously. "He want to arrest her. That is what he want." He looked over at Celia. "Tell him to leave. He listen to you, signora."

He might, more than Nicholas Greaves ever did. "I do not understand what is going on, Mr. Taylor."

"Neither do I, ma'am. Not exactly," said Mr. Taylor. "But it's got something to do with a dead man."

✂ CHAPTER 4 ✂

"Greaves. There you are." Dr. Harris, bent over Shaw's body, looked over when Nick entered the room. He must have rushed to get there, his hair sticking up on the crown of his head, his shirt clumsily tucked into his pants.

"Sorry to have disturbed you so late," said Nick.

"Don't worry about the hour, Greaves. Death rarely arrives at a convenient time, and I'm used to that," said the coroner, tidying his shirttail. "What's the story with our gentleman here?"

"This is Mr. Ambrose Shaw, a banker and politician, lately a member of the Copperhead party," said Nick. "In residence at this establishment to treat a heart condition and other illnesses of a personal nature."

"Mr. Shaw here looks to be the right age and physical condition for such problems," he said. "So why am I here, if the fellow died in his sleep of heart failure?"

"Suicide was initially suspected," said Nick. "The gas had been turned on, and Mr. Ross claims Shaw had been agitated recently."

"But you're thinking foul play."

"Shaw came into the station recently to report that somebody had been stalking him," said Nick. "Plus, one of the patients reports spotting an intruder outside Shaw's room not long before his body was discovered."

A person who might've been Mina Cascarino, he should've added. Harris didn't need to know her name, though, and Nick wasn't ready to believe she could be involved. Despite the evidence of a shawl that he'd last seen draped over her shoulders.

"An intruder or one of Mr. Shaw's fellow patients?" asked Harris.

"The patients have been accounted for. Plus, we think we've figured out how a trespasser got into the building. There's a private entrance and Shaw was given a key, but we can't find it anywhere." The street cop who'd discovered Mina's shawl had thoroughly searched the suite. "The intruder must've gotten ahold of Shaw's key somehow."

"Ah," murmured Harris. "What time was the intruder observed?"

"About seven thirty. Maybe a little later."

"Not even an hour and a half ago . . ." Harris dragged his fingertips through his graying beard. "I would have guessed the fellow has been deceased longer."

"He didn't die around seven thirty?" asked Nick.

"I'm saying I'm not positive he's only been dead for an hour and a half," he replied. "But it's possible."

"What about gas exposure?"

"I'll have to do an autopsy of course, inspect the air passages for inflammation and phlegm, but I believe it's common for rigidity to set in during cases of coal-gas poisoning, which I don't see here beyond the usual rigor mortis that is beginning to occur." Harris crossed to the dressing table and peered inside the pitcher on top of it. "When was Mr. Shaw last seen alive?"

Nick thought back to what Mrs. Wynn had reported. "Around six thirty."

"And his body was discovered at seven thirty, after an intruder was spotted?" he asked. "An hour's not enough time to have died from exposure to coal gas, Greaves. Not even if the gas flow was extremely high."

Interesting. "So the gas was meant to make us think he'd tried to kill himself?"

The coroner poured water into the adjacent basin to rinse his hands. "I suspect Mr. Shaw was already dead from another cause, and the gas was turned on for one of three reasons—to ensure Shaw died, to make his death appear accidental, or, lastly, to look like suicide, as you say."

"So how *was* Shaw killed?"

Harris dried his hands. "It's just a thought, but how he might've come to die from that here . . ."

"Care to be more specific, Harris?"

"Sorry about being vague, Greaves," he said, flashing an apologetic smile. "Note the redness around Mr. Shaw's nose, as though the skin had been exposed to a chemical that had inflamed it," he pointed out. "The last time I saw redness like that was on a woman who'd visited her dentist and had received chloroform as an anesthetic. Too strong a dose, as it turned out. Dangerous stuff in the wrong hands. Even in the right hands."

"Chloroform?"

"Just a hypothesis, and I'm not all that sure it makes sense. Although I did find this wedged beneath Mr. Shaw's body." He pulled a white linen handkerchief, its edge embroidered with gray thread, from his vest pocket. "Perhaps soaked with chloroform and applied to his face to sedate him. Unfortunately, the substance is highly volatile and the smell dissipates rapidly. The man had good taste in handkerchiefs, though."

"What happened to that woman who visited her dentist?" asked Nick.

"Oh, didn't I say? She died," said Harris. "When her heart failed."

• • •

"Who is the deceased, Mr. Taylor?" asked Celia.

It had taken an age to calm the uproar his comment about a dead man had caused, but somehow Celia had settled the Cascarino family. Reluctantly, Mr. Cascarino had given her use of the parlor to speak in private with Mr. Greaves's assistant. Celia was not so naive, however, as to imagine many ears were not pressed against the closed door between them and the entry area.

Mr. Taylor stood in the center of the room, his heavy policeman's shoes depositing dirt on the floor's threadbare oilcloth. He was unable to sit as every chair and table was covered by scraps of material waiting to be sewn into shirts, which would be sold to supplement the

Cascarinos' meager income. He gripped his hat and looked as distressed as Celia felt.

"Mr. Ambrose Shaw, ma'am," he answered.

"The politician?" *What an amazing coincidence.* "I'd heard he was unwell and receiving treatment at the Hygienic Institute."

"Seems so. But he's gone and died in a suspicious fashion."

"What has his death to do with Mina?"

"Mr. Greaves wouldn't say, ma'am," he replied. "He just wanted me to find her as quick as I could and report back when I did." He glanced at the door as though he hoped to make his escape right then.

"Mr. Greaves must have a reason to connect Mr. Shaw's death to Mina," she pointed out. "Some clue or evidence linking her to the fellow."

Mr. Taylor hesitated, his mouth twisting.

"You can tell me, Mr. Taylor," she said. "I expect I shall learn the story from Mr. Greaves himself soon enough."

"Well, I heard from the local policeman who patrols the area around the Institute that he found a shawl in the alleyway next to the building."

"A shawl." That was the evidence? Nicholas Greaves must have a strong reason to believe the item belonged to Mina, though.

"Was Miss Mina here all evening, ma'am? Do you know?" Mr. Taylor asked, sounding hopeful she might reply in the affirmative.

"She was not, Mr. Taylor," she answered. "She stumbled home sometime before eight with a concussion and no recollection of the evening's events."

Other than to mutter about something terrible having occurred.

He frowned. "That's not good, ma'am."

"No, it is not, Mr. Taylor."

• • •

"This is absolutely horrible, Detective," said Ross, pacing the rug spread across his office floor. "Do you have a report from the coroner?"

"He'll have to perform an autopsy to be certain of the cause of death, but it does look suspicious," Nick answered.

"That trespasser . . ." Ross took a seat on the nearest chair and pulled off his spectacles. "Oh my. Oh my, oh my."

"I'm hoping you can answer a couple of questions, Mr. Ross."

"What could I possibly tell you, Detective?" He blinked nearsightedly at Nick. "I was at home while all of this transpired."

They'd be confirming that, too. "The private entrance to the side staircase . . . we've searched for Mr. Shaw's copy of the door key and it's missing."

"Oh, that," he said. "Mr. Shaw informed me yesterday that he'd lost his key. I sent to have a copy made, but I haven't received it yet."

"Did Mr. Shaw have any visitors this week?" Somebody who'd helped themselves to the fellow's key, planning on coming back later and making use of it.

Ross dug out a handkerchief to wipe his glasses before returning them to his nose. "His family had been to visit. His wife, son, daughter."

"Any other visitors? Lady friends, for instance?"

"Ladies visiting here?" Ross clawed at his shirt collar like it was choking him. "I do not run that sort of establishment!"

"Of course not. Just thought I'd ask." Nick examined the room, took in the polished furniture, the books on shelves and tables. A set of porcelain statues purchased in the Chinese quarter. The worsted damask curtains at the window. All in all, tasteful and comfortable. And expensive to sustain. "You don't store chloroform on the premises, do you, Mr. Ross?"

"Chloroform? I don't comprehend why you're asking . . ." The reason dawned on him. "It has to do with Mr. Shaw's death, doesn't it? He wasn't killed by gas asphyxiation?"

"Do you store chloroform on the premises?" Nick repeated.

"No. Not at all. We don't make use of the substance." Ross's eyes were weirdly large behind the lenses of his spectacles. "His assailant brought it with him. Isn't that what occurred, Detective?"

"Maybe so, Mr. Ross."

• • •

"You may not speak with Mina this morning, Mr. Greaves," said Celia, entering the Cascarinos' sunlit parlor and closing the door behind her.

After Mr. Taylor's visit last night, she'd anticipated that the man he worked for would eventually turn up. She wished, though, that Mr. Greaves had waited until she'd had a chance to have a cup of strong black tea. She'd spent the night sleeping–attempting to sleep–on a chair next to Mina's bed and every muscle ached with exhaustion.

"Good morning to you, Mrs. Davies," he replied, dragging his hat from his head. The gaze that met hers revealed little emotion. Nothing beyond the cool aloofness he often and easily enwrapped himself with, as readily as drawing on a coat. "You look well. Taylor told me you were here."

She waited for him to say more, which he did not.

What did she expect? That he might claim to be pleased to see her? That he'd missed her these past months, even though he had said goodbye? She'd gotten used to not seeing him, and now to be face-to-face once more . . .

Stop with the sentimentality, Celia. Mina was in trouble, which had to be her primary concern.

"I would return the compliment, Mr. Greaves, except that you look rather tired." Weary, worn out, his soft brown eyes shadowed. "Addie told me you'd gone to Sacramento. You have family there, I believe."

"Taylor's been gabbing."

"Should he have not mentioned that you were away?" she asked.

"My father died. That's all."

He meant to sound flip, but she heard the misery in his voice. "And you regret not seeing him before he passed away." Her guess struck home, if she read his responding expression correctly. Which was never an easy thing to do.

41

"I do regret not mending fences with him before he died, but what's done is done," he replied. "And I'm not here to discuss my trip to Sacramento."

"You are here to speak with Mina, of course. Her condition has improved from last night, but her concussion has left her with amnesia and she cannot explain what took place," she said, yawning behind her hand. "Mr. Taylor relayed that Mr. Ambrose Shaw has died. Suspiciously, I gather."

"Harris thinks so."

"Then it must be the case," she said. "Please do sit down, Mr. Greaves, because I fully intend to." She dropped onto a chair across the room from him.

He removed a bundle of shirts, in the middle of being sewn, from a stool and sat. "When did Mina arrive here last night?"

"One of the children came to fetch me to tend to her about eight in the evening," she replied, feeling for unpinned strands of hair and wrestling them back into place. His eyes, she noticed, traced the movement of her hands as they worked. "I would guess Mina had arrived ten minutes earlier. Possibly more."

"Ten minutes . . ."

She could see him calculating what the hour meant, and the solution to his calculation was not encouraging.

"You suspect her of involvement in a man's suspicious death because you found a shawl, Mr. Greaves?" she asked. A loud gasp followed by a murmur of young voices rose in the entryway beyond the parlor's closed door. Mina's siblings must have gathered outside to eavesdrop. Mr. Cascarino called to them in Italian from another part of the house, and several of them pattered off.

"An intruder was seen outside Shaw's room around seven thirty, Mrs. Davies," he replied, turning his hat through his hands. "His body was found shortly afterward. Her shawl was discovered out in the alley."

"The intruder has been identified as Mina Cascarino?"

"No, but the shawl we found is the blue one she always wears," he said. "She didn't have it on when she showed up here last night, did she?"

"I shall have to ask," she replied, acutely aware she hadn't noticed a blue shawl in the bedchamber Mina was currently occupying. "But many women own blue shawls, Mr. Greaves. How can you be so positive the one found is hers?"

"Until you prove it's not hers, ma'am, I'm going to suspect it is," he said. "She knows Shaw, based on the box of candy I saw in her possession yesterday afternoon signed 'A.S. . . . with affection.' Pretty damning, if you ask me."

"A shawl and a box of candy."

"And a concussion," he added.

"There could be an entirely innocent explanation for her concussion, Mr. Greaves." Hair pinned as well as she could manage, Celia lowered her hands to her lap. "Furthermore, a murderer is not likely to promptly smack themselves on the back of the head after committing the crime, are they?"

"I'd say that would be unusual, ma'am," he replied. "More likely she was an accomplice."

"Oh, Nicholas, honestly. You truly believe that of her?"

He began to knead the spot on his arm, the location of a wound he'd endured during the war, which tended to ache when he was unsettled. "I *have* to suspect her, Mrs. Davies. And there's more. Taylor went to Bauman's last night before coming here and running into you. She left around six thirty because she had 'plans.'"

Over an hour elapsing with no explanation of where she'd gone or what she'd done. "You are positive there was an intruder at the Hygienic Institute."

"Our witness is positive," he replied. "On top of that, the outside door to a private staircase leading to Shaw's exclusive first-floor suite was discovered unlocked and the man's copy of the key, missing."

"You are assuming the intruder made use of this missing key, which they'd acquired . . . how?"

"They'd either taken it from his room—his wife and children had gone to visit him at the Institute—or Shaw had given the key to them," said Mr. Greaves. "Not expecting the person might use it in order to kill him."

She'd have to search Mina's things for that key.

"How precisely did Mr. Shaw die?" she asked. "His daughter, Miss Rebecca Shaw, told me he was being treated for a weak heart. And before you ask how I know her, Barbara and I happened to have been at her photographic gallery having our portrait taken yesterday afternoon."

He chuckled wryly and gave his arm a final rub before dropping his hand. "Why am I not surprised, Mrs. Davies, to learn you know the Shaws?"

"I have met his daughter, that is all," she said. "How did he die?"

"There are what appear to be chloroform burns on Shaw's face," he said. "His heart may have failed as a result, but the person responsible wasn't taking any chances and turned on the gas in his room to be positive. Or to make us think it was an accident."

"Chloroform." What a curious choice of weapon.

"Mr. Ross, the proprietor, informed me he doesn't use it, so Shaw's killer had to have brought the chloroform with them."

She was fatigued and not thinking clearly, but the events he'd outlined seemed implausible. "If I may, Mr. Greaves, the scenario you are proposing is as follows—Mina, who'd somehow obtained Mr. Shaw's key, crept into his room, managed to subdue him with chloroform, which may have resulted in his death, turned on the gas, fled, dropping her shawl, mysteriously ended up concussed, and stumbled home."

"A tidy summary, Mrs. Davies."

It was. Too tidy. "Have I described the actions of the Mina Cascarino you know, Mr. Greaves?" she asked. "Tell me the truth. Would she do this? For I suspect she would not."

"It doesn't matter what you or I think, Mrs. Davies," he replied. "Because, so far, the only evidence we have points to her."

"We must prove her to be innocent, Mr. Greaves. We must find who is actually responsible."

"'We,' Mrs. Davies?" he asked with the slightest of smiles.

"'We,' Mr. Greaves. One more time," she replied earnestly. "For Mina's sake."

• • •

For Mina's sake.

"Well, sir?" asked Taylor, trailing Nick into his office, a steaming cup of coffee in his hand.

"Mina Cascarino still doesn't remember what happened last night." He picked up the shawl his assistant had left atop his desk, disturbing a stack of papers, which fluttered onto the floor. Last night, he'd been positive it was Mina's. This morning . . .

"You saw Miss Mina?" asked his assistant.

Nick lifted an eyebrow. "'Miss Mina,' Taylor?"

"I go to Bauman's, sir. She's got a nice voice."

"She does." He dropped the shawl back onto the desk. "Oh, and Taylor, you don't have to keep Addie Ferguson apprised of every blessed thing I'm doing, okay?"

His assistant blushed a darker red than Nick had ever seen on his face, and Taylor had done an awful lot of blushing in the many months he'd worked for Nick. "She asks about you. I'm not gonna not reply."

Damn. "It's all right. I'm just being irritable," he said, bending down to retrieve the papers. He noticed an ant crawling across the floor and crushed it with his boot. "And to answer your question, I didn't see Mina. Mrs. Davies wouldn't let me."

Taylor started to laugh but quickly stifled the sound, pretending instead to be overtaken by a bout of coughing. "She wouldn't let me see Miss Mina, either."

"You told Mrs. Davies about finding the shawl."

"She insisted that she'd get you to tell her about the case if I didn't," he said. "So I did."

"That's okay too, Taylor." The woman had a way of convincing the most reluctant individual to blab. An ability that had come in handy before and might again. She had looked well that morning, he thought. And damn if he hadn't missed her.

"I gotta be honest, sir," said Taylor, pausing to sip from his coffee. "I can't imagine Miss Mina getting tangled up in a mess like this. Or why she'd get involved with some fellow like Mr. Shaw."

Why *would* she be interested in a man old enough to be her father? Maybe Shaw had been charming, sensitive, generous. All the things Nick had never been.

"Did you have a chance to check on Platt's story about being downstairs until Mrs. Wynn came looking for him?"

"The other patients confirm that they were in the parlor until . . ." He set down the cup and consulted his ever-present notebook. "Until a few minutes before seven thirty, sir. They were pretty sheepish about the mess they'd caused, and that both Mary Ann Newcomb, the cook, and Mr. Platt had to clean up. One fellow saw Miss Newcomb leave the building while Mr. Platt was still in the parlor, sweeping up broken glass."

"So maybe we can exclude Platt and the cook from consideration, although I'd like to hear her version of events," said Nick. "Did any of the other patients report spotting this trespasser?"

"No, but would they have if he'd come in through that private side door?"

"Had to ask."

Taylor closed his notebook. "What do we do next, sir?"

"Tell Mullahey to question Miss Newcomb, specifically to learn if she can back up Platt's story and if she noticed an intruder," he said. "Meanwhile, we go visit the Shaws."

"I hear they've been told Mr. Shaw died from a simple heart attack," said Taylor. "Why would we show up at their house to ask questions?"

"His wife and children dutifully visited him at the Institute earlier in the week, and Shaw's key—the one he'd been supplied that unlocked the private side entrance—is missing. Maybe one of them took it."

"They won't admit to taking that key," Taylor pointed out.

"No, but we do need to get their alibis for last evening. If they can provide any. I also want to ask them about the threatening individual Shaw reported following him. If Mina isn't involved in Shaw's death, despite the evidence against her so far, then maybe that person is," said Nick. "Maybe they'd intended to do more than simply scare Shaw, Taylor. Maybe they'd wanted him dead. And now he is."

• • •

"Mrs. Davies, you're back," said Mina.

"That I am," said Celia. She'd stopped in at home to ensure that Barbara's new tutor had arrived, disappointing Addie when she'd not paused to talk about Mina's situation. "I hadn't a chance to check on you earlier this morning. You were still asleep."

Mrs. Cascarino vacated the chair next to the sickbed. "Did that policeman leave?"

"He left a while ago, Mrs. Cascarino," said Celia.

"Nick? I thought I heard his voice," said Mina, elbowing herself upright, the color in her face draining from the effort.

Celia gently eased Mina back against her pillows. "Mina, you must not try to get up."

"Her stomach is still . . ." Mrs. Cascarino gesticulated to indicate nausea. "But her head does not hurt her so much. And she cannot remember—"

"I can answer for myself, Mama," said Mina. "I'm still woozy, Mrs. Davies. And confused."

"My poor *piccola*." Mrs. Cascarino bent down to arrange the pillows propping up her daughter's back. While Celia had been next door, someone had dressed Mina in a clean white nightgown, her black hair worked into two plaits that hung down over her shoulders. The braids made her seem childlike, as young as her little sister, peeping around the edge of the bedchamber doorframe.

"Your recovery needs time." Celia glanced at Mrs. Cascarino. She'd gone to speak with Mina's little sister and her back was turned, but she still had ears. "Mina, I have an important question. Do you recall going to the Hygienic Institute yesterday?"

"What is this place?" asked Mrs. Cascarino, rushing back to Mina's bedside. "This . . . this institute?"

"I can't . . ." Mina pressed her palm to her forehead. "I can't remember."

"Mrs. Davies, you see? She has pain. Her head, it hurts her." She scowled. "Please do not ask questions."

"Mrs. Cascarino, perhaps you can help me and fetch a fresh pitcher of water?" Celia motioned at the nearby pottery jug. "For Mina. If you will."

The woman grabbed up the jug. "Do not ask my Mina questions. She is sick," she said and stomped off.

Celia waited for Mrs. Cascarino's footsteps to fade then scooted her chair nearer to the bed. "Mina, I must know if you can remember planning to meet Mr. Ambrose Shaw at the Institute last night."

Mina's eyes searched Celia's face. "Ambrose?"

"So you do know him."

"He's been in occasionally. At Bauman's."

"Does he give you gifts?" *Like chocolates from a confectioner's?* "Flirt with you?"

"He's never given me gifts," she said. "Who's said he has?"

"Mr. Greaves."

"Nick's wrong about that." Mina hugged her arms about her waist. "Why does it matter if I know Ambrose Shaw? What's happened?"

Why not tell her? The news might even be written about in the Italian papers. "Mr. Shaw has died, Mina."

"*Oddio!*" She blanched. "How?"

"His heart failed," said Celia. "But the police believe his death may not have occurred naturally."

"And I'm to blame?"

"A guest of the Institute saw someone outside his room last night," she said. "And your blue shawl was found in the alley near an unlocked door to the building."

"My shawl?" Her gaze scoured the bedchamber. "It's got to be here. I never went to visit Ambrose Shaw at the Hygienic Institute. Why would I go see him? That's not what happened. Or did it?" Her brow furrowed. "Why am I so confused? Why don't I know what I did?"

"Concussions can cause amnesia, Mina," said Celia. "But you believe you never visited him there earlier this week, or were given a key."

She rubbed her temples with her fisted hands. "I do remember leaving Bauman's early last night. And I remember coming home. That's all. I never went to visit him. He didn't give me a key."

"Last night, you kept mumbling the word 'terrible,'" said Celia. "Do you recall saying that? What it was that happened?"

"No. Honestly, I don't."

Celia sat back. She was accomplishing nothing by questioning Mina, who was not the only person who needed to be patient with her recovery. Patience and time. But, at the moment, she could spare little of either. She needed proof that shawl was not Mina's.

"Where is the clothing you wore last night, Mina? Maybe your shawl is with your dress and other things." The checked tan gown Celia remembered Mina wearing last evening was not in the bedchamber.

"My bedroom, maybe? The one I share with my sisters. At the end of the hallway," she said.

Celia exited the room, relieved to see that the door to Mina's bedchamber stood open and she would not need to explain why she wanted access. Her sister followed Celia inside, the little girl's eyes wide and watchful.

"You have all been taking such good care of Mina," said Celia, though she doubted the child understood all but a few words of English. Mina's dress, along with a pair of mended stockings and a thick petticoat, lay on the largest bed, tucked against the wall beneath the window. "Your sister will recover all the more quickly because of your love and kindness."

The girl, barefoot, padded over to the bed and stared as Celia lifted the gown. The shawl was not beneath it, nor anywhere else in the room. *Gad.* Maybe the shawl the police had found was Mina's after all.

"Is this not a lovely, lovely dress?" she asked Mina's sister, whose unblinking gaze hadn't shifted away from Celia's face for a single instant. "Your sister is so fortunate to own a dress so fine."

Celia held the gown in her hands, afraid of her next step. The step that might prove more damning than the lack of a blue shawl in this room. Running her hands over the gown, she searched for a pocket and found one, discreetly sewn into the side seam. She felt a lump and reached inside. Cool metal met her touch, and a chill swept over Celia. It was a key. An ornate brass key.

Bloody hell.

℘ CHAPTER 5 ℘

"Why did Miss Mina have some key in her pocket, ma'am?" asked Addie, moving to the far end of the porch, away from the open parlor window that might permit Barbara or her tutor to overhear. "She canna be connected to this politician's murder. I'll nae believe it."

"I wish I had an answer, Addie," said Celia, wrapping her crimson shawl tightly around her body even though the day was mild. "Perhaps it is not the key to the Institute that Mr. Greaves is looking for and there is a completely innocent explanation. She did not recognize the key when I showed it to her, however, but that might be expected, due to her amnesia."

"Plus, the shawl the police discovered might not be hers," said Addie. "And that box of candy Mr. Greaves noticed might not be hers, either."

"Very true, all of that." Celia glanced at the newspaper Addie had tucked under her arm. "The news of Mr. Shaw's death has not made it into the papers yet, has it?"

"Not that I've seen, ma'am. I was hoping there'd be an update from Mr. Twain and his excursion to the Holy Land, but there isna one yet," she replied, tapping the newspaper. "How strange, though, that only a week ago, I read about a poor woman whose heart stopped because of chloroform used by her dentist. A story like that could give people ideas."

Especially if that person was aware that Mr. Shaw had a weak heart.

"It might have done," said Celia, grateful her housekeeper was such a keen reader of newspapers.

"Nonetheless, Miss Mina canna be responsible, no matter the key you found," said Addie, bound and determined to defend the young woman. "I suppose you have to tell Mr. Greaves, though. The evidence canna be kept from the police. Doing that would make us—"

"Accomplices," finished Celia. "Yes, Addie, I shall have to inform him at some point." *After I discover whether it works the lock on that private door.*

"Will you need me to collect your portrait from Miss Shaw, then, because you are busy tending to Miss Cascarino?" asked her housekeeper. "Miss Shaw sent a note that it is ready."

"Mina's family is providing excellent care, which means I have the time—and the perfect excuse—to return to Miss Shaw's studio and ask some questions," said Celia. "I may be gone for a while, so do not worry about me."

"Wait, you mean to interrogate the fellow's daughter?" asked Addie, her voice full of disapproval.

"Rebecca Shaw is the only one of the Shaw family members I know," she said. "The woman is as good a place as any to begin my search for the man's real killer."

Addie eyed her skeptically. "So long as she's not the killer herself, ma'am."

• • •

"Detective Greaves, Officer Taylor, this is my son, Leonard," announced Mrs. Delphia Shaw with a half-hearted flip of her hand.

She had high cheekbones, made pallid by the inky blackness of her brocade gown. Her skin was remarkably free of the sorts of wrinkles that had creased Nick's mother's face. Wrinkles from too much time exposed to the winds and the sun. Too much worry brought on by life with an unforgiving husband.

Leonard Shaw greeted Nick and Taylor with a brief, grim smile. He was tall, lean, and muscular for a man who worked in an office all day as a banker. His dark suit of clothes was made of high-quality material, tailored to fit perfectly. "Gentlemen."

"'Gentlemen'?" muttered Taylor at Nick's back. "Well, there's a first."

Shaw slid closed the drawing room pocket doors and crossed to where his mother sat, the massive wing-back chair she occupied a monstrosity of gold-and-red brocade. There were touches of gilding everywhere in the drawing room—the frames on the paintings hanging from the picture rail, the candlesticks on the mantel, the clock. Nick wondered if the choice in furnishings reflected Mr. Ambrose Shaw's taste or hers.

"Perhaps you can explain why you and your fellow police officer are here, Detective Greaves," said Leonard Shaw. "My father . . . my father perished from a sudden failure of his heart."

"Our condolences, by the way, Mr. Shaw," replied Nick.

"Thank you, but why are the police interested?"

"They are suspicious, Leonard," said Mrs. Shaw. Two large jet earrings dangled from her earlobes, bumping against her square jaw each time she moved her head. They matched the jet brooch pinning her neckerchief. She might be in mourning, but she wasn't about to neglect her appearance. "What else?"

Her tone was sharp, and her son flinched. Up close, Nick could see how much the fellow resembled his mother, his equally square jaw, broad face. Shaw had been to a barber already that morning; he smelled of bay rum.

"Do you mind if we all sit down, Detective?" asked Shaw, indicating the nearby sofa and chair. He groaned as he lowered onto the chair. "I'm still in shock over my father's death. I only heard the news thirty or so minutes ago, when I returned from my morning appointments. From another policeman."

Nick removed his hat and took a seat on the sofa. "News like this is never easy to hear, Mr. Shaw."

Taylor found a spot to stand near the fireplace where the Shaws wouldn't notice him taking notes.

"Maybe you can explain what you're suspicious of, Detective," said Shaw.

"I'll get to that, Mr. Shaw," he said. "You both went to visit Mr. Shaw at the Institute earlier this week. How did he seem?"

"He was enjoying his little holiday away from the cares of the world," replied Mrs. Shaw.

"Not anxious or agitated?"

"Detective Greaves, these questions are distressing my mother," said her son. "We're mourning the loss of my father and a great man. This is no time for the police to be nosing around."

"He was untroubled, Detective," said Mrs. Shaw, her voice awfully steady for somebody who was supposed to be distressed. "My husband was not someone easily agitated, or who'd find himself in low spirits. Ambrose was strong-willed and optimistic. Which is why he wasn't initially interested in visiting the Institute, thinking he didn't require Mr. Ross's services, but I convinced him that the treatments would be best for his health. He had many goals to achieve, Detective, and neither of us wanted him to have to slow down."

"I suppose the Institute's private entrance was convenient for you and your husband to make use of, Mrs. Shaw," said Nick. "A good way to keep from being observed by people out on the street."

"What private entrance?" she asked, looking over at her son as though he'd been remiss in not mentioning it.

"You weren't given a key for it?" Nick asked.

"No," she replied.

Leonard Shaw shook his head. "Mr. Ross never provided me or my mother with a key to some private entrance, Detective Greaves."

"Why was Mr. Shaw staying overnight at the Hygienic Institute instead of returning home each day?" he asked.

"Mr. Ross explained that the treatment would be most effective if Ambrose stayed for the week, where his diet and the quietness of his mind could be best monitored," she said. "He was supposed to come home tomorrow."

Taylor flipped a page of his notebook, the snap of the paper startling her.

"Detective Greaves, I'm still trying to understand why you're asking questions," said Leonard Shaw. "We were told my father had a heart attack. Didn't he?"

"Mr. Shaw came into the police station last week to report that he was being followed." Nick slid the brim of his hat through his fingers, turning it in slow circles. The movement was a habit of his, but he'd discovered its ability to unsettle folks he was interviewing, so he'd never tried to break himself of the mannerism. "What can either of you tell me about that?"

"My husband didn't want me to be alarmed, but in the past few weeks, on more than one occasion, he noticed someone trailing him when he was out in the evening." Delphia Shaw pressed her lips together for a second before going on. "At first, he thought he was imagining things. But by the third or fourth occurrence, he decided to go to the police."

"Who didn't act interested in investigating," added her son.

"Did Mr. Shaw ever suggest a reason somebody might be following him?"

"Ambrose kept his own counsel," said Mrs. Shaw. "But Leonard and I developed a theory."

"And?"

"We're convinced that Mr. Elliot Blanchard had either been following Ambrose or had hired someone to," she said.

"Who is Elliot Blanchard?"

"You haven't heard of him?" asked Shaw. "He plans to run against my father in the upcoming elections, and he's done everything he can to ruin my father's chances."

"*Planned*, Leonard. Not plans," said Mrs. Shaw. "Your father has passed, if I need to remind you."

"Why would Mr. Blanchard try to frighten your husband by stalking him, ma'am?" asked Nick.

"You'd have to ask him, Detective," she replied. "The fellow's a scoundrel."

"Opposing your husband's politics doesn't make him a scoundrel, Mrs. Shaw," said Nick.

"He *is* a scoundrel, Detective," she asserted, her eyes narrowing. "Mr. Blanchard has run scathing articles in the newspaper and confronted my husband in public with the worst insults. I urged Ambrose to take out a complaint against the man, report him to the police, but he resisted. He laughed off my suggestion, saying that arguing about citizenship and universal suffrage heated men's blood and to not worry, since Mr. Blanchard's party was not going to win. And it didn't in the recent elections, so Ambrose was correct. People do not want citizenship nor the right to vote extended to former slaves in every state in this country."

Taylor grumbled, but he was too far away for Nick to hear exactly what he'd said.

"Elliot Blanchard started a brawl inside the billiard room at the Bank Exchange. Struck my father with his walking stick," said Leonard Shaw. "So you can understand why we'd accuse him of stalking my father, Detective Greaves."

"Mr. Blanchard is a violent man," said Mrs. Shaw. "A man who undoubtedly decided that insults and attacks weren't enough to stop my husband from pursuing his political ambitions. So he moved on to threatening behavior. A coward."

"Eventually your husband did file a complaint, though," said Nick.

"He did. Late last week," said her son. "I wonder if Blanchard found out."

I do, too. "While Mr. Shaw was staying at the Institute, did he report seeing Blanchard or tell you he thought he was being watched?"

Mrs. Shaw's eyes widened. "Mr. Blanchard went to the Institute and frightened Ambrose to death, didn't he? Caused my husband's heart to fail."

"Mr. Shaw's death is suspicious, ma'am," said Nick. "That's all I'm able to say."

"Blanchard has to be responsible for my father's death, Detective," said Leonard Shaw. "He must be arrested."

"We'll speak with the fellow, Mr. Shaw, and see what he has to tell us," said Nick.

"Undoubtedly he'll lie to you, Detective Greaves," he said.

Nick kept his hat brim turning through his fingers. "Do you mind if I ask where you both were last evening between the hours of seven and eight?"

"Why would you ask us a question like that?" asked Leonard Shaw.

"Just answer him, Leo," said his mother. "I retire early and was likely in bed by eight, Detective. Our domestic can confirm the exact time, because she helps me undress. Leonard came in from a social engagement around nine."

"You were awake and checking the clock, Mrs. Shaw," said Nick. Taylor flipped to a new page of his notebook, quietly this time.

"I leave my watch on a stand atop the little table right next to my bed," she answered.

"You live in this house, Mr. Shaw?" asked Nick.

"I have a room on an upper floor. No reason to leave my parents alone in this rambling place," he said. "My stepsister, Rebecca, operates a photographic gallery in the city. My brothers have mining interests in Nevada. I intend to stay here until I marry and set up a household of my own."

Mrs. Shaw's expression didn't reveal her opinion of her youngest son's decision to remain at the family homestead.

"Did your domestic see you come in around nine, Mr. Shaw?" asked Nick.

"I managed to slip in without her spotting me," he replied. "Had a brandy in the upstairs parlor, then went to bed. Sorry if I disturbed you, Mother."

"Ah," said Nick. "Where was this social engagement you attended before you returned home last night, Mr. Shaw?"

"I was at a supper with several friends. A meeting of the San Francisco Club at the Parker House," he replied. "I'm sure any of them can tell you I was there."

"And can also tell me when you left."

Mrs. Shaw scowled at Nick. "Of course they can, Detective," she said. "Rather than interrogate us, you should spend your efforts on proving Mr. Blanchard's involvement. Unless you sympathize with his politics and refuse to imagine him culpable for Ambrose's death."

"I wouldn't let my sympathies interfere with my duties, ma'am." Nick stood, and Taylor closed his notebook, stowing it away inside his coat. "I think that's enough for today. And again, our condolences."

Mrs. Shaw rose as well. "Mr. Ross sent a note around requesting that we come to the Institute as soon as possible to collect Ambrose's possessions. We've barely had time to process my husband's death, and he's sending demands like that."

"Maybe he needs to free up the room for another guest."

"Oh, I doubt that," she replied.

Nick tapped his hat onto his head, leveling the brim with a sweep of his fingers. "We'll keep in touch, ma'am. Once the coroner has reached a conclusion on your husband's death, we'll let you know."

Mrs. Shaw inclined her head. "Leonard, please accompany the policemen to the door, if you will."

"Gentlemen," he said, striding for the parlor doors to tug them open.

Nick paused at the doorway. "Oh, ma'am, I forgot to ask you something. Have you ever heard of a woman named Mina Cascarino?"

"No," she answered. "Should I have?"

"Just curious."

Taylor bid the Shaws a good morning and scurried out of the house after Nick. "You think one of them could've been the intruder Mrs. Wynn saw last night, sir?"

Nick paused on the front steps of the house. "I can't rule them out, even though Delphia Shaw acted like she didn't know about that private entrance." He didn't want Mina to be guilty any more than Mrs. Davies did.

He descended to the sidewalk, Taylor on his heels.

"Suppose they'll both inherit a lot of money," said his assistant, patting down his coat pockets and fishing out a cigar and a match. "Never seen so much gilding in my life."

"I expect they will," said Nick, turning down the steep incline of the road.

"I also gotta say Leonard Shaw didn't look all that upset about his father's death, sir . . . Mr. Greaves, sir."

"Maybe he's good at keeping his emotions under control."

Taylor looked over at him. "You think so?"

"Not really."

• • •

Who was aware that Ambrose Shaw had a weak heart?

Celia strode down Montgomery, bound for Miss Shaw's gallery. All of the Shaws would know, for a start. Mr. Ross at the Institute and possibly one or more of his employees. Close acquaintances, she presumed, but beyond them . . .

At the gallery, the shades were up and the front window displayed an *Open* sign. Celia stepped inside, setting off the bell above the door. Within seconds, Miss Shaw exited her darkroom, a thick apron tied over her dress and leather gloves on her hands. The smell of photographic processing compounds wafted out.

"Mrs. Davies, you've come to retrieve your portrait," she said, peeling off the gloves and setting them aside. Despite their protection, her fingernails were stained from photograph development chemicals. "It has turned out very well. I think you and your cousin will be pleased. I have it right over here. Please take a seat."

Miss Shaw went to a cabinet against the wall and opened it. As discreetly as possible, Celia examined the woman as she moved about. Was she a trifle pale? Or was she oddly unperturbed by the news of her father's death? Unless she'd not yet been informed.

"Here you are." Miss Shaw handed over the picture, the print attached to a rectangle of thick paper approximately four by six inches in dimension. "It's called a cabinet card. They've become very popular since they were introduced. I can also sell you a frame to display it, if you'd like."

Celia had never had a portrait taken, and it was disconcerting to see her image staring back from the glossy surface of an albumen print, her hand resting on Barbara's rigid shoulder. Her cousin was quite lovely, but the two of them could not be more of a contrast—Barbara relatively petite and dark of hair and eye, while Celia was taller than she enjoyed being, her own hair and eyes cast eerily pale against the background.

"Don't you like it?" asked Miss Shaw. Up close, Celia could see that the young woman's eyes were red-rimmed. From crying?

"No, it is quite perfect. Thank you," she replied, giving the print back to Miss Shaw for wrapping. "I simply have never seen myself beyond what I observe in the mirror of my dressing table."

"I also printed four cartes de visite for you to send to friends and family."

Would Celia's aunt and uncle in England want a photograph of their wayward niece and their brother's half-Chinese daughter? Not likely.

"Barbara will be thrilled to be able to send one to her friend, who is away at the Young Ladies' Seminary in Benicia," she said. "And I shall purchase a frame for the cabinet card. A simple one. Nothing too showy." Nothing too expensive.

Miss Shaw set the cabinet card atop the glass case and hunted for a frame among those on display inside.

"I must tell you about the oddest coincidence, Miss Shaw," said Celia, rising up on her toes to keep the woman's face in view. "An acquaintance of mine turns out to be a friend of your father's. A Miss Mina Cascarino. Do you know her as well?"

Miss Shaw's expression gave no hint she recognized Mina's name.

"I've never heard of her, Mrs. Davies," she replied and straightened, frame retrieved. "But then my father has a great many friends. Even female ones."

Ones he enjoyed sending boxes of candy to.

"Certainly," said Celia. "She recently expressed to me how worried she is about your father's health, though."

"Oh?" the other woman asked, her fingers trembling now.

"Miss Shaw, are you quite all right?" asked Celia.

"What do you mean?"

"I am a nurse and it is my habit to be observant," she said. "You appear upset. Is it your father? Has he has suffered a turn for the worse?"

Miss Shaw clasped her hands at her waist. "It *is* my father. The police were here this morning . . . a dreadful business."

"The police?" asked Celia, doing her best to sound appalled.

"Yes," she said. "My father has died. Suddenly. His heart."

"Oh my goodness," said Celia. "But why did a police officer come?" Miss Shaw eyed her. *Blast, I've gone too far with my questions.* "Have I misspoken, Miss Shaw?"

"Why *are* you here, Mrs. Davies?"

"To collect my photographs, of course," she replied, wishing she'd been more interested in participating in the amateur theatrics her neighbors used to stage when Celia was a child. "If I had been aware you were suffering a recent bereavement, I'd not have done."

"You must think I'm heartless, leaving my business open under such circumstances."

"Your father's death came as a shock." *Did it not, Miss Shaw?* "The routine of work can be comforting."

"I'll close once I've taken care of my appointments this afternoon." She stared at the frame she'd forgotten she was holding and set it down. "Delphia will want help planning the funeral."

"Delphia?"

"Mrs. Shaw. My father's second wife."

Not referred to as her stepmother, Celia noticed. "Undoubtedly she shall," she said. "At least you had an opportunity to visit him at the Institute not long before he passed away. A comfort."

Her eyes narrowed. "How do you know I went to visit him?"

Calm, Celia. Be calm. "You mentioned it yesterday when Barbara and I were here." *Exude calm despite the mistruth you just told.* "Do you not recall?"

"I don't remember saying anything about my visit to you, because I didn't actually talk to my father," she responded. "He didn't want to see me, and I left after a few minutes."

Perhaps their relationship was not as "sufficiently amicable" as Miss Shaw had yesterday claimed. Furthermore, perhaps she'd not had an opportunity to take her father's key from his room. Which meant the one currently stored in Celia's reticule had found its way into Mina's pocket by some other mean than Miss Shaw giving it to her. If that key even was the one missing from the Institute.

"Do be kind to yourself, Miss Shaw. Losing a father can be hard," said Celia, smiling gently. "Both of my parents passed away when I was young. To this day, I feel their loss keenly."

"Hard? I suppose you're right, Mrs. Davies," she replied, retrieving a sheet of paper to wrap Celia's photographs. "I wonder, though, if Delphia and Leo will agree."

ꙮ CHAPTER 6 ꙮ

"I appreciate you taking the time to see me, Jane," said Celia, settling onto one of the deeply cushioned chairs in her friend's parlor.

"I'm grateful for the company," Jane Hutchinson replied, taking the settee opposite, her magenta silk gown billowing around her. "With Grace away at college, it's been very quiet around here. I even think Frank misses her."

"Of course he misses her, just like Barbara misses her. Grace is a joy," said Celia. "Your husband only pretends to be annoyed by his daughter's spirited nature."

"If so, he's very good at pretending." Jane leaned toward her. "Celia, were you able to . . ." She glanced at the closed parlor doors, shut tight against the rest of the household. "Were you able to pay that fellow the money he was owed?" she whispered.

Mr. Griffin. The recent upheaval had caused her to forget about him and Patrick's debt.

"I was. Thank you for your help," said Celia, her voice as low as her friend's. Frank must not be aware that Jane had lent her money. "I shall make good my obligation to you as soon as possible."

"Don't worry. There's no rush. Honestly."

Celia smiled. Kind, generous Jane. A true friend.

"Oh, wait. I've a present for your stepdaughter." She unwrapped the bundle she'd brought from Miss Shaw's gallery and handed Jane one of the cartes de visite. "Barbara and I had our photograph taken yesterday by Miss Rebecca Shaw. You've heard of her studio, no doubt."

"I have. I was wondering what you had wrapped in paper there." Jane took the portrait and smiled over it. "Grace will be thrilled to get this. I'll send it to her today." She placed the carte de visite on the side table. "Would you like some tea? Hetty's around here someplace."

"There's no need to fetch your servant. I've not come for tea nor to simply give you that photograph."

Her friend lifted a brow. "You're here to discover what I know about someone." Her smile vanished. "Oh, no, Celia. Who is it who's died now?"

"Am I so transparent?"

"Not at all. I've just grown used to the fact that you usually only show up at the house unexpectedly when you need my help on one of your cases."

"My 'cases'? I am *not* an investigator."

Jane laughed. "You could've fooled me, Celia."

"I must be cursed, Jane. What a dreadful year it's been."

"Have you heard from Patrick?" she asked.

"No. He has apparently gone to the Colorado Territory in search of gold." Which did not mean he'd not return to San Francisco someday. "My visit has nothing to do with him. I'm here to ask how well you know Ambrose Shaw and his family. Aside from having heard about his daughter, the photographer."

Jane sat back and began to toy with her wedding ring, twisting it around her finger. "Oh. Them."

"What about them?" Celia asked.

"I don't know the Shaws well, since Frank doesn't agree with Ambrose Shaw's politics," said Jane. "A few years ago—before you came to San Francisco, Celia—I tried to convince Delphia to join the Ladies' Society of Christian Aid. When she learned we occasionally collect funds to support the Chinese Mission House, she declined to participate."

Which would make Delphia Shaw like other ladies unwilling to offer charity to the Chinese women in the city. Several members of the Society were not comfortable with Barbara, either, whispering about Celia's cousin on the limited occasions she'd agreed to attend a meeting.

"I'd not like her, then."

"Probably not, although the few times I've interacted with Delphia Shaw she's been cordial and pleasant enough," said Jane. "As for the other Shaws, I've only met Ambrose Shaw and just one time. Strolling through the City Gardens. Broad smile, large teeth. Ready to pump a person's hand, as Frank might refer to the fellow's handshakes, like so many politicians. But quick to hold a grudge against those who oppose him."

"How do others feel about Ambrose Shaw, Jane? Do you know?"

"It's said that Ambrose is hot-tempered. As is his son, Leonard, from what I hear. Like father, like son, I suppose. Frank dislikes the both of them and refuses to do business with their bank." Jane's eyes widened. "Ambrose Shaw is why you've come. What's happened to him?"

"You must keep what I tell you in confidence," said Celia. "I am uncertain what the police intend to tell the newspapers about the event."

"You know you can trust me."

She could. Utterly.

"Ambrose Shaw was discovered dead last evening at the Hygienic Institute," she said. "From an apparent heart attack. However, the gas jet in his room had been opened, possibly to feign an accident or a suicide attempt. The coroner believes Mr. Shaw may have been rendered previously unconscious—or dead—from chloroform. With Mr. Shaw's weak heart, the substance could have killed him. Furthermore, an intruder was spotted outside his room not long before his body was discovered."

"Mr. Shaw, murdered. My, my," Jane said, as calmly as if she were commenting upon the state of the roses in Celia's garden. "What does Mr. Greaves have to say?"

"He has informed me that one of my neighbors' daughters is under suspicion," she replied.

"Then you have spoken with Mr. Greaves."

"Do not get that look in your eye, Jane," said Celia. "There can be nothing between us. Ever."

"Because of Patrick's untimely return from the dead?"

Celia felt the involuntary uptick of her pulse, noted the way she held her breath at the mention of Patrick's name. As though the sound of an indrawn breath might inform her husband where to locate her, and he would materialize right then and there, striding across the thick carpet of the Hutchinsons' parlor, his blue eyes snapping with life.

"Yes, Jane. Because of him."

"It's been three months since you imagined catching sight of Patrick, Celia, and not a word from him," said Jane. "Maybe he's not actually alive or gone to the Colorado Territory, despite what you've been told."

"Patrick's current circumstances are irrelevant, and I'd prefer to not think about him at all," she replied, irritation rising, the sentiment as good a marker as any of how she'd often felt about her husband. *We should never have wed.*

"What do you plan to do next?" asked Jane, honoring their friendship by dropping the subject of Patrick Davies.

"I intend to clear my young friend of suspicion, and in order to do that I must discover who may have had a reason to wish Mr. Ambrose Shaw dead," said Celia. "She was acquainted with him but has no motive to harm him that I can discern. Perhaps Mina was an innocent pawn in another's scheme."

"He was a wealthy man, Celia, who also wasn't afraid of engaging in heated political debates," said Jane. "All sorts of people might have wanted him dead."

"Precisely," said Celia. "Rebecca Shaw made a curious comment about her stepbrother Leonard and Mrs. Shaw. Questioning if they'd be upset about Mr. Shaw's death."

"There are rumors that Ambrose was disappointed with Leonard. Money troubles, I think. However, Leonard works at the family bank, so their relationship couldn't have been all that bad."

"Shall he inherit the business?"

"Probably, pending approval of the other officers. I gather his older brothers are located in Nevada—successful mining operators, I believe— and might not be interested in running the bank here," she replied.

"Either way, Leonard Shaw should inherit a tidy sum of money. A motive to want his father dead, Celia?"

"Perhaps," said Celia. "Delphia Shaw should become a wealthy woman, and Rebecca Shaw as well, I presume."

"Rebecca and her father did have a falling out," said Jane.

"She'd told me they were on decent terms."

"Not at all. He prevented her marriage to a local wine merchant, Mr. Elliot Blanchard, when she was still young enough to require her father's consent. Their relationship became strained as a result," Jane explained. "Interestingly enough, Mr. Blanchard became one of Ambrose Shaw's political opponents."

"I wonder if the two events are somehow related," said Celia. "I am surprised, though, that Miss Shaw, as strong-willed as she seems to be, did not simply wait until she was old enough to wed Mr. Blanchard without needing her father's permission."

"Rebecca may have intended to wait, but Mr. Blanchard married another," she replied. "It was bold of her to suggest her father's death might not upset Leonard or Delphia, when she has as much reason to shed few tears."

"Bold? Or cunning?" Or both? "Although killing her father now makes no sense. The timing seems a trifle late, if she sought to clear a path to wedding her beloved, who is married."

"Maybe she is suddenly also in need of her inheritance. Or . . ." Jane raised a forefinger, her thoughts changing direction. "Or she recently learned she might be cut from the will and decided to strike now."

"A chilling thought, Jane."

Celia leaned back, the chair cushions plump and soft, the midday sunlight falling warmly upon the polished wood floor, the parlor mantel clock chiming genteelly, Hetty's voice quietly greeting Jane's husband in the entryway beyond the closed door. The epitome of peace and calm. But all around them, Celia felt encroaching dark intrigue and danger. *When the sun sets, who doth not look for night?*

Indeed, Mr. Shakespeare.

"Celia, you haven't explained why your young friend is suspected of murdering Ambrose Shaw."

Celia refocused on Jane's face. "Her shawl—or one very much like it—was found outside the Hygienic Institute," she said. "Furthermore, I found a key in the pocket of her dress, which could possibly unlock a door leading to Mr. Shaw's room at the Institute. Or may not."

"All of which sounds bad, Celia," said Jane. "Will you be able to help her?"

Celia considered her friend. A woman who was far more bold and daring than her delicate features and polite manners might lead one to believe. *Addie will never forgive me if Jane is harmed in any way. However, nothing ventured, nothing gained.*

"Jane, are you busy the next hour or so?"

• • •

"There you are, Mr. Greaves. You rushed off so early this morning I didn't have a chance to get some breakfast in you," said Mrs. Jewett, sweeping in from the rear of the house, where the kitchen was located. She'd rolled up her dress sleeves, and flour speckled her skin. "I've made a pie. Apple. Your favorite."

Was apple his favorite? Maybe it was. "You didn't need to."

"Well, of course I didn't need to, Mr. Greaves. I wanted to," she replied, wiping her fingers on the edges of the apron tied over her middle. "I thought a small taste of your childhood might bring you some comfort."

He also didn't recall ever telling her about his childhood in Ohio. Maybe he had, because if he hadn't, the woman was a mind reader. Which was a scary thought. "Sorry I ran out of here before you could feed me this morning. Police work."

"Another awful murder?" she asked.

"Can't discuss it, Mrs. Jewett."

"Of course not. I understand. Wait. A telegram came. I put it . . ."

She flapped aside the apron and dug into the pocket of her checked merino skirt. "Ah, here it is."

Located, she waved it at him. He grabbed the telegram and stuffed it into a pocket.

"Aren't you going to read it?" she asked.

Only his sister sent him telegrams, and he'd said all he had wanted to say to Ellie when he'd departed the dock in Sacramento yesterday morning. "Later. No time right now. I just stopped by to let Riley out and to grab a bite to eat."

He had plans to meet Taylor back at the station in a half hour, hopefully with Elliot Blanchard in tow. After the Shaws' accusations about the man, Nick wanted to question him before the afternoon papers came out with the news of Ambrose Shaw's death.

"I'll make sure to have some of your apple pie later, Mrs. Jewett."

Sighing, she peered at him with her gentle, motherly gaze. "You can't keep working so hard, Mr. Greaves. No rest. No decent meals. It's not good for your health."

He smiled, though moving his lips into the expression was about as easy as dragging a plow through mud. "I've got your pie to look forward to, Mrs. Jewett. That shall fix up my deficient health perfectly."

"I can see you're in one of your moods, Mr. Greaves. Maybe I should get out my extract of buchu instead of making you a pie."

"I'm not ill, Mrs. Jewett. I'm working on a new case."

She leaned closer, looking for all the world like she wanted to pat him on the cheek. He wasn't the son she'd lost in the war, though, as much as she wanted Nick to be. "Working too hard." She tutted.

"Maybe I should go to the Hygienic Institute and be restored," he said, heading for the stairs up to his second-floor rooms.

"That place? Oh, you shouldn't go there, Mr. Greaves. I hope you're not serious."

He paused on the steps. "Why do you say that? Are there problems there?" Problems other than the one Ross was already dealing with?

"Well, one of the ladies at our benevolent society had a piece of jewelry stolen when she stayed there overnight. Two weeks ago? Or was it three?" She scrunched up her face as she tried to remember. "And I believe the husband of another friend learned that an acquaintance of his was robbed of a very fine engraved gold pen while staying at the dreadful place, as well."

Well, this was interesting. "Did your friends report the thefts to the police?"

"I didn't ask for details, Mr. Greaves," said Mrs. Jewett, giving every indication she wasn't sure he understood that it was impolite to interrogate one's friends. "That's all I know. Somebody who works at that place is a criminal, if you ask me. A complete criminal."

• • •

"The middle of the day, Celia?" asked Jane, who'd been ready for an adventure until they had disembarked the horsecar and Celia had finally divulged what she intended to do. "You are going to see if that key fits one of the doors to the Hygienic Institute in the middle of the day, in broad daylight?"

"My actions would be even more suspicious if I slunk down that alley and fiddled with the lock after dark, do you not agree?"

Across the road from where they stood, the Hygienic Institute occupied what had once been a corner hotel. Comprised of three limestone stories above the ground level, large pedimented windows fitted with awnings processed across the two façades, and the entire building was overtopped with a green-painted dentil cornice. A structure grand enough to evoke comfort and confidence but not so grand as to be intimidating. There was no indication it had been the scene of a crime, aside from the shutters that had been closed over the street-level windows, suggesting that the proprietor sought to hamper passers-by from peeking inside to satisfy their curiosity. The news of Mr. Shaw's death had yet to reach the papers, though; there was little risk at the moment of intrusive sightseers.

"Have you prepared an explanation for the policeman who will eventually stroll by, Celia?" asked Jane.

"I will maintain that I am a guest of the establishment, making use of the private entrance for reasons I'd prefer not to expound upon," said Celia. "Besides, my experiment should only take a few seconds. Hopefully a policeman will not stroll past in that amount of time and observe me."

"Then what am I here for?"

"In case I am mistaken about the frequency with which policemen make their rounds."

"You want me to distract a police officer while you commit what is undoubtedly a crime?" Now she sounded aghast. "Celia!"

"Thank you, Jane."

Celia, the key clasped in one fist and her skirts in the other, dashed across the road. She dodged horse manure and a snapping dog that had taken a sudden interest in her. She'd already determined that the private entrance had to be located in the narrow alley between the Institute and a two-story building alongside, which housed a shop selling coconut matting and rugs. Head held high, which hopefully signaled that she had every right to be entering the alleyway, Celia plunged into the shadows cast by the surrounding structures.

She glanced over her shoulder and saw that Jane had—reluctantly—followed at a more stately pace.

"Well, hurry up," Jane hissed, pausing at the mouth of the alley to peruse the contents of the coconut-matting retailer's windows. Not items a woman in deep magenta silk with a matching bonnet might normally be interested in, but despite her protests, Jane was not about to allow Celia to proceed without her.

Celia smiled and quickly located the door in question, a discreet sign reading *Private* nailed to the wood. She prayed the door did not actually let onto a service room or Mr. Ross's personal office. She tried the doorknob—locked—and inserted the key. It did not fit well, and she jiggled the handle to see if she could get the wards to slip into place.

Footsteps crunched along the alley. "It may not actually fit this door lock, Jane. Although . . . wait a moment . . ."

"What are you up to?"

The man's voice startled her, and Celia jumped backward, the key flying from her hand. He lunged for where it had fallen, grabbing it before Celia could successfully battle the constrictions of skirts and a corset. *Bloody . . .*

Cheeks hot, she returned the man's stare. He had a heavy jaw, a disjointed nose that looked as though it had once been broken, and a very unwelcoming expression on his face. "Might I have my key back? I am a patient here—"

"No, you're not." He pocketed the key. "So you'd better tell me exactly who you are and what you're up to before I find a cop and report you."

Behind him, Jane was gesturing wildly. "Oh, Celia! My goodness, you did wander far off. What are you doing? Is she causing trouble, sir? You have to forgive her." Jane slipped past the man and took hold of Celia's elbow. "Come along. We should go home now and have your tea. You'd like that, wouldn't you? Do forgive us, sir. She hasn't been at all well lately."

"Home?" asked Celia. Heart pounding, she rushed for the alley's exit alongside Jane. "Yes, let us go home, sister."

They ran out into the sunlight and across the road, Jane slowing to look back.

"Do not slow, Jane. We must get away before he decides to make good on his threat to find a policeman." Celia hurried her along until they reached the safety of the next street and turned down it. "That was quick thinking on your part. Although I am not certain I enjoy being marked out as a madwoman."

"It worked, didn't it?" asked Jane, panting as she leaned against the nearest empty wall.

"Yes, it worked."

"It was the only excuse I could think of when I spotted him charging down the alley. I have no idea where he came from," said Jane, retying her bonnet ribbons, which had come undone. "What about the key, though? Did it fit the lock?"

"I believe it did, Jane." Unfavorable news for Mina's innocence. "I hate to say so, but I do believe it did."

• • •

"I don't understand what the police want with me, Detective . . . I didn't catch your name," said Elliot Blanchard, seated on the edge of the chair in front of Nick's desk.

He was trying to sound calm, but his body betrayed him. Everything about the man was a tightly wound coil, from the taut way he held his shoulders to the flexing of the muscles beneath his clean-shaven jaw. Maybe Blanchard was always tense. Maybe folks admired that about him. Saw his pent-up energy as a sign he was a politician who meant to get things done. Personally, the man was setting Nick's teeth on edge.

"He's Detective Greaves, Mr. Blanchard," said Taylor, leaning against the wall behind Blanchard. Right next to the closed door to Nick's office, a barrier to any thoughts of rushing off Blanchard might get.

"Yes. Detective Greaves. Thank you," he said. "As I was saying, I don't understand what the police want with me. I already spoke with an officer about the burglary at my house last week. Unless you've found the person responsible?"

"I wasn't aware you'd been burglarized, Mr. Blanchard." Such cases weren't Nick's usual jurisdiction.

"A strange situation, frankly," he said. "The person went to a lot of effort to break in and rummage through my possessions, but I can't tell what they took. I wasn't going to bother to file a report, except my wife insisted."

"Ah."

Taylor scribbled notes. He'd follow up on Blanchard's report and brief Nick later.

Nick leaned back in his chair, which creaked in response. "Tell me about your interactions with Ambrose Shaw, Mr. Blanchard."

"I've been brought here because of that argument we had at the Bank Exchange, haven't I?" He scoffed. "But that was weeks ago. I thought Shaw had decided to let bygones be bygones. Has he lodged a complaint after all?"

"You admit to arguing with him," said Nick.

"I'd be pretty stupid not to. There were plenty of witnesses."

Nick rested his elbows on the chair arms and tented his fingers. "What was the fight about?"

"I'd rather not say."

"'There were plenty of witnesses . . .'"

"All right. Shaw made an allegation about my wife. That she is a mulatto," he replied, his gaze fixing on Nick's face. *Watching for my reaction?* "He'd like to ruin my chances at ever getting elected to any post, Detective Greaves. Announcements like the one Shaw made will undoubtedly turn some voters against me, and he knows it."

"*Is* she a mulatto?" asked Nick.

Blanchard scowled. "Does her race matter?"

"Not to me personally, Mr. Blanchard, but marriage between a white person and a mulatto is a crime in this state."

"I am aware of that, Detective," he said, the words crisp. "She's South American, but some folks look at her and think she might be mulatto. More of them, now that Shaw's insinuated she is. She's afraid to leave the house. That burglary rattled her even more."

"So Shaw makes the claim aloud inside the billiard parlor at the Bank Exchange saloon, in front of everybody there, and you hit him."

"We'd both had a few too many whiskeys. I lost control. I'm not proud of it," he replied. "I punched him. The man weighs a good thirty pounds more than I do, Detective. I don't know how I managed to knock him down, but I did." He scoffed again, louder this time. "Maybe he faked the fall. He was muttering 'my heart, my heart.' Looking for sympathy, I assume. Trying to cast me as the aggressor."

Nick shifted in his seat and contemplated Blanchard. "But then you decided to start following him, late at night, to scare him . . ."

"I've never . . . That's ridiculous!" he exclaimed. "Is he accusing me of following him? I demand to know."

"Mr. Shaw came to the station a few days ago to report that someone had been stalking him when he'd go out at night. He became alarmed," said Nick. "Given your past history with the fellow, you've been proposed as the culprit."

"By who?" he asked. "Let me guess. Leonard Shaw."

Taylor's pencil scratched furiously.

"Where were you last evening, Mr. Blanchard?" asked Nick.

"Not out stalking Ambrose Shaw."

"Where were you last evening, Mr. Blanchard?" Nick repeated. "Between, oh, seven and eight o'clock?"

"I was at my house," said Blanchard. "Reviewing the day's business receipts after dinner. I'm a wine merchant."

"You don't review your receipts at your business office?"

"It's quieter at my house," he said. "I'm usually at home in the evening. My wife and I don't socialize much. Especially lately."

"She can confirm you were home," said Nick.

"She's gone to visit her mother in Yuba City. She left on Sunday after church," he replied. "She wanted some time away from the city and all the gossip. The hateful whispering."

The timing of her departure was unfortunate for Blanchard . . . or convenient. "Do you have any domestics who can vouch for you, Mr. Blanchard?"

"We have a woman who cleans and cooks for us during the week, but she leaves by seven, Detective Greaves."

"No prying neighbors?"

"Look, I've told you I was not following Ambrose Shaw last night, trying to scare him," said Blanchard. "Why don't you believe me? What's going on?"

Nick retrieved his battered watch from his vest pocket and flipped open the lid. Not yet twelve. In a few hours the *Evening Bulletin* would be out on the street, the paperboys yelping the news about Shaw's sudden death. Blanchard wouldn't have to guess why the police were interested in him once the story got out.

He tucked the watch back into its pocket. "Last night, around seven thirty, Ambrose Shaw was discovered dead in his accommodations at a medical facility where he's been staying."

Blanchard turned as white as a proverbial ghost.

"Oh my God." He shoved back his chair, tipping it over in his haste to get to his feet. "My God! You think I've killed him!"

"Why would you conclude that he'd been murdered, Mr. Blanchard?" asked Nick.

Blanchard's brows tucked low. He had even features, the sort of face you might find on a shop clerk. Somebody you might ignore when passing on the street. Pleasant enough but not worth noticing. Even and unremarkable, until he fixed his large gray eyes on a person with an intensity that was almost maniacal. Except Nick didn't think the man was any sort of a maniac, merely earnest and smart.

"What else would I conclude from the statements you've made, Detective? Your questions?" he asked. "If a reporter has spotted me coming into the station . . . Damn it all." Blanchard dropped onto his chair again.

"Can anybody vouch for you, Mr. Blanchard?"

"Nobody will vouch for me, Detective, but the absence of an alibi isn't enough of a reason to blame me for Shaw's death," he answered, his color slowly returning. "Obviously, we've had our differences. I've admitted as much. But I'm no fool. I wouldn't go to the Hygienic Institute and assault Shaw. Has somebody claimed they saw me there? Have they?"

Nick studied Blanchard. "Did I mention that Mr. Shaw was at the Hygienic Institute?"

"It wasn't a secret. Everybody knew he'd gone there because of his heart," he said. "Guess his opportunity to learn if their treatments work got cut short."

"Have *you* ever partaken of the water cure at the Institute?" Had use of a key to a private entrance, perhaps. A key he hadn't returned.

"I've never had the need, Detective," he replied flatly.

"Ah." Nick got to his feet. "Taylor, escort Mr. Blanchard out. And make up a story for the reporters, if there are any outside, about why he's been to visit us."

Taylor put away his notebook and took the man's elbow.

"And, Mr. Blanchard," added Nick, "don't make any sudden plans to leave San Francisco. Do you understand?"

"Yes." The fellow shook off Taylor's grip. "They're lying, though, Detective Greaves. The Shaws. Lying about Ambrose Shaw being followed. Lying about me."

"Why would they do that, Mr. Blanchard?"

"Because they want to destroy me. Even now. Even after Ambrose has died," he said. "And hell if they aren't going to succeed."

CHAPTER 7

"Miss Campbell, I apologize for not properly greeting you when you initially arrived." Celia paused in the parlor to hand the wrapped photographs to Addie, which she'd had to fetch from Jane's house where she'd left them.

Her housekeeper raised her eyebrows, a silent query about what Celia had learned from Miss Shaw and why it had taken her so long to return home.

"Later, Addie," whispered Celia, stripping off her gloves and bonnet and handing them to Addie as well.

Miss Olivia Campbell, Barbara's tutor, rose from the chair she'd taken at the dining room table. She wore a severely dark dress, rather old-fashioned in its cut, the color of which caused her to appear sickly, especially given her thin, ash-brown hair. Her attire was likely chosen to make her seem older and more mature than her four-and-twenty years.

"That's quite all right, Mrs. Davies. I didn't mind. It gave me a chance to talk to Miss Walford for a few minutes before we began the assessment."

She cradled her left hand in her right, holding it tight against her waist. The arm was thin and frail, partially paralyzed from a childhood disease. Diphtheria, perhaps. Celia hadn't requested the specifics when Miss Campbell had interviewed for the position last week.

"Nonetheless, I do apologize," said Celia, sitting opposite her and Barbara.

"Thank you for engaging me to assist your cousin," said Miss Campbell, retaking her seat. She had bright eyes but a reluctant smile. Perhaps she was used to being judged and found wanting; the effort of a smile wasted upon people who could not look beyond her limp hand to observe the good, the intelligence in her. Little different than the way people looked at Barbara. "My assessment this morning tells me that Miss Walford is very intelligent."

Barbara shot Celia a glance questioning if Celia had instructed Miss Campbell to make that claim.

"I've heard nothing but good about you, Miss Campbell," said Celia.

"Have you? Not everyone is willing . . ." Her words trailed off.

To speak well of you or employ your services because of your physical flaws?

"I do not care what everyone else is willing or not willing to do," said Celia. "I only care about how you can help Barbara."

"My cousin seems to think I need to add to my education," said Barbara. "I was dismissed from the nearby grammar school two years ago when some of the parents complained about my being there. Because my mother was Chinese."

"I'm sorry," said Miss Campbell.

"Their reactions are not your fault, Miss Campbell," said Celia.

"Nonetheless, I am sorry," she replied. "Despite your past experience, I hope you're looking forward to our lessons, Miss Walford."

"My cousin has convinced me they're necessary."

"And you don't believe they're necessary? But they are, Miss Walford," said Miss Campbell, her voice rising on a tide of passion. "Education is the rebuttal to those who'd limit who we can be or what we can do. Don't you agree, Miss Walford? You simply must agree."

For the first time in weeks, since Grace Hutchinson had gone off to the Young Ladies' Seminary in Benicia and left her bereft, Barbara smiled. A warm, wonderful smile. *I have not chosen wrong.* She had chosen precisely the right young woman to instruct Barbara.

"Yes, Miss Campbell," Barbara said. "I agree."

"Thank you," said Miss Campbell. "If it's acceptable to you, Mrs. Davies, I'd be happy to begin my work with Miss Walford immediately."

"It is completely acceptable, Miss Campbell," said Celia. "Tomorrow morning?"

"Perfect. Thank you," the young woman replied. Her gaze took in Barbara. "Miss Walford promises to be an excellent student. I'm looking forward to our time together."

"No Chaucer, though," said Barbara.

Laughing, Miss Campbell stood. "No Chaucer, Miss Walford." She tugged on her cotton thread gloves, her weak left hand struggling to ease the crochet-work over her right. Task completed, she collected her small leather case. "I'll be going, then."

She exited the house and descended the steps to the street.

"Libby's okay," said Barbara, once Miss Campbell was out of earshot.

"Libby?" asked Celia.

"Miss Campbell said I could call her by her nickname." Barbara waved at her tutor, who'd paused on the pavement to look up at the house. Miss Campbell waved in return before proceeding along the road, the small leather case she carried swinging at her side.

"I am glad you like her."

"So am I," said her cousin, striding back inside.

Addie exited Celia's examination room. "*Weel?*" she asked, once she was certain Barbara had strolled out of earshot.

"Miss Campbell will be most excellent."

"That's not what I was asking, ma'am."

"I have lost that key, Addie," she replied. "But not before discovering that it did fit the lock in a private side door to the Institute."

"I'll nae believe it of Miss Mina."

"The police will." Even Nicholas Greaves, who knew the young woman far better than either she or Addie did. "I cannot fathom how she obtained it, though."

"But what was Miss Mina's motive? To be rid of some annoying fellow who'd been giving her candy? If we believe that box at Bauman's was even hers." Addie folded her arms, unwilling to be swayed. "Not Miss Mina. She'd have thought of another solution."

"Addie, she'd not be the first woman to strike out in desperation," said Celia. "But before you accuse me of giving up on her, I shall go and speak with Herr Bauman. He will know if Mr. Shaw had indeed been bothering Mina, and if she'd been upset as a result. And if she indicated she'd planned to go to the Institute to confront the man."

"And what if you find she had planned to go there, ma'am?"

"As they say, I shall cross that bridge when I come to it."

• • •

Nick climbed the steps leading from the basement station to the side alley and strode over to where Taylor waited at the curb.

"Mr. Blanchard took a cab back to his house, sir," he said around the lit cigar clenched between his teeth. Smoke puffed from his mouth. "There weren't any reporters outside, which made him happy."

Nick paused to scan the streets around the station. It was another habit of his, this endless watchfulness. As was typical for the middle of the day on a dusty Portsmouth Square, the surrounding streets were busy with pedestrians. The usual hubbub, including a street vendor hawking "magic razors." Preferable to the one last week selling rattlesnake oil. He should have an officer make sure the man had a license.

"Inform the cops who work Blanchard's neighborhood to keep an eye on him. Just to make sure he doesn't pack up and catch a train out of town," said Nick. "Also, check if Shaw even remotely hinted when he made his complaint that Blanchard was the person tailing him. We need to confirm Leonard Shaw's accusation."

"Will do, sir," he said. "Why'd you let Mr. Blanchard go free, though? He's got a motive and he doesn't have an alibi."

"Hating a man because he insults your wife doesn't always lead to acts of revenge, Taylor." *Thank God.* "And we can't get around the fact that all the evidence we so far have points to Mina Cascarino."

Taylor plucked his cigar, smoked down to a stub, out of his mouth. "Want me to try to talk to Miss Mina this afternoon?"

Because Mrs. Davies might let Taylor up to see her, when she'd thrown up barricades preventing Nick?

"I need you to check on that robbery at Blanchard's house, find out what you can learn. If it's even relevant." *Which I'm not sure it is.* "I'm going to Miss Shaw's photographic studio and see what she knows about Elliot Blanchard and her father. Then I'm off to the Hygienic Institute. I've learned that a few patients have had belongings stolen while staying there. I need to hear what Ross has to say. Find out if we've had any reports about thefts at the Institute too, Taylor."

"What's somebody stealing from patients got to do with Mr. Shaw's death though, sir?"

"Maybe Shaw was the victim of a robbery attempt gone bad," he said. "But that's what we need to figure out."

"Detective Greaves!" A policeman in his gray uniform hailed him from across the street. He ran over once the traffic allowed.

"Did you have a chance to speak with Ross's cook, Mullahey?" Nick asked him.

Mullahey greeted Taylor with a nod. "I did, Mr. Greaves. She confirmed what the others have said—that she didn't see a stranger inside the building after visitin' hours. She also told me Mr. Ross left around quarter past seven. He stopped in the kitchen to speak with her before he went home. After that, she helped Mr. Platt tidy up the parlor until he told her she could go. Before seven thirty."

"The same as what Platt said," said Nick.

"She didn't know at all about the ruckus Mrs. Wynn caused, or that Mr. Shaw had died, until this mornin' when she arrived for work at the Institute," Mullahey added.

"So the intruder *had* to have used the private staircase in order to not be spotted by Mr. Platt or Miss Newcomb. Or by any of the other patients. Right?" asked Taylor.

Mullahey leaned in. "Unless this person was a ghost, Taylor."

"Very funny, Mullahey."

Nick thanked him and, tugging the brim of his policeman's cap, he strode off.

Taylor dropped his cigar stub onto the sidewalk and crushed it with the heel of his boot. "Where does this leave us, sir?"

"Well, it seems Platt and the cook have vouched for each other." If they were both telling the truth. "Also, the other patients—aside from Mrs. Wynn, busy discovering a trespasser on the premises—were in the parlor having a rousing game of cards and Ross was on his way home. That's where we're at."

"Suspecting an intruder," said Taylor, frowning. "Like Miss Mina."

• • •

Rebecca Shaw's photographic gallery stood on Montgomery, two short blocks south of the police station. Nick arrived just as a young couple in their Sunday best strolled out of the studio. The man nodded a greeting and murmured to the woman at his side, something amusing that made her giggle.

A memory of a long-ago visit to a photographer stirred, the sound of Meg's voice as she teased Ellie about the dress she'd chosen to wear for the portrait, Ellie chiding her to try to settle herself for once, Nick laughing at both of his sisters. But it was a memory so fleeting it could have been the hastily detected scent of a passing woman's perfume, or a barely sighted sparrow darting from shrub to shrub, and he was grateful when it vanished as quickly as it had entered his mind.

At the ring of the bell above the shop door, Rebecca Shaw stepped through a side doorway with a smile, a heavy apron tied over her dark, plain dress. She was tall—taller than he'd imagined for a reason he couldn't fathom—and had a confident bearing. The light streaming through the window caught in her rich auburn hair.

"Are you looking to make an appointment to have your portrait taken?" she asked.

Nick crossed the sunlit space, beneath a dozen somber faces staring down from the walls, peering out from frames propped on tables and easels, the smell of chemicals sharp in the air.

"No." He flipped back his coat to show his badge. "I'm Detective Greaves."

Her smile slid off her face. "A policeman has already been here to tell me about my father. So if you don't mind, I have work to finish before I close."

She turned on her heel and headed for the room she'd come from. Marched past her camera and the painted canvas backdrop—a fanciful scene of a hillside—that had probably been used for the couple he'd encountered on the sidewalk.

"Miss Shaw, I need to ask you some questions," he said.

"It's not convenient for me right now." She ducked inside the room, and Nick followed. The overpowering tang of chemicals, the small window cut into the exterior wall inadequate to air out the space, caused him to cough.

"I must be used to the smell by now," said Miss Shaw, examining the photographs suspended by clips to dry.

Porcelain and glass dishes were arrayed on a table, and bottles of chemicals—glacial acetic acid, alcohol, distilled water, cyanide of potassium, nitrate of silver—lined wood shelves. Salted paper sat alongside a supply of frames. All of it carefully arranged. A reflection of Miss Shaw's personality, perhaps.

"I can't help that it's not convenient, Miss Shaw," he said. "I need to talk to you."

She slid him a look. In the darkness of the space, it was hard to read her expression, judge if her confusion was genuine. "Is it normal protocol for the police to intrude upon grieving family members?"

It is when they might have critical information. "How about we return to the main room where we'll both be more comfortable, miss."

Reluctantly, she left, stripping off her heavy apron as she walked. She tossed it onto a large glass case in the center of the gallery. "I don't know how I can help you, Detective."

"I spoke with your brother and Mrs. Shaw this morning."

"My stepbrother," she corrected, toying with a slim gold bracelet she wore on her left wrist. She had long fingers with short nails, discolored by chemicals. Many women would be embarrassed to show their hands, if they looked like Rebecca Shaw's. She didn't strike him as a person who cared what others thought. "What did Leo and Delphia have to say about my father's sudden death? Something that has given you a reason to come here and ask questions."

"What can you tell me about Mr. Elliot Blanchard?"

"What has he got to do . . . my father's death was not natural, was it?" she asked. "Was it, Detective?"

"As you guessed, the coroner suspects foul play."

"And Leo has implicated Elliot . . ." She let out a mirthless chuckle. "He's always hated him."

"You know Mr. Blanchard well, Miss Shaw?"

"We have a close acquaintance," she replied. "*Used* to. No longer, since he and my father ended up on opposite sides politically."

"Did your father ever complain to you about a suspicious person following him?"

Her expression didn't change; maybe the idea of somebody stalking her father wasn't remarkable. "A suspicious person like Elliot, you mean? If Delphia and Leo have blamed Mr. Blanchard, they're lying," she stated. "And my father never complained to me, because we haven't spoken in months, Detective Greaves."

"I was told you'd visited him at the Institute this week."

"I did—upon his request—but after a few minutes of waiting in the Institute's parlor, I figured he'd decided against meeting me after all. So I left."

"The parlor? You mean he didn't give you a key to use?" asked Nick.

She gave him a strange look, tilting her head the way Riley would sometimes do when the dog was trying to process something Nick had said. "My father didn't give me a key to use, Detective Greaves. The front door was unlocked. I went straight in."

Okay. "What about your stepmother's relationship with your father?" he asked. "Was it a happy one?"

She surprised him by laughing. "I'm sorry. That was rude of me."

Enough of an answer to his question.

Outside, a fire engine clattered past on the street, its bell ringing.

The commotion drew her attention, giving Nick time to better study the interior of the gallery. Examine the carefully arranged portraits and the few landscape photographs on display. If they were her work, she had talent. He wondered who'd financed the place.

"They've gone a ways up the street, thank God," she said. "I'm always afraid of fires. And earthquakes."

"Don't you have insurance for your business here, Miss Shaw?"

She answered his question with one of her own. "How much longer is this going to take, Detective?"

"Almost done." He smiled, even though his smiles weren't worth half of the ones Taylor could muster. "A person was spotted outside your father's room last night. They could have critical information about Mr. Shaw's death and we'd like to locate them. Any idea who it could've been?"

"Somebody like Elliot, you mean?" she asked. "I'm sorry, but I don't have any idea who it was."

"What about a mistress, Miss Shaw? Your father sent candy to saloon girls," he replied. "I've seen a box myself."

"For all his sins, Detective, he was not a philanderer. He simply enjoyed sending gifts. To young ladies. To political supporters. Sometimes even to his enemies." Rebecca Shaw turned aside and retreated behind her glass display case. She bent down to search among its contents. "Ambrose Shaw was a complicated man."

He couldn't detect animosity in her demeanor; just a straight-forward assessment of her father's personality. More gracious and forgiving than Nick had ever been when it came to his own father.

"One last question, Miss Shaw," he said. "Where were you last night, between seven and eight?"

"I closed my studio not long after seven and then went to my rooms above this shop, Detective," she answered quickly. She straightened, a leather carte de visite cover in her hand. "My neighbor who lives in the flat across from mine can vouch that she spoke with me near my usual dinnertime. Around seven thirty, I suppose," she added, without him even having to ask. "I have another question for you, Detective. How *did* my father die?"

"Painlessly, miss, if you draw any comfort from that."

"That's good." She rolled her lips between her teeth. "That's good."

"Who stands to gain the most from your father's death, Miss Shaw?"

Her eyes—a deep blue that bordered on green and were quite engrossing, if he wanted to spend time admiring them—considered him closely. "Who'd be the happiest? Or who'd be the richest?"

"Your choice on how to answer."

"They are probably one and the same, Mr. Greaves," she answered. "And I'd be a fool to name names when I have no more of an idea than you apparently do."

• • •

"I need your help, Cassidy."

Caleb Griffin hung back in the gloom cast by the boardinghouse balcony overhead, his hat tugged low. Owen had never known Caleb to lurk in shadows, trying to not be noticed. Heck, he'd even taken to wearing a plain charcoal-colored vest instead of his red one that made him as noticeable as a robin hopping about in a tree. He still smelled of rose water, though, and the Sozodent he used on his teeth. Some things a fellow just couldn't give up, Owen supposed.

"My help?" asked Owen, recoiling in anticipation of a blow that might come in response to his question. Caleb usually issued orders and folks were just supposed to obey. Not ask questions.

Caleb didn't hit him, though.

"Yes," he said. "Your help."

"Oh . . . okay."

Shoot, Cassidy. Why'd you go and agree like you don't have a lick of sense? Plus, why did a person like Caleb Griffin even need help from him? The idea bothered Owen. About as much as the notion that Caleb knew where he lived and had been able to send a message to his lodgings requesting this here meeting.

"I mean . . . I mean . . ." stuttered Owen. "I mean I'll see what I can do, Caleb. I've got a job at a confectioner's store now, you see, and I can't be missing work. I need the money."

Caleb scowled. He had a downright mean scowl. That much hadn't changed, either. "Don't be wasting my time, Cassidy. I can't afford to be standing around jawing with you."

"Somebody after you, Caleb?"

Shoot! What is wrong with me, asking a question like that?

This time, Owen cringed *and* shut his eyes. Caleb barked a laugh. Which Owen hadn't been expecting at all.

He peeled open one eyelid. "What do you need me to do, Caleb?" He had to give the man a chance to explain; Owen owed Caleb his life, and he wasn't going to go and be so ungrateful as to forget.

"I need you to give a fellow a message for me. This is where you'll find him."

Caleb dug a folded scrap of paper and a coin from his pocket, shoving the items at Owen, who grabbed them before they fell into the muck of the side street. As it was, the soles of his brogans—he'd only last week had new heels put on—were sticking to something he didn't fancy identifying.

He stared down at the coin, heavy and solid in his fist, before stowing it away. A silver dollar? A whole silver dollar?

"There'll be another one of those if you do what I'm asking right," said Caleb.

Owen's fingers shook as he stuffed the coin into his brogan, safer there than inside one of his pockets. It was sorta alarming, if Caleb was paying him that kind of money.

The note had an address on it. "What's the message?"

"Watch for a fellow with red hair." Voices approached, drawing Caleb's attention off Owen until the owners passed the end of the side street without bothering either of them. "His name is Platt. He works at that address. Tell him I want my money."

Who didn't owe Caleb Griffin money? Even Mr. Davies had, and look at the trouble it had caused Mrs. Davies.

Owen stuck the note into his brogan alongside the dollar coin. His foot was hot and damp, as sure a sign of his rattled nerves as the shaking of his fingers. "But, Caleb, like I already told you, I need to get to my job at the confectioner's soon. Can't I just leave your message at this fellow's lodgings?"

"He's not there. I already checked," he said. "Which means he's still at his place of employment but could be leaving any minute."

"You sure I can't just drop the message at his work place, then?" Was he whining, now? Did he sound like he was whining?

"Are you gonna help or not, Cassidy?" asked Caleb, the tone of his voice implying Owen had better answer yes.

Owen swallowed. "Um, okay. I expect you'll want me to get a response from him, too."

"I knew I could count on you, Cassidy."

Tugging his coat collar tight against his jaw, Caleb bolted into the sunlight and sprinted up the road like a pack of wild dogs was snapping at his heels.

• • •

The Institute's front door was unlocked—just as Rebecca Shaw had supposedly found it on her visit—and Nick stepped into the entry hall. "Hullo?"

The parlor was empty, dust motes spinning on a narrow band of sunlight stealing through a chink in the closed shutters. Angry voices echoed down from the upstairs rooms, and pots clanged in the kitchen. He didn't need to be shown to Ross's office, though. He knew where it was.

Nick knocked and entered the room. "Have a minute, Mr. Ross?"

"Oh, it's you again, Detective Greaves." He'd been staring out the window, his back to the door. The view was very fine, looking out on the limestone-clad walls of a church across the way, one stained-glass window a jolt of vivid cobalt blue and crimson red among the expanse of creamy stone. "Has the coroner finally issued his report on Mr. Shaw's suspicious death?"

"I expect he'll be finished with his examination sometime today."

"And then the newspapers will hear," said Ross. He produced a handkerchief to mop across his forehead. The fellow sure did sweat a lot. "A reporter was here this morning, wanting to know why the police have been spotted coming and going. I'll be ruined. No one will come to my Institute again. Ever. And my wife is distraught that one of your officers came to our door at daybreak this morning, asking her to vouch for my whereabouts last evening."

Mullahey, up and about early, aware that morning sleepiness sometimes encouraged folks to blurt out the most honest statements. "And what did she answer?"

He flushed. "That I was at home, as I said, Mr. Greaves."

"Why don't you take a seat, Mr. Ross. You don't look well."

Ross happily dropped onto the chair behind his desk. "I've spoken with my daytime assistant about Mr. Shaw's missing key, Mr. Greaves."

"And what did you learn?"

"He intended to retrieve a new one from the locksmith today, to replace the one Mr. Shaw lost," he said. "However, before he did, the fellow chose instead to quit. Not fifteen minutes ago. Once he'd heard . . . well . . ."

That Mr. Shaw had died under suspicious circumstances, Nick supposed.

"And now I've had to ask Mr. Platt to remain past his usual departure time, to help with the patients who've decided to cut short their stays." He glanced at the ceiling, the direction of rooms soon to be vacated by angry—and loud—occupants. "They've all decided to leave after lunch. Actually, one of them left right after breakfast. I'll be ruined."

Nick let Ross moan over his misfortune for a few seconds before moving on.

"I've spoken with Miss Shaw about her visit here," he said. "She tells me she never met with her father."

"I believe, sadly, that was the case," replied Ross, confirming her story.

"And Mr. Shaw definitely had no other visitors? Besides his wife and son." Somebody who might've helped themselves to a key.

"We limit visitors, Detective," he said. "My patients require comfort and quiet."

"Certainly," said Nick. "It's come to my attention that several of your former patients had personal items stolen while they were inmates here. What can you tell me about that?"

"I . . . I do recall a patient . . . umm . . . making that claim," he stuttered.

"More than one, according to my information."

"More than one? No, no. Just one."

"Okay, what about that one?" asked Nick, sure he sounded as impatient as he felt.

"She was being treated for a nervous disposition, Detective," he said. "Her husband assured me that she has flights of fancy, which is why I didn't notify the police."

"Your patient mustn't have agreed with her husband's assessment that she was suffering from a flight of fancy, because she told her friends about the theft."

"Oh. That's how you heard."

"I've also been told that a male patient had an engraved gold pen stolen," said Nick.

"Nonsense!" Ross's face flushed a dangerous-looking shade of red. "No other thefts. Most certainly not. I don't operate an institution occupied by thieves!"

A rapid knock sounded on the doorframe and Mrs. Shaw barged into the office. "I'm glad to see you, Detective Greaves. I'd like to report a theft. My husband's gold watch and fob chain are missing from the possessions he brought with him to this . . . this horrible place!"

CHAPTER 8

"Captain Eagan was looking for you, sir," said Taylor, following Nick into the detectives' office. He closed the door behind him. "Got wind we were investigating Mr. Shaw's 'natural death,' as he put it, and wants to know what you're up to."

"And what did you tell him?" asked Nick, tossing his hat onto the desk.

"That Dr. Harris thinks it's suspicious," he replied. "The captain didn't say anything after I told him that."

"Good." He dropped onto the chair at his desk while Taylor took the one opposite. "Miss Shaw was at her gallery. She's adamant that Delphia and Leonard Shaw are lying about Blanchard being the person who'd been following Ambrose Shaw."

"I looked through our records, sir," said Taylor. "Mr. Shaw never named who he'd suspected of stalking him. I'm surprised he didn't take the chance to accuse Mr. Blanchard, seeing how much they disliked each other."

So was he. "Miss Shaw also said she hadn't been given a key. In fact, she didn't even speak with her father when she visited the Institute, which Ross has backed up," said Nick. "I checked her alibi for last night. Her neighbor confirms speaking with Miss Shaw around seven thirty."

Taylor jotted in his notebook. "So we can eliminate Miss Shaw?"

"Maybe," Nick replied. "Mrs. Shaw happened to show up while I was in Ross's office. Her husband's expensive gold watch and fob chain are missing from among his possessions, and they didn't go with the body to Harris's morgue. The fellow was only in a nightshirt last night."

"Another theft." Taylor whistled. "We did get a report on one of those other incidents at the Institute, sir. Looks like there's been a problem at the place for a while."

Except this time the thieving might've turned into murder.

"Ross's wife has vouched that he was safely at home by seven thirty."

Nick leaned back, the casters squealing. One day maybe he'd remember to take some oil to them and stop their cussed noise. "So he might be a thief but he's not our killer."

Taylor peered at him. "Miss Mina can't possibly be responsible either. Right?"

Mina. *Damn.* "I think I will head over to the Cascarinos', Taylor. See if she's got Shaw's watch." Hopefully Celia Davies wouldn't be there this time to stop him.

"And a key?"

Nick's stomach soured. "And a key."

Just then, a shadow appeared on the other side of the office door's glass. The man rapped on the door and opened it. "Greaves, Taylor," said the coroner. "Might I interrupt?"

Nick gestured for him to come in. "You're finished with Shaw's autopsy?"

"Enough to give you some answers, I believe."

Taylor jumped up and offered Harris his chair.

"First of all, Ambrose Shaw did die from heart failure. That much is clear," said the coroner. He withdrew a folded piece of paper from the inside pocket of his coat and consulted it. "Furthermore, there was a quantity of alcohol in his stomach along with a small amount of his supper. One or two sheets in the wind, if you ask me."

"That much easier to knock out with chloroform," said Nick.

"It wouldn't hurt."

"He was also robbed of an expensive gold watch and chain, Harris," he said. "Perhaps his assailant wanted to render him senseless in order to have time to hunt around for the man's valuables before finishing him off with a good dose of coal gas fumes."

Harris refolded his notes and stowed them away. "Sedating someone in order to steal from them really isn't as simple as what's reported in the papers, Greaves. Those sensational stories about innocent victims having an assailant sneak up behind them with a chloroform-soaked rag and rendering them instantly unconscious," he replied. "It normally requires several minutes of administration to anesthetize a person, especially a man of his size."

"Shaw helped them out by not only being drunk but keeling over from heart failure."

"He didn't perish immediately," said Harris. "I found a faint contusion on the back of his right wrist where he struck it against something, or someone. In addition, I discovered a number of scratches on his cheeks, near his ears. I couldn't find any skin beneath his fingernails, so the scratches were likely caused by his assailant."

"While holding the cloth against his face," said Taylor. "That linen handkerchief."

"That's my supposition, Mr. Taylor. He must've been too drunk to fight off the person," said Harris. "Unfortunately, chloroform doesn't leave a telltale smell in the blood or tissues of its victims, so I'm having to go with my instincts on the cause of his heart failure. The abrasions on his face. The slight chemical burns on the sensitive skin around his nose. The lack of stiffness that I'd associate with excess gas exposure. That handkerchief."

"Enough to convince an inquest jury he was murdered?" asked Nick.

"Depends on the jury, Greaves," he replied. "Finding the chloroform bottle in Mr. Shaw's room would've been helpful, though."

"Why not just crack Mr. Shaw on the head and then turn on the gas to finish him off?" asked Taylor. "Rather than use chloroform."

"Because an obvious wound makes it hard to pretend his death had been an accident caused by a gas leak," said Nick.

"But the perpetrator stole his watch, sir," protested Taylor. "Once we discovered it was gone, we'd *have* to conclude Mr. Shaw's death was murder. Right? I mean the fellow didn't throw his gold watch and fob chain out the window before succumbing to gas fumes."

"Unless the killer and the thief *are* two different people, Taylor." But was one of them Mina Cascarino?

Harris stood. "A fascinating Gordian knot I'll leave to you two gentlemen to unpick. Do you need anything else, Greaves?"

"When do you intend to call the inquest?" asked Nick. "I'd like time to investigate without the reporters howling that Shaw was killed." The results of the jury's findings would be in the papers as soon as they could slap ink on the presses.

"I can't hold off much longer. Tomorrow morning at the latest," he said. "I have another inquest to conduct, so maybe I can claim I'm just being efficient in holding them at the same time. A suicide, the other one." He shook his head. "When will folks stop killing themselves in this town?"

As soon as they stop feeling desperate and lost, like Meg . . .

"Thanks, Harris," he said, embarrassed to hear his voice shake. Harris didn't appear to notice, though.

The coroner left, quietly shutting the door behind him.

"It's all pretty confusing to me, sir," said Taylor, frowning over his bewilderment. "By the way, I had a chance to look into that burglary at Mr. Blanchard's house. The report matches what he told us. Somebody broke in, rummaged around, tossing things everywhere, left without anything. One of the officers who investigated found a broken window, but that was all he discovered."

Nothing taken, but enough of a mess to make sure the occupants of the house knew that somebody had broken in . . .

"What if it wasn't actually an attempted burglary, Taylor?" asked Nick. "Blanchard said it scared his wife. Maybe that's all the perpetrators intended."

"Could be, sir." Taylor scratched his neck with the edge of his notebook. "I guess."

Nick exhaled and spun his chair to look out the office window and its basement view of passing legs. Maybe one day he'd get a promotion that provided an office on an upper floor, with windows offering a better prospect than an up-close view of a sidewalk. Or maybe he'd just go out and find another occupation, one that didn't leave him inhaling the dirt blowing in off the street, or regularly dealing with the cruel and the criminal.

"A burglary at Blanchard's house with nothing stolen," he mused. "Thefts from patients at the Hygienic Institute. Someone reportedly following Shaw in recent weeks, alarming him, his family accusing Blanchard of being responsible. Shaw now dead from a heart attack probably brought on from chloroform exposure, gas turned on in his room, his watch and fob chain stolen. Mina Cascarino concussed, her blue shawl outside in the alley, a box of candy from A.S. in the dressing room at Bauman's . . ."

"Are *all* those events connected, sir? All of them?"

"You know what I always say about coincidences, Taylor." *Don't ever trust them.*

"A heckuva mystery, sir."

"Yes, Taylor." Nick tugged the sash down, rattling the cast-iron window weight. "One that doesn't make any sense. Not yet."

• • •

"Mrs. Davies?" Mina looked over at the door, an expectant smile on her face. It slid off when she realized it was Nick. "Oh."

"How are you feeling?" he asked, shooting a look at the chair pulled alongside her invalid bed. Too close to her for comfort.

"You're not here to ask after my health." Propped up in bed, she'd been holding a book when he'd entered. She tried to set it on the bedside table, but she missed and the book slid onto the floor.

Nick bent down to retrieve it. *Leaves of Grass* was embossed on the spine. "I didn't realize you read poetry, Mina."

"You never realized a lot about me. Give it back." She grabbed the book from his hand, wincing at the suddenness of the motion, and set it back on the table. The curtains had been drawn, leaving the bedroom cool and shadowed, but he didn't need sunlight to observe her irritation.

Knuckles tapped rapidly on the half-closed door. "Mina?" called her mother through the opening.

"I am fine, Mama. Go downstairs."

They exchanged a few words in Italian before Mina convinced Mrs. Cascarino it was okay to let Nick stay.

"I can't believe she even let you in the house," said Mina.

"I can be persuasive."

She smiled again, and this time it didn't look pained but genuine. "Don't I know it," she replied. "But I don't want to talk to you."

"I'm not here to rehash what we said to each other at Bauman's yesterday."

"I barely remember what we said." She rearranged the pillow at her back, sliding him a sideways look as she did. "You're here to ask about Ambrose."

"I would've spoken with you this morning, but Mrs. Davies refused to let me upstairs."

"I wish she was still here to prevent you again." She pinched her eyes closed and pressed her knuckles against her temples.

"Are you all right?"

"A dizzy spell. It'll pass. They always do after a bit." She pulled in a few breaths, which seemed to steady her. "My head hurts to move. The light bothers me. My brothers and sisters . . . the noise makes my brain pound. I'm starting to wonder if I'll ever be well again and it scares me."

"It'll get better. Trust me." He waited for a few seconds before continuing. "Have you been able to remember anything at all from last night, Mina?"

"Bits and pieces. It's like I have a flash of a memory, but by the time I try to latch on to it and hold on, it's gone like it never existed."

"What about a key, Mina? Did Ambrose Shaw ever give you one?" he asked, afraid of the answer.

"Mrs. Davies asked about a key she'd found," she replied. "In my skirt pocket. I didn't recognize it, though. I don't know where it came from."

Damn, damn.

And blasted woman. When was she planning on telling him? Mina had to be somehow involved, though, and Mrs. Davies had arrived at the same conclusion. Which was why she hadn't exactly rushed to the station with a key she'd discovered.

"Did Mrs. Davies also mention finding a man's watch and chain?" he asked.

"No."

"What about purchasing chloroform . . . have you recently for any reason?" he asked.

She eyed him warily. "I don't use chloroform. Why would I buy any? Was it used on Ambrose Shaw? Is that what happened?"

She wasn't so concussed that she couldn't reason clearly. "Do you mind if I search through your clothes?" he asked.

Her eyes flashed like the Mina he'd always known. "What if I told you no?" She frowned and pointed to her left. "The end of the hall."

A couple of Cascarino children watched him from the stairwell as he strode down the hall and into the room. A small but tidy space, flower-print curtains at the window to cheer it, Mina's clothing folded neatly at the end of the largest bed.

He lifted her tan gown, unfolded the rest. He'd touched her stockings, her petticoats before—she favored fine linen undergarments, the best she could afford. A small luxury in a cruel world, she'd explained. And he'd been vain enough to think her purchases had been meant to please him. *You deserved better than me, Mina. You still do.*

But the folds of her clothes and pockets were empty.

"Well?" she asked when he reappeared at the bedroom doorway.

"No watch." Maybe Celia Davies had taken it, too.

"I didn't do it, Nick. I had nothing to do with Ambrose Shaw's death," she insisted, her face ashen. "I'm positive."

"How can you be, Mina? You keep telling me how fuzzy your memory is."

"I'd remember something as horrible as that." Her eyes locked on his, pleading with him to believe her. To believe *in* her. "Wouldn't I?"

• • •

Owen leaned against the slice of brick wall between the windows of a liquor retailer and a watchmaker's store, cleaning his teeth with a wood toothpick like he had all the time in the world and wasn't in any rush to return to some menial job like a poor slob. Even though he *was* in a rush to get back to the confectionary store.

Dang. When is that fellow gonna leave the building so I can give him Caleb's message?

A side door to the Hygienic Institute opened, and a woman stepped through with a bucket. She tossed its contents out onto the alley, looked around, spotted Owen staring at her—*shoot!*—scowled, and went back inside.

Owen slunk against the bricks, which didn't exactly offer any cover but did succeed in getting a customer marching out of the adjacent liquor store to notice him skulking like a criminal. A not very good criminal, at that.

"What are you doing there, boy?" the man shouted. As if he owned the spot on the sidewalk or something.

Owen yanked the toothpick from his mouth and straightened. "Enjoying the weather, sir."

"Move on, or I'll find the nearest police officer and report you for loitering."

"I got a right to stand and enjoy the sunshine," said Owen, jutting his chin.

The fellow turned an ungodly shade of crimson. "We'll see about that," he snapped and charged up the road. In search of the nearest cop, no doubt.

The corner newspaper boy, who'd been shouting the headline about some Shaw fellow who'd gone and died, had overheard and doubled up with laughter.

"What are you cackling about?" asked Owen, angrily kicking at a broken chunk of brick and sending it skittering across the plank sidewalk into the gutter.

The boy, still laughing, dashed out into the road to hawk papers to the passengers descending from a stopped horsecar, leaving Owen to scowl after him.

Durn it all.

He should get going, because that fellow from the liquor store would be showing up with a cop soon enough, and it might not be one of the officers Owen was friendly with. Just then, a woman loaded down with a bulging carpetbag and a small trunk pushed through the front door of the Hygienic Institute and headed down the street.

A fellow with bushy whiskers and spectacles chased after her. "Mrs. Wynn, please reconsider," he yelled. "I assure you, you're perfectly safe."

Safe?

She halted and said something to the man, but the bells of the church a block away took to clanging the hour right that very second and Owen couldn't hear a single thing. Not that he was close enough to hear much anyway, and not that he was sure he should be bothering with eavesdropping on them, either. She looked hopping mad, though. Finished with her response, she turned on her heel and continued her march down the road. The bushy-whiskered fellow shook his head and went back inside.

Huh.

He couldn't stand there much longer. That fellow would be back with a policeman, and Mr. Roesler would be wondering why Owen was late for work.

Sighing, he started down the street, bound for the candy store, which happened to be the same direction Mrs. Wynn was heading. He shot her a glance before turning onto the street where the store was located. She'd rounded the corner across the way when a red-haired fellow came striding down the road. The fellow Caleb had wanted Owen to give a message to! He scuttled around the same corner where Mrs. Wynn had gone and stopped her.

Ain't . . . isn't that interesting?

Tucking his hands into the pockets of his pants and whistling the first tune that came to his head—"Camptown Races," as it turned out—

Owen strolled across the road, hustling at the last moment to avoid being hit by a fast-trotting buggy. Mrs. Wynn and her companion didn't notice him sauntering their way. Heck, most folks didn't pay any mind to a kid walking along. Unless he looked like he wanted to sell 'em something or pickpocket them.

Owen halted a few feet away and bent down to tie his bootlaces. Near enough to overhear; far enough to not draw their attention.

"Where's the watch?" the fellow hissed, his voice echoing off the window at the woman's back.

"What in heaven's name are you talking about, Mr. Platt?" asked Mrs. Wynn, sidling away from the fellow.

"It's gone. Along with the fob chain," said the man, sounding sorta menacing. "Where is it?"

"I don't know why you'd be accusing me of stealing Mr. Shaw's watch," she spat. "Please leave me alone."

"Owen! Why you there?" a voice called from up the road.

Shoot! What is Angelo Cascarino doing in this part of town?

Mrs. Wynn shot Owen an alarmed glance. "Cease bothering me, sir," she said to Mr. Platt, hiked her skirts, and dashed for the horsecar coming to a stop in the street.

Her companion noticed Owen. "What do you want, kid?"

"Um . . . Mr. Griffin says to pay him the money you owe. Now."

The fellow bared his teeth, sorta like an angry dog, and brandished his fists. "Get the hell outta here or else."

Owen didn't require a second invitation to do just that.

"Go home, Angelo," he snapped at the boy, wide-eyed over Mr. Platt's threat, and scurried off. He didn't dare check if Mr. Platt was chasing.

• • •

"Mr. Greaves, is it true about Mina?" asked Bauman, wiping his hands on a clean rag as he came out from behind the saloon's long bar. "One of the girls tells me she is very ill. Mr. Taylor did not tell me that last night when he was here."

Nick couldn't recall ever seeing Bauman from head to toe. It seemed the fellow was always standing behind the bar, a barrier between his clientele and him. Or between them and his beer taps and precious supply of liquor. Currently, the saloon was empty aside from Bauman and his wife, cooking in the tavern's kitchen, getting ready for the men who'd soon arrive for a meal after work.

"She's got a concussion," Nick replied, taking off his hat.

"Not good. I need her here. Giulia sings instead of Mina, but the customers complain." He pulled a face. "She must return."

"Hopefully she will soon." And not need to be slapped in jail. "Has a Mrs. Celia Davies been here? Blonde, British woman?" After visiting Mina, he'd gone next door and pried Mrs. Davies's plans out of Addie Ferguson, who'd reluctantly relinquished the information.

Bauman shook his head. "No."

"Well, I expect she'll turn up soon enough."

Nick looked around. At the neatly arranged tables and chairs, the recently cleaned wood floor gleaming a warm golden brown, the spotless framed mirrors on the paneled walls reflecting the gas lights. It was a nice place, the sort of place respectable men—and sometimes women—would feel comfortable in. Respectable men like Ambrose Shaw.

"Was Ambrose Shaw a regular here, Herr Bauman?" he asked.

"The politician? The man who died yesterday?"

The news had reached the papers. Even the ones a German saloonkeeper read. "Yes. Him."

"Three . . . four times." Bauman finished wiping his fingers on the cloth and tucked it into the band of his apron. "No more."

"Were he and Mina . . . you know . . ."

Bauman raised his thick eyebrows. "Friends?"

"You could put it that way," he said. "The sort of friend who gives gifts of chocolates."

"I doubt Mr. Shaw ever gave gifts to Mina," he said, despite the box

Nick had seen for himself. "He did like to talk to the girls, though."

"Did his attention make her angry?" Enough to want to permanently get rid of the annoyance?

Bauman chuckled. "Mina? She is afraid of no man."

That was Mina, all right. Fearless. A trait he'd always admired. A trait Celia Davies had, too. In abundance. "How was she yesterday? Upset, for instance?"

"Her mind was not on her work."

Distracted by her plans, perhaps. "You told Taylor that she left around six thirty," said Nick. "Did she say where she was going? Maybe to the Hygienic Institute? Have you ever heard her talk about the Institute?"

"She never spoke about that place. Last night, she only said she had important business and did not seem happy." He scowled. "My wife had no one to help until Giulia came in at seven."

"Do you mind if I search through the dressing room in the back, Herr Bauman?" asked Nick.

The saloonkeeper narrowed his eyes. "It is open, Detective."

He felt the man's gaze on his back as he strode down the hallway. Frau Bauman paused her cooking to stare at Nick, too.

Damn.

Not much had changed since he'd been inside the room yesterday. There were still chairs stuffed in the corner, although the number of beer casks looked to have decreased. San Francisco never lacked folks fancying a drink or two. Or more. The dressing table had been tidied, the hair ribbons and pins, the pot of rouge all stacked to one side. The cracked mirror also remained, but the box from Roesler's was gone. It wasn't in the repurposed basket being used as a waste can. It was possible one of the others girls had helped herself to the candies. Mina's blue shawl wasn't in the room, either.

The dressing table chair, one leg shorter than the rest, wobbled as he sat. He located a box of percussion matches and lit the lantern, the sulfurous smell of the burnt match head lingering in the air. The table had a single drawer, and he rummaged through its contents—some hair combs, a dry brass inkwell, and an old tin of sugared almonds—but nothing incriminating. Nick dragged over the wastebasket. Somebody had dropped torn shreds of paper into it. He picked them out and spread them flat on the table. A restaurant receipt. A note addressed to Giulia—Mina's inadequate replacement—praising her beauty and suggesting they meet someplace private after work. A scribbled list of items to purchase at the grocers. No instructions from an accomplice detailing a plot to murder Shaw. No receipt for chloroform. No evidence that proved the fearless Mina Cascarino was guilty. Or innocent.

• • •

Celia paused on the pavement outside the basement entrance to Bauman's *lagerbier* saloon. The door was open, and the sound of voices and clinking dishes drifted out onto the street. It was early for an evening meal, but clearly patrons were gathered inside. She'd been delayed by a brief visit to a patient, or else she would have arrived before the place was busy with customers.

She reached for the banister that would guide her down the steps but did not budge.

Why am I standing here as though my feet have been nailed to the planking?

She knew the answer. She was afraid she'd embarked upon discovering a truth about Mina Cascarino she did not want to learn. That Herr Bauman would tell her Mr. Shaw had been bothering Mina, and the young woman had come to fiercely resent the man.

"Enough to wish to be rid of him," she murmured aloud. A girl passing on the street, a basket laden with vegetables tucked beneath her arm, gave Celia an apprehensive glance and hastily scurried past.

Celia glanced around to see if anybody else was staring at her and thinking she was a raving madwoman. Fortunately, the majority of the people on the road were more interested in their own affairs than those of a well-dressed Englishwoman who had a habit of talking to herself.

She closed her gloved fingers around the iron handrail—evading an unidentifiable residue splattered on the railing's surface—and charged down the stairs.

The most delicious smell of grilling sausages met her as she stepped inside. The flare of a solitary gas lamp, suspended in the hallway at the far end of the space, provided a meager supplement to the light coming through the open front door. A moment passed before her eyes adjusted from the brilliant sunshine outside to the gloom.

After several years spent residing in San Francisco, Celia was used to the stir she created whenever she entered an establishment such as Bauman's, the sudden hush from the male occupants followed by a whirl of whispers. That the reaction passed so quickly this time was the only surprise.

A barrel-chested man, a white apron tied over his thick waist, looked over from where he stood behind the long bar. *"Ja?* Can I help?" he asked, his accent heavily German, his smile warm and broad.

"Yes, you may be able to help me," she replied. "I am seeking information on a young woman who works here. A Miss Mina Cascarino."

"Well, Mrs. Davies, finally here," said a very familiar voice from a shadowed corner. "Now how about you hand over that key?"

✂ CHAPTER 9 ✎

"What were you planning on accomplishing at Bauman's, Mrs. Davies?" asked Nicholas Greaves, his long strides forcing her to scurry alongside him in order to keep up.

"Mr. Greaves, is it absolutely necessary for you to dash along the road at this pace?" she asked, cursing the tangle of her petticoats around her ankles. "Consider that, if I fall behind, I am more likely to turn around and go back to the *lagerbier* saloon."

He pulled up short. "You didn't have to come with me because I asked you to."

"Because you *told* me to," she rebutted. "And I would not mind hearing the reason *you* were there, Mr. Greaves."

"Do I have to remind you that I am the investigator in a case of murder and that Mina Cascarino is a suspect?" he asked. "And I demand you tell me what you were doing at Bauman's. I don't think you were stopping in for a beer."

"As if I've not been inside establishments like Herr Bauman's before, Mr. Greaves." And worse places than his clean and tidy tavern. "I went to inquire about Mina's possible relationship with Mr. Shaw, though she has denied one. Unfortunately, I got no farther than five feet inside the saloon before I was stopped from my task."

"Bauman claims she ignored the fellow, so make of that what you want. However, he also informed me that Mina was distracted and unhappy when she left the saloon yesterday," he replied. "Upset because of what she intended to do, maybe. She and her accomplice, the one who gave her that concussion."

What was it Mina had said last evening? *It's terrible. What has she . . .* She slid Mr. Greaves a glance. She should tell him, but he would only believe those words were more evidence that Mina was guilty.

Maybe, Celia, she is.

"Despite her distracted state of mind, I truly cannot comprehend why Mina would wish to kill Ambrose Shaw, Mr. Greaves," said Celia. "Even if she had a motive, I expect she could not have readily subdued the fellow. She is rather petite in stature."

"There's evidence of a struggle, but Shaw was drunk. Maybe he wouldn't have required much subduing." They'd attracted the attention of a street sweeper, who'd been creeping closer with his broom the last few seconds. Mr. Greaves scowled at the kid. "We'd better keep walking, ma'am. And while we're walking you can tell me about the key you found in the pocket of Mina Cascarino's dress."

He held out his hand.

"You may hold out your hand for hours, Mr. Greaves, but I cannot conjure what I do not possess," she replied. "A fellow with red hair, who may work at the Hygienic Institute, snatched it away."

"Platt. Ross's evening assistant," he said, his strides lengthening once more. "Well? Did the key fit the lock? Because I'm sure that's what you were up to when you ran into Mr. Platt."

"It may have done," she admitted. "Did you find Mina's shawl at Bauman's?"

"No, I didn't find her shawl at Bauman's, so the one from the alley is most likely hers," he said. "Between that and the key, we have to conclude she was there."

Gad. Until Mina's amnesia lifted and she could explain her actions, she appeared to be very guilty.

"You didn't happen to also find a watch in her skirt pocket, did you?" he asked.

"No. A watch, you say?" asked Celia, pausing at the edge of the road. She caught sight of a pair of young girls running across an empty lot, leveled and readied for yet more new construction. They called out to one another, carefree. Seemingly untroubled by the sorts of concerns weighing on Celia's mind. *How fortunate for them.*

"Mrs. Shaw insists that her husband brought his valuable gold watch and fob chain with him to the Institute, but now it's gone," he answered, taking hold of Celia's elbow to hurry her across the cobbled street, his grip tighter than required.

"I am safely across now, Mr. Greaves," she said. "You may release my arm."

"Yes, ma'am," he said and charged on at the same pace as earlier. "There have been other thefts at the place, though."

Sighing, she hurried to catch him up. "So was Mr. Shaw the victim of a robbery gone horribly wrong?" Committed by whomever had been responsible for the prior thefts. The red-haired fellow, perhaps? Mr. Ross? Someone else?

"Working on that possibility, ma'am."

"In addition, Mina Cascarino is not a thief," she stated. "Perhaps the theft of the watch and his death are not intimately connected."

"Taylor and I are also considering that idea."

At least they were agreeing on something. "The witness who observed that intruder outside Mr. Shaw's room . . . at what time did she observe them?"

They arrived at Portsmouth Square, the location of City Hall and the central police station, and Mr. Greaves halted on the corner across from the building.

"Not long after seven thirty," he said.

"If Mina left Bauman's at six thirty, what took her so long to reach the Institute? Presuming she is the interloper your witness noticed," said Celia. "The distance between the tavern and the Hygienic Institute is a fifteen-minute walk, no more. I cannot imagine Mina arriving there any later than six forty-five."

"Simple. She spent an hour someplace else first," he said. "Meeting her accomplice to review their plot."

"You are impossible, Mr. Greaves," she said, impatience flaring. "I am going to make a proposal and you are going to not scoff. Agreed?"

"I'd have to first hear your proposal before I agreed, ma'am."

She offered a smile that was more of a grimace. "Here is my proposal. Namely, that the same person who gave Mina her concussion also left that key in her pocket," she said. "Our murderer—who may or may not additionally be a thief—wishing to discard a critical piece of evidence."

He stared off into the distance, reflecting on her comment. He had a profile that could break hearts, if hearts were susceptible to a handsome man's face.

"What do you want me to say, Mrs. Davies?" he finally asked, gazing at her.

"That you will consider my proposal a good one."

"Deal," he said, inclining his head.

"Good. Well, then. Back to our other suspects. What have the Shaws had to say about Ambrose Shaw's sudden death?" she asked. "Miss Shaw has implied that her stepmother and stepbrother may not be distraught. Further, I might add, she denies ever having heard of Mina Cascarino."

"Rebecca Shaw has an alibi, you'll be pleased to hear. A neighbor spotted her outside her rooms above her gallery around seven thirty," he said. "As for Leonard and Delphia Shaw, they've accused a fellow named Elliot Blanchard. He and Shaw are political enemies with a recent history of brawling at the Bank Exchange saloon. No alibi for where he was last night, either."

"How intriguing. Jane shared an interesting tidbit with me concerning Mr. Blanchard and Miss Shaw," she said. "At one time he intended to marry Rebecca Shaw, but her father managed to sever the engagement."

"Blanchard is married now, though," he said. "He can't still be holding a grudge about the broken engagement."

"Who understands the hearts of men?"

"Shakespeare, Mrs. Davies?"

"The Bible, Mr. Greaves," she replied. "More precisely—'for what man knoweth the things of a man.'"

"Or of a woman, Mrs. Davies."

Indeed.

The girls had chased each other along the road and ended up at

Portsmouth Square, where their mother waited at the far edge of the park. She bent to tidy their curls. Such gentle affection, and utterly dissimilar from the bitter animosity and pettiness that had surrounded Ambrose Shaw.

"Did you question Herr Bauman about that box of candy you noticed, Mr. Greaves?" she asked. "If it was a gift to Mina from Mr. Shaw? She says she never received candy from him."

"That box from Roesler's is gone, but Bauman doesn't think Shaw ever sent her presents," he replied. "However, he might not be aware."

"Roesler's?" she asked. "What a coincidence. Owen works there."

He frowned at her. "Don't be getting any ideas, Mrs. Davies."

"I am merely remarking upon the coincidence that Owen works at the same confectioner's that Mr. Shaw likes to frequent." If she could prove Mr. Shaw had never gifted Mina with chocolates from Roesler's, it would be one less piece of evidence to use against her. She smiled with all the innocence she could muster, which made Mr. Greaves scowl more fiercely. "That is all."

• • •

"The blasted Mrs. Davies found the key to the Institute's private door in Mina Cascarino's skirt pocket." Nick yanked back the chair next to Taylor's desk and sat. "And I doubt she meant to ever tell us."

"Miss Mina *is* the killer, sir?" He glanced over at the booking officer, standing at his desk. The fellow was cleaning his fingernails with the point of his pocketknife and acting like he wasn't eavesdropping on their conversation. "She was the person Mrs. Wynn saw."

"Mrs. Davies has proposed that the killer stashed it in Mina's pocket after he—or she—knocked her out."

"Oh!" Taylor's entire face perked. "That could be what happened, don't you think, sir?"

"Mina might not have killed Shaw, but we still need to figure out what she was doing outside the Institute around the same time the man was being chloroformed to death." The door to the detectives' office was closed. Nick would prefer to have this discussion in there, but the shut door meant Briggs was occupying the room. "Her shawl wasn't in the back room at Bauman's, but at least she didn't have Shaw's watch on her. If I can trust Mrs. Davies about that."

"While you were with Mrs. Davies, sir, I had a chance to talk to the fellow who oversees the rooms at the Parker House. The ones that the San Francisco Club uses." Taylor fished around in his coat pockets and pulled out his notebook to consult. "He recollects Leonard Shaw attending last night's meeting, but says he left a lot earlier than the rest of the club members. Right after dinner, in fact, which had finished around seven."

"Maybe Ambrose enjoyed a surprise after-hours visit from his not-so-loving son." Had Mina conspired with Leonard Shaw? The idea was unsettling.

The alley-side door swung open, and Owen Cassidy hurtled down the steps. "Mr. Greaves! Glad you're in." He tipped his cap at Taylor. "I mighta overheard something important just now. About that politician who died. The one all the afternoon newspaper boys are squawking about."

Nick sat up straight. "How do you manage, Cassidy?" The kid was just as adept at being in the right place at the right time as Mrs. Davies.

"I didn't hear all that much, Mr. Greaves, but I was . . . uh, enjoying a late lunch near the water cure place when I came across this lady talking with a fellow—Mr. Platt, I think his name was—about a watch—"

"A watch?" interrupted Taylor.

"Why were you busy listening in on a couple of strangers having a private conversation?" asked Nick. "Wasn't by chance, I'd bet."

"Umm." The kid stuck his tongue in the side of his cheek and scuffed a toe across the dirty station floor. "Umm . . . uh . . ."

"Cassidy, spit it out."

"Caleb paid me."

Well, well, Mr. Griffin. It's you again. Back to cause more trouble.

"Dang it, Owen!" shouted Taylor, causing the booking officer to look up from his fingernails.

"Sorry, Mr. Taylor, Mr. Greaves."

"He paid you to do what?" Nick asked the boy.

"To give Mr. Platt a message that Caleb wants his money."

Figures. Absolutely figures. "Go on about the woman and Platt, if you will."

"Well, Mr. Platt was asking the lady—her name was Mrs. Wynn—where the watch was, and she said she didn't have it. Made it sound like he was accusing her of stealing it or somethin'."

Nick looked over at Taylor, who cocked an eyebrow but didn't take his attention off his notebook. "Mrs. Wynn. You're positive?"

"I am. That's what the whiskered gentleman from the water cure place had called her," said the boy. "She'd come out of the building just a few minutes before I heard her talking with Mr. Platt."

"Did you overhear anything else?"

"She said—which is why I came straight here to tell you before I headed back to work at the confectionary store—that she couldn't understand why he was accusing her of stealing Mr. Shaw's watch. That's the dead fellow, isn't it?" he asked. "She also demanded that Mr. Platt leave her alone, which made him mad as thunder. Mad as thunder, Mr. Greaves."

• • •

"You were at the police station house?" Mr. Roesler's eyes goggled at Owen. Just like a beetle's might, dark and dancing about.

"Yes, sir," he replied. "One of the . . . uh, detectives there is a relative. A cousin. I had a note for him from his . . . aunt. Thought I'd stop in quick. Sorry it took so long, sir."

"You have relatives in San Francisco?" he asked. "I thought you were an orphan."

Owen hated that word. Plum hated that word.

"Yes, sir, I do have relatives," he said. "Don't care to mention my cousin, though, because of his police duties."

Mr. Roesler's beetle eyes scanned him. "Hmph," he declared. "Get to work. And don't expect to be leaving on time today."

He stormed into the back room, the heavy blue velvet curtains that separated it from the main room swishing shut behind him.

Owen exhaled. That was close. He unhooked his apron from its peg on the wall, tied it around his waist, and grabbed one of the cleaning rags. He took to polishing the display case along the wall and let the smells and colors of the confections on display calm him.

He loved being inside Mr. Roesler's store. He'd gotten lucky, landing a job here, and a day didn't go by that he didn't pause and just stare at it all. When he could get away with pausing and staring, which only was when Mr. Roesler was in back. Owen would gaze at the candies lined up in their glass jars, colorful as snippets of a rainbow captured and put on display for folks to ooh and ahh over. Inhale the aroma of sugar and chocolates—sorta faint, but he could smell it, he was sure—licorice and cinnamon and caramel. Glistening gumdrops and sugar flowers, stuff too pretty to eat, he thought. Displays of fancy nuts and dried fruits, some he'd never before seen and couldn't name to save his soul. 'Course, *he* wasn't supposed to be sellin' to customers, so it was okay he didn't know what everything was; he'd been hired to keep the store tidy, the counters clean, the paint on the display benches touched up wherever it got chipped or scuffed, the blue-and-red carpet runner swept, the pans of the brass weighing scale spotless, the window glass sparkling, every jar polished clean of fingerprints. *Dazzle them, Cassidy. Dazzle them.* That's what Mr. Roesler said to him every time he arrived for work. His notions got results, because the ladies couldn't go by the front door of his sliver of a store without stopping and coming inside.

Yep, it sure was better than when he'd worked at Mr. Hutchinson's company. Which had been nice enough in the office, all polished wood and comfortable chairs. Except Owen's job had been to install a brick floor in the cellar, where he'd gone and found a buried dead body . . .

Best not to think about that.

Owen started whistling as he rubbed at a spot on the case covering the rows of fancy candies, dreaming of the day he could save up enough money to buy himself a pound of chocolate creams. Caleb's silver dollar would come in handy. Or maybe a pound of the cordial candies. The chime of the bell above the door startled him out of his reverie.

"Mrs. Davies. What are you doing here?" He gulped. Had she already heard about him working for Caleb?

"Good afternoon, Owen." She closed the door and glided into the store. A lot of the time, she did sorta glide. Not when she was hurrying to visit a patient, though, because then she charged ahead faster than any other female he knew.

Mr. Roesler had heard the bell and parted the closed curtains. "Ma'am, how can I help you?"

"I have come to speak with Owen. For just a moment," she said, smiling sweetly. "If you do not mind."

Mr. Roesler gaped. "Are you a relative, too, ma'am?"

"Owen and I are close acquaintances, Mr. Roesler," she said. "I have some important news that he has been waiting to hear, and, as I was in the vicinity, I thought I would stop in and share it with him. Just a moment. If you do not mind. And I will be happy to make a small purchase of marzipan when we are finished," she added, which succeeded in pacifying him.

"Of course," he said.

She placed a hand on Owen's back and propelled him toward the door. "Outside, Owen."

"You've got news about my parents, ma'am?" His voice squeaked because he was so excited. "This ain't . . . isn't about Caleb?"

He scoured the street for any sign of Caleb. Just in case he was hiding someplace nearby, like behind that stack of crates over there, or in the doorway of the liquor store down that way. Knowing Caleb, he could be.

"Caleb? You mean Mr. Griffin?" she asked, moving to stand with her back to the store window. "Why would you presume I was here to talk about him?"

His cheeks got so hot it was like a flaming torch had been thrust at his face, or something. "Uh . . . no reason, ma'am," he sputtered. "So, have you located my parents?"

"Regrettably, no, Owen," she said. "I am sorry, but claiming I had news was the first excuse to pop into my mind."

"Oh," he replied, his hopes squashed. One day he'd find his parents, though. One day.

"I am here because I have a task for you," she said.

"A task?" Why in tarnation did everybody want to hire him for 'tasks'? *Maybe 'cause you're good at getting things done, Owen Cassidy.* The thought cheered him. "What sort of task?"

"You know Mina Cascarino?"

"Of course I do. Everybody does," he said.

She got a funny, pinched look on her face, which he didn't understand. "Everyone."

"What about her, ma'am?"

She turned to face the store window, pretending to have a need to adjust her hat, using the glass as a mirror. "She currently is a key suspect in the death of a fellow at the Hygienic Institute."

"Mr. Shaw!" he blurted out.

She glanced over at him. "You have heard the news."

"But the papers said he died of a heart attack." Unless . . . *that* was why Caleb had wanted him to give that message to the red-haired fellow who worked there. It hadn't really been about a debt, but because Mr. Shaw had been murdered. And Caleb was somehow connected to it.

Shoot!

"Owen, is there something you are not sharing with me?" Mrs. Davies asked. "Something to do with Mr. Shaw or the Institute?"

He didn't dare tell her about Caleb hiring him. It was bad enough that Mr. Greaves and Mr. Taylor were disappointed. He couldn't bear having Mrs. Davies disappointed, too. She was like a mother to him.

The only person who cared, since his actual parents had decided to up and dump him like a sack of old clothes not worth nothin' . . . anything.

"It's nothing, ma'am," he said. "What's the task you want me to do?"

"I want you to examine Mr. Roesler's customer accounts to discover who Mr. Ambrose Shaw sent candies to in the past, say, two weeks."

Owen felt his eyebrows leap straight up his forehead. "If Mr. Roesler catches me poking through his books, he'll toss me onto the street quick as a wink!"

Mr. Roesler must've been watching from inside the store, because she smiled and nodded. She retied the bow of her bonnet and turned to face the street again.

"Owen, I must identify other women Mr. Shaw may have sent confections to," she said. "Because a box of candy from Roesler's, a gift supposedly sent by Ambrose Shaw to Mina Cascarino, is an important piece of evidence linking her to the man and his suspicious death." She peered at him. Miss Barbara liked to say her eyes were as frosty as ice chips, but Owen had never thought so. "Please, you must help. I am relying upon you."

A fellow would have to be stony-hearted to refuse.

So he said yes.

• • •

"I'll question Platt on my own, Taylor," said Nick.

After Cassidy's account, he'd sent for Mullahey to meet him and Taylor at the Hygienic Institute. Ross hadn't objected to Nick's request to use the parlor. It was as comfortable a space as Ross's office—thickly carpeted, the walls covered in flocked paper, a large fireplace at one end, a round table in the center, and at least a dozen cushioned armchairs scattered about. Nick dragged a toe across the carpet near the table. No leftover shards of broken glass; Platt and the cook had tidied up well.

"What do you want me to do, sir?" asked Taylor, taking in their surroundings, the luxuriousness of a room inside a medical institution that was likely way nicer than any in Taylor's place.

"I need you to search outside, see if you can find any evidence the officers might have missed last night. Something that might help us identify who it was who concussed Mina Cascarino, for instance," he said. "Maybe you'll even find a discarded chloroform bottle."

Taylor hurried out of the parlor, crossing paths with Platt.

"Ah, Mr. Platt, there you are," said Nick.

"What do you need from me now, Detective Greaves?" he asked, halting beneath the curved branches of the unlit brass gasolier. "I'd like to head home and get some dinner. It's been a long day. At least I don't have to come back later; we don't have any patients left."

Mullahey appeared in the hallway beyond the parlor. Nick jerked his head, indicating the officer should proceed with searching the sleeping room Platt used at the Institute. Mullahey grinned, further distorting the crooked nose he'd once broken in a scrap with a pickpocket, and dashed off.

"I'd like to give you a second chance to tell me all about your acquaintance with Mrs. Wynn," said Nick.

Platt's eyelids twitched, a modest reaction. Maybe he'd been anticipating the question. "Like I said before, she's a frequent patient here," he replied. "So?"

"Do you regularly confront Mr. Ross's patients out on the street and accuse them of stealing, Mr. Platt?" asked Nick. "A watch, in this case."

"What?" Platt scoffed. "That's ridiculous."

"One of my associates observed you questioning Mrs. Wynn about the location of a watch," he replied. "Mr. Shaw's watch, I believe. The one Mrs. Shaw has told the police is missing."

"Your associate doesn't know what he's talking about."

"Here's something else I'd like an answer to, Mr. Platt—why might Mrs. Wynn demand that you leave her alone?" Nick asked. "Have you two worked together in the past? Maybe stealing from the patients here then fencing the goods?"

Platt's face went a pasty shade. "This is ridiculous."

"Excuse me if I find your conversation with her rather suspicious, Mr. Platt. Accusing her of stealing from a man who'd passed away at this fine medical institution you work at. Makes me think the two of you are keeping a secret about the poor fellow's death." Nick folded his arms and regarded Platt. "Are there secrets?"

"No secrets, Detective," Platt replied. "I saw that Mrs. Wynn and Mr. Shaw were friendly with each other from the very first. Sitting together at lunch. Chatting in the private parlor past when the other patients had retired for the night. Made me suspicious."

"Of what?"

"That she'd been buttering up Mr. Shaw because she saw he was an easy mark," he said, starting to sound more confident about his story. "So when she bolted out of here today, I decided to confront her about the watch Mrs. Shaw reported stolen. I accused Mrs. Wynn of taking it."

"And murdering him?"

Platt shrugged. "If the shoe fits . . ."

"Why not inform the police rather than confront her yourself, Mr. Platt?" asked Nick. "It's our job to pursue criminals."

"I guess I haven't been thinking clearly since I found Mr. Shaw, Detective," he replied.

He was too calm for Nick's taste. Too confident that he was innocent . . . or had done a thorough job of pinning his crimes on somebody else.

Knuckles rapped on the doorframe, and Mullahey poked his head through the opening. "Nothing, sir."

"No gold pen or pieces of jewelry?" The other items reported stolen.

"No, Mr. Greaves."

Damn.

Platt's eyes narrowed. "You had an officer search my room."

"Mr. Ross gave us permission," replied Nick blandly. "This is his building, I believe. Mullahey, I'll need you to get a search warrant for Mr. Platt's lodgings. And I'd like to talk to the cook, if she's still here."

"She's gone home already, Mr. Greaves," said Mullahey.

"Then bring her by the station first thing in the morning."

"Will do." He tapped fingers to the brim of his police cap and trotted off.

"What do you expect Mary Ann to tell you, Detective? That I'm a thief?" asked Platt.

"We mean to figure that out, Mr. Platt."

"Well, you didn't find anything in my room here, though, did you?" challenged Platt. "Because I'm not the crook. Mrs. Wynn is. You're barking up the wrong tree, Detective."

Pinching his mouth into an ugly red line, he turned and shoved past Taylor, who'd already returned from his search.

"Nothing in Mr. Platt's room, sir?" he asked.

"Apparently not." Nick gestured at the object in Taylor's grasp. "What have you got there?"

"A clue," he replied, bouncing on the balls of his feet with excitement. "In the weeds out in the alley. Only ten feet or so from the private side door."

He handed over his discovery. It was the broken-off neck of a bottle, the paper label that had once secured a stopper ripped, only two words legible. *Pure.*

And *chloroform.*

✂ CHAPTER 10 ✂

"Maybe that piece of glass isn't from the bottle of chloroform that our killer used," said Taylor, sounding dejected. He slowed to light a cigar, the wind funneling between the tall buildings lining the road spoiling his attempts.

Nick had wrapped the broken-off part of a bottle in a handkerchief and stashed it in his coat pocket. "It is possible that it could just be somebody's trash."

They turned down the street leading to Mrs. Wynn's lodging house. Up ahead rose the towering edifices of banks and assay offices along California Street, the grandiose headquarters of steamship lines on Sacramento. A collection of lavish buildings capable of making a person forget the crowded alleyways of the nearby Chinese quarter or the teeming docks to the east. Areas where the honest bustle of commerce would soon be replaced by less respectable activities as night fell.

"But don't get too discouraged, Taylor. Because where is the rest of that bottle?" asked Nick.

"What do you mean, sir?" Realization dawned, and Taylor's mouth dropped open into an O. "I see. The killer came back and snagged it, trying to get rid of the evidence. So it *is* our bottle."

"Anybody scavenging for glass to sell would've found all the pieces, Taylor." One and a half cents paid per pound. "Only somebody in a panic would've left that bit behind."

Taylor gave up on lighting his cigar and tucked it away. He squinted at the street. "Can we trust Mr. Platt's accusation about Mrs. Wynn being the thief, sir? Mr. Greaves?"

Trust and *Platt* were two words that should probably not be used in the same sentence. "I suppose we'll find out, Taylor, when we question her."

A newspaper boy dashed across the street toward them, waving a copy of the paper he was selling. "Ambrose Shaw dead!" he shouted, dodging a wagon hauling brick up the road. "Copperhead politician Ambrose Shaw dead!"

"Here. I'll take a copy," shouted Nick. He took a paper from the boy's ink-stained hand and tossed him a dime.

The boy pocketed the coin and ran off in search of more customers. Nick skipped over news of the arrival of the steamship *Constitution* and the upcoming events planned for the state fair, locating the article about Ambrose Shaw.

"What does it have to say, sir?" asked Taylor, leaning over Nick's shoulder.

"Not much, thank God." Nick folded the paper and handed it to his assistant. "Just that Shaw's been found dead and that the police have been to the Institute to investigate. Tomorrow morning's papers, though . . ."

Taylor tucked the newspaper under his arm. "The reporters are going to conclude Mr. Shaw's death is suspicious, with us showing up at the Institute."

"Maybe they can figure out who's responsible."

They located Mrs. Wynn's lodging house, wedged between a gunsmith's and a liquor store, not anywhere near as fine as the nearby banks and assay offices. They climbed the steps, the last rays of sun glinting dully off the windows. The glass needed a cleaning. The entire wood exterior could use a scrub, the paint faded and grimy from coal smoke, leaving the place tired and worn-looking. Maybe Mrs. Wynn wasn't quite the well-heeled, influential lady Mr. Ross thought she was.

Nick twisted the bell, which rang with an off-key jangle.

"Yes?" The woman who answered goggled at Taylor's uniform. She was short and wiry, her gray hair wrapped in a yellow bandana, and gaped the way most folks did when police showed up but hadn't been summoned. "Officers?"

"We'd like to speak to Mrs. Wynn," said Nick. "According to the City Directory, she lives here."

"She does live here, but what's she done?"

"Is she in?"

"Nope," the woman answered.

"You're positive."

"Of course I'm positive." She stared at Nick and Taylor like she questioned the intelligence of the police. Hell, *he* doubted the intelligence of the police some days. "I'd know who's currently in their rooms at my own lodging house, wouldn't I?"

"Yes, ma'am, you would," said Taylor, who never missed a chance to smooth the ruffled feathers of someone they were speaking with.

"I haven't seen her since she returned from that medical place she was staying at," she said. "Turned up not long after lunch then hightailed it back out of here."

"I'd like my assistant to look through her room," said Nick. "As part of an investigation we're conducting."

"You got a warrant for that?" she asked.

Why, *why* did everybody make that their first question when he attempted a search? Were the lawyers conducting classes on proper police procedures that he wasn't aware of? "We're not planning on removing anything, ma'am. Just a look around."

A young woman, small and dark-haired and very pretty, descended the stairs at the landlady's back. "What's going on? Why are the police here?"

"They're conducting an investigation, Miss DiPaolo. Want to speak with Mrs. Wynn for some reason." From the depths of the boarding-house came the sound of pottery crashing to the floor. "*Now* what's going on in the kitchen? I can't leave for a second."

"Go see to that, Mrs. M.," said Miss DiPaolo. "I'll talk to the officers."

The landlady smiled gratefully and rushed off.

"'Mrs. M.'?" asked Nick.

"She has a lengthy Polish last name I've never been able to master," she answered with a musical laugh. She had a dimple in her left cheek, and her eyes were the color of ripe hickory nut shells. Warm and watchful. "I'm Giulia DiPaolo. Maybe I can help you."

Giulia . . .

She stuck out her hand for Nick to shake. Her skin was soft, as though she'd never known rough work.

Taylor was studying the young woman. "Don't I know you from someplace, Miss DiPaolo?"

"It's always possible, Officer."

"I know where!" he exclaimed. "You work at Bauman's *lagerbier* saloon."

"Yes, I do," she said, dimpling. Taylor blushed. Of course.

She had to be the Giulia whose name had been written on a torn-up note in a wastepaper basket. Bauman's inadequate vocalist.

"You must know Mina Cascarino," said Nick.

"Certainly I do. She sings most nights, so I work alongside her quite often," she replied. "Expect to see her there tonight, in fact. I'll be on my way to Bauman's as soon as I've had a bite to eat."

"She won't be at Bauman's tonight, Miss DiPaolo. She's ill."

"I had no idea. Will she be okay?"

"I'm not a doctor," said Nick. "Taylor, go fetch the landlady back to let you into Mrs. Wynn's room." Rather than moon over pretty *lagerbier* saloon girls.

"Yes, sir." With a parting nod for Miss DiPaolo, he dashed off.

"We were hoping to speak with Mrs. Wynn, Miss DiPaolo," said Nick. "However, your landlady says she's not here at the moment."

"Oh, Althea. Strange bird."

"Any idea where she might be?"

"No, Officer. I haven't a clue," she said. "She keeps to herself. Very private, quiet woman."

Didn't sound like the Mrs. Wynn Nick had met. The woman was proving to be full of mysteries. "You didn't happen to see her today when she returned to the boardinghouse after her stay at the Hygienic Institute, did you?"

"I didn't," she replied. "I don't only work at Bauman's, Detective. I have a job at a bakery during the day, and I didn't leave there until three this afternoon. She wasn't around by the time I got back."

"Has she ever mentioned a Mr. Platt to you? Had any male visitors?" he asked.

"Mrs. Wynn? Male visitors?" Her eyes sparkled with amusement at the idea. "And I've never heard her mention a Mr. Platt. As I said, she's a fairly private person."

Private? Or secretive? "Did you work at Bauman's last night, by any chance?"

"Yes."

"Did you see Miss Cascarino there?"

Taylor returned with the landlady and climbed the stairs behind Miss DiPaolo.

"No, because she left earlier than usual and I didn't start until seven. I gather she had an engagement of some sort," said the young woman. "I figured it was with a man, but she didn't tell me who."

"Does she chat with the male customers at the saloon?" asked Nick. "A man named Ambrose Shaw, for instance."

"Lots of men try to flirt with us, Detective, but we're careful to ignore them," she said. "Herr Bauman doesn't want his employees socializing with the customers. None of us would risk our jobs by ignoring his rules. It's a good place."

It *was* a good place. "What sort of a mood has Miss Cascarino been in lately?"

"She's been anxious and agitated lately." Miss DiPaolo puckered her forehead. "I've caught her staring off, deep in thought. And if I ask her what's wrong, she snaps at me. I'd been worrying that she was in trouble. That maybe she'd fallen in with the wrong sort of people. And now you're here, which means I must've been right."

The landlady clomped back down the steps, Taylor on her heels.

He shook his head. "Nothing, sir. No watch or any of the other stolen items."

Another dead end. Unless Mrs. Wynn had pawned everything already.

Miss DiPaolo's gaze darted from Nick to Taylor and back again. "I do hope Mina's not in too much trouble. Or Mrs. Wynn, either."

"Are you finished here, Officers?" asked the landlady, folding her arms. "I've got work to do."

Nick returned his hat to his head. "Notify the police immediately if Mrs. Wynn returns, ma'am."

"'If?'" she asked. "She'd better return. She owes me a month's rent!"

• • •

Fog crept between the buildings, chilling Owen's neck as he swept the sidewalk. *Durned Caleb Griffin*. It was Caleb's fault he'd been forced to work late. All because of that message he'd had to give to Mr. Platt, which had kept him away from the shop for too long. Mr. Roesler hadn't been happy at all, and now he was out here cleaning the planks in front of the store at a god-awful hour. He was going to miss dinner, durn it all.

Stomach rumbling, the cold air encouraged him to sweep faster just to get warm. Although pondering how he'd be able to poke around in the store's account books without Mr. Roesler catching him should've been a thought nerve-racking enough to heat his skin. He'd been thinking, though, about Mr. Roesler's habits. He often went down to the docks near to closing time to check on the next day's incoming shipments. He was down there right now, in fact. And sometimes on his way back, he stopped at Ghirardelli's to purchase cocoa, which Mr. Roesler then packaged in fancy tins with his name on it, claiming the chocolate was his special formulation. All of which should give Owen time—

"Hey! Cassidy!"

Owen halted sweeping and looked around. Who was calling him? He didn't see anybody he recognized. Just the usual folks hustling past on the sidewalk, the hawker down the street out pushing his hair tonic—"garrunteeed to grow your hair back!"—the lady at the mantilla store cajoling the last of the day's shoppers to come inside.

"Cassidy!" the voice shouted. This time its owner peered around the corner of the store and gestured at him.

Shoot. Caleb.

Owen hurried over to where Caleb was waiting. "I only got a second. Mr. Roesler's gonna be back any minute."

Caleb Griffin had drawn his collar up, hunkering down into his coat like a turtle wanting to hide inside its shell. "Well?"

"I gave him the message, Caleb. Once he was done talking to Mrs. Wynn."

"Wynn, huh? You didn't hear them mention me, did you?"

"No. They didn't say nothing . . . didn't say anything about you, Caleb. Not a word." Owen instinctively stepped away from him. "You didn't kill that Shaw fellow, did you?"

"Me? Kill Ambrose Shaw? Are you crazy, Cassidy?"

He swallowed, his tongue sticking to the roof of his gone-dry mouth. "Yep, Caleb. Crazy," he managed to stammer. "But do you know who *did* kill him?"

"You think I'd tell you?" Caleb barked a laugh.

Nope. "Should I be worried, Caleb? Is there gonna be a dangerous person after me now?"

"I'd keep my head down if I were you, Cassidy. But that's always good advice."

With that, he turned and legged it, splashing through a puddle of wastewater tossed onto the street by the nearby hotel's domestic. Owen didn't have the guts to call out and remind Caleb about the other silver dollar he owed him.

• • •

I do hope I've not risked Owen's job.

Celia's pace slowed as she turned down Vallejo. On her way home from Roesler's Confectionary, she'd stopped in on a patient whose lodgings were situated between the candy shop and Celia's house.

Which meant the sun had sunk behind the western hills and Owen was likely finished with work and gone home. It was too late to return to the shop and tell him she'd rather he did not examine those ledgers and risk his position at Roesler's.

"Just be careful, Owen," she murmured.

"*Weel*, home at last, ma'am," called Addie, fists on her hips, from the porch.

The lamp in the parlor had been lit, shedding a warm and welcoming light behind her. Next door, a candle burned in the room Mina occupied, but the rest of the house was quiet and dark. The only time the Cascarino home was quiet was when the children were engaged in eating.

"We've been waiting dinner on you," her housekeeper added.

"I am sorry, Addie," said Celia, gathering up her skirts to climb the steps. "I visited my patient who is due to have a baby, which took longer than I'd anticipated."

Addie harrumphed loudly enough for Celia to hear. Smiling, she ascended the steps. A rectangle of white stopped her. She bent down to retrieve it.

"What do you have there, ma'am?"

"A note. Addressed to me," she said, climbing the rest of the way to the porch.

"I didna see it earlier when I swept the steps," said Addie, staring mistrustfully at the plain piece of folded paper.

"Curious." Celia ran a thumbnail through the wafer gluing the flap shut and held the note up to the light coming through the parlor window. *Leave us alone.* Spelled out in precisely printed letters, as though meaning to obscure the author's identifiable cursive handwriting.

But who was "us"? The Shaws? She hadn't met nor spoken with any of them, aside from Rebecca. Who else, then?

She scanned the darkened road, searching for the person who'd dropped the note on the step. There wasn't a soul within sight who looked out of place. Life as normal, the fog bell ringing, a man hauling a cart up the street's steep incline for his final delivery of the day, the priest from St. Francis wandering out of his rectory, bound for dinner at a parishioner's.

"What does it say, ma'am?" asked Addie impatiently.

"*Leave us alone.*" She refolded the note and tucked it away. "With no signature."

"Threats again?" asked Addie. "*Och*, ma'am, this always happens whenever you get involved in one of Mr. Greaves's cases."

"Not always, Addie." *Or did it?* "All in all, a rather pointless request when I've no idea who *us* refers to."

"'Tis unchancy, ma'am," her housekeeper replied. "Unchancy."

. . .

Squinting against the early morning sunshine, Nick yawned into his fist and ambled over to the chest of drawers against the wall. He hadn't slept much since he'd returned from Sacramento, thoughts about his father's funeral swarming his brain like ants angling for space on a dropped piece of food. Hard to believe it had been less than a week since the funeral. Two days since he'd said goodbye to Ellie.

"Just two days." Goodbye to a city he'd likely never visit again. He'd miss his sister, though. "Maybe I should tell her she's welcome to come here, after all, Riley."

Riley got up from where he'd been sprawled beneath the window, a spot he favored, where he could sniff the smells of the city drifting in when Nick opened it to the breeze. The dog trotted over to Nick and looked up at him.

"Don't mind me, Riley." He scratched the dog's head, which caused a mighty thumping of his shaggy tail. "You know how my moods are."

Nick slid open a drawer and rummaged through his overshirts, each one as wrinkled as the last. He never cared to spend money on having somebody press his clothes. Mrs. Jewett had offered, but he didn't want to be beholden to her.

And that's the problem with you, Nick. Maybe you should let folks help.

He shoved the calico shirt he'd pulled out back into the drawer, his knuckles brushing against a crumpled scrap of paper. The unread telegram Mrs. Jewett had handed him yesterday. He tore open the envelope. It hadn't come from Ellie, like he'd expected, but from the ex-wife of his deceased Uncle Asa.

"Never thought I'd hear from you again." The telegram had been sent from St. Louis, which implied the woman who'd gone off with an army officer had grown weary of life in Indian country with the fellow. The news of Nick's father's death must have been posted in the papers there, although he couldn't figure why. Maybe Ellie had notified their aunt . . . their *former* aunt. She'd always liked the woman for some reason.

*Deepest sympathy on your father's parting. He spoke
often of you with pride. As did Asa. Love.*

"My father, proud of me?" Nick crushed the telegram into a ball and threw it against the wall. Riley went to fetch it. "Go ahead. Chew it up, if you want," he said. "Wait, wait. Never mind, Riley. Give me that."

He grabbed the slobbered piece of paper and flattened the creases, staring at the words. He should reply to her. Just not today. Not when a case was calling, which had always been his best excuse for brushing aside all the guilt and the pain.

"You look well enough this morning, ma'am," said Addie, her tone a trifle critical, and set out Celia's breakfast. "Despite receiving a threatening note last evening."

"I cannot permit the note to upset me, Addie," said Celia. "And perhaps it has nothing to do with Mr. Shaw's death."

Addie poured her a cup of tea. "Because folks are always dropping off unsigned notes requesting that you leave them alone."

Best not to reply, she thought and reached for the butter and toast.

"Have you seen the news this morning?" asked Addie, laying a copy of the *Daily Alta California* on the dining room table alongside Celia's plate.

"Not yet." Celia finished the bite of toast she'd taken and patted her mouth with her linen serviette. "What is it?"

"There on the front page." She tapped the article of interest with a fingertip. "An article about Mr. Shaw and his unexpected demise."

Celia picked up the paper and read aloud. "'Mr. Ambrose Shaw was found deceased in his room at the Hygienic Institute Wednesday night. Authorities refuse to respond to rumors the fellow met an untimely end. Mr. Ross, owner and operator of the Institute, disputes claims that the gas jet in Mr. Shaw's room had been turned on and caused Mr. Shaw's demise, despite the noticeable smell of fumes outside his room. His political opponent, Mr. Elliot Blanchard, has been questioned by the police and released. Our readers may recall an unfortunate dispute between the two men at the Bank Exchange saloon that came to blows. Mr. Blanchard maintains his innocence in this most recent event, asserting that Mr. Shaw perished from natural causes and any insinuation he is involved in the man's death is slander meant to smear his reputation.' Well," said Celia, dropping the newspaper onto the table. "The news is out."

"Maybe Mr. Greaves doesn't believe Miss Mina is guilty, after all."

"He hasn't sufficient proof of Mr. Blanchard's guilt, however, if he released him," she replied. "Jane had some interesting information about the fellow. She told me he and Rebecca Shaw had once planned to wed, until her father brought the engagement to an end."

"He's had his revenge against Mr. Shaw, then."

"I might agree, except Mr. Blanchard has married another." *The hearts of men . . .* which could be so fickle.

"Oh, Mrs. Davies. There you are." Libby Campbell entered the dining room, her leather satchel clutched at her waist. "I knocked, but when no one answered, I tried the door and found it unlocked. I suppose I should have rung the bell."

"You are very early, Miss Campbell." Celia indicated the chair across from her. "Please sit while I finish my breakfast. Hopefully you do not mind."

"I'm the one who should be apologizing for intruding," said the young woman, leaving her satchel near the doorway. With her good arm, she pulled out the dining table chair, struggling as its legs snagged in the thick carpet underfoot. Her cheeks pinking, she glanced at Celia and Addie to see if they'd observed the difficulty she was having. Celia perused the newspaper as though she'd not been paying Miss Campbell any attention. "I was excited to begin Barbara's lessons."

"Unfortunately, Miss Campbell, my cousin is not an early riser." Celia looked over at her housekeeper. "Addie, tell Barbara her tutor is here and bring Miss Campbell some tea."

Addie hastened out of the room, the crisp patter of her footfalls receding up the stairs.

"There's no need to offer me tea, Mrs. Davies," said Miss Campbell.

"It will be awkward for me to sit and eat my breakfast while you have nothing, Miss Campbell," said Celia, smiling at her to ease the tight furrow between the young woman's eyebrows. "Besides, you shall be a regular visitor here. I'd never be so impolite as to not at least offer you tea."

"Not all employers would offer their employees tea."

"Addie is the only person I have ever employed, Miss Campbell, so I've little experience in what behavior is considered proper or not," she said. "Not that I much care what might be proper behavior between employer and employee."

"Mr. Blanchard used to say that we are all to be treated equally," she declared. "Sadly, not enough people agree with his viewpoint."

"You previously worked for Elliot Blanchard?" Jane had never told Celia the name of the person who'd recommended Miss Campbell's services.

"Why, yes." Libby gave the newspaper, folded open at Celia's elbow, a quick look. "Is that a problem?"

"Not at all." But how very, very intriguing . . .

"Miss Barbara should be down soon, ma'am," said Addie, bearing fresh hot water and a china teacup for Miss Campbell. "Here you are, miss."

The tea served, Addie retreated to the kitchen again.

"I saw the story in the paper this morning," said Libby, reaching for the porcelain sugar bowl. "Mr. Blanchard is an energetic and passionate man, a demanding employer, but it's incomprehensible that anybody could implicate him in Mr. Shaw's death. Incomprehensible and a downright lie." Color once more washed over her cheeks. "I'm sorry, Mrs. Davies. I'm being too free with my opinions. It's a problem I have."

"I am often too free with my opinions as well, Miss Campbell. You're among friends here," she said. "What was your role at the Blanchard household? I was not aware they had children to tutor."

"I tutored his wife," she replied, dropping a spoonful of granulated sugar into her tea and stirring. "She is from South America. Mr. Blanchard wanted my assistance improving her English so that she'd be more comfortable in society. He has political ambitions, and . . ." The clink of her spoon against the porcelain decreased its frequency until it stopped.

"And his South American wife might be a hindrance to his prospects?" said Celia.

"Only for those who are small-minded, ma'am," she replied. "The petty and ignorant. People like Ambrose Shaw, who has said unkind things about her."

More reason for Elliot Blanchard to despise the fellow, perhaps. "These are contentious times, Miss Campbell," said Celia. "The outcome of America's recent war appears to have aroused a fresh round of animosity rather than provided any hoped-for peace."

"We all saw what happened in the recent elections, ma'am. Retaliation for attempting to ensure that freed slaves should be considered citizens."

"So noted, Miss Campbell. Contentious times."

Libby Campbell carefully placed her spoon onto the saucer. "Mrs. Blanchard is very lovely. Such shiny dark hair and eyes. I felt sorry for her. The way people would look at her on the street when we'd go walking."

Like they looked at Barbara. With hatred and resentment.

Celia eyed her over the brim of her teacup. "Why did you leave Mr. Blanchard's employ, Miss Campbell?"

"I would've continued if his wife hadn't made plans to stay with her mother in Yuba City. To get away from San Francisco for several weeks. It's warmer and drier there, I hear," she said. "Mrs. Blanchard suffers from chronic pain, and the chill makes it worse some days."

"Barbara has a bad foot. The weather also bothers her, at times."

"She does? The water cure might help," she said. "I tried to get Mrs. Blanchard to go, but she wouldn't."

"Oh?" asked Celia, lowering her cup, her gaze fixed on the young woman's face. "Are you familiar with the Hygienic Institute's treatments, Miss Campbell?"

"Oh no, not me. I couldn't afford a place like that. I've heard about the Institute from a friend." She glanced at the newspaper. "Although Mr. Shaw's sudden death will be bad for the place."

"It most certainly will," said Celia.

"Working at the Blanchards' was gratifying, and I enjoyed my time with them," she said, abruptly resuming their prior line of conversation.

A more suitable topic, perhaps, than Mr. Shaw's highly suspicious death. Which certain circles had implicated Mr. Blanchard in. "Mrs. Blanchard was an eager student, and Mr. Blanchard has so many interests besides the wines he sells. He has a huge collection of insects, butterflies, preserved reptiles, and the like. They're stored in glass cases in his display room. He calls it his 'cabinet of curiosities.' I've never heard such a phrase."

"I have. A family friend in England kept a taxidermy display of every mammal native to Hertfordshire." She used to balk when her aunt arranged a visit to their friends' home, her reaction infuriating her uncle and giving Celia's brother an excuse to tease her for days afterward about being a coward. She'd encountered far more startling scenes, far less genteel displays of death in the years since.

"So you're familiar with collections like his." The young woman leaned forward, her eyes bright. "Quite amazing, aren't they? It's like visiting a museum except you don't have to go any farther than a room in your house! At first Mr. Blanchard's exhibits made me queasy, all those dead eyes staring, the bugs looking ready to skitter free of their pins and glue, but I got used to it."

"It is a fascinating hobby." The work of a disciplined mind.

"Mr. Blanchard caught a lizard out in the garden one day, and he wanted to show me how he intended to preserve it. He meant to store the creature in a jar with carbolic acid and arsenic, I believe. Before removing the insides, stuffing the body with bran, and mounting it." Libby gave a shudder. "But the smell of the chemicals in his workroom was overpowering. Plus, I rather pitied the poor thing and couldn't bear to watch!"

Her description gave Celia pause. "Does he keep many chemicals in his workroom, Miss Campbell?"

"He has all sorts, along with his other supplies," she said. "Why?"

"Merely curious."

• • •

"Any news on Mrs. Wynn?" asked Nick, striding into the detectives' office, Taylor hustling inside behind him. The room was, thankfully, empty of Briggs, who never showed up early at the station.

"Maybe she's skipped town," said his assistant. "Even though her clothing and whatnot were still in her room."

"Let's head back over to her lodgings; maybe we missed a clue."

"Detective Greaves?" One of the station's policemen stood in the doorway with a woman, a cheap straw bonnet on her head, red-knuckled hands clenched at her waist. Freckles dotted her round face. "This young miss is here to talk with you."

"You must be Miss Newcomb. Thank you for coming in," said Nick.

"I got your message at my lodgings last night that you wanted to see me." She nervously scanned the interior of the office, anxious as an animal caged in a trap. Most folks tended to look that way when they'd been summoned to speak to him. "I came as soon as I could this morning."

"And we appreciate that." He gestured for her to take one of the chairs near his desk. "I'd offer you coffee, but I don't think any has been made yet."

"That's okay."

Taylor scrambled to help her sit.

"I'm not sure how I can help you though, Detective," she said. "I already spoke with one of the police officers yesterday."

"I had a few more questions, since I haven't had a chance to meet with you myself," said Nick, dropping onto his chair. "First off, I believe you and Mrs. Wynn were the last two people to see Mr. Shaw alive. Does that sound correct?"

"I suppose that's true."

"How did he seem?" he asked. "Did he appear to be expecting a visitor, for instance? Or acting rattled, maybe?"

"He was down to his vest and shirtsleeves when I brought his dinner to the small parlor, looking ready for the evening," she replied. "Behaving like his usual self. Not a polite man. Not to me, at least."

"You told Officer Mullahey you didn't notice any trespassers in the building Wednesday night."

"Mrs. Wynn saw an intruder," she replied.

"What about you?" he asked.

"I didn't see anybody, but after I talked with your officer, I got to remembering some footsteps I'd heard," she said. "Right before I left for the night."

"You left around seven thirty, wasn't that what you told Officer Mullahey?" asked Nick. At his side, Taylor's pencil scratched across the paper of his notebook.

"A few minutes before." She glanced at Taylor, likely curious about what he was recording. "I'd finished helping Mr. Platt in the parlor, put away the lovely tureen I'd used to serve the soup jardiniere I'd prepared for dinner, collected my purse and bonnet, then heard those footsteps, scurrying across the flagstones. The noise was coming from the end of the hallway, near the side door that leads out onto the alleyway."

"The private entrance that the occupants of the suite are able to use," said Nick.

She nodded. "Yes, but I didn't see anybody. I called out, but nobody replied, so I thought it must've been Mr. Platt and left."

"Except Mr. Platt was still in the parlor tidying up the broken glassware."

"Which is why I now realize I'd made a mistake," she said. "It had to have been the intruder Mrs. Wynn saw. I wish I'd spotted them. Then maybe we'd know who it was who'd been inside Mr. Shaw's room."

"Speaking of Mrs. Wynn, do you know how we can contact her?" Nick asked. "She wasn't at her lodgings last evening, and we'd like to speak with her about some thefts at the Institute."

"Why would you want to talk to her about those?"

"You were aware of them, Miss Newcomb?" asked Nick. "Mr. Ross has been trying to keep the thefts quiet."

"I didn't want to snitch on him," she said. "It's hard to get decent work in this town, if you're an unmarried female like me."

Nick considered the young woman. "He's been stealing from his patients?"

"I don't mean to imply Mr. Ross is the thief, Detective! Oh Lord, no!" Her hands flew to her face. "It's just that it would be bad business for him if folks learned that there have been problems at the Institute."

"Problems like expensive items being lifted from patients' rooms."

"It's awful," she replied, fidgeting in her chair, ruffled by all his questions.

"Who do you think the thief could be, Miss Newcomb?" he asked.

"I don't like to point fingers, Detective."

"Nobody does." Hell, that wasn't true. A lot of folks loved to point fingers. "But since you've been brave enough to stop in our station this morning, why not go ahead and tell us who it is you suspect, miss."

Being called brave seemed to please her, and her expression perked up.

"It has to be Mr. Platt. He has horrible debts, Detective. He gambles. Bets on boxing matches and horse races," she explained. "A gentleman . . . I shouldn't call him that. True, his teeth were clean and he smelled good, but he was no gentleman." She shook her head. "He's come to see Mr. Platt sometimes. I've seen them together when I've left the Institute after finishing up in the kitchen. Whispering out in the alleyway. Arguing about money. Money I believe Mr. Platt owed him."

"We've heard about this fellow and the debts Mr. Platt owes him," Nick replied. "Funny, though, that Mr. Platt has accused Mrs. Wynn of being the thief."

"He would, wouldn't he?" she asked sensibly. "Although if Mr. Platt had been the person outside Mr. Shaw's room, Mrs. Wynn would've recognized him. Unless he'd put on a disguise. Don't criminals wear disguises sometimes, Detective?"

"On occasion, miss." More often in novels than in real life, though.

"It's all really dreadful, isn't it?"

Yes. "I have another question for you. It's about an item my assistant discovered in the alley outside the Institute." From a drawer in his desk,

Nick retrieved the broken bit of chloroform bottle and held it out for her to see. "I've been told that Mr. Ross doesn't use chloroform at the Institute, but maybe I've been told wrong."

"No. Not in a long time. We don't keep it on hand anymore," she said, staring hard at the piece of glass. "I don't know where that came from, but lots of folks throw rubbish into the weeds out there, Detective. I'm chasing them off all the time."

"Ah, of course."

"Is Mr. Ross in trouble too, Detective Greaves?" she asked, watching him closely as he returned the bottle to the desk drawer. "Because of some broken bottle of chloroform?"

He locked the drawer and leaned back. Mary Ann Newcomb's fidgeting had turned to trembling. *What is it you're keeping from me, Miss Newcomb? What is it you're afraid to reveal? Who is it you're scared of?*

"Is there anything else you'd like to tell us, Miss Newcomb?" he asked.

"No, sir," she said. "I just hope you find whoever it was who killed Mr. Shaw. It's not right that there's a murderer on the loose. Not right at all."

• • •

"Yes, ma'am?" asked the woman who'd answered the bell at Mr. Blanchard's home. She scanned Celia from tip to toe, her perusal hesitating when it encountered the leather-bound notebook clutched in Celia's lace-gloved hands.

"Is Mr. Blanchard in this morning? I am Mrs. Celia Davies. Collecting monies for the Orphans' Asylum," said Celia, summoning her most proper English accent, which had the effect of hiking the woman's eyebrows. *Do not over-egg the pudding, Celia.* She smiled and pressed on. "I was told by a mutual acquaintance that Mr. Blanchard would be most generous with his support. After the reports in the newspapers of the amount raised by Mr. Higgins on his march up Montgomery last week, we have found many of the excellent citizens of

San Francisco clamoring to add their names to the list of noble contributors."

"Mr. Blanchard?" she asked. "You sure you have the right fellow?"

Celia stepped back and surveyed the nearby houses clinging to the steep incline of the road. "This *is* the address I was given. Mr. Elliot Blanchard, correct?"

"That's him."

"One of my associates came by here Wednesday evening, but she was unable to petition Mr. Blanchard directly," she said. *Oh, you are getting too good at these mistruths, Celia.* "Her name is Mina Cascarino. Did you happen to speak with her?"

"Never heard of a Mina Cascarino," she answered without hesitation. "And I leave after dinner, so if she rang past six, I don't know why Mr. Blanchard didn't answer."

"But he is here now."

"Yes, ma'am." Sighing, the maid pulled wide the door. "He was out for a bite of breakfast at Empire State—he does that whenever Mrs. Blanchard is away—but he's just come in before he goes on to his downtown office. I'll ask if he'll see you. He's an awfully busy man, though."

"Certainly, certainly," said Celia, pushing into the entry hall before the woman could change her mind about admitting her. The space was thick with quiet, the noise of the street outside muffled. "I am most appreciative. My thanks."

"Don't thank me, ma'am," she responded. "Not until we discover if Mr. Blanchard's willing to talk to you."

Celia glanced around. A staircase rose ahead of her, and a narrow hall stretched ahead. At its far end, a door to the dining room stood open, shedding light across the polished wood floor and the mauve-and-blue carpets extending from its doorway to the entrance vestibule. Among a row of portraits—mounted in a bewildering variety of gilded and painted frames on the papered walls—a large clock ticked imperiously. A man's black cassimere hat lay on the padded seat of a curved-back chair, as if its owner had been in a rush to discard it and had tossed it there, rather than hang it on the waiting stand.

"Such a welcoming space," said Celia, nodding approvingly in supposed appreciation for what was, in truth, a typical entrance to a respectable home.

"Hmm."

The housekeeper strode into the parlor at their right, and Celia followed. Its curtains were drawn against the upholstery-fading California sun. Everything in the room was heavy—the sofa and its fringed cushions, the stuffed armchairs, the wide pilasters of the black cast-iron fireplace mantel, the brocaded ottomans and marble-top tables, more wallpaper with a dense pattern of geometrical flowers. Was Elliot Blanchard equally heavy and fussy, with a thick watch chain draped across a stout belly, his broad cheeks bristling with whiskers? More like a stodgy businessman, perhaps, than the ambitious fellow she'd imagined a woman like Rebecca Shaw would fall in love with. Or the man Miss Olivia Campbell had found so fascinating. Unless the furnishings reflected the taste of the woman he'd married, attempting to prove her Americanness through the decor.

"You can wait here." The housekeeper gave a hasty flick of her hand to indicate an appropriate spot on the Brussels rug and left.

Her footsteps ascending the stairs indicated where she'd gone. Celia's task was now to find Mr. Blanchard's workroom, filled with possibly incriminating chemicals. Where, though, to locate his "cabinet of curiosities"? A bright room at the rear of the house and overlooking the garden that ran alongside the home, she supposed. Hopefully that room was on this level.

As quietly as possible, Celia leaned into the hall and peered up the stairs. Distant voices, those of the housekeeper and a man, echoed off the paneling from a second-floor room. The sound rose and fell in the rhythm of a disagreement. She only had minutes—perhaps less—to find the workroom and search his collection.

She sped down the hall on her toes, pausing to peek into the next room she passed. It was outfitted as a library, bookcases climbing halfway up three walls. A few bottles of wine occupied a rack near a large desk. No other types of bottles or cases of pinned insects, though.

Celia hurried on, into the dining room at the end of the entrance hall. More light and less fussiness in this space, outfitted practically with a rosewood table and chairs, plain marble fireplace, and sideboard. The door adjacent likely led onto the kitchen. It was the closed one to her right that might take her to her destination.

Overhead, wood boards creaked, and her pulse leaped. But no one came down the stairs into the hallway. She opened the door and discovered a glass-fronted piazza, display cases stretching from one end of the space to the other. Chairs and tables were scattered around the piazza to allow the inquisitive to sit and survey particular creatures of interest. Perhaps take a moment to closely examine the display of—Celia leaned nearer to read the description cards—of various *Epinotia* moths. Beyond the windows, the side garden bloomed with late summer roses. The space was stunning, and she wished she had time to study the arrangements of iridescent beetles and peculiar walking sticks, the butterflies in brilliant oranges. She had dawdled enough, however.

She spotted another door and tried the knob. The door swung open on well-oiled hinges, the odor of alcohol greeting her, to reveal a narrow cupboard of a space. The ceiling overhead was made of glass, as were the walls on three sides, rather like a miniature conservatory. A workbench was pushed against the windows, and various implements sat on its surface—pincers and tweezers and a small forceps that brought to mind the birthing instrument she owned, several scalpels, a stack of specimen boxes, glass vials and a handful of wide-mouthed bottles with cork stoppers. Pins of various sizes and lengths of silver wire. A board had been laid atop the table and a dragonfly was pinned to the surface, its spread wings shimmering opalescent in the morning light. On the wall hung shallow shelves filled with rows of bottles and jars. Strangely, there was a gap where an item was missing.

Celia set down her notebook and began examining the labels, one after the other. Alcohol. Carbolic acid. Thick glycerin. A small jar of arsenic powder. *As Libby had mentioned and most intriguing.* Gum arabic, for adhering the creatures to paper or board, she presumed. Ether.

She arrived at the gap in the bottles. Glass glinted at the back, and she rose onto her tiptoes to drag it forward to read its label.

"What in God's good name are you doing in here?" a man shouted.

Celia whirled to face him, narrowly avoiding sending the whole lot of bottles crashing onto the flagstone floor. He stood in the doorway, tall and lean, a tight cap of dark curls silhouetted against the stronger light of the room behind him. Not the face or form of a stodgy businessman, but a man whose even features were twisted with outrage.

"Oh!" Her face went hot. "I do apologize, Mr. Blanchard."

"Get out before you break something." He stood aside. Celia snatched up her notebook—it was one of her patient ledgers, and she did not want to leave behind proof she hadn't arrived to collect a charitable donation—and strode past him into the piazza. He banged the door shut behind her. "When my housekeeper informed me you were here, she neglected to mention you planned to rummage through my house."

"I . . . oh, dear. Yes, this does look bad." She smiled apologetically. "However, a friend told me about your collections. I could not resist the temptation to see them for myself."

"Well, you've seen them." He extended a hand in the direction of the front of the house. He had large, almost protuberant, eyes. They glared at her with a fierce intensity. "And now you can leave."

He stood behind her and began to slowly move toward the door she'd left ajar, herding her like a wayward sheep.

"Does this mean you are not interested in donating to our cause?" she asked, dragging her feet against the inexorable force removing her from the piazza. "Delphia Shaw indicated you would be most receptive. The poor orphans are so worthy."

He scoffed. "Why in heaven's name would Delphia Shaw send anyone to my house seeking charitable contributions? Is this some sort of a joke?" He took her elbow and pushed—shoved—her into the dining room.

"I apologize for my error. I imagined her recommendation a sincere one, but . . ."

"Tell Delphia I'm not amused any more now than I ever have been with her antics." He managed to steer her through the dining room and back into the entrance hall. "And who was it who told you about my collection? Not Delphia Shaw. The Shaws have never been invited here."

Oh? "No, not Mrs. Shaw. A friend I'll not name, as I do not wish you to be as angry with her as you currently are with me."

He shuffled her down the hall. His housekeeper, waiting in the doorway to the parlor, raced off when she saw them coming. Undoubtedly, she'd be due a tongue-lashing for permitting Celia to enter the house.

Mr. Blanchard threw open the front door. "As much as I'm used to being gossiped about, Mrs. Davies, tell your friend to keep her tittle-tattle to herself."

Celia stepped over the threshold and out onto the front step. "Again, I am deeply sorry, Mr. Blanch—"

Before she could finish her sentence, he slammed the door on her face. No matter. She had learned what she'd come to discover.

• • •

"So who did steal Mr. Shaw's watch, sir, and those other items from the Institute's patients?" asked Taylor, smoke swirling off the cigar clenched in his teeth as they walked. "Mr. Platt?"

"Mary Ann Newcomb fancies him to be the thief, although the conversation Cassidy overheard contradicts her," said Nick. "At least as far as Shaw's watch is concerned."

Taylor puffed thoughtfully on his cigar. "Hope that Mrs. Wynn is at her lodgings this morning, so we can get a straight story."

"If she's not there, Taylor, she's probably on a train by now." Nick turned the corner, the bustle of a nearby fruit stand sending up a hum of noise. Apples, pears, figs, and plums were piled neatly in wood baskets, the smell of fruit warming in the sun drifting their direction. "Might be headed to Arizona, for all we know."

Or Mexico, like Patrick Davies had done when he'd abandoned Celia and left San Francisco.

"We've got Tokay grapes," called the stand owner, women in head-scarves and thick shawls crowding around him. "And fresh apricots today."

"I like grapes," said Taylor. "Wonder if I should get some to take home."

"Since when do you like grapes?"

"Well, Miss Fer— ahem." He cleared his throat. "I've always liked grapes, sir."

Right. "Later, Taylor."

They arrived at the lodging house, no more impressive-looking in the foggy morning light, and climbed the short flight of stairs to the door.

Nick pointed at Taylor's cigar. "Put that out."

"But I'm not finished, sir . . ." He frowned. "Yes, sir."

He bent and stubbed it out on the stone step while Nick rang the bell. A harried young woman—a girl, actually, around fifteen or sixteen years old—answered, a wet washrag dripping in her hand. Not the landlady, this time.

"What? Oh, my," she said, taking in Taylor's uniform.

"We're here to speak with Mrs. Wynn," said Nick.

"I can . . . um . . ." The chambermaid hunted around for somewhere to drop the rag, decided the empty boot rack in the entryway worked, and wiped her damp hands across her apron. "I can take you to her room, Officers."

"She's here?" asked Taylor.

"So much for Mrs. M. notifying us that the woman had returned to her lodgings, as we'd told her to do," said Nick.

A female resident in a drab cotton dress wandered out of the dingy parlor at their right. "What's going on?"

"The police are here to see Mrs. Wynn," said the girl who'd answered the door.

"Again?"

"Oh, dear," the girl exclaimed and scuttled up the fraying carpet covering the stairs, trailing the smell of beeswax and strong lye. Nick and Taylor climbed after her, all the way to the top floor and the rooms tucked beneath the eaves.

"She didn't come down for breakfast, so I guess she's still in her room. The one at the end." The girl pointed. "There."

Taylor rapped on the door. "Mrs. Wynn? Police." He leaned his ear against the door and rapped again. "Mrs. Wynn? Nothing, sir."

"Do you have a key?" Nick asked the chambermaid.

"Sure." She rummaged through a pocket and produced a key ring. "Should be . . . let's see . . . this one."

The girl, her hand shaking, slipped the key into the lock and turned. "Mrs. Wynn, sorry to—why, she's not in here, Officers. And all her stuff's cleared out!"

Nick stepped into the empty room just as a woman outside released an ear-splitting scream. He sprinted to the window and yanked it open. Down in the cobbled yard, a young woman, a pile of laundry at her feet, noticed him.

"She's dead!" she screeched, pointing toward a shed. A pair of booted female feet protruded, the rest of their owner's body hidden by the building's overhanging roof. "She's dead!"

CHAPTER 12

"Got here as soon as I could, Greaves," said Harris, exiting the rear door of Mrs. Wynn's lodging house.

"Thanks, Harris," said Nick, standing next to the shed to block the view of the bloodied woman on the ground behind him. Residents gawked from every window that faced the yard, even though most couldn't actually see the body because of the building's overhang. Occasionally, a face popped over the alley wall. Nosy passersby. "The victim's back here."

The coroner pushed aside the drying bed linens, which flapped on ropes tied between the lodging house and the side fence.

"Well, that's a mess." He squatted next to the body and felt the skin of the woman's face. He then dipped a finger into the puddle of blood that spread dark red across the gravel beneath her head, rubbed it against his thumb. "Body's cold. Blood fairly well congealed. She's likely been dead a couple of hours at most. Do you know who she is?"

"Althea Wynn. The woman we'd interviewed as a witness in the Ambrose Shaw case," answered Nick. "We also found a gold man's watch and fob chain in a concealed pocket of her petticoat. Likely his."

The items weighed down Nick's coat pocket. Worth enough, if pawned, to support an unpretentious person like Mrs. Wynn for at least a year. He'd have to inform Mullahey they weren't going to need that warrant to search Platt's lodgings for the watch, after all.

"Well, this was the perfect space to stash a body, if you didn't want it discovered right away," said Harris. He gently removed her blood-soaked bonnet, crushed from the blow to her head, and prodded the damage done to her skull. "Struck with some force. Good thing Officer Taylor isn't out here to get nauseated."

His assistant had a weak stomach. As it was, the sight of Mrs. Wynn's hair caked with gore was turning Nick's. He'd seen too much blood during the war, too often smelled its metallic tang to ever tolerate the sight or smell again. He looked away.

"Mrs. Wynn had been attempting to leave town," said Nick, nodding at the carpetbag and small trunk resting near the alley gate where she'd set them while she'd undone the latch. "Her room was emptied of all her belongings some time after we tried to speak with her yesterday."

"Sadly, she didn't get far." Harris gently lowered Mrs. Wynn's head to the ground and pulled out a cloth to wipe his hands.

"Let me get somebody to bring you a washbasin." Nick ran back to the lodging house and shoved open the rear door. The frizzle-haired cook, who'd been skulking on the other side, jumped backward. The kitchen—the dry sink crowded with dirty breakfast dishes, a pot bubbling on the cooking stove against the wall—smelled of grease and rotting vegetables. "We need a basin of water out here."

"Yes, sir," she squeaked.

"I don't think our victim was killed in this exact spot, Greaves," said the coroner once Nick returned. "Based on the disarray of her skirts and the snags on her stockings, she was dragged behind the shed. In fact, you might observe faint lines from her heels in the gravel there."

Disgust tugged at Nick's gut. "Was she assaulted, Harris?"

"Sexually?" Harris frowned and glanced at the body. "I'll check, of course, but I don't think so. Murdered and hauled to this spot where she might not be noticed right away."

The cook elbowed a path through the hanging laundry, the tin basin she carried splashing water as she scuttled across the yard. She set it next to Harris, shot a glance at the blood on his hands, went white, and ran back off.

Harris rinsed his fingers, staining the water red. "I suspect she was struck with a heavy rough-edged object, like a broken brick or cobblestone. There was some residue on the bonnet. It absorbed most of the blood she'd shed."

"Can you tell if the assailant was a man or a woman?"

The coroner considered the question. "Given the angle . . . not a short person," he said, emptying the basin onto the ground and getting to his feet. "Although our victim here is rather small herself."

The rear door opened again, and Taylor led Giulia DiPaolo through. A long braid of her hair hung over her shoulder, and she clung to it, her hand trembling.

"Miss DiPaolo heard something, sir," he said.

"This is dreadful, Detective Greaves," she said, her voice trembling as much as her fingers. "Poor Mrs. Wynn. Who could've done this to her?"

"What was it you heard, Miss DiPaolo?" asked Nick.

She swallowed hard, her gaze darting at Mrs. Wynn's prone corpse before hastily shifting back to Nick's face. "I heard a cry around sunrise. My room is the one right there." She turned to point at a window two floors below Mrs. Wynn's room. "The sound woke me up. I thought it was the gate hinges squealing, at first. But then there was a truly eerie noise, like a screech from a wounded animal. I went to the window and saw a shadow moving in the alleyway, but it was so dark. I may also have heard a voice, a man's—"

"A man. Are you sure, Miss DiPaolo?"

"Pretty sure," she answered. "At the time, I assumed I'd heard the alleycats fighting and went back to bed, even though I had to get up not long after." She bit her lower lip. "I'm sorry. Truly. I wish . . ."

"I doubt you could've prevented what happened, Miss DiPaolo," said Taylor, soothing as usual.

"Taylor, take Miss DiPaolo back inside, if you will. And ask if anybody else heard noises at sunrise or saw somebody out here," said Nick. "When you're finished with the lodgers, question the neighbors."

"Yes, sir." Taylor led her back inside, the door opening to a rush of questioning voices before they were cut off by it shutting again.

"Taylor discovered a broken part of a discarded chloroform bottle outside the Hygienic Institute, Harris," said Nick, waiting as the coroner finished drying his hands. "We can't prove it's the one used in Shaw's death but my money's on it."

"I didn't imagine it would ever be found, Greaves."

"Wish I could identify who's responsible for killing him and Mrs. Wynn, though. Here. Let's go see what we can find out in that alley." Nick tugged open the gate, sending more busybodies scattering in all directions, their heels kicking up gravel. "Hey, hey! Police! I need to talk with you," he shouted, trying to get any of them to stop and answer questions. None of them obliged. "Damned nuisances. They've probably trampled any evidence out here."

"However, I believe we've located our murder weapon." The coroner pointed at a pile of stones and crumbling bits of brick against the fence. "There, Greaves."

"I believe you're right, Harris," said Nick and retrieved the broken half of a cobblestone, one edge smeared with blood.

● ● ●

"Detective Greaves is out, ma'am," said the lone officer in the police station. "Only Mr. Briggs is in right now," he added, pointing his pencil at the closed door to the detectives' office.

"I shall leave a message for Mr. Greaves, then," said Celia.

"Fine by me, ma'am."

Celia went over to Mr. Taylor's desk, wondering where all the rest of the policemen were, for there were desks aplenty in the room, indicating the number of officers employed by the force. However, those desks and chairs were almost always empty whenever she came to visit. Even the turnkey who also booked new jail arrivals was absent from his corner standing desk. Odd that she did not know his name, given all the times she'd been to the station. Perhaps one day she would ask Mr. Greaves about the fellow.

Or perhaps you will not, Celia. The sooner she accepted that she'd see little of Nicholas Greaves in the future, the better.

She sighed, which caused the policeman to peer at her. "I shall be out of your way soon, Officer. Do not worry about me."

149

"I wasn't worried."

Lovely.

She stripped off her gloves and searched for a pen, ink, and notepaper on which to write. She needed to inform Mr. Greaves about Mr. Blanchard's supply of chloroform—she'd only glimpsed the label of the bottle, but it was clear what she'd read—as well as his domestic's confirmation that he had no alibi for Wednesday evening.

"Need help there, ma'am?" asked the officer, leaning back in his chair.

"Did Mr. Greaves or Mr. Taylor mention where they were headed this morning?" She located what she required and took a seat in Mr. Taylor's chair. The objects atop his desk smelled strongly of cigar smoke. A much more pleasant aroma than the general stink of the room.

"I'm not allowed to say. But maybe *I* can help." He stood and squinted at her note. "Have you got a crime you'd like to report?"

"Oh, dear, I'm not allowed to say, Officer."

He muttered something uncomplimentary and sat back down.

Should she include in her message that she'd received a warning note from an unknown sender? Mr. Greaves would only chastise her for getting involved in police matters. Deciding against informing him, Celia finished writing and went over to the closed door to the detectives' office. It suddenly swung open, and she jumped backward.

"Sorry to startle you, ma'am," said the fellow who'd opened the door. Portly and rather short, his eyes met hers at nearly the same level. He dragged his fingertips through his beard—a doughnut crumb trapped deep within its mesh of hairs—as he examined her. "Aren't you—"

"Yes, I am, Detective Briggs." She'd met him before and misliked him nearly as much as Nicholas Greaves did. "I am Mrs. Davies." She held up the note. "I was hoping to leave this message for Mr. Greaves."

"He isn't here, but I can see he gets it, once I'm finished."

He stuck out his hand, and Celia snatched the piece of paper out of his reach. "The message can wait."

A man stepped into view behind the detective, his fingers busy reseating his hat upon his head. "Thanks for all your help, Detective. I appreciate it."

"Not a problem," said Mr. Briggs, his smile what some would describe as oily. "Not a problem at all, Mr. Shaw."

Leonard Shaw? What could he want and why was he speaking with Detective Briggs and not Mr. Greaves?

Before Celia could pose the question to him, he'd doffed his hat at her and marched past, quickly crossing the police station on his way to the main staircase.

"Was that Mr. Leonard Shaw?" she asked Detective Briggs.

"Yep."

"I read about his father's death at the Hygienic Institute," she said. "What an astonishing incident and quite suspicious. Was he here to discuss it with you?"

Mr. Briggs dropped the grin he'd been wearing. "That is police business, ma'am."

"Oh. Of course," she replied, coquettishly touching the sleeve of his coat. "Silly of me to presume you might share your opinion on the matter."

He glanced at her hand. "Well, I might be able to tell you one or two things, ma'am."

The alleyway door opened and Nicholas Greaves descended the steps, a broken cobblestone in his hand. Celia straightened, her cheeks hot.

"Mrs. Davies?" he asked. His gaze took in the detective at her side. "Briggs."

"Greaves," the detective replied in a tone as hard as Mr. Greaves's had been. "This here lady's got a note for you."

"Don't let us interrupt your doughnut-eating, Briggs," he replied.

"Ha ha." He smirked and stomped back inside the detectives' office.

Mr. Greaves turned to her. "What exactly was going on there with Briggs, Mrs. Davies?"

"Nothing at all, Mr. Greaves," she replied. "And may I ask why you are holding a cobblestone?"

"You may." He looked down at the broken stone. "It was used to murder Mrs. Wynn."

. . .

"Mrs. Wynn stole Mr. Shaw's watch and fob chain?" asked Mrs. Davies, her skirts hiked in order to match Nick's pace, her boot heels rapping crisply on the wood sidewalk. "As least we have resolved who stole the items, but so many other questions do remain."

"And if I find answers, I'll be sure to share them with you."

"No need for sarcasm, Mr. Greaves."

The morning had turned warm and fair. He'd prefer that they were strolling someplace pleasant, like paths at the Willows or admiring plants inside one of the hothouses at Woodward's Gardens, rather than trudging down Kearny toward the Hygienic Institute. He'd also prefer that Jack Hutchinson, his closest friend, hadn't died during the war, that Meg was still alive and their father had forgiven Nick before he'd passed away, that Patrick Davies hadn't returned to torture them both. But he rarely got what he wanted.

"Nevertheless, her death and Mr. Shaw's are clearly connected, Mr. Greaves," she said, oblivious to the miserable wanderings of his mind.

"Hard not to come to that conclusion." He glanced over at her. Her jaw was set, her brain no doubt attempting to outstrip his in a race for solutions. "You know you don't have to accompany me, ma'am. You're free to return to your clinic."

"I am fully aware I need not accompany you, Mr. Greaves, but you've not permitted me the opportunity to relay what I discovered this morning."

Here she was doing police work again. He'd scold her but his warnings never stopped her. Maybe he was glad they didn't. "You *could* just hand me your note."

"I do not comprehend why you are being so difficult."

Don't you? Don't you understand why being near you bothers me so much? "What did you learn, Mrs. Davies?"

"Firstly, Mr. Blanchard's domestic departs at six, verifying that he has no alibi for Wednesday evening."

"He's already admitted that, ma'am." But he did appreciate her confirming what they'd been told.

"Secondly . . ." Her mouth turned upward in a self-congratulatory grin. "Mr. Elliot Blanchard collects insects."

"*That's* what you discovered?"

"Obviously, Mr. Greaves, I learned much more than that piece of information," she replied tersely. "Apparently, there are certain substances used to suffocate the creatures in order to halt their flutterings, which would damage their wings."

"How fascinating," he said, stepping around a grocer's clerk dragging a loaded handcart through a doorway and out onto the sidewalk.

Mrs. Davies nimbly skirted the man, as well. "I am going to ignore your continued sarcastic comments and tell you that one of those substances is chloroform," she said. "In the room Mr. Blanchard uses to prepare his displays, he maintains supplies of various substances. Including chloroform. A gap in the tidy row of bottles hinted that one was missing."

"Taylor found part of a discarded chloroform bottle in the alley outside the Institute yesterday. Not far from the private entrance."

"A rather reckless disposal of evidence for a man who appears to have a meticulously organized and scientific mind, but perhaps he was startled," she mused. "By Mina unexpectedly showing up, perhaps. Incidentally, his domestic did not recognize her name."

"If Blanchard knows Mina, you think he'd be inviting her over to his house? Introducing her to the servants?" he asked. And yes, he was being sarcastic again.

"Mr. Blanchard was also absent from his house this morning," she continued. "Breakfasting at Empire State, supposedly."

"Out and about around sunrise, perhaps taking a side trip to bash in Mrs. Wynn's head."

She looked over at him, taking her attention off the uneven planks of the sidewalk and stumbling on a protruding piece of wood.

Nick grabbed her elbow to steady her. "That was a crude remark. Sorry about that, ma'am."

"I tended soldiers sent to the Army hospital during the war, Mr. Greaves. I am not so easily shocked. Simply a momentary distraction," she said, easing her arm out of his grasp with a tight smile. "Regarding the unfortunate damage Mrs. Wynn's skull suffered, I can attest to Mr. Blanchard's ready temper. Although his anger was likely due to finding me nosing around where I was not meant to be."

"I can't imagine anybody being angry with you about that, ma'am," he quipped. Her smile was fleeting, but reward enough. "Our witness to the attack on Mrs. Wynn thinks she heard a man's voice."

"Perhaps we can now narrow the list of suspects, Mr. Greaves, and eliminate Mina from consideration. At least so far as Mrs. Wynn's death is concerned," she said. "Besides not being male, she is far too unwell to have risen at dawn, made her way to the woman's lodgings, and cracked her over the head with a cobblestone."

"She might not be responsible for killing Mrs. Wynn, ma'am, but she's the only one of our suspects I can definitely place at the scene of Mr. Shaw's murder," he reminded her. "And you don't need to scowl at me. I honestly don't want Mina to be guilty, either."

"I am pleased to hear you say so, because I can never be confident," she replied. "I do hope you consider that Mr. Blanchard could be the source of the chloroform used to subdue Mr. Shaw, and that Mrs. Wynn was merely an opportunistic thief. The fellow has no reliable alibi for the evening of Mr. Shaw's death and possibly for this morning, as well."

"My opinion of your orderly, scientific fellow is that he's too clever to commit a crime as brutal as what happened to Mrs. Wynn," he said. "Even with his ready temper."

"We know better, do we not, than to presume appearances are truthful?" she asked. "'One may smile, and smile, and be a villain.'"

"Shakespeare this time, ma'am?"

"Yes. From *Hamlet*," she replied. "I wish I'd known to inspect Mr. Blanchard's clothing to assess if any items were dirty or blood-spattered."

"Mrs. Davies, the day you become clairvoyant is going to be a scary one."

She chuckled and waited for the street sweeper to finish scooping horse manure into a nearby cart, the scrape of his shovel against macadam an irritating rasp. The path he'd opened across the road wouldn't stay clear of muck for long.

"Ross's cook suggested that Platt had stolen Shaw's watch. Obviously she was wrong, but maybe he is involved," he said. "Cassidy overheard him accusing Mrs. Wynn of stealing it, and now we've found it in her possession. So . . ."

"Owen has been spying on these people?" she asked.

"At Griffin's request, it seems."

"No wonder he–" She clamped her mouth over the rest of her sentence.

"'No wonder he' what, ma'am?"

She perked her chin. If he never saw her again, it'd be the one thing he missed most. That and the spark in her clear blue eyes.

"Given that Mr. Griffin is paying him to snoop, no wonder Owen was reluctant to accept another job, one that I had for him. A request to search Mr. Roesler's accounts to identify all the recent recipients of Mr. Shaw's gifts," she said. "I aim to prove, Mr. Greaves, that Mina Cascarino was not one of them."

He grinned. He couldn't help it. She never failed to astonish him. "I'm glad you're on my side, ma'am. That's all I can say."

"All that aside, Mr. Blanchard *must* be the one who murdered Mr. Shaw," she stated. "Then Mrs. Wynn stole the man's watch upon realizing he was deceased."

"And Blanchard killed *her*, even though she hadn't identified him?" he asked. "Hadn't even given us a description."

"He panicked after you questioned him."

It wasn't impossible. "He is your favorite suspect, isn't he, Mrs. Davies?"

"Chloroform, Mr. Greaves," she said. "And a lengthy history of professional—and possibly personal—hatred of Ambrose Shaw. Furthermore, he possesses no good alibi for either murder. Means, motive, and opportunity."

"How did he get the key to the Institute's private entrance, though?" he asked as they crossed the cleared path in the street. "Don't think he made a friendly visit to his ailing political opponent and had a chance to swipe the man's copy. The key, I remind you, that you found in Mina's pocket."

"I believe we made a pact to agree that the killer left it there, Mr. Greaves."

"No comment, ma'am."

"Here is where Mr. Blanchard's orderly, scientific mind would come in handy, though. The fellow is resourceful and would find a way to obtain it. Perhaps he'd enrolled Miss Shaw's assistance." Her mouth twisted, turned down. "I wish now I'd questioned her about that key when I was at her studio yesterday. Before I lost it."

"She'd have denied recognizing it, ma'am," he said. "More importantly, Mr. Ross confirms that she didn't meet with her father."

"Mr. Greaves, she could be lying. She could have snuck upstairs, for example, while Mr. Ross was otherwise engaged."

He exhaled. "If the police force ever hires female officers, Mrs. Davies, I'll be sure to put your name in."

"You are not being sarcastic again, are you, Mr. Greaves?"

"Not at all, ma'am."

"Well, we need not worry about my becoming a member of the constabulary," she replied. "The police force will never hire women, I suspect."

They rounded the corner. Halfway up the street stood the Hygienic Institute, its green awnings unfurled to protect the windows from the sun. Nick didn't understand the need for the awnings; most of the rooms' shutters were closed. He doubted business was good. Although the trade in gossip was going strong, based on the clumps of folks collected along the street who were chattering together and pointing.

Celia Davies surveyed the onlookers. "What an unfortunate turn of events for Mr. Ross, would you not agree, Mr. Greaves? One patient dead on the premises of his medical establishment then another grotesquely murdered. And now his assistant among those suspected," she said. "One could almost imagine that someone wished to destroy his reputation and ruin his business."

"There have got to be easier ways to accomplish a man's ruination, Mrs. Davies, than by murdering folks," he replied.

The Omnibus Railroad horsecar rattled up the street, slowing as it passed the Institute. Letting all the passengers gawk, Nick supposed. What was going to happen once folks learned that a second patient had died, this time clearly murdered? He'd have to alert the local police to increase patrols in the area.

"Do you have an opinion as to why Leonard Shaw was visiting Detective Briggs while I was at the station, Mr. Greaves?"

"He was?"

A murmur swept through the crowd huddled outside the Institute's front door, and she rose on her toes to better see. It was only Ross, glaring as he pulled down the blinds covering the large ground-floor windows.

"You did not notice him?" she asked. "I suppose you must not have done. Mr. Shaw left the station by the main staircase, so you'd not have crossed paths."

"He was in talking to Briggs . . ." Nick's wound took to aching, and he reached up to rub his arm. "All I need is for him to be interfering in one of my cases."

"I did try to ask why Mr. Shaw was in the station, but Mr. Briggs refused to tell me," she said, settling back onto her heels. "Although he may have revealed all after a few more minutes of persuasion."

"Flirting, you mean."

"I was not flirting."

Right. "Thanks for trying, ma'am, but as annoying and incompetent as Briggs can be sometimes, he's not stupid. Well, not completely stupid," he said. "Speaking of Leonard Shaw, his alibi for Wednesday evening has gotten shaky. Left the meeting he was attending early. Maybe as early as seven."

"Well, that is intriguing."

"Putting it mildly."

Ross finished closing all the blinds facing the street. The crowd, deciding the show was temporarily over, began to drift away.

"I should return to my clinic after all, Mr. Greaves. I have an appointment in about fifteen minutes to prepare for," said Mrs. Davies, consulting the watch that she pinned to the waist of her dress. "But I must remark that I am struck by the coincidence that, at the very moment Mrs. Wynn departed her lodgings this morning, her killer showed up. The timing—"

"Is mighty convenient."

℘ CHAPTER 13 ℞

A strip of black crepe had been draped over the *Closed* sign in the window of Rebecca Shaw's photographic gallery. The blinds were drawn and the interior, from what Celia could see through the gaps, was dark and empty. She'd intended to return home, but her walk to the Institute with Mr. Greaves had brought her too near the studio to resist the temptation to speak with Miss Shaw again. Perhaps she knew why her stepbrother had been at the station that morning, or why a bottle of chloroform was missing from among Elliot Blanchard's supplies. Was prepared to admit she had, possibly, taken her father's key to the private entrance and passed it on to her former fiancé. Or that she had critical information about who had murdered Mrs. Wynn.

"Are you lookin' for Miss Shaw?"

The voice belonged to a clerk from the adjacent general merchandise shop, a fellow so lean his apron strings had been wrapped twice around his pinched waist.

Celia never ceased to marvel that, first of all, people took notice of her peering through windows and, secondly, were all too happy to assist. The average San Franciscan was either extraordinarily helpful, unabashedly inquisitive, or excessively suspicious of strangers.

"I am, but I see that she has closed her gallery," she said. "Because of the death in her family, I presume."

"That would be right, ma'am. Her father's gone and died," he said. "Murdered by somebody who didn't like his politics, I'd bet. I woulda voted for him."

She forced a smile; she wasn't here to discuss the rights of former slaves with this man.

"Do you know where I might find Miss Shaw?" she asked. "This is a difficult time, and as an acquaintance, I wish to extend my condolences, leave a small note. Perhaps she resides nearby."

"She lives in the apartment right above her studio." He jabbed his thumb toward the pertinent windows. Their blinds were also closed. "The street door might be unlocked. The woman who lives on the top floor leaves it open for her daughter, who comes and goes an awful lot and don't have a key."

Sometimes unabashed nosiness paid off. "Thank you."

He politely tapped fingers to the brim of his cap. "My pleasure, ma'am."

Celia waited for him to return to the general merchandise shop before trying the street door, located between Miss Shaw's gallery and a tailor's on the other side. As the clerk had predicted, it was unlocked.

A steep staircase, lit only by a gloomy skylight, wound up the building's four stories. At the first landing was a door to what had to be Miss Shaw's flat, located immediately over her gallery.

Celia rapped on the doorframe. *Please answer. Please.*

A door opened on the floor above, and feet pounded down the steps.

"Is that you, Miss Shaw? I got that coffee for you," said the woman, her tawny skirts lifted as she descended, revealing her scuffed half boots. A yellow tin of J. A. Folger Pioneer Coffee in her hand, she abruptly halted when she spotted Celia outside Miss Shaw's door. "Oh. I'm sorry, I thought I heard Rebecca down here."

She spoke through thinly parted lips, as though ashamed of her teeth.

"I was hoping to extend my condolences on the loss of her father, but she does not appear to be at home," said Celia.

"No, she went out early this morning. Probably to look in on her stepmother. The funeral's tomorrow." The woman lifted the tin of coffee. "I offered to buy her some coffee. She never seems to have the time to take care of herself."

"When was it that she left, would you say?" Around sunrise, when a widow was attacked? "I ask because I wonder when I might expect her to return. I do truly wish to speak with her."

"Before six, I think it was. I rise early to do my shopping before I head to the primary school on Pine, where I'm an assistant. I was just getting ready," she explained. "I was surprised to see her. She's not usually up and around at that hour."

Before six. Only if Mrs. Wynn's boardinghouse was nearby, however, would Miss Shaw have had enough time to get there and commit the crime prior to the sun rising. Celia peeked at her watch. Almost nine. *Where have you been for the last three hours, Miss Shaw?*

"Do you know if she ever returned home?" asked Celia. Or has she been gone the entire time?

The woman's gaze narrowed. "That's a strange question. What's it matter?"

"Perhaps it does not. I believe I shall wait until tomorrow's funeral service to extend my condolences to her," said Celia. "A more proper opportunity, rather than intruding upon her today."

"Might be better tomorrow," she agreed. "Although you're not the only one who's been looking for her this morning. I heard them knocking on her door, but they left before I could see who it was."

"Ah." And who could that have been? "This may come as another odd question, but have you ever heard her mention a Mrs. Wynn?"

"Don't think so, but then she is fairly private."

"What about a young woman named Mina Cascarino?" she asked, pressing her luck that Miss Shaw's neighbor would tolerate all the queries. "She is an acquaintance of Miss Shaw's whom I've been attempting to locate in the city. An old friend I lost touch with."

"Was she one of those young women who came to her gallery for their portraits?" she asked. "For an exhibit she'd hoped to hold someplace."

"How fascinating. I'd not heard of this exhibit."

"Working-class girls, they were. They come by to visit her every so often." The woman glanced toward her room, somewhere up in the shadows of the stairwell. "I do have to hurry, ma'am, or I'll be late to school."

"I am sorry for delaying you."

Celia retreated down the steps and back outside. The windows of

Miss Shaw's studio had been emptied of all but a handful of photographs set in front of the closed blinds. She leaned down to examine them, the faces of strangers. One was of two women, attired in simple dresses, their arms around each other's waist. Those working-class girls Miss Shaw's neighbor had spoken of? None of them were Mina, though, providing a connection between her and Miss Shaw. Celia did not recognize a single one, save for the image of a man captured in emulsion upon tin. A man who was Elliot Blanchard.

"What a curious portrait to display in your window, Miss Shaw." *An image of your former fiancé.*

Nearby, a church bell rang the hour. She was going to be late for her appointment. She hurried past the general merchandise shop, where the clerk spotted her through the window and nodded. On the pavement ahead, two women huddled together, oblivious to the pedestrians having to sidestep them.

One of the women was familiar. In fact, she looked to be Miss Shaw, dressed in black mourning attire. And the other person with her . . . Celia squinted to see better. Her deep bonnet shielded her face from view, though. She was gesturing frantically, however, Miss Shaw gripping her arm to calm her.

How very, very curious.

Celia increased her pace, drawing nearer to the two of them. "Miss Shaw!"

At the sound of her name, she looked over and scowled. She exchanged a few hasty words with the other woman and sped off, down the road that crossed Montgomery, her companion heading the other direction. Celia chased after Rebecca.

"Please wait, Miss Shaw!" she shouted, weaving through the pedestrians obstructing her progress, who glared at her unladylike headlong sprint down the street.

"Pardon me," she said to a woman holding the hand of a small child Celia had collided with. When she looked up, she realized she'd lost track of Miss Shaw.

Just then, a horsecar pulled away from its stop, and a tall woman in a black dress bolted from a side alley and jumped aboard before it picked up speed.

Blast.

• • •

"Sorry to disturb you again, Mr. Ross," said Nick, watching the man from the doorway of the ladies' bathing room. "I see that you're busy."

"I'm having to do the work of our cleaning staff myself, because I was forced to let them all go. Hopefully temporarily," said Ross, scrubbing out one of the room's two cast-iron tubs, his cuffs covered by sleeve stockings and his face red from the exertion. The space was tight and warm, the air smelling faintly metallic, and water condensed on the outside of the cold water pipe that fed one of the taps. Ross was sweating, too. Occasionally, a drip fell from the showerhead that arched over the tub he was scouring. "Have you resolved Mr. Shaw's murder, Mr. Greaves?"

"Not yet," he replied. "Although it is fascinating that the coroner detected alcohol in the man's stomach."

Ross went even redder. "I . . . I . . ."

"It's okay, Mr. Ross. Your secret's safe with me," said Nick. "I'm here because of Mrs. Wynn. You told me she had lots of friends and acquaintances. Did any of them visit her while she was taking the cure?"

Somebody who'd learned when the woman intended to flee San Francisco and stopped her before she could make good on her escape.

"I don't recollect anyone visiting. The day she arrived—Monday—was a very busy day for me, however. There was a leak in one of the pipes, so there were workers down here I had to supervise." He flourished the scrub brush he'd been using, which splattered soapy water onto the black-and-white tiled floor. A few sudsy drips slid down the nearby tiled wall. "And of course Mr. Shaw was also set to arrive that day. I had to oversee that his room was prepared to the highest of standards."

"No doubt," Nick replied, starting to sweat himself, the cloying damp and heat of the room seeping through his clothing. "I'm afraid I've got more bad news for you, Mr. Ross. Mrs. Wynn has been murdered."

"Oh my heavens!" He dropped the scrub brush, and it clanged against the bottom of the tub. "Do the newspapers know yet?"

Probably. Although how they managed to be so well-informed was a mystery to Nick. "Where were you this morning around sunrise?"

"I'm a suspect?"

"We're going to ask everybody, Mr. Ross. It's normal."

He retrieved the brush. "At home. I was just getting out of bed, I'd say. My wife can confirm that."

He'd be making sure she could. "We've recovered Mr. Shaw's watch and fob chain," he said. "In Mrs. Wynn's possession."

"Oh . . . oh . . ." Mr. Ross swayed, his empty hand flailing for the lip of the tub, using it to steady himself. "A regular patient. A faithful client. I trusted her . . . how could she?"

Nick dragged over a nearby stool for the man to sit on. "Wish I could answer that question."

Ross's shoulders drooped. "She abused my welcome. I trust my patients. I thought she was a respectable woman."

Who liked to nick expensive watches. "I have some questions about Mr. Platt, Mr. Ross. Such as a rumor I heard that he's the person who's been stealing from your patients. What do you think about that?"

"But Mrs. Wynn took Mr. Shaw's watch," said Ross, the scrub brush, forgotten in his hand, dripping water onto the tiles. "You just told me that."

"She and Platt were observed deep in conversation yesterday," said Nick. "Maybe they were in cahoots."

"I cannot fathom that being the situation, Mr. Greaves. Mr. Platt has been nothing but the most reliable of employees," said Ross. "He's been with me four years and I've never had any trouble with him."

Except Platt was in debt to Griffin, so his willingness to cause trouble might've changed for the worse. "I should also inform you that my assistant discovered part of a chloroform bottle out in the alley here."

"A chloroform bottle?" Ross used his forefinger to adjust his spectacles on the bridge of his nose. "I have no idea how it got there, Mr. Greaves. I repeat that we do not use the substance."

"Then you won't mind if I have a look at your supplies and prove that to myself, will you?"

"If you insist, but you won't find any." Ross stood and balanced the brush he'd been holding on the edge of the tub. "The storage room is down the hall."

Nick followed him into the whitewashed hallway, gas jets flaring overhead, a series of closed doors on either side. More bathing rooms. Out here, the air was just as cloyingly damp, and he was glad when they reached the far end of the hall and a door labeled *Supplies–Private*.

Ross unlocked it, crossed to the room's narrow window, and retracted the blinds. Pulling them open didn't offer much light, though, and Nick surveyed the shadows.

"As you see, Mr. Greaves, we have no need for harmful substances. Pure water is our cure."

The walls were lined with wood shelves holding clean rags, fresh linens, stacks of towels, soft brushes. For scrubbing skin, Nick supposed. Another set of shelves held washing powder and bar soaps. Hill's Chemical Olive Soap. Soda and a small container of lime.

Ross sidled in close behind Nick. "If the killer used chloroform on Mr. Shaw, Mr. Greaves, they did not obtain it from my supplies. I assure you."

Just then, Mary Ann Newcomb barged into the room. "Oh! I'm sorry, Mr. Ross. I didn't realize you were in here with Mr. Greaves," she said. "I need to fetch some washing powder for the table linens."

"We're finished, Miss Newcomb," said Nick, tidying the stack of towels he'd started to search through. He swept past the both of them, out of the room.

"An excellent idea, Mary Ann," Ross replied. "We may as well clean the entire facility while we have no patients."

She scurried inside the supply room.

"If you have any information about Mrs. Wynn's next of kin, Mr. Ross, I'd like to know," said Nick. "We need to contact them."

The cook's gasp was so loud it echoed off the room's walls. "Next of kin? Has Mrs. Wynn passed away?"

"She died this morning," said Nick. "Attacked outside her lodging house while attempting to flee town."

"Oh, no!" Her eyes went wide, showing the whites around the irises like a panicked horse. "That's what she'd been trying to tell me. That she was scared and needed my help. But now it's too late!"

• • •

"What bad has happened now?" asked Jane, ascending the street's incline alongside Celia. When she'd arrived at the Hutchinsons', her friend had been discussing dinner plans with her servant, but hadn't objected to rushing off. "You're practically sprinting, so it must be awful."

"Something awful *has* happened, Jane," she said. "And I have a question for you that may or may not shed light on the event. Is it possible that Rebecca Shaw and Elliot Blanchard are still involved with one another? Despite the fact that he has married. She has his portrait on display at her studio."

"What a scandal *that* would be if they've resumed their *affaire de coeur*." She sobered. "It actually would be really shocking, and detrimental to his political ambitions."

"As though romantic affairs have ruined other politicians' careers, Jane."

Jane waited to respond, having caught the eye of a neighbor across the road, who tipped his stovepipe hat at them. "Not the person to encounter right now. He's a terrible snoop," she murmured. She smiled a greeting and slipped her hand into the crook of Celia's arm, tugging her forward.

"Mr. Blanchard means to not be like other politicians, Celia. More noble. More righteous," she said. "Frank is a serious supporter of his. He'll be upset if it's true that Elliot Blanchard and Miss Shaw remain in close communication. I haven't heard any rumors, however."

A lack of rumors did not lessen Celia's conviction that the two remained friendly. A friendliness that may have gone too far . . .

"Mr. Blanchard keeps an amazing insect collection," she said, as blandly as when she'd announced the same to Mr. Greaves.

"I've heard about it from Frank. However, he thinks hobbies like that are pursued by men with way too much time on their hands," said Jane. "I didn't realize you'd ever been invited to Mr. Blanchard's house to see his insects."

"I was *not* invited."

Jane laughed. She had the happiest, most honest laugh of anyone Celia knew. "How did you manage to get inside? Outside of his political work and his wine business, he's a very private person, from what I understand."

"I pretended to be collecting monies for the Orphans' Asylum early this morning."

"And he agreed to see you?"

"His maid let me into the house," said Celia. "Against her better judgment."

They turned into the breeze sweeping down off the western hills. Carrying the salty smell of the ocean, thought Celia, although her perception of the aroma might be due more to her wishful thinking than reality. *As soon as this case is resolved, Barbara and Addie and I must visit Cliff House again.* Laugh at the sea lions at Seal Rock. Strip off their stockings and wade in the cold ocean water . . .

Jane nudged Celia with her elbow. "Celia, are you listening?"

"Evidently not. Did you ask me a question?"

"Why did you want to see Elliot Blanchard's insect collection?" she asked. "A sudden interest in entomology?"

"No. Curiously enough, when Miss Campbell arrived for Barbara's lesson this morning, she made a comment about the collection," she said. "You hadn't mentioned that she used to tutor Mrs. Blanchard."

"That was how I'd heard about her. Or rather how Frank heard about her," said Jane. "From Mr. Blanchard, who heaped praise on Olivia. She speaks Spanish, it seems, and Mrs. Blanchard hails from South America. He felt she needed assistance with her English."

"Anyway, Miss Campbell mentioned Mr. Blanchard's collection and all of the chemicals he keeps to both stun and preserve the creatures," said Celia. "Do you recall that Mr. Shaw passed away after being overcome with chloroform? Well, Mr. Blanchard keeps a supply of the substance. Furthermore, it appeared to me that one of the bottles was missing. So . . . voilà!"

Jane slowed her steps. "You don't think . . . wait, Celia. A missing chloroform bottle from among Mr. Blanchard's supply doesn't mean *he* was the one who took it down from its shelf. His domestic could've taken the bottle, for instance. Maybe she suffers from chronic pain or has severe asthma and uses the substance to ease her symptoms. Or . . ." She came to a complete stop and unwound her hand from Celia's arm. "There was a burglary at his house not that long ago. A week or so, maybe? I read about the incident in the *Morning Call*. What if somebody stole from his chloroform supply? Somebody who'd also previously seen his insect collection and knew about the chemicals he keeps."

"Why might someone steal chloroform, Jane, when it can be readily purchased at the nearest apothecary?"

"I guess I prefer imagining some burglar is responsible for that missing bottle than Mr. Blanchard making use of it," said Jane, retaking Celia's arm and continuing up the road.

"He is my primary suspect, but we still have a wealth of others." She felt as much as observed Jane's small, tight smile at Celia's offhand use of "we." "Not only in Mr. Shaw's death but in the murder of the only witness. Around sunrise today."

"Silenced because of what this witness knew?"

"The woman was attempting to flee the city, so she must have feared for her life," said Celia. "She was bludgeoned in the alleyway behind her lodging house. Just as she was making her escape."

"'Bludgeoned' does seem like the sort of attack a man would engage in."

"To be fair, women can be just as capable of brutal assaults, Jane," she said. "I spotted Miss Shaw this morning speaking with another woman I could not identify. A woman who was very agitated."

"Are you suggesting their conversation is connected to this morning's murder?"

"Perhaps I am reading guilt where there is none."

They reached a high point along the road, where they could see and hear the commotion of the city yet feel distant and removed, and Jane came to a stop. Smoke belched from manufactory stacks. Ships, spied through the fog that veiled the hills, crowded the harbor. Bricklayers were hard at work on the street below. The endless industry of San Francisco, which never seemed to rest. As restless as the thoughts churning in Celia's brain.

"I should also tell you about a note I received last evening, Jane. An unsigned note that read *leave us alone*." She looked over at her friend. "Frankly, I do not know what to make of it."

"A warning message sounds dangerous, Celia."

"Addie would agree."

"But who could be the author?" asked Jane. "I mean, are any of the suspects aware of your involvement in the investigation?"

"I would say that Miss Shaw is suspicious. I presume Mr. Blanchard is as well, after my visit to his insect collection," Celia replied. "Mina is aware, of course, but she'd never leave me a warning note."

"She *did* have that key, though, Celia," said Jane skeptically.

"I'm of the opinion that it was stashed in Mina's pocket by the actual perpetrator," she said. "After the person unexpectedly encountered her out in the alley."

"I can see that." Jane grabbed her bonnet as a gust of wind whirled along the street. "If we're focusing on Rebecca Shaw and Elliot Blanchard, how did either of *them* get ahold of that key?"

"I proposed to Mr. Greaves that Miss Shaw had managed to pilfer it from her father's room," she said. "But it could also be possible that someone who works at the Institute gave it to one of them." An idea that had just sprung to mind.

"If I had to make a guess, Celia, I'd suggest that redheaded fellow," said Jane. "A shifty character, if you ask me."

A man embroiled in Mr. Griffin's world, according to Mr. Greaves. *Very shifty.*

"I wish I was acquainted with Mr. Ross, the proprietor of the Hygienic Institute," said Celia. "Or understood if the layout of the building would permit Miss Shaw to have snuck upstairs to grab her father's key without being observed."

Jane sighed. "Celia, I know what you're going to say . . ."

"You do not have to go with me, Jane."

"And miss out on the excitement?" she asked. "If that redheaded fellow spots us, though, he'll get us tossed out."

"Then let us hope Mr. Platt is not at the Institute tomorrow," she replied. And winked.

℘ CHAPTER 14 ℚ

"Here, miss," said Nick, handing Mary Ann Newcomb a glass of cool water he'd scavenged from the captain's office without him noticing.

"Thank you." She gulped the water as though Nick had rescued her from the desert, not simply brought her over from the Hygienic Institute. Finished, she set down the empty glass and turned to Nick with a guilty look on her face. "I suppose I should've told you this morning when I was here that Althea and I were friends, Detective. Have been for months, ever since her first stay at the Institute last year."

"Yes, you should have, Miss Newcomb," he replied. "You said she was scared and might've wanted your help. With leaving town?"

"She came into the kitchen yesterday around lunch to say goodbye. I could tell something was bothering her, but she wouldn't explain. All she said was she wouldn't be visiting the Institute ever again, but I wasn't to worry. That she was heading to Crescent City to live with the only family she had. Except now she won't be," she added gloomily. "I would've helped her if she'd asked me to. She must've finally realized she knew who the intruder was and got scared. Awfully scared."

"Did Mrs. Wynn have any enemies?" he asked. Mary Ann Newcomb was proving to be a frustrating witness—full of information but lacking in the details that would make a difference to his case. "As her friend, I expect she'd confided in you."

"She hadn't an enemy in the world, as kind as she was," she insisted. "But then, I suppose some folks aren't always what they seem, are they, Mr. Greaves?"

What was that phrase Celia Davies had quoted? *One may smile, and smile, and be a villain.*

"Perhaps Mrs. Wynn was one of those folks, after all, Miss Newcomb." Nick considered the young woman seated across from him. "We discovered Mr. Shaw's watch and fob chain on her."

"Are you positive?" she asked. "I mean . . . how could she have taken them from Mr. Shaw?"

"The fellow had conveniently died."

She shook her head. "No. It can't be like that. She wouldn't have had the time," she said. "She was down in the kitchen with me for nearly the whole evening, aside from when she was at dinner with the others. She always stops in to chat when she's with us."

"She came into the kitchen to talk to you Wednesday night?" he asked, not recollecting if Mullahey had learned that already. Regrettably, Taylor wasn't here to consult his notes.

"She did. Right about the time I returned to the kitchen after taking Mr. Shaw's tray up to the small parlor," she said. "She wanted to see what I was preparing before going to the dining room."

"What time was that again?" he asked.

"Around six." A frown darted across her face. "She was in a blue funk that evening—Mr. Ross had hoped partaking of the cold dunk baths would cure her of her melancholia—and she got into an argument with one of our male guests. I could hear their raised voices where I was in the kitchen. Mr. Ross must've heard them, too, because he rushed in to make peace. But everybody's hackles had been raised, so Althea got up from the table and went to her room. She'd hardly touched her food and didn't even get to enjoy the dessert I'd prepared. One of her favorites. Rice pudding."

"She might've gone straight to Mr. Shaw's room to rob him at that time." Although the small, middle-aged woman Nick had met seemed even less capable of subduing Shaw than Mina. "And not Mr. Platt."

"So I was wrong about him stealing Mr. Shaw's watch," she conceded. "But Althea couldn't have either, because Mr. Shaw was still alive when she went upstairs then."

Mrs. Wynn had claimed to notice Shaw in the private parlor, finishing up his meal around six thirty. "How did the watch end up in her possession, do you think, Miss Newcomb?"

Her gaze darted around the room as if searching for a response.

"Somebody planted it on her."

Or the woman had found the time to steal the watch later, between noticing a trespasser and alerting Platt.

Nick rested his elbows on the arms of his chair and tented his fingers, contemplating the cook over their tips. "Let's say it was Mr. Platt who killed Mrs. Wynn," he said. "How could he have learned she intended to leave town this morning? Would she have told him?"

"I doubt it, Detective." She scrunched up her face. "I wonder, though, if he overheard us talking in the kitchen yesterday. About her plans to go to Crescent City."

A distinct possibility. "Did she have any other confidants, anybody else she might've revealed her plans to?"

"She had friends, lots of friends," she replied. "She could've told any one of them. And I suppose other folks knew about her family in Crescent City. She enjoyed talking about them. Called them true pioneers."

"You don't have a name of a particular friend, though."

"I don't. I'm sorry. I wish I could tell you more." Tears welled in her eyes and she bit her lower lip, trying to stop them from falling. "She must've been trying to protect me, by saying so little. Because of the person who ended up killing her."

Nick lowered his hands and leaned forward. "I have to ask where you were today around sunrise, Miss Newcomb. Before you came into the station," he said. "Procedure, you understand."

"Do you mean . . . you mean . . ." she stuttered. "I was getting ready to come here, Detective. You can ask my landlady. When I was done talking with you, I went straight to the Institute. To give the kitchen a good scrub. It needs it. And now's as good a time as any," she replied. "Do you think we'll ever have patients again, Detective? I sure do need my job with Mr. Ross."

"Folks will eventually forget, Miss Newcomb." Another scandal, another shocking crime always came along to distract people from the last scandal, the last crime.

Her tears spilled over to trail down her freckled cheeks. "It's so awful, Mr. Greaves. Did she suffer, do you think?"

He'd been asked that question before. He'd never come up with a ready answer that would satisfy the grieving friends, the grieving family left behind after some wretch had stolen the life of their loved one. An answer that would satisfy him.

"Her death was probably quick, Miss Newcomb," he replied, just as he had all those other times. Even if the response hadn't always been the truth.

"To think she'd been so happy the night before, coming down into the kitchen to make her apology about the fuss she'd caused arguing with the others, to chat with me while I washed the pots and the dishes," she said, swiping her tears off her face. "If only I'd known what was going to happen. If only she'd been upstairs the whole time, instead of in the kitchen with me. Maybe she'd have scared off that trespasser and Mr. Shaw wouldn't be dead. Maybe she wouldn't be dead, either."

• • •

"You're not planning on wandering off to the police station this afternoon, are you, Mr. Cassidy?" asked Mr. Roesler, removing his white apron, the material as pristine as a fresh dusting of snow. He hadn't seen snow since he was a little kid, thought Owen with a dash of black melancholy.

"No, sir," he replied, rousing himself. "I'm not going anywhere this afternoon."

"Good. Watch the store while I'm out." Mr. Roesler looked around the interior of the store, the glass cases sparkling, the candies glimmering like edible jewels in their jars, his eyes full of affection like a father for his child. His expression shifted. "Or maybe I should close up and send you home—"

"I'll be able to manage, sir," interrupted Owen. This was gonna be his chance to look through the customer account ledgers for Mrs.

Davies. He couldn't miss it. "Besides, it's not that busy around this hour. You'll be back, won't you, before the fellows heading home from work stop in to buy confections for their sweethearts?"

His boss eyed him. "You sure, Mr. Cassidy?"

Owen puffed out his chest. "Yes, sir, I can take care of things here. And if anybody has a complicated order, I'll tell them that you mean to return . . . when exactly do you mean to return?"

"An hour."

Would that be enough time for what he had to do? It should be, as long as customers didn't actually come into the store. "Not a problem at all, sir."

Mr. Roesler scanned him, pursed his lips skeptically, and grabbed his hat from the hook by the front door. "Don't take a single piece of candy, Mr. Cassidy. I count them all first thing in the morning and last thing at night and reconcile the numbers against sales."

And he did; Owen had seen him.

"No, sir. I wouldn't dream of it." Was he never going to leave?

"All right, then. An hour." He put on his hat and strode out the door, the bell tinkling.

Owen counted to ten before scuttling outside to make sure Mr. Roesler was actually gone. He didn't see him anywhere and ducked back inside.

"Now, where does he keep his books?" he mused aloud, scooting behind the long counter where Mr. Roesler tallied the customers' purchases and settled their accounts.

The current account book sat at the edge of the counter, and Owen pulled it over. He rifled through it, but the entries only went back the past couple of days. Not even to Wednesday, the day Mr. Shaw died. Owen shoved it aside and squatted onto his haunches. Two rows of shelves filled the space underneath the counter, and Mr. Roesler had stacked several paperbound ledgers on the sagging wood. Along with tins of Jenkins' Hair Restorative—he did have a bald spot, come to think of it—and peppermint lozenges for his throat, and a stoppered glass container of Dr. Spencer's Fragrant Sapoine for the teeth and breath.

"Huh." Had to be presentable for the customers, he supposed.

A shadow passed the store window, and Owen straightened, his heart thumping like the rear leg of a dog scratching at fleas. But it was only an elderly fellow strolling past, admiring the beribboned candy boxes on display before moving on. Pulse returning to normal, Owen grabbed the ledgers. As quickly as possible, he thumbed through the book. How far back should he look? Maybe just to the first of September. A couple of weeks, Mrs. Davies had said. Holding the pages open, he hunted around for a writing utensil and some paper.

"You shoulda planned better, Cassidy," he muttered to himself.

He found a short stack of notepaper and a pencil on the shelf and began to search through the records for Mr. Shaw's purchases. It didn't take long. The man seemed to buy candies from Mr. Roesler almost every day. He scribbled the names, scowling at his handwriting–Mrs. Davies was going to be disappointed when she saw how childish it was. At least he didn't find Miss Mina's name. He didn't recognize any of the names, but maybe Mrs. Davies would. He wrote as fast as he could, chewing his bottom lip as he concentrated, hoping she'd find his efforts useful.

"What are you doing, Mr. Cassidy?" Mr. Roesler's voice boomed through the store.

Owen jolted upright, the pencil he'd been holding dropping to the floor. He'd been focusing so hard he hadn't heard the bell. "You're back already, sir."

"Lucky for me, it appears, that I'd forgotten some paperwork I needed." His boss stomped across the room. "Are you looking through my ledgers? What are you up to? I knew I never should've hired an Irish kid." His eyes narrowed down into slits. "Are you attempting to steal customer names? Has somebody paid you to poach my customers?" He snatched the logbooks out of Owen's reach. "Well?"

The Irish comment had stung. "No, sir. I'd never do that. I was just . . . uh . . ."

Mr. Roesler pointed at the door with his free hand. "I'm not going to listen to your excuses. You are released from my employ. Leave now."

Shoot. Shoot! "Yes, Mr. Roesler. I'm sorry, Mr. Roesler."

Head hanging low, he shuffled past him.

The fellow trailed him to the front of the store. "And don't be expecting to receive a recommendation from me, Mr. Cassidy."

"No, sir."

Owen slunk out onto the sidewalk, Mr. Roesler slamming the door behind him. *Well, durn it.* Another job lost. But not everything had been a bust.

He looked down at his fist, clenched around the notes he'd made for Mrs. Davies, and let himself grin. He'd succeeded at one thing. He stuffed the papers into his pocket and hurried up the road.

• • •

"Althea Wynn was upset yesterday, all right, but she didn't say much more to Mary Ann Newcomb than she meant to head to Crescent City and never return," said Nick, leaning against his assistant's desk. Across the station, the booking officer was idly flipping through his ledger, looking up on occasion to eye them or to react to shouts echoing from the holding cells off to his left.

"Had to have been frightened about Mr. Shaw's killer, sir," said Taylor. "She must have recognized the person, after all."

"Wish she'd told us, rather than decide to go on the run. And here, by the way, is the likely answer to how her attacker knew what time she'd be making her escape." He unfolded the newspaper he'd brought into the main station room and dropped it on Taylor's desk. He tapped the column labeled *Ocean Steamships*. "Boats don't leave San Francisco very often for Crescent City. Only twice a month, according to the ship tables. But there was a steamer heading out this morning."

"All they had to know was that she had family there and she meant to leave town," said Taylor. "Would the Shaws be aware of that?"

"Platt told me that she and Ambrose Shaw were awfully friendly. Maybe they were acquainted outside of their shared time at the Institute. If Platt's telling the truth," said Nick. "I have several questions for the Shaws, aside from whether Mrs. Wynn was an acquaintance. Such as why Leonard Shaw was here this morning and talking to Briggs. Out and about early rather than over at the bank."

"Have you asked Mr. Briggs?"

Nick had to laugh. "He wouldn't tell me if I threatened violence," he said. "I also want to hear Shaw's reason for why he left the Parker House long before the meeting of the San Francisco Club had concluded Wednesday night."

"Miss Mina couldn't have killed Mrs. Wynn this morning. We're sure about that, at least," said Taylor. "So who did? Mighty frustrating that Miss DiPaolo is the only one who's claimed to have heard Mrs. Wynn getting attacked. All the rest are tight-lipped as clams."

"They either didn't witness the woman getting attacked or aren't willing to admit they did, Taylor," said Nick. He massaged his old wound, which ached. Hell, it always ached these days. "Anything else for me?"

"Mullahey got an alibi for Mr. Ross," said his assistant. "His wife says he didn't leave for the Hygienic Institute this morning until around eight."

"Quick work. Both of you. Good job, Taylor," said Nick, his assistant beaming over the compliment. "Mrs. Davies favors Blanchard as the perpetrator. A man with a motive to kill Shaw and no alibi for the time of his murder or that of Mrs. Wynn's this morning. Mrs. Davies stopped in at his house, early, and learned he'd been away."

"Maybe he *is* our killer, sir."

Nick shrugged. "Why does it seem our list isn't narrowing, though, Taylor? Why aren't we making any progress?" How many more people would have to die before he figured out who was behind the deaths?

"This doesn't tell us who the killer is, sir, but Dr. Harris sent a message around saying there was no evidence that . . . um . . ." Taylor cleared his throat. "That Mrs. Wynn was assaulted. If you know what I mean."

Taylor's only weakness was a too-soft heart and stomach. But was sentimentality such a failing? "I do know what you mean."

"Also, he wanted us to know that he's released Mr. Shaw's body to his family," he said. "Already been announced there'll be a funeral tomorrow."

"Wonder who's all going to be in attendance." Nick straightened and reached into his coat pocket, retrieving Shaw's watch from where he'd stored it. Carved with intricately intertwined vines that surrounded Shaw's monogram, it was cold and heavy in his hand. "I've been carrying this around all day. Put it someplace safe. When I'm at the Shaws', I'll inform them it's been recovered, but we need it as evidence for a while longer."

Taylor examined the watch, depressing the latch holding the lid shut, springing it open. "I don't get why Mrs. Wynn's killer didn't take it, sir."

"They either weren't interested in that watch or were interrupted before they could locate it," he said. "She'd hidden it inside a deep pocket sewn into her petticoat. Would've taken some searching."

Taylor closed the watch lid with a click. "Doesn't seem right, does it, sir? That a widow lady had become a criminal."

"No, it doesn't seem right, Taylor. But life isn't always fair or pleasant or easy," said Nick, gloominess stealing over him. He shook it off before the feeling took hold. "While I'm at the Shaws', I need you to question Platt about where he was this morning. He wasn't at the Institute like usual, because Ross didn't need him to come in. He'd accused Mrs. Wynn of stealing Shaw's watch, so I have to ask if he'd decided to go get it from her."

"What do I do if I find Mr. Platt hasn't got a good explanation for his whereabouts, sir?" asked Taylor, locking the watch and chain in his desk.

Nick rubbed the ache in his arm. "Arrest him on suspicion of murder, Taylor."

• • •

"Thank you, Mrs. Davies. For everything." The young woman drew her shawl about her shoulders, wrapping it over her chest and tying the ends at her low back. "I did mean to go to the fellow who offers the electromagnetic cure, but after seeing what happened at the Hygienic Institute with that politician, I've decided not to trust any of those types of places."

Celia returned the calomel powder to her glass-fronted cabinet of medicines and supplies. "The water cure is generally harmless and may have even helped, in your case."

"That's what doctors want you to believe about what they prescribe, too. But look how many of *them* have killed their patients," she said, pursing her lips.

"Accidentally, of course," said Celia, defending a group of men she rarely felt inclined to vindicate.

"Blundering and cocky, is more like it."

Yes. Celia escorted the woman to the front door. "Please return tomorrow morning so I might assess if the calomel is effective."

"Aye, ma'am."

Celia bid her farewell and returned to her examination room.

Addie strode in from the kitchen, an enameled-tin basin in her hand, sloshing with sudsy water. "Were you able to help that poor creature?"

Were they not all poor creatures? The women who came here, most of them impoverished and unable to afford a physician's fees. Perhaps her patient had been correct about some doctors, their medical degrees conferring arrogance rather than a sincere desire to help each and every patient who came to them. Regrettably, Celia had met physicians whose education had failed to teach them that females were equally worthy of the quality of care provided the typical male.

"She has nettle rash from eating something that disagreed with her. I advised her to be careful with her diet and gave her a few grains of calomel to take later today, if the rash does not subside on its own. I hope she has the patience to wait it out." She pushed away from the door. "The woman has six children, Addie. How will she ever find the time to tend to herself properly?"

Addie clucked her tongue against her teeth and set the basin next to Celia's examination table. "'Twas ever the same for me mother. Tending to all the wee bairns. Wore her down to skin and bones."

Homesickness darkened her housekeeper's voice. *I wish I had the spare money to send her on a journey home to Scotland to see her family.* But she did not. She barely had enough spare money to provide treatments for her patients.

Celia patted Addie's forearm; a hug would be more appropriate, but Addie would not allow such an intimate gesture from her.

"I shall be having an outing with Jane tomorrow, Addie," she said. "Once I have returned from Mr. Shaw's burial service. Hopefully I've no patient appointments that will require canceling."

"I presume you mean to attend the burial to nose about."

"I have questions, Addie."

"As ever," she said, fetching a cloth from the glass-fronted cabinet. "*Weel*, your outing with Mrs. Hutchinson does sound pleasant. I'm glad you've decided to tend to yourself for a change."

Celia made no response and sat at her desk to jot notes on her patient.

"You're not having an outing with Mrs. Hutchinson as a treat, are you, ma'am?" Addie asked, a displeased edge to her voice. "This has to do with Mr. Shaw's death."

Celia shifted to face her housekeeper. "There's been another murder, Addie."

"Am I to feel better now?" she asked. "And might I ask where you and Mrs. Hutchinson are going tomorrow?"

"To the Hygienic Institute, to make some enquiries," she replied, feeling rather sheepish. "We shall only be visiting Mr. Ross's establishment for an hour or so, and I sincerely doubt we shall come to harm."

Addie lifted one eyebrow into a perfect brown arc. "And was that not what Mr. Shaw must have thought, too?"

⌀ CHAPTER 15 ⌀

"Please tell me you do not require much of my time, Detective Greaves," said Delphia Shaw, her eyes remarkably clear, her head high, her skirts billowing across the settee in great ebony waves. All in all, a regal effect. "It is nearly dinner."

He'd never before met a widow who had an appetite so soon after their husband's death. *Maybe I shouldn't be so harsh on the woman. Maybe I should learn to be less cynical.*

Nick dragged his hat off his head. "Depends on how quickly I get my questions answered, ma'am."

"What are your questions, Detective?"

"We've recovered your husband's watch and fob chain," he replied.

"Not a question, but I am happy to hear you have," she said. "I want to give the watch to Leonard, to pass on to his children when the time comes."

"If Mr. Shaw's will doesn't direct otherwise," he observed.

"Obviously I would never go against my husband's wishes. Dearest Ambrose."

Her gaze swept the room, packed with flowers, white lilies and roses mostly, their aroma dense and overpowering. Vases, crosses, wreaths, and crescents festooned with ribbons covered tabletops, perched atop stands, filled corners. Outpourings of fondness and respect, he supposed. Or the necessary show from folks eager to stay on the good side of the man who would inherit the business from his father. Who, despite the hour, was still at his office. Mourning for Ambrose Shaw was not speeding his youngest son home from the bank. Maybe he didn't want to face all the flowers.

"I'll send one of the officers over with the watch and chain when we no longer need it as evidence, ma'am," said Nick.

"I presume the person who stole them is also responsible for my husband's death."

"We haven't worked out the details yet," he said. "Unfortunately, we won't get any assistance from the person whose body we found them on."

"Body?"

"The person who'd taken Mr. Shaw's watch and fob chain was found dead early this morning, ma'am."

"I see," she said, her tone flat, not bothering to feel sympathy for a criminal. Not many folks did. Even if they had been a widow woman. "Do I know this person, by any chance?"

"You might. Mrs. Althea Wynn."

"My goodness," she said. "Why am I not surprised?"

"We'd heard that she and your husband were friends."

"I wouldn't ever refer to them as friends, Detective," she replied, sounding appalled at the suggestion that a woman of Mrs. Wynn's station might be friends with a man of Shaw's. "They were acquaintances. He'd met her at a fundraising event. In fact, it was Mrs. Wynn who'd initially recommended the Hygienic Institute to Ambrose. He always had been swayed by females he found . . ."

"Attractive?" Mrs. Wynn had been a good-looking woman.

Her mouth puckered, Nick's observation as sour to her as sucking on a lemon. "Did she murder my husband, Detective? Or was she in collusion with Mr. Blanchard?"

Between Delphia Shaw and Celia Davies, he didn't know which of them was more certain of the man's guilt. "As I've said, ma'am, our investigation is ongoing."

"Elliot Blanchard was stalking Ambrose, assaulting him in public, openly adversarial . . . has he an alibi?" she asked. "He had reasons to wish my husband out of the way. What else do you need?"

"Speaking of reasons, Mrs. Shaw, why didn't you inform me that Mr. Blanchard and your stepdaughter had once been engaged to marry?"

"An episode Ambrose and I . . . the entire family wished to forget, Detective Greaves," she replied, disdain clear on her face. "I suppose he still resents us. Even though he married that woman."

That woman. "You disapproved of Miss Shaw's relationship with him."

"The man's actions verify that we were right to disapprove," she said. "I always suspected Mr. Blanchard had pursued Rebecca solely to irritate Ambrose, and I was proven correct."

From behind one of the floral arrangements came the muted chime of a mantel clock, the sound drawing her attention. She sighed and dabbed at her eyes with a hastily retrieved handkerchief. There hadn't been many flowers at Nick's father's funeral, just a handful of small bouquets from family. Maybe Abraham Greaves hadn't been as admired as Ambrose Shaw. Maybe nobody had reason to curry favor with Nick or his sister Ellie.

The chiming stopped, and she turned back to Nick. "I trust you've concluded your questions, Mr. Greaves. I am quite drained of energy from my husband's unexpected passing and would like to rest before my evening meal."

"Just a few more items, ma'am," he said. "Your son was in the police station this morning. Do you know why?"

"Leonard doesn't have to inform me of every single one of his activities, Detective Greaves. I trust him. I *must* trust him, now that he will take over my husband's share of responsibility for the bank," she said. "Undoubtedly he was complaining to another of the officers about the lack of progress in obtaining justice for my husband."

Stay calm, Nick. Don't react. "What time did he leave the house this morning?"

She paused, not much longer than required to inhale and exhale. Perhaps connecting his question to the news that Mrs. Wynn had been found dead earlier that day.

"Before I arose. However, I don't know the precise hour," she replied.

"I thought you kept your watch next to your bed."

"I was too weary to check the time."

A predictable response. He'd have to ask the maid on his way out. "And you weren't away from home this morning, I suppose, Mrs. Shaw?"

A tick of annoyance tightened the skin around her eyes. "I am grieving my husband, Detective. Not out socializing."

"Certainly." He returned his hat to his head. "Thank you for your time, ma'am. I'll make sure you get your husband's watch as soon as possible."

She slowly rose to her feet. "One of the servants will be waiting to show you out."

Not to help him find the front door, but because Delphia Shaw wanted to make sure he used it.

The parlor doors slid open the instant he reached them. Proving that the female servant, who wore what looked to be a newly purchased black-print dress—even the staff was expected to be in mourning—had been lingering on the other side.

She led him to the front entrance. Nick paused on the threshold, the air outside downright fresh after the choking heaviness of a roomful of flowers.

"I've got a question for you," he said to the maid. "Do you know when Mr. Shaw left the house this morning?"

She pinched her lips tight and shot a glance over her shoulder, back in the direction of the parlor.

"It's okay," said Nick. "Mrs. Shaw won't mind you speaking with me."

"If you're sure." She had an accent that reminded him of a lieutenant he'd known during the war, who'd been from someplace back East; he regretted thinking of the man right then. "I don't want to get in trouble."

"It'll be fine," he assured her, even if he doubted it would be fine. "Do you know when he left?"

"Before sunrise. Early for Mr. Leonard, but things haven't been the same around the house since Mr. Shaw died."

"How so?"

"Just . . . different. Unsettled. Especially with Mr. Leonard," she answered. "I guess that's normal after one of the family has died, although I've never been in a situation exactly like this before."

Wasn't every day a servant's employer got murdered. "Did Mr. Shaw return to the house this morning?" *Looking, let's say, dirty from having smashed Mrs. Wynn's skull then dragging her dead body behind a shed?*

"No, sir. He must've gone straight to the bank after having breakfast."

Before sunrise? What restaurant in town was open then? The same one that Elliot Blanchard had dashed off to? And why hadn't Leonard Shaw stopped at the house afterward like he had yesterday?

"Likely so," said Nick. "One final question for you. Have you ever heard any of the Shaws mention a young woman named Mina Cascarino? Not that you'd be eavesdropping on their conversations, of course."

She glanced toward the parlor again and leaned in close so she could whisper and be heard. "There's been arguments at supper about some young lady that Mr. Leonard's been associating with, but I haven't heard her name," she said. "Don't tell them I said so. They'd dismiss me for certain."

His stomach tightened around the information. Not Mina and Ambrose Shaw, but Mina and Leonard Shaw. "I won't tell them where I heard. I promise you."

"Is that all, sir?" she asked hopefully. "I need to polish the silver."

"Yes, that's all. Thank you. You've been very helpful." *Very helpful.*

• • •

Leave us alone.

Seated on the porch rocking chair, the wind spilling over the summit of Russian Hill cool if dust-laden, Celia reread the note she'd been left. The three words were no more revelatory this afternoon, though, than they had been last night. *What group of people am I to be avoiding? Leaving alone?*

With a sigh, Celia returned the note to her pocket just as the planks of the Cascarinos' porch creaked under someone's weight. Barbara, after completing her lessons with Miss Campbell, had gone to visit Mina and was descending the steps. Out in the road, a pair of girls were playing graces before they were called in to eat dinner, tossing the narrow hoop to each other and trying to catch it with their sticks. Barbara glanced in their direction, girls who'd never invite her to play even if she were nearer their age, and set her jaw. One slanted looks at Barbara as she walked, her gait stiffening as she fought her limp. It was rare for anyone on this street to speak aloud what they must think when they noticed Celia's cousin. The weight of their opinions, though, was always palpable.

"How is Mina?" she asked when Barbara reached the porch.

"Better, but not much."

She gestured at Barbara to take the seat adjacent to the rocking chair, but her cousin declined. "Her amnesia has not improved?"

"I didn't probe, Cousin Celia," she replied. "I don't want to be an investigator. That's your interest, not mine."

"I apologize for asking, Barbara," she said. "I should not be involving you in these matters."

Her cousin shrugged. "It's okay. Sorry I snapped at you."

Barbara glanced at the girls, who'd collected the hoop, which one had flung too far down the road, and were whispering together. Celia wished she had the words to ease her cousin's heartache. But her words more often magnified Barbara's unhappiness than lessened it.

Barbara pulled her attention off the girls. "Actually, Mina now remembers going to the Hygienic Institute on Wednesday night."

Celia sat up, tipping the rocking chair forward on its runners. "She does? Did she explain why she went?"

"She thinks she'd gone there because she was worried about someone or something," said Barbara. "That's all."

"Worried . . . not angry or vengeful."

"No. The word she used was 'worried.'"

Worried about Mr. Shaw . . . or what she herself intended to do? "Thank you, Barbara," said Celia. "Now that you've returned home, please let Addie know that she can set out dinner."

"Has Owen been invited?" She leaned over for a better view of the corner where Vallejo intersected with Kearny. "Because that looks like him coming up the street."

Celia stood. "He is invited now."

Barbara returned Owen's wave and went inside the house.

"Hullo, Mrs. Davies," he said, bounding up the stairs.

"You have the list of names from Roesler's."

He grinned and pulled a very crumpled piece of paper from his trouser pocket. "Yep!"

"Come inside. Let us peruse this at the dinner table."

He happily followed her into the house, pausing first to scrape muck from his boots before continuing on to the dining room. "Miss Mina's name isn't on it. Mr. Shaw did send some to 'all the ladies at Bauman's,'" he quoted, "but not to Miss Mina in particular."

The box of candy Mr. Greaves noticed had to have been that one. "Thank goodness she'd never received any."

She took a chair and Owen chose another. He plucked his ragged wool cap from his head, his tawny hair crushed from its snug fit, and hooked it on the chair back.

"Addie, set a place for Owen," she called. "He is joining us for dinner."

Celia spread Owen's notes on the tablecloth, flattening out the creases. "I hope you did not get into trouble collecting these names for me," she said as she scanned the paper. She looked up when he did not reply. His head sagged and his freckles had disappeared into the wash of color spreading over his cheeks. "Owen?"

"I, um, got dismissed. Mr. Roesler caught me," he said. "But it's okay, ma'am, honest it is! I'll find another job."

"Oh, Owen. I was afraid that might happen."

"'Tis glad I am to see you, laddie." Addie collected a set of dishes from the sideboard and placed them in front of Owen. "Though you look like you need a good meal."

"Nobody cooks like you do, Addie."

Addie winked at him and bustled off, the sound of utensils against pans soon echoing from the kitchen.

"What shall we do about your predicament, Owen?" asked Celia.

"Like I said, I'll find another job."

"How about I inform Mr. Roesler you were only reading through his customer logbooks as a favor to me and the police," she said. "I shall even ask Mr. Greaves to speak with him and explain that the information you obtained may bring a killer to justice."

Although Mr. Roesler might rightly ask why the police department had not come directly to him to get the list of names, rather than employ a shop boy to dig around in his books.

"Will it?" asked Owen. "Will it bring a killer to justice, ma'am?"

He looked so eager and innocent. She reached out to straighten the tuft of hair that always stood up above his forelock. But he shied from her touch; he was not a child any longer.

"Your information has, at least, aided Mina's cause," she answered. "Now to the others on this list."

There were over a dozen names, some male, mostly female, addressed to the recipients at restaurants and boardinghouses and saloons, many saloons in addition to Bauman's. In the beginning of September, Mr. Shaw had sent a small box of candied fruits to Mrs. Wynn. *How intriguing to see her listed.* The remainder of the names were unfamiliar. Except for one.

"Oh, my."

"What is it, ma'am?" asked Owen, craning his neck to see. "Is it somebody you know?"

"Yes." What would her cousin make of the name Owen had recorded? *What do I make of it?* "The familiar name belongs to Barbara's new tutor. Miss Olivia Campbell."

• • •

"I can explain," said Libby Campbell.

Full of bravado, she stared back at Celia, only the feathers trimming her bonnet trembling revealingly. Before they had even touched dinner, Celia had sent Owen to fetch the young woman here. She'd been prompt in arriving.

"Please do explain, Miss Campbell," said Celia, taking the chair opposite the parlor settee occupied by the young woman. "You may begin by telling us how you know Mr. Shaw."

"You're going to tell my cousin that it's all a ridiculous mistake, aren't you, Libby?" asked Barbara, seated in the chair near the parlor piano. "That box of candy sent to you. You never received it, right?"

Miss Campbell's gaze flickered, but she didn't respond to Barbara's question.

"Go on, Miss Campbell," prodded Celia.

"I met Mr. Shaw when I was out walking with Mrs. Blanchard one day. At the City Gardens," she said softly. "He was extremely friendly, even though I could tell Mrs. Blanchard didn't like him. She was curt, tried to walk on, but he wouldn't let her. Let us. I think she mistrusted his overtures."

"Given the political rivalry between her husband and Mr. Shaw, she had every reason to mistrust his actions," said Celia.

"He asked my name—I don't know why—and I told him. I couldn't be impolite and refuse. The request seemed harmless, at the time." She cradled her weak arm, hugging it to her waist. A protective response. But what was it she was protecting herself against? "Maybe he thought sending me that box of candies would be amusing. Maybe he thought I'd tell Mr. or Mrs. Blanchard about receiving them and they'd be angry. Upsetting them would've pleased Mr. Shaw, I suspect. According to Mr. Blanchard, he was a cruel man. Petty and vindictive."

"Did you ever tell your employer about the gift?"

"No, I didn't," she said. "And I never responded to Mr. Shaw. But I did eat the chocolates. They were really good."

"You shouldn't have, Libby," stated Barbara, anger flaring. "You should've sent him a note demanding he leave you alone and thrown them away."

Libby shrank into the settee cushions, taken aback by Barbara's criticism.

"Barbara, I believe Miss Campbell handled the situation appropriately, given the circumstances," said Celia.

Her cousin frowned. "Would *you* have calmly accepted a gift from some pushy man? A man getting enjoyment out of pestering women who didn't want his attention?"

"No, I would not have done. But in my position, I risk little by rejecting their advances," she responded. "Pushy men tend to punish those who openly rebuke them, Barbara. Miss Campbell cannot afford to have her life destroyed by a man who may have happily done so. The world is not always fair to women. As well you know."

Barbara opened her mouth to continue her argument, but subsided. "I'm sorry, Libby. I shouldn't have criticized you."

"It's all right," she replied. "I should have told you, Mrs. Davies, that I'd met Mr. Shaw. But I was embarrassed about it and didn't think my knowing him mattered. Does it? I mean, have you changed your mind about having me tutor your cousin?"

"Not at all," Celia assured her. "I am satisfied with your account."

She relaxed. "Thank you, because I enjoy teaching her."

Earlier that day, Barbara would have smiled at Miss Campbell's remark. Instead, she sulked, disappointed that someone she'd quickly become attached to, someone she had come to admire, had proven to possess flaws. Celia let her gaze drift to her uncle's ever-smiling portrait. *You left your daughter at too young an age, Uncle. She needs more love and attention than I've been able to provide.*

"Have you met any of the other Shaws, Miss Campbell?" asked Celia.

Barbara groaned. "Cousin, must you?"

"I don't mind answering, Barbara," said Miss Campbell. "I haven't."

"What about Rebecca Shaw? Did Mr. Blanchard ever mention her?"

She shook her head. "Not around me."

"Ah. I was under the impression that Miss Shaw and Mr. Blanchard were old friends."

"I can't imagine why they would be," she was quick to reply.

"Miss Shaw is very pretty," interjected Barbara. "We went to her studio to have our portrait taken, and I liked her. If I were Mrs. Blanchard, I'd be jealous if I ever heard rumors that her husband was friends with Miss Shaw."

"He'd never do anything to hurt Mrs. Blanchard. Never."

Spoken with considerable heat. "I've also learned that the Shaws have accused Mr. Blanchard of harassing and stalking Ambrose Shaw."

"That's a bald-faced lie, Mrs. Davies," Miss Campbell spat. "True, they'd had that fight at the Bank Exchange saloon—it was in all the papers, which is how I heard, because nobody was to speak a word about it at the house—but for any of them to claim that Mr. Blanchard had been stalking Mr. Shaw . . . it's a lie. He'd never do that. Mrs. Blanchard was right that Mr. Shaw would try to provoke him, hoping to make Mr. Blanchard do something reckless and appear volatile and unstable."

Celia contemplated the young, passionate woman across from her. "*Did* Mr. Blanchard do something reckless, Miss Campbell?" she asked quietly.

"He didn't go out the evening that Mr. Shaw died. He didn't kill him," she insisted.

"How can you be so positive?"

She blanched and clutched her weakened arm. Did the limb pain her like Mr. Greaves's wound pained him? Like Barbara's foot ached when foul weather approached? A sign, a portent of deeper, more forbidding troubles.

"I can be positive, Mrs. Davies, because . . ." Her chin abruptly went up, a decision made. "Because I was at his home Wednesday evening. With him."

✄ CHAPTER 16 ଓ

"Is Mr. Shaw still here?" Nick asked the teller, occupied with locking the gate in an ornate metal screen spanning the length of the bank's chest-high walnut counter. The counter was at least two feet deep, which must not have been judged an adequate safeguard against felonious customers.

"I'd have to check, sir," the teller said, speaking through the gate rather than unlocking it again, which might encourage Nick to loiter.

"I'd appreciate that. Police matters." He went through the motions of showing his badge to the fellow, who jerked his head back in surprise. "Detective Greaves."

There'd been a message waiting at the station from Taylor, who'd gotten an alibi from Platt. *Sound asleep in room at boardinghouse. Landlord confirms.* Disappointing, because Nick really would have enjoyed arresting Platt for murder. Instead, he got to spend more time with Leonard Shaw, interrogating him.

One of the other employees, an older fellow sporting a black mourning armband, his puffed-out chest signifying a level of importance—assumed or actual—wandered over. "What's going on here?"

"This police detective wants to speak with Mr. Leonard."

The older man narrowed his eyes. "I will see if Mr. Shaw is in his office, Detective. You may wait there."

He gestured at a row of angle-top desks against the wall—there weren't any chairs to sit on—and hustled off.

Nick waited until the man disappeared into the bank's rear offices before turning back to the teller. "Nice place."

He scanned the room as though he was a connoisseur of banking establishment interiors. In addition to the fancy teller screens and deep walnut counter, the floor was paved with clouded marble. There was a quarry in Tehama; maybe the stone had come from there. The ceiling was pressed tin, like at Bauman's, and the walls were papered in an elegant blue-gray geometric pattern. At the room's far end, a door stood ajar, the bank's massive cast-iron safe visible through the opening. The name of its manufacturer was painted in curling gold letters across the front. From *Cincinnati, O.* Reassuringly solid, for those customers needing reassurance. Wall clocks ticked. Portraits hung in prominent locations. One was draped in black. The last time Nick had seen that face, it had been resting slack-jawed against the plush mattress of a bed at the Hygienic Institute.

"Mr. Ambrose Shaw, correct?" he asked the man peering at him between the screen's bars.

"Yes." The teller glanced up at the painting. "A tragic death. So sudden."

"A good man to work for, I imagine."

"He was a fair man who demanded the best from his employees," the teller replied. "Although he'd recently begun to focus his attention on politics, his guiding hand at the bank will be missed."

"No doubt. No doubt," said Nick. "But I'm sure his son is prepared to step right in."

"Mr. Leonard worked alongside his father every day."

A statement that might or might not confirm Nick's comment. "His fiancée must be eager to see the whole business settled so they can plan for their wedding."

"Mr. Leonard? Getting married?" The man tipped his head to one side. "I didn't know he was walking out with anyone. Are you sure?"

"Maybe I misunderstood what I was told." The Shaws' servant wouldn't have lied about overhearing arguments concerning Leonard Shaw's choice in women, though. "I'm hoping Mr. Shaw can see me. I've been trying to speak with him all day, but when I stopped in this morning, he wasn't around."

"You were here this morning?"

Nope. "I spoke with somebody else."

"Mr. Leonard arrived at his usual hour, around nine," he said. "I don't understand how you missed him."

"I don't understand it either." A few hours to account for, then. Breakfast and a stop at the police station shouldn't have taken so long. "Anyway, we received a report that a man who resembled Mr. Shaw was observed tussling with a fellow in an alley not far from here. A possible attempted mugging. Mistaken identity, undoubtedly, but we have to be sure it wasn't him."

"Mr. Leonard made no mention of such an incident, and he didn't at all look like he'd been involved in a tussle," he said. "His clothes were immaculate, and he'd been to the barber for his morning shave."

The teller had provided the information Nick had been after with his made-up story. However, clean clothes didn't exonerate Shaw of bashing in Mrs. Wynn's head; he may have changed before arriving at the bank. But where? Not at home.

"A man of few words."

"He doesn't usually talk to us at all, Detective."

"Well, I suppose the witness to the scuffle was mistaken, but I'll wait over there to confirm with Mr. Shaw," said Nick. "Wouldn't want a crime to go unreported. Could be dangerous for other folks around here, to have a mugger on the loose."

He wandered back to where he was supposed to have been standing the entire time. The teller sidled over to another man, partially hidden by rectangles of opaque glass set in the metal screen, and took to whispering. Nick leaned against one of the desks, nicely outfitted with brass inkwells, pens, and writing paper, and wished the men would talk louder so he could hear their conversation.

The door leading to the bank vault opened wider, and Leonard Shaw stepped through. Looking immaculate, as reported. Fresh as a daisy, as Nick's mother used to say when describing folks but not always in a kindly way.

"Mr. Greaves, what brings you to the bank?" he asked, striding toward Nick with an outstretched hand. The tellers behind their metal screen watched with undisguised curiosity.

"Let's go outside and talk for a couple of minutes, Mr. Shaw."

Nick exited the bank to stand on the sidewalk beneath the overhang of an awning. Any conversation they had would be drowned out by city noise, buzzing with commotion as workers spilled out onto the streets at day's end, shutters and blinds snapping shut, saloons and restaurants cranking to life.

"Is there news?" asked Shaw. "Have you identified who murdered my father? It's Blanchard. You've arrested him, haven't you?"

He and his mother were consistent in their accusation. "When did you leave your house this morning, Mr. Shaw?"

"What does that have to do with my father's death, Detective Greaves?"

"Humor me."

Shaw rolled his tongue around in his mouth before answering. "I departed the house around sunrise."

Smart to be honest, figuring Nick might already know the answer to his question. "Seems early, Mr. Shaw."

"I couldn't sleep." He paused to tip his hat at a pair of young women strolling on the sidewalk, their belled skirts brushing against Nick's calves as they passed. "Pointless to stay in bed when there are numerous matters to attend to before my father's funeral tomorrow."

"Where did you go between sunrise and arriving at the bank?" he asked. "Aside from stopping in at the police station."

"I did stop at the station immediately before breakfast," said Shaw. "You weren't there."

"You spoke to my colleague Mr. Briggs instead." Nick eyed him. "What about?"

"Personal matters unrelated to my father's case."

"Ah," Nick replied. "And after you departed the police station?"

Shaw groaned, already tired of Nick's questions. He couldn't be anywhere near as tired of them as Nick was.

"I went to breakfast and then on to my barber. My usual routine," he answered. "I arrived at the bank around nine. I like to get to my office before opening. As my father always did, although sometimes he'd start at eight or even seven. A man dedicated to his business."

"Three hours of briefly meeting with a police detective, breakfasting, and sitting in a barber's chair." None of which, in Nick's opinion, had much to do with getting ready for his dedicated-businessman father's funeral tomorrow. "Interesting."

"I ran across several acquaintances while I was out, offering their condolences," he said. "I insist that you tell me why you care where I was this morning, Detective Greaves."

Just then, a newspaper boy, peddling the remainder of his copies of the *Evening Bulletin*, shouted, "Widow woman murdered."

A providential response to Shaw's request, thought Nick.

One of the tellers, departing the bank for the evening, overheard the boy's cries and dashed across the road to snap up a paper.

"That's why you're questioning me. Because a woman was murdered today." Shaw cursed under his breath. "I didn't kill her, whoever she was, or my father."

"Then you'll be happy to provide more details on your movements this morning, Mr. Shaw," said Nick. "Because I doubt you spent an entire three hours engaged in what you'd like me to believe."

Shaw stared out at the street. On the other side stood a tobacconist's; maybe when Nick was finished with Shaw he'd stop in and buy some cigars for Taylor. The booking officer was prone to stealing from Taylor's supplies and he was always running out.

"I went for a long walk," he finally said. "To think, Detective."

"A long walk. Thinking." The most unlikely alibi Nick had ever been offered in his years as a cop.

"It's true," insisted Shaw. "Thinking if it's possible Rebecca had a hand in our father's death."

Well, well. "You and Mrs. Shaw have been expending a lot of breath blaming Blanchard for murdering your father," said Nick. "Are you now telling me you imagine Miss Shaw could've plotted with him? Is that what you concluded after your lengthy walk?"

"They were in love. Once. She and that rabble-rouser." There was venom in his tone. "A man 'giving voice to the oppressed.' Ha. Blanchard only ever gave voice to his own ambition."

Like a typical politician, if Nick were to offer his opinion. "Why imagine that Miss Shaw had schemed with him? They're not still in love, right?"

"I've heard rumors . . ." He didn't finish the sentence; he didn't need to. "Rebecca's obstinate. Mother calls her wayward, but that makes her sound like a child, which she definitely isn't. If Blanchard asked for my stepsister's help, I've no doubt she'd give it."

Nick couldn't tell, for the life of him he couldn't tell at all, if Shaw was upset about the possibility his stepsister had been involved. Or if he was leading Nick on. No love lost between Shaw and Rebecca, perhaps, since families didn't always love one another. God only knew the hatred Nick had sometimes felt for his father. Misguided hatred, maybe, borne from his own guilt over Meg's suicide. But for all that depth of dark feelings, he'd never have accused the man of murdering someone. Unless he was actually guilty.

"You might be interested to learn, Mr. Shaw, that we found your father's watch and fob chain on the woman who died this morning," he said. "Her name was Mrs. Wynn. Your mother says she was acquainted with your father."

"I . . ." Shaw rubbed his forehead. "What? Mrs. Wynn? How did she get Father's watch?"

"I see the information is shocking, Mr. Shaw," said Nick. "Especially when you've been so keen on accusing Blanchard—and now Rebecca—of a plot to murder Ambrose Shaw."

"Maybe they were all working together," said Shaw. "A conspiracy to kill off my father."

"A conspiracy, Mr. Shaw?" asked Nick. "Or is this convoluted tale an attempt to hide your own guilt?"

"Why would I want to kill Father?"

"For the inheritance?" Nick suggested. "Or maybe because he also stood between you and a romantic attachment he didn't approve of. Just like he hadn't approved of Rebecca's relationship with Elliot Blanchard. Did you and this young woman work together to do away with your father, only to discover you'd been spotted? By a widow whose cold, dead body is now with the undertaker?"

Shaw's neck went red first, spreading across his skin until the flush reached his face—as slowly as a dry cloth dipped in a crimson liquid, the color diffusing through the material. "I don't know what you're talking about."

"You spent three hours this morning wandering about, deep in thought, then went to the station and then breakfast, where you'd like me to believe you kept encountering acquaintances who wanted to extend their condolences, then on to your barber's. Three hours, Mr. Shaw?"

"That's how long it took. I don't know why that's so damned hard to believe," he spat. The door to the bank opened, and the rest of the tellers exited the building, casting sideways glances at their boss and the police detective. Shaw turned his back to them and lowered his voice. "I don't know why what I've said is so hard to believe, Detective Greaves."

"Well, because we've also discovered that you left your meeting at the Parker House right after dinner on Wednesday. Around seven," said Nick. "You didn't arrive at home until nine. Two hours. Another mysterious lapse of time I'd be happy to have you explain."

Shaw's nostrils flared as he sucked in a breath. "I went to visit a lady friend whose name I'm not going to provide, so don't even bother to ask."

"Ah, your paramour, who your parents disapproved of."

"I'd prefer to leave her out of this."

"She's your alibi, Mr. Shaw. You sure about that?"

"I am very sure about that." Shaw stepped closer, the smell of bay rum cologne drifting off his clothes. "If you've got proof I'm responsible for my father's death or Mrs. Wynn's, charge me, Detective Greaves. Otherwise, leave me alone. My father is being buried tomorrow. I'd like to be able to mourn him, alongside my mother, in peace."

Nick fixed an innocent expression on his face. "Is that why you smell so good, Mr. Shaw? You're planning on spending the evening with your mother, recalling all the better days with your father?" he asked. "Or did you have other plans? Maybe with your lady friend."

"Leave me alone, Detective Greaves."

He stalked off, the tails of his frock coat flapping against his legs.

Nick counted to twenty before he followed. A gift of cigars for Taylor would have to wait.

• • •

"Miss Barbara's hidden away in her room and willna speak to me, ma'am," said Addie, setting a small glass of dark purple wine at Celia's elbow. Bramble wine, made using a recipe Addie had brought from Scotland. "She may talk to you, though."

"If she'd not speak to you, Addie, she will not speak to me." She sipped from the glass. "Your wine has turned out well."

"Thank you, ma'am. I should have a nip myself to calm my nerves," she replied, eyeing the cut-glass decanter she held. She lowered it onto Celia's examination room desk before she gave in to her impulse. "But what are we to do about Miss Campbell now?"

The young woman's confession had stunned them all. None more so than Barbara, who'd shouted at Miss Campbell before dashing up to her bedchamber, where she slammed her door so firmly that the sound reverberated through the downstairs rooms. Libby Campbell, in tears, had sworn that nothing untoward had happened between her and Mr. Blanchard before springing from the settee and running from the house. Celia had not attempted to stop her.

"She may be lying to protect him, Addie," said Celia. "I would question Mr. Blanchard myself about Miss Campbell's assertion, except that after my visit to his house this morning, he'll likely never agree to speak with me again."

Addie tutted. "And I'd come to like the lass."

"What a predicament we are in, Addie."

"Aye, but you'll find a way to fix matters, ma'am," her housekeeper replied, filled with confidence. "You always do."

She slipped out of the room, softly closing the door behind her.

Celia drained the bramble wine, the sweet liquid burning down her throat, and set the empty glass aside. Time to think. Time to work through the puzzle surrounding Mr. Shaw's murder. The death of Mrs. Wynn, as well.

She opened the drawer in her desk and pulled out a table book, opening it to an empty page. She inked a pen and began to inscribe her thoughts. Suspect. Motive. Clues for or against their guilt. Starting with Mr. Shaw before turning to Mrs. Wynn, whose murder Celia had significantly less information about. A man whose demise had been brought about by a very unlikely weapon—chloroform. The killer had been aided by the fact that Mr. Shaw had been drunk, according to the coroner. Less time and effort needed, perhaps, to bring about his death. Mr. Shaw had briefly struggled, if she properly recalled what Mr. Greaves had told her. The struggle itself may have been the cause of his fatal heart attack.

Where to start . . .

Proceed one by one, write down your thoughts. Starting with the suspect Miss Campbell desired to protect.

Elliot Blanchard, she wrote. Motive—acrimonious political opponent of Ambrose Shaw, who'd broken off Mr. Blanchard's engagement to Miss Shaw. Might also have despised Mr. Shaw for insulting Mrs. Blanchard. In possession of chloroform, a bottle missing from his supply. Possibly aware of Mr. Shaw's poor health and susceptibility to heart failure. Still uncertain how he might have acquired the key to Mr. Shaw's room. His whereabouts Wednesday evening accounted for by Miss Campbell, whose truthfulness as a witness was, however, questionable. *I fear she is somewhat in love with the man.* Out of his house around the time Mrs. Wynn was struck down.

Leonard Shaw. Motive—inheritance money and difficult relationship with his father, according to Jane. Dubious alibi for the evening of Mr. Shaw's death. Had visited his father at the Institute, providing an opportunity to take the key. Encountered Mina outside, struck her down, stowed incriminating key in pocket? Open question as to where he may have obtained chloroform. Would know of his father's heart condition. At the police station this morning, but what was his alibi for the exact time of Mrs. Wynn's death?

"I do wish I'd had an opportunity to meet him and Mrs. Shaw," Celia whispered, tapping the end of her pen against her lower lip. "Form my own impression of them. Another reason to attend Mr. Shaw's burial service."

It would be enlightening to observe not only the Shaws but the other mourners. Who might count themselves as a friend of Ambrose Shaw?

Celia resumed list-making.

Delphia Shaw. Motive—terminate a possibly unhappy marriage, gain inheritance monies as well. She'd also visited Mr. Shaw at the Institute. May have been able to depart and return to her home Wednesday evening without any servants, if they had live-in domestics, marking her absence. Would definitely be aware that her husband's heart was weak.

She'd have to enquire what the staff situation was at the Shaw household. She might be able to ask someone about it at the cemetery tomorrow. *Who would speak to you about such a matter at a funeral, though, Celia? Honestly.*

Back to Mrs. Shaw—and Leonard Shaw. Did they possess chloroform? Celia surveyed her cabinet of medicines, bandaging, mixing vessels. Among her own supplies was a bottle of the substance, which she'd purchased to assist in delivering babies but had not yet used. Recommended for women in extreme discomfort, its action reportedly slowed labor, rendering the substance counterproductive. The Shaws, however, might keep a bottle in their home for another purpose. Was Delphia Shaw tall enough to smash Mrs. Wynn's skull?

"Gruesome, Celia."

Rebecca Shaw. Motive—inheritance money, useful to support her photographic studio, and revenge against the man who'd denied her the chance at happiness with Elliot Blanchard. But why remove the obstacle to their marriage at this point, years after the engagement had been broken? Her alibi for Wednesday evening was an interaction with her neighbor around seven thirty.

"The time the intruder was spotted."

Rebecca may have obtained chloroform from Mr. Blanchard, either with his knowledge or without, or purchased it. She was tall and likely sufficiently strong to overwhelm her unhealthy and drunken father—taking him by surprise, no doubt—and kill Mrs. Wynn. *And that key . . .* she'd proposed to Mr. Greaves that Miss Shaw could have snuck upstairs while at the Institute. It was a scenario she planned to assess while she and Jane were visiting the place.

Mr. Platt. Celia knew almost nothing about the fellow. Motive—attempting to steal from a wealthy patient. Accidentally killed Mr. Shaw with chloroform meant to sedate the man, perhaps. Mr. Ross had denied keeping a supply on hand as part of his treatment regimen, however. As an employee of the establishment, Mr. Platt could gain ready access to Mr. Shaw's room. Owen had overheard him arguing with Mrs. Wynn about Mr. Shaw's watch.

"And now Mrs. Wynn was dead." Celia considered her paper. "Ah, Mr. Platt, that does not bode well for you." Yet he was not the person found in possession of Mr. Shaw's watch. Perhaps he'd dashed out of Mr. Shaw's room in a state of shock when the fellow died, leaving it behind. Ran downstairs and threw open the private entrance door, feigning an interloper's means of entering the building. Spied Mina outside and . . .

"Gone back to fetch the all-important key and hide it in her skirt pocket?"

Sighing, Celia re-inked her pen and moved on.

Mr. Ross. Motive—Unknown. Also had access to Mr. Shaw's room, obviously, but why kill his patient? An old animosity Mr. Greaves had not uncovered? An argument got out of hand concerning the efficacy of Mr. Ross's treatments? Obviously knew of Mr. Shaw's medical condition. Or had *he* sought to steal from his wealthy client in order to pay outstanding debts? Yet it was Mrs. Wynn who'd been found with Mr. Shaw's watch and fob chain. Had they conspired together, but then he murdered her in order to silence her?

"I am catching at straws."

She retrieved a second piece of paper to continue her list, grown cumbersome in its length.

Mrs. Wynn. Motive—theft. Had occupied a room down the hall from Mr. Shaw. Could have easily monitored his comings and goings. She'd provided the information about an intruder, a possible fabrication. Body found with his watch and chain. Obtain chloroform from apothecary or Mr. Ross's disputed supply? Aware of Mr. Shaw's poor health? Obviously, she'd not killed herself that morning, which meant there were either two murderers or she had to be removed from suspicion as Mr. Shaw's killer. Same issue as Mr. Platt's concerning the key in Mina's pocket.

Mr. Griffin? What was his role in this affair? He had paid Owen to contact Mr. Platt, who owed him money. No known motive to harm Ambrose Shaw. He was, of course, certainly clever enough to gain entrance to the Institute and Mr. Shaw's room, but a chloroform-soaked rag was an unlikely instrument for a criminal like him. A knife was more direct.

"Perhaps he'd intended to render Mr. Shaw unconscious in order to kidnap him and hold him for ransom." His plans thwarted by the fellow's unfortunate and sudden heart failure. Yet he'd need to haul away the man's insensate body without being observed. A difficult task, even with the availability of a private entrance.

"Now you truly *are* catching at straws, Celia. How fantastical an idea." She scratched out his name.

And what about Mina Cascarino? She had no motive that Celia could discern. She could not, however, deny that Mina had been at the

Institute, having gone there in a state of anxiety around six thirty. What was her relationship with any of the other suspects, aside from an acquaintance with Ambrose Shaw? They'd likely never resolve how that dashed key had ended up in her pocket until she regained her memory, though. Mina was not, however, culpable for Mrs. Wynn's death. The only one on Celia's list who could be cleared of suspicion in the woman's murder.

Celia's pen hovered above the page as she pondered one final possibility.

Olivia Campbell. Motive—to prove her loyal affection for a man she could not have, Elliot Blanchard, by removing his political opponent. A young woman whom Mr. Shaw had sent chocolates to, his motivations contemptible and hurtful. Had she come to hate him as a result of that unwanted gift? She'd known that Mr. Blanchard possessed chloroform. Had witnessed its effect upon living creatures. But how might she have become aware that Mr. Shaw's heart was failing him? Information required to even begin to believe dosing the man with chloroform might kill him. Question about how *she* could have come into possession of the key. Her alibi for Wednesday evening that she'd spent it with Elliot Blanchard, who'd surely deny she had been with him, whether or not that was the truth. With a weak arm, could she have struck down Mrs. Wynn? Only one strong arm was required to wield a heavy cobblestone, though. Had arrived to tutor Barbara at a strangely early hour this morning . . .

It cannot be possible, thought Celia, her pen inscribing a heavy, blotchy circle of ink around Miss Campbell's name. *Can it?*

• • •

Leonard Shaw proved ridiculously easy to trail. Nick didn't even need Taylor's skills to track the man through the downtown streets and alleyways. He never once looked back to see if anybody was following him. He might just be walking home. Innocent as a lamb.

But Shaw didn't turn south toward the home on Stockton he shared with his mother. Instead, he headed north. Toward the Barbary. Turning onto a street Nick had often walked.

It was only when he neared the tavern that Shaw glanced around to see who might be monitoring his movements, unfolding the velvet collar of his coat to hide behind. Why then? It wasn't a crime to stop in a saloon, and nobody would care that some politician's son, the heir to a bank, wanted to imbibe a lager beer or two. Although Nick would guess the fellow's taste leaned toward scotch whiskey.

Shaw didn't notice Nick watching and trotted down the shadowed steps into the basement, his body temporarily blocking the light from the freshly lit gas lamps as he crossed the threshold. Nick pushed away from the wall where he'd been leaning. He didn't have to follow the man inside. He'd ask Bauman later who Shaw had come to visit at his saloon.

∅ CHAPTER 17 ℞

"Mr. Greaves." Miss DiPaolo stood up from the chair she'd been occupying. "I'm glad you're here. I wasn't sure you would be, on a Saturday."

"Sometimes I even work on Sundays. Could you fetch Miss DiPaolo some coffee?" Nick asked the booking officer, leaning against his desk and eyeing the young woman who'd come into the station early on a Saturday morning. "From upstairs."

"Am I one of your lackeys now, Greaves?" he shot back. "And what's so bad about the coffee down here?" He jerked his head in the direction of the white enamel pot heating on the corner stove.

"Thanks for helping out," Nick replied. Grumbling, the booking officer stamped up the stairs. "There's no need for you to keep standing, Miss DiPaolo."

She smiled, which made her eyes shine. If Taylor were here, he'd be blushing. "Mina always has said you're blunt. I don't mind, though," she said, retaking her seat.

Mina talked about him to the other girls at Bauman's? "How can I help you this morning, Miss DiPaolo?"

"I wanted to let you know I'll be taking charge of Althea's body," she said. "She doesn't have any other family in town. At least, none that I'm aware of."

"Her nearest relative's in Eureka, I hear," he said, waiting to see if she'd correct him, trying to discover just how many people knew about Althea Wynn's family in Crescent City.

"Are they? Pretty far away," she said. "I want her to get a decent burial, and the other women at the lodging house chipped in to help pay for one. I didn't want Althea's body sent to a medical college so they could . . . well, you know."

"I do." Bodies getting buried at public expense could be claimed by medical students unless the dying person had stated they didn't want to be a part of anatomy instruction. Mrs. Wynn hadn't exactly had the opportunity to make her wishes known. "I'll inform the coroner. Is that all?"

"I . . . I . . ." She paused to compose herself. He hadn't realized that she and Mrs. Wynn had been such great friends. Couldn't have been that close, if she didn't know about the relatives in Crescent City.

"Take your time, miss."

"I'm finding it awful hard to believe what the papers are reporting about Althea," she said. "That she was a thief."

Damn. He'd like to know who'd leaked the information to the reporters about Shaw's watch. Probably Briggs, just to rile him.

"We don't have any other explanation for how Mr. Shaw's watch and fob chain ended up in her possession, Miss DiPaolo," said Nick. "Do you?"

"I don't understand it at all. Unless . . ." She stared at him. Giulia DiPaolo had lovely, clear, intelligent eyes. "Unless that man who came by to talk to her the other night is to blame. Maybe he pressured her to steal from Mr. Shaw. That must be it."

"You told me Mrs. Wynn never had male visitors."

"I wasn't completely honest, Detective, because then I'd have to admit how we—the other lodgers and me—manage to have fellows visit without Mrs. M. finding out," she said.

Mullahey thudded down the stairs, a steaming cup of coffee in his hand. "The booking officer told me I was to give this to you, Mr. Greaves. He had some other words, as well, but 'tis best I not be tellin' you those in front of a young lady, sir."

"The coffee is for Miss DiPaolo." Obviously the fellow had found his own lackey.

"Here you go, miss," he said, handing the mug to her. "I've news for you, sir. About one of our suspect's alibis."

"Oh?" asked Nick, observing Miss DiPaolo's inquisitive sideways look. "Please excuse me for a moment."

He rose and motioned for Mullahey to join him out of her earshot.

"What have you learned?"

"Mr. Blanchard was at Empire State restaurant yesterday morning, like you'd heard." Mullahey grinned fleetingly. "Having a bit of a row with Mr. Leonard Shaw, as it turns out. Apparently Mr. Blanchard is a tad upset that the Shaws have been accusin' him of being a murderer. One of the waiters had to stop their argument from turnin' into a round of fisticuffs."

The fight a detail Shaw had omitted from his description of how he'd spent yesterday morning.

"Thank you, Mullahey." Nick returned to his chair opposite Giulia DiPaolo, engrossed in sipping her coffee. "So who was Mrs. Wynn's male visitor? Have a name?"

"He was a scruffy fellow, with a crooked nose and reddish hair. Do you know him?"

"Yes, I believe I do." Platt, again. "Did you overhear their conversation?"

"I didn't, but I've been thinking back on yesterday morning, and I believe . . ." She rolled her lips between her teeth. They flushed pink when she released them. "I believe he was the shadow I saw in the alleyway, Detective. The man whose voice I heard."

"Mullahey!" Nick called over to the policeman before he disappeared up the stairs, stopping him in his tracks. "I need you to bring Platt in." Past time they arrested him, his supposed alibi be damned.

Mullahey nodded and rushed off.

Nick turned back to Miss DiPaolo. "Were you at work last evening?" Her arrival at the station may have saved him a trip to Bauman's to ask about Leonard Shaw's visit. Which might no longer be important, if Platt was the killer, but a broken thread worth tying off.

Her expression changed. Not her expression, actually, but her posture, which had been drooping as expected for somebody upset over the brutal murder of a friend. A subtle, wary stiffening of her spine.

"I was, because Mina's still recovering from her concussion and hasn't returned yet," she said, a slight edge to her voice. Resentment, probably.

"A man stopped in last evening. A fellow I'm interested in. Broad face. Dark, narrow-set eyes. Clean-shaven. Dresses well," he said, describing Leonard Shaw. "Do you know who I'm talking about?"

She set the coffee on the desk behind her. "You mean Leo Shaw."

"He's a regular, then." Mina *had* to know him, in that case.

"He's only taken to stopping by in the past few weeks," she said. "I guess he heard about the saloon from his father."

"Did Leonard Shaw spend last evening alone, enjoying your singing and Herr Bauman's lager?" he asked. "Or was he joined by a friend?"

"Nobody joined him, Detective," she said. "Mr. Shaw came in, sat alone for around an hour, and left."

Leonard Shaw had slathered on bay rum in order to have a lager or two, alone, at Bauman's? "You're positive."

"I didn't notice him talking to anybody, Detective," she said. "But then I was busy without Mina there. Awfully busy."

• • •

The morning had dawned damp, mist drawing a gray veil across the sky as though even the heavens themselves wept for Ambrose Shaw.

Celia, you have grown poetical. Or morose. Or both.

She stared out the window of the Central Railroad car, steadily climbing toward the western hills and the flank of Lone Mountain, the cross at its peak a landmark beckoning them onward. The number of buildings and houses gradually reduced, replaced by an increasing quantity of flimsy fences and stakes marking out lots for future buildings and houses. Ahead rose the imposing bulk of the recently constructed Ladies' Relief Society Home, its grandness incongruous among the patches of greasewood and sagebrush and sand. Standing alone like a guest who'd come early to the party and was awkwardly waiting for the rest to arrive.

Celia consulted the watch she'd pinned at her waist. Not long before they would reach the cemetery. Mr. Shaw's funeral services had gotten underway midmorning. Mindful, perhaps, of the business hours of those who'd be attending, and who likewise might wish to return to their offices—even on a Saturday—after sympathizing with the Shaws. Friends had been called to visit the family home at nine o'clock and from there to proceed to the cemetery. No church service had been planned, which Celia found unusual for a man in his position. She would have attempted to call at the Shaws' home—she'd been bold enough to spy on a murder victim's church service before—but she'd had an appointment with the patient she'd yesterday treated for nettle rash.

Celia surveyed the occupants of the horsecar compartment, wondering if any of her fellow passengers were headed to Mr. Shaw's burial. Women in black, their faces veiled, wept into handkerchiefs, consoled by family members. Men with armbands or hatbands of black sat in sober, somber silence. Most of those invited to attend Mr. Shaw's burial, though, would be sufficiently prosperous to own carriages or procure a private hackney coach rather than subject themselves to the ignobility of a gritty ride on public transport.

Would Mr. Blanchard be in attendance in order to disprove the reports of ill will between the families? Not likely. The owner of the Hygienic Institute, Mr. Ross, would likely also not be at the graveside. And, for that matter, neither would Miss Olivia Campbell. How might Rebecca Shaw respond to Miss Campbell's assertion she'd spent Wednesday evening with Miss Shaw's former fiancé? The best way to learn would be to ask.

A solitary, grim-faced fellow across the aisle and a few seats ahead, a pair of wire-framed spectacles perched on his nose and his face sprouting bushy whiskers, might be one of Ambrose Shaw's mourners. He must have sensed her staring, for he glanced over his shoulder and met her gaze. She inclined her head. He scowled and looked away, blotting his forehead with a handkerchief even though the interior of the car was not warm.

Curious.

Soon, a long white picket fence came into view, rising and falling over the undulations of the hill. The area it enclosed was a sea of crosses, tombs, and marble mausoleums. Laurel trees dotted the grounds, and a chapel stood near the road. The horsecar eased to a halt, stirring Celia's fellow passengers to reluctant life.

"Laurel Hill Cemetery," called out the driver. "Calvary Cemetery to your left. Odd Fellows beyond that."

As a unit, the passengers rose and shuffled out of the car, the man with the spectacles hurrying to the front of the crowd. Celia got to her feet, her back stiff from the lengthy four-mile ride. Brushing off her skirts, which had managed to collect dust and sand through the open windows of the horsecar, she exited the omnibus. At least the drizzle had ceased. A row of carriages, adorned with tall black feathers and ebony bunting, lined the road alongside the cemetery. Perhaps they had conveyed Mr. Shaw's funeral party.

The damp air chilled her face, and she hugged her shawl tighter around her shoulders. From where the hills descended to the shore, the fog trumpet erected near Cliff House sounded, its tone deep and mournful, warning ships approaching the entrance to the Golden Gate. The scent of the ocean drifted on the air along with the sound of the fog warning. When she crested the next rise in the road, she would be able to spy the Chinese burial grounds. A friend lay buried there. A young woman whose murder had plunged Celia into a world of criminal investigation and danger she'd never sought to be a part of.

I wish it had stopped with her. Despite Barbara's insistence—and Mr. Greaves's as well—that she enjoyed the occupation far more than she should, she prayed that the murders of Mr. Shaw and Mrs. Wynn were the last two cases she ever had cause to involve herself with.

Her musings had distracted her, and she'd lost sight of the bespectacled fellow. Just as well. If he was indeed one of Ambrose Shaw's mourners, she would encounter him at the graveside. As she reached the gateway leading into Calvary Cemetery, a hackney coach came to a halt behind her. Rebecca Shaw clambered down before the driver could open the door for her. She was alone, having chosen, it appeared, to not share a conveyance with her stepmother and stepbrother.

"Miss Shaw," Celia called out. Much to her amazement, Rebecca Shaw waited for Celia to catch her up.

"Mrs. Davies," she said, the sheer black netting drawn over her face obscuring her expression but not her annoyance. "I'm surprised to see you here."

"I wished to extend my condolences to your family, Miss Shaw," replied Celia, falling into step alongside the woman.

"Oh?" she asked, sounding doubtful. "Well, the only family in attendance besides me will be Leonard and Delphia. When my brothers were informed of Father's death, they opted to not make the journey from Nevada."

The path wound along an incline, its gravel crunching beneath their feet. Celia spotted the bespectacled man several yards ahead.

"Is that fellow one of your father's acquaintances?" she asked. "I saw him on the horsecar. An oddly anxious man."

Miss Shaw peered at him. "Mr. Ross from the Hygienic Institute. What gall, to think he's welcome here."

He trailed after a middle-aged woman. Mrs. Shaw, perhaps. She was of average height—too short to attack Mrs. Wynn with a cobblestone?—and possessed a confident bearing. The young man accompanying her looked to be Leonard Shaw. Mr. Ross was attempting to have a conversation with him, but Mr. Shaw brushed him off.

Celia ducked beneath the branches of a tree planted too near the path. "Is that Mrs. Shaw with your stepbrother?"

"Yes, it is. I didn't realize you'd met Leo."

"I encountered him at the police station yesterday morning," she said. "Very early. Do you know what he was doing there, by any chance? The detective he was visiting is not the one in charge of your father's case."

"I don't, and I wouldn't advise asking him this morning." She pressed her lips into a grim line for a brief moment. "That's why you're here. Because the police haven't yet arrested anybody for murdering my father and you intend to poke around. I haven't forgotten what your cousin mentioned about your meddling in police affairs, Mrs. Davies."

"You need not have waited for me, Miss Shaw," Celia pointed out. "You could have continued on and ignored me. As you did yesterday morning when I stopped by your apartment, only to find you absent."

"You want to know why I ran off?" she responded. "Don't look startled. Of course I noticed you yesterday and I *did* choose to ignore you."

"Yet now you are willing to speak with me." Perhaps she'd had time to construct an excuse.

"Where might I go and hide?" Rebecca Shaw swept a black-gloved hand before her, its movement encompassing the sparsely vegetated hillside. There were more headstones than shrubs and trees. "Behind that row of crosses?"

"I am persistent, I admit," said Celia. "So why have you changed your mind?"

"Because you're persistent," she said. "What is it you're so curious about?"

"Why do you have a tintype of your former fiancé in your studio window?" asked Celia.

"Mr. Blanchard has always been supportive," she replied. "Nothing more, Mrs. Davies. Our relationship is concluded."

"And what of that woman I noticed you with . . . she seemed very agitated," she said. "Because of Althea Wynn, perhaps?"

"Who?" the woman walking alongside was quick to respond.

"Haven't you read the papers?" Celia asked.

"I've been too busy lately to read newspapers."

"Of course." Celia glanced at Miss Shaw's hands, the fingers gripping the strings of her black lace reticule, and tried to envision them clutching a broken cobblestone. Smashing it down upon Mrs. Wynn's head. The image was not too difficult to conjure. "It must be distressing to see the newspapers linking Mr. Blanchard to your father's death."

"It's outrageous."

Two women defending the man.

"Especially considering that your father perished from a seizure of his heart brought on from exposure to chloroform. How could Mr. Blanchard have known about Mr. Shaw's poor health and his vulnerability? Unless you'd informed him." They reached the crest of the hill and continued along the path, which dipped down the other side. Thirty or so yards away, a grave had been opened, a canopy stretching overhead. A clergyman mingled among the gathering crowd. "Furthermore, there is the unfortunate fact that Mr. Blanchard possesses a supply of the substance. A bottle is missing from his house."

"You're being ridiculous, Mrs. Davies," said Miss Shaw.

Did I truly believe I could make her implicate him? Celia changed tack. "I received a note Thursday evening at my house. Did you leave it for me?"

"I don't have any reason to send you missives, Mrs. Davies," replied the woman tersely.

"I suppose you do not," said Celia, cautious with her steps on the descending path, gravel slipping beneath the leather soles of her shoes. "Do you know Miss Olivia Campbell?"

"You have a lot of questions, Mrs. Davies, and I'm getting pretty tired of them."

"You do know her, though." *I am indeed persistent, Miss Shaw.*

"Elliot . . . Mr. Blanchard hired her to tutor his wife and improve her English," she said. "Why?"

"She has stated that she was with him Wednesday evening, providing him an alibi."

Miss Shaw came to an abrupt halt. "What?"

"I believe you heard me, Miss Shaw," said Celia. "Miss Campbell says she was with Mr. Blanchard the night your father died. However, I am uncertain whether to believe her. She could be lying in order to protect him."

"Oh my God, Mrs. Davies." Rebecca Shaw burst out laughing,

which took Celia aback. "You know what? Perhaps you should leave the police work to the professionals. That's what I think is the only truth in this whole wretched mess," she said and marched off to join the others at the grave.

• • •

Nick leaned against a marble monument, a squat obelisk tucked beneath an oak tree that hadn't obliged the family by growing tall enough to provide shade. The monument was dedicated to the memory of—he squinted at the name carved into the stone—dedicated to the memory of T. Vincent. *Loving husband and father.* All he and Ellie had been able to afford for their father was a puny granite headstone whose surface would erode in the harsh sun and dusty wind of Sacramento. *Abraham Greaves* eventually worn down to where, some decades from now, it'd be hard to tell who'd been buried at the edge of the cemetery. Tell if he'd also been a loving husband and father.

He spoke often of you with pride . . .

Nick shook off the recollection and contemplated the scene unfolding at the grave. The ceremony was wrapping up, the requisite handful of dirt tossed onto the lowered coffin followed by a small bouquet of flowers Delphia Shaw had been carrying. Rebecca Shaw had chosen a spot far enough from her family members to avoid speaking with them but not so far that she'd be accused of disrespect. Mr. Ross was among the mourners, he'd noted. A unexpected visitor. Elliot Blanchard, unsurprisingly, was absent. Also unsurprising was the presence of a blond-haired woman in a deep blue gown who'd never learn to leave police business to the police.

Just then, she dipped her chin and shot a look in Nick's direction. He saluted her with a wave of his hat.

She retreated from the group gathered around the grave, where the clergyman was offering final words, and climbed the incline to where he stood. "Good day to you, Mr. Greaves," she said. "Mr. Shaw has received a lovely graveside service. His widow and son appear genuinely bereft."

"What about Rebecca Shaw?" he asked when she joined him, her attention fixed on the people who'd come to see Shaw's casket descend into the ground. The contours of her face could only be described as elegant, and her eyelashes . . . *damn, Nick. Not the time. Not ever the time.*

"Obligation has brought Miss Shaw here." Celia Davies narrowed her eyes as she observed the woman, who was beating a hasty retreat. "I went to Miss Shaw's yesterday to question her about her stepbrother's visit to the police station."

"I thought you'd planned to go straight to your clinic."

"I changed my mind," she said. Unapologetically.

"Leonard Shaw explained to me he was at the station on an unrelated, private matter, which he didn't care to elaborate on."

"Ah."

Right then, Rebecca Shaw glanced in their direction. Behind her black veil she was probably glaring.

"Miss Shaw was not at her apartment when I visited," continued Mrs. Davies as the woman hurried down the path toward the waiting carriages. "Her neighbor, who appears to closely monitor Miss Shaw's comings and goings, mentioned she'd gone out unusually early. However, as I prepared to depart, I noticed her with a woman I did not recognize. Miss Shaw was keen to avoid me and they both ran off."

Interesting.

"Her stepbrother has decided to implicate her, which makes a change from blaming Elliot Blanchard." At the moment, the man was leading his mother away from the grave, Delphia Shaw leaning on his arm. "Both men had a busy morning yesterday. He and Leonard Shaw were at Empire State, arguing. Almost came to blows over the Shaws blaming Blanchard for Ambrose Shaw's death."

"A demonstration of the extent of his temper," she said. "However, I thought you were focusing on Mr. Platt as the perpetrator. Which means I must ask what you are doing here?"

"Paying my respects."

"Certainly," she replied with a hasty smile. "I have other news, Mr.

Greaves. Owen obtained a list of recent purchases of candy made by Ambrose Shaw. He did not send that box you saw at Bauman's to Mina; it was addressed to 'all the ladies.' He'd not singled her out for attention."

"I remind you about her shawl and the key, Mrs. Davies," he said. "Plus her concussion. She's involved, all right."

She glanced up at him, past the brim of her deep bonnet. "Mina does now recall heading to the Institute in a state of anxiety. Worried, she told Barbara. Perhaps she'd become aware someone meant to harm Mr. Shaw and intended to intervene."

"Or Shaw had invited her there," he said. "Maybe even sent her that key."

She frowned. "The candy was not intended for her, Mr. Greaves."

"Okay, okay, Mrs. Davies. Point made."

"Thank you."

"Maybe Mina had learned that Platt meant to harm Shaw," said Nick, returning to his "perpetrator." "A young woman—a Giulia DiPaolo—who lives at Mrs. Wynn's boardinghouse thinks she spotted him at the time of the woman's murder. Plus, we have Cassidy's testimony about Platt and Mrs. Wynn arguing over Shaw's watch."

"Was Mr. Platt a regular customer of Bauman's?" she asked.

Nick massaged the sudden ache in his arm, the wound that managed to hurt at the strangest—or most perceptive—of moments. "I get why you're asking, ma'am."

"I would indeed be happy to have you prove that Mr. Platt is the murderer, Mr. Greaves, but in order for Mina to learn of a plot to harm Mr. Shaw, she most probably acquired the information at the saloon," she explained. "And if Mr. Platt never went there, how had she heard?"

"Mina Cascarino doesn't spend all her time at Bauman's, Mrs. Davies."

The mourners had all vacated the gravesite, strolling in groups of two and three back to their carriages. Leonard Shaw and his mother walked alone.

"I should also inform you that Barbara's new tutor, a Miss Olivia

Campbell, used to work for the Blanchards. She acted as companion and English teacher to Mrs. Blanchard," said Mrs. Davies, watching them depart. "She has made an astonishing declaration that she was with Mr. Blanchard on the evening of Mr. Shaw's death."

"No wonder Blanchard didn't provide an alibi; he didn't want anybody to know he'd been with a woman who wasn't his wife."

"I queried Miss Shaw about the likelihood Miss Campbell told me the truth," she said. "Miss Shaw laughed at me."

"No one should laugh at you, Mrs. Davies."

Color washed over her cheeks. "Thank you for saying so, Mr. Greaves. However, it was not the first time nor, I suspect, shall it be the last," she replied. "I do fear Miss Campbell sympathized with Mr. Blanchard's hostility toward Ambrose Shaw. She was another recipient of Mr. Shaw's gifts of chocolates. A gift to hurt her and draw the ire of her employers, the Blanchards."

"The more I hear about Ambrose Shaw, ma'am, the more I despise the fellow."

"However, we must consider that Miss Campbell is lying in order to protect Mr. Blanchard."

"You don't want to think she's a young woman who might spend the evening with a married man," he said.

"No, I do not," she answered. "Should you question her, please do be kind."

"Am I usually unkind, Mrs. Davies?"

"At times, you take on a fierce expression when you interrogate people, Mr. Greaves," she said. "I experienced your scowl myself the first time we met."

When he'd questioned her about her brother-in-law's role in the murder of a Chinese girl. That time seemed like years ago instead of just a few months.

"No need to worry about my expression, ma'am. I don't need to speak with Miss Campbell." Platt was the murderer, sure as the year came around. A woman striding across the cemetery caught Nick's eye.

She was heading straight for the Shaws. "What's Giulia DiPaolo doing here? She was just at the station."

Mrs. Davies twisted about to see who he'd spotted. "That woman in the green dress, do you mean? The young lady who noticed Mr. Platt," she said. "She looks familiar. I cannot fathom why, though."

Giulia DiPaolo didn't get any closer than twenty feet to Mrs. Shaw and her son. They veered off at a right angle, unaware she'd been making a beeline in their direction. Rebecca Shaw noticed her, though, and dashed for the line of waiting carriages. Miss DiPaolo slowed before changing course and heading for the small stone building near the main gate. The receiving vault for the temporary storage of corpses.

"Maybe she's here to arrange Mrs. Wynn's funeral," he said. "She's taken charge of the woman's body."

"I suppose you are right."

He hated when she said that; it usually meant she didn't agree.

"You know, ma'am, our discussion about Miss Campbell and Rebecca Shaw is all very interesting, but I'm convinced that Platt's behind both murders and have sent Mullahey to arrest the fellow," he said. "He might not have meant to kill Shaw, but he wanted that watch to settle his debt with Griffin. Except Mrs. Wynn beat him to it. When he overheard that Mrs. Wynn was going to flee San Francisco, he figured she'd realized he'd killed Shaw and also that she had the man's watch in her possession. She had to be dealt with. So, Mrs. Davies, I'd say we're finished."

"Are we, Mr. Greaves?" she asked. "I feel as though I've been handed a critical piece of this puzzle-map but have discarded it as irrelevant."

"I'm going to throw Platt in jail, Mrs. Davies," he said firmly. He'd finally gotten his hands around this case and here she was, causing it to crumble in his grasp.

"Do what you must, Mr. Greaves," she answered, unruffled, her chin up. "And I shall do likewise."

❦ CHAPTER 18 ❧

"Mina, how are you today?" asked Celia, stepping into the bedchamber Mina occupied, Mrs. Cascarino's footsteps fading in the hallway beyond the room.

Mina set aside the book she'd been holding. "Better. A little," she replied. "I suppose Barbara told you about my memories starting to come back."

"She did." Celia took the bedside chair, her dark blue skirts crowding against the bed itself. She'd come straight from the cemetery, the dust of the journey on the hem of her dress and her shoes. "Have you recalled any more since she visited?"

"Not much. Just that I was anxious and in a rush to get to the Institute," she said. "But exactly why I felt that way, I don't remember."

"Could it have been concern over Mr. Shaw, perhaps?"

Mina gazed up at her. She had dark and captivating eyes, fringed with thick long lashes. They were not the eyes of a guilty woman. Or so Celia dearly wished to believe. "You mean, did I know that he was going to be murdered?" she asked.

Celia sat back. "That is what I mean."

"How could I have known?"

"Have you ever heard of a Mr. Platt, Mina?" She watched the young woman closely; Mina's reaction would be revealing. But she did not cringe nor glance away, convey any hint she had ever heard his name.

"The name's not familiar," said Mina.

"He works at the Hygienic Institute. Mr. Greaves intends to arrest him for the murder of Mr. Shaw and a Mrs. Wynn, who was killed yesterday morning," said Celia.

"Then Nick believes I'm innocent, after all," she said, sounding hopeful.

Celia knew she should be content to see the man accused and possibly convicted. But if Mr. Platt was not responsible, hanging an innocent man did not feel like justice to Celia, even if Mina was spared.

"Not completely, Mina," she replied. "There remains the matter of your shawl and the key I found, which worked the lock on a private door at the Institute."

Mina pinched her eyes closed. Perhaps to rebel against the cruel trick her unhealed brain was playing by not permitting her to completely remember, crippling her efforts to defend herself. "Nick thinks I'm an accomplice."

"Did you love him, Mina?" It hurt to ask that question. Like countless other jealous women, though, Celia desperately wanted the answer. "Never mind. I should not have asked. Your prior relationship with Mr. Greaves is irrelevant to this particular situation."

"Is it?" she asked. "I did. Once." Her smile was fleeting. More a trace of a smile than an actual one. "He was hurting after he returned from the war and discovered his sister had died by her own hand. Consumed by the pain, which left no room for me."

Celia considered the young woman resting on the bed, surrounded by the small comforts of a family poor in earthly goods but rich in tenderness and warmth. Someone had cut the last fading blooms of a rosebush and tucked the flowers into a glass vase for Mina to enjoy. One of her siblings had sketched a picture of a sunny garden and left it on the bedside table. A woman deeply loved by her family and who would love deeply in return.

"I am sorry, Mina," she said.

"There's no need to apologize for Nick, Mrs. Davies," she replied. "Besides, he cares far more for you than he ever did for me. I can tell by how he speaks your name."

Her heart contracted, but what could she do with the sensation, the emotion? Nothing.

"Enough about Nicholas Greaves, Mina, other than to tell you I've confirmed that those candies he saw at Bauman's were not meant for you," said Celia. "Mr. Shaw had them sent to 'all the ladies,' according to the customer records at Roesler's."

"They were actually meant for Giulia." Mina gasped at her sudden recollection. "I remember now, Mrs. Davies. He'd sent them to her."

"Is Giulia's last name DiPaolo?" The young woman who'd endeavored to chase down the Shaws at the cemetery that morning. The young woman who'd supposedly observed Mr. Platt in an alleyway around the time of a murder.

"That's her, and despite some record that Mr. Shaw had sent those candies to 'all the ladies,' they were definitely meant for Giulia. How she laughed when that box showed up." She frowned. "I should've told Nick, but I remember now I was so mad that he'd presumed those candies were a gift for me."

"Miss DiPaolo was at the cemetery this morning," said Celia. "Does she know the other Shaws?"

"She's met Leonard, because he comes into Bauman's every once in a while. Flirts with him," she said. "I don't know about the others."

"Are she and Leonard Shaw in a relationship?" she asked. The pieces of the puzzle-map were hovering nearer, readying to fall into place, and the recognition made Celia's pulse tick upward.

"She probably wishes she was, a rich man like him, but I don't . . ." Mina stopped, her brow furrowing.

Celia seized Mina's hand, as though clutching her fingers might squeeze the memories out of her brain. "What is it, Mina?"

"Nothing." She shook her head, which made her wince from the movement. "I don't remember anything. I thought I might be . . . but I don't."

"You were worried and went to the Institute because you feared what Giulia meant to do, didn't you, Mina?" Celia asked. The young woman who knew both Ambrose Shaw and Leonard Shaw. Who'd accused Mr. Platt of murdering Mrs. Wynn. "That night, you kept muttering 'terrible, terrible.' But you also said something like 'what has she . . .' Mina, did you mean Giulia DiPaolo?"

"Giulia can't be involved in those murders. She can't." Mina paused to massage her temples; perhaps the conversation was making her head ache. "That's not who she is."

"What other 'she' would you have been upset about?" asked Celia. "She knew Ambrose Shaw, perhaps more intimately than you were aware. Most critically, she lives at the same boardinghouse as the second victim, Mina, and is the only witness pinning the crime on Mr. Platt. What else can we conclude?"

But were those the pieces of the puzzle-map that were meant to fit together, or was she forcing them into place?

• • •

"How was Mr. Shaw's funeral, sir?" asked Taylor, hopping up from his desk.

"Grand," replied Nick. "Thanks for coming in on a Saturday, Taylor. Has Mullahey brought Platt in yet?"

"He's in one of the holding cells, sir. Mr. Greaves, sir," he replied, nodding toward the barred door. "Not happy one bit. Guess you decided his alibi didn't work out."

"Guess so."

The booking officer's desk stood empty; maybe he'd decided to leave early on a Saturday. Nick rooted around in the papers atop it for his keys. Not finding any, he pounded on the door to the holding cells. A middle-aged fellow snoozed on a stool at the end of the six-foot aisle separating the two rows of cells.

"Hey, I need to talk to a prisoner," said Nick through the iron crosspieces barring the window. "The booking officer's not here to let me in. Did he give you the keys?"

"Yeah, yeah." The jailer grudgingly got up from his chair. "I'm coming. Stop banging on the door, Detective Greaves." He trudged along its length, dodging the outthrust hands of prisoners trying to grab his keys. "You're after Mr. Platt, our brand-new guest, I suppose."

His keys clanked in the lock and he swung open the door. Nick squeezed past. He hated this place, the damp darkness and the chill, the mold and the squeak of rats, the stink of slop jars and sweating men—and women. At times Nick couldn't decide if it was worse in here or at the main jail on Broadway. This was bad enough.

"Which cell?" he asked the jailer, who was thudding the door shut again.

"I'm right here, Mr. Greaves," said Platt, pressing his face against the floor-to-ceiling grate of a cell two spaces down. He'd been brought in before he'd had a chance to shave and brownish-red hairs prickled his cheeks. "So I'm guilty, huh?"

Three cells down, a young man—not much older than a boy, actually—strained to catch sight of the new prisoner and the cop come to talk to him.

"What're you looking at?" Platt shouted at the kid, causing him to jump back and bump into the cot behind him. A grizzled fellow across the aisle—a drunk and one of their regulars—cackled so hard it made him cough. The jailer banged a thick wood baton against the nearest grate, the clang reverberating off the weeping stone walls, which quieted things for all of a minute.

Nick stared at Platt, who scratched fingers through his beard stubble and stared back. "You were seen by a witness at Mrs. Wynn's yesterday morning," said Nick. "Slinking through the alleyway."

"Nope, sorry. Wasn't me," he said. "And I'd like to know who this witness is."

"Do you suddenly have a solid alibi, Platt?" Nick asked.

"I was at my lodgings, asleep. Just like I told your assistant when he stopped by to visit yesterday," he said. "And I'm not going to be railroaded for a crime I didn't commit."

"This is how I see it," said Nick, shifting his stance and putting his back to the occupants of the other cells. "You brought chloroform into Shaw's room, meaning to knock him out and steal his watch. Except—surprise!—you killed the fellow. You turned on the gas to make it look like an accident or that he'd killed himself. Couldn't take the watch now, because then it would be clear the man had been murdered."

Platt chuckled. "One problem, Detective. I never would've needed to use chloroform on Shaw in order to pilfer his watch. I could look at the treatment schedule and learn when he'd be down having a cold soak. Go in then," he said. "Or enter his room in the middle of the night. I'd hear him snoring away when I'd walk by his suite on my rounds. I probably could've stolen the shirt he slept in without waking him."

Nick continued on. "Griffin was pressing you for the money you owed him. Maybe you panicked and decided against those more sensible options," he said. "Sadly, Althea Wynn saw you running out of Shaw's room. When she crept inside to steal his watch and found him dead, she realized you'd killed him. Right, Mr. Platt?"

"Sounds like you got it all sorted out, Mr. Greaves," he replied, his expression flat. "What do you want me to say? I confess?"

"Would be helpful," said Nick. "How did Mrs. Wynn reply when you demanded to know if she'd taken Shaw's watch? Did she tell you that she'd seen you? That she knew you'd killed him? And you discovered that she meant to flee to Crescent City. On a ship headed out of town yesterday morning. A quick trip to her lodging house to murder her then back to your bed, where you could pretend to have been sleeping like a baby all along."

"Perfect explanation, Detective." He pressed his face against the cell bars. "However, somebody else killed Shaw. But apparently I'm the one who's going to pay."

• • •

"Ma'am!" cried Addie, startled as Celia burst into the entry hall.

"Jane will be here at any moment, but we have an additional visit to add to our agenda," she said, removing her black gloves and tossing them aside with her shawl. "A side trip to Miss Shaw's photographic studio."

Addie caught the gloves and shawl before they landed on the floor. "Why there?"

"My quest involves a witness who has blamed the evening attendant at the Hygienic Institute for murdering our second victim."

"Then you've nae need to go to that dreadful place today, after all," said her housekeeper.

"Ah, but I feel that witness is no longer reliable," said Celia, hopping on one foot as she struggled to remove the half boot on the other. "According to Mina, the young woman was the recipient of the candy Ambrose Shaw sent to Bauman's. Which might play into a scheme to murder the fellow."

"Miss Mina knows her?"

"Yes, and I have to ask if Miss DiPaolo was the reason Mina had gone to the Institute Wednesday." Both boots freed, she handed them to Addie. "Maybe Mina had followed her that evening to stop her from going through with her plans."

And here I was beginning to suspect Miss Campbell.

"So what does this Miss DiPaolo's involvement have to do with your hurried need to go to Miss Shaw's studio?" asked Addie, Celia's discarded clothing bundled in her arms.

"She was at Mr. Shaw's burial service this morning and looked familiar to me," she answered. "I have a hunch why, and the resolution might be found at Miss Shaw's gallery. Among the images of working-class women arrayed in the window."

What if, thought Celia, it had been *Rebecca* Shaw Miss DiPaolo had been seeking to intercept at the cemetery? Unresolved business concerning the deaths of Mr. Shaw and Mrs. Wynn, perhaps. *Moreover, what if she was the woman I saw with Rebecca yesterday, frantic and upset?*

"Just because she's been photographed by Miss Shaw doesna make her a killer, ma'am," Addie pointed out. "No more than you and Miss Barbara are murderers for having your portrait taken by her."

"The note, Addie. *Leave us alone.* What if she and Miss Shaw are the 'us'?" asked Celia. "I have to figure out where I've seen Miss DiPaolo before." And what it might mean, once she did settle the question.

Addie frowned. "'Tis certain you'll find trouble, ma'am."

"Do not fret, Addie."

"You're off on one of your schemes," she replied. "How can I not fret?"

True.

Celia bounded upstairs in order to change into her crimson flannel Garibaldi blouse and holland skirt. The outfit she had often worn before she'd taken on widow's clothing. Wool and linen and sturdy cotton to gird herself in. Armor to provide courage, which had been sorely lacking since Patrick had arisen from the dead.

The front bell sounded; Jane had arrived.

"You're going to wear your nurse's costume to the Institute, Celia?" she asked when Celia stepped into the parlor.

"I feel more comfortable in these clothes, Jane." Celia rested her hands at her waist, the blouse freeing her from the strict confines of a tight corset. She could readily breathe; how glorious a sensation. "But first, a brief stop at Miss Shaw's studio is required."

Jane glanced at Addie, standing in the doorway to the parlor, who shook her head. "It'll be closed, Celia."

"I do not require the gallery to be open. I shall explain on our way there," she said. "Unless you do not wish to accompany me, after all."

"As I said yesterday, I wouldn't want to miss the excitement," Jane replied, winking. "But where's Barbara?" She peered into the dining room, visible through the open doors. "I wanted to give her a letter from Grace."

"You can leave the letter on the entry hall table for her," said Celia, tying the ribbons of her hat beneath her chin. "She is keeping to her bedchamber because of some startling news Miss Campbell shared with us yesterday."

"You'll have to tell me about that, too."

The Hutchinsons' tilbury waited outside on the curb. Joaquin, who lived across the street and was always on hand for tasks, stood holding the reins. He'd been whispering to the horse—a lovely bay—and caressing the animal's forelock. He snapped to attention when he heard Celia and Jane descending the stairs.

"Before I left the house, I read the notice of that widow's death in the paper," said Jane, taking the reins and leading the carriage horse back down the street. "The article mentioned that she'd been a frequent—and recent—patient at the Hygienic Institute."

"Interestingly, Mr. Ross was at the cemetery today," said Celia. "I expect he will be quite upset over the newspaper stories."

"Hopefully not *too* upset."

"We've nothing to fear from Mr. Ross, Jane." *I think.*

Reaching more level ground, they climbed onto the carriage seat. Celia provided the address of Miss Shaw's photographic gallery, and Jane steered the tilbury in its direction.

"So tell me why we're going to Miss Shaw's studio first," said Jane.

"Because Mina Cascarino has recalled going to the Institute Wednesday evening, and I have an idea who it was she may have followed there." Celia relayed what she'd learned about Giulia DiPaolo. "I recognized her at the cemetery, and the probable reason is because I'd seen her photograph at Miss Shaw's gallery."

"A photograph doesn't prove she conspired with Miss Shaw to murder Ambrose Shaw, Celia," said Jane, much as Addie had done.

"No, but it does prove they knew each other, which could be important in revealing the author of that warning note I received."

"I'd nearly forgotten about that note."

"I wish I could."

Jane steered the horse onto Montgomery, slowing as pedestrians—gingerly stepping around horse droppings not yet cleaned away—crossed the street ahead. "I'm afraid to ask about Miss Campbell's news."

"She has made a stunning admission," said Celia. "She offered herself as an alibi for Mr. Blanchard's movements the evening of Mr. Shaw's death. She maintains that she was with him."

"What?" asked Jane, disbelieving. "A young woman like Miss Campbell would never behave so foolishly."

"She cares for him enough to be willing to sacrifice her reputation," said Celia. "That much is clear."

They arrived at Miss Shaw's photographic gallery and studio. Jane reined in the horse and halted the tilbury before the shop door.

Celia hopped down, as did her friend, who tied the reins to a nearby hitching post. The blinds were lowered to the level of the row of photographs on display, the studio behind dark, as expected. Miss Shaw would not be at her camera today.

"Here, these are the images I wanted to examine," said Celia, studying the faces mutely staring back. The young women in their plain dark dresses and simply coifed hair. Evoking the reality of a working-class girl? Or seeking to project a preconceived notion of what a woman forced to earn her living looked like?

"Miss Shaw does good work," said Jane. "Are any of the girls Miss DiPaolo?"

"I believe she is that one, there." Celia tapped the window glass in front of the portrait propped in the center of the row of pictures. "This *is* where I recognized her from."

"She is lovely." Jane squinted at the photograph. "That young woman with her is Olivia Campbell. Don't you recognize her? She's dyed her hair dark. Probably for the benefit of the photograph; light hair doesn't always show up well. But that's definitely her."

Celia leaned closer to the glass.

"Yes, that is Libby Campbell." A shiver danced over her skin.

"Maybe she's not so innocent after all, Celia," whispered Jane, her warm breath clouding the window glass.

"She mentioned a friend who'd visited the Hygienic Institute," said Celia. "What if instead *she* had been the patient, receiving treatment for her weak arm? Learning the daily routine. Becoming aware of how to most easily arrive at a private suite. Perhaps even managing to acquire a critical key to that room."

Jane looked over at her. "Could Miss Campbell be the culprit?"

"Perhaps. Or at least, one of them." Celia pondered the image of two women, their arms about each other's waist, looking bold and brave. "Moreover, Jane, we may have identified the authors of that note. What if *these* ladies are the 'us'?"

· · ·

What if Platt isn't guilty? What if Giulia DiPaolo is lying?

Nick stared out the window behind his desk, barely noticing the passing pedestrians or hearing the barker parading in front of the nearby gentlemen's clothing store hawking its wares. "Doeskin pants for you, sir. Blue flannel coats. Doeskin pants." He'd had other witnesses ready to swear on their family Bible that they'd caught sight of a suspect at the scene of a crime, only to discover twenty-five other folks ready to swear that the person had been drinking at the saloon with them or had been attending a church picnic . . .

"Sir?" Taylor called around the half-open door of the detectives' office. "Can I come in? You didn't hear my knock, I guess."

Nick looked over his shoulder. "Lost in thought, Taylor." He dropped onto his chair and spun it to face his assistant. "Of course you can come in. What is it?"

"I wanted to let you know that Mullahey and one of the other fellows have been looking into whether Mrs. Wynn was at the Institute when those patients reportedly had possessions stolen," said Taylor. "Looks like she was, sir. Could be coincidence—"

"You know what I always say, Taylor."

"Not a coincidence," he said. "So she's likely been the thief and took advantage of Mr. Shaw's sudden death to steal from him too. Right?"

"Probably," he replied. "Platt may have planned to steal that watch from Shaw then blame the theft on Mrs. Wynn, who we eventually would've connected to the other thefts at the Institute."

"Well, that's resolved at least," said his assistant, doing his best to sound chipper. "And we've got our killer locked away."

Nick frowned and rubbed his arm. "We've got Platt locked away."

"Is Mr. Greaves here?" called a familiar voice out in the main station. What in hell was she doing there now? Hadn't they discussed everything at the cemetery?

Taylor jogged over to the door. "In here, Mrs. Davies."

"Ah, Mr. Greaves." She'd taken the time to change out of her somber blue dress and into the outfit he'd first seen her in, her businesslike Garibaldi blouse and brown skirt. Taylor offered his chair, but she declined. "I am glad you are in your office."

Mrs. Hutchinson was not far behind her. "Hello, Mr. Greaves."

"Is she embroiling you in one of her schemes, Mrs. Hutchinson?" he asked, getting to his feet.

"Nothing dangerous," she answered, with a playful smile. "We went to visit Rebecca Shaw's photographic gallery."

"I have discovered a connection between Rebecca Shaw, Giulia DiPaolo, and, sadly, Barbara's tutor, Olivia Campbell," said Celia Davies. "The latter two women were subjects for an exhibit Miss Shaw had planned but never put on."

Taylor located his pencil and notebook among his coat pockets and started writing.

"So?" asked Nick.

"So, according to Mina, it was Miss DiPaolo who was the intended recipient of Mr. Shaw's gift of candy, Mr. Greaves. Miss DiPaolo whom Mina was likely following to the Institute Wednesday night," she said. "When I was called to Mina's bedside that evening, she was muttering that something terrible had happened, and 'what has she . . .' Unfortunately, by the next morning Mina had completely forgotten what she'd said. I can only surmise she'd learned of Miss DiPaolo's involvement in the scheme to harm Mr. Shaw and sought to stop her."

"Giulia DiPaolo needed a key to that private entrance and Shaw's room, though," he said. "How'd she get it?"

Mrs. Davies's eyes lit. *Damn, she has an answer for that, too.*

"Perhaps her friendship with Olivia Campbell is the answer. Miss Campbell has a partially paralyzed arm, from a childhood illness, I suspect," she explained. "She may have recently been a patient at the Institute, in pursuit of relief. Time spent at the facility that could have come in handy if one wished to discover how to access Mr. Shaw or obtain the key to his room."

"You'd proposed to me that Rebecca Shaw had taken it," he said.

"I have not ruled out that scenario, Mr. Greaves."

Of course she hadn't.

"Don't you agree that Celia has devised an excellent explanation?" asked Jane Hutchinson, beaming with pride over her clever friend.

"I don't know what to make of it, Mrs. Hutchinson."

"What about Mr. Platt, sir?" asked Taylor, looking up from his notes. "Isn't he guilty, after all?"

"Not now, Taylor."

"Tell him about the note, Celia," said Jane Hutchinson.

Nick's old wound throbbed. "What note, Mrs. Davies?"

She hesitated, so the woman who'd accompanied her filled in the blanks. "A message telling Celia to 'leave us alone.'"

Damn. "If you're hiding any other snippets of information, ma'am, I wouldn't mind hearing them right now."

"I do not possess any other 'snippets of information,' Mr. Greaves, although I've come to suspect it was Miss DiPaolo I observed deep in frantic conversation with Miss Shaw yesterday morning," she replied. "While you attend to her, Jane and I shall collect Miss Campbell and persuade her to come to the station and give an account. And Mr. Taylor here can interrogate Miss Shaw."

"Whoa, no you don't, Mrs. Davies," he said, stretching out his hand. He'd lunge over the top of his desk and tackle her if that's what it took to stop her recklessness. "Mrs. Hutchinson, please take your friend back to her house and make sure she stays there."

Jane Hutchinson gave Celia Davies a quick look. "I'll do what I can, Mr. Greaves."

Mrs. Davies was busy scowling at him. "You do comprehend the criticality of my information, do you not, Mr. Greaves?"

He comprehended that her critical information was about to derail his entire case. If she was right. Which she quite often was.

"Taylor, bring Miss Campbell in. I'll go to Miss DiPaolo's. We'll attend to Miss Shaw later." Nick turned to the woman whose scowl hadn't let up. "Mrs. Davies, can you promise to stay at your house, or do I need to find a policeman to guard you?"

"Where might I seek to go, Mr. Greaves, as you intend to interview the two women I am primarily interested in?" she asked, smiling innocently.

Nick grabbed his hat off his desk and used it to point at her. "Stay. At. Home."

He swept past her, stomping from the room, Taylor on his heels.

• • •

"Well?" asked Jane, interweaving her fingers to tighten her gloves. "Do we still intend to visit the Hygienic Institute? Since it seems you've resolved everything."

Celia waited for the slap of the closing alleyway door to finish reverberating through the police station before replying. "I've no intention of twiddling my thumbs at home, awaiting news from Mr. Greaves, while I have questions to answer."

"I didn't think you'd want to go home."

A police officer, seated at one of the desks out in the station, inspected them as they strolled through the room. "Ladies."

Celia inclined her head and kept on walking, straight for the alley door, and sped up once she reached the stairs. Out onto the street, she glanced both directions, in case Mr. Greaves or his assistant were nearby.

"Is it clear?" asked Jane, stealing out into the alleyway behind her.

"I do not see either of them."

She and Jane hurried up the alley and around the edge of the building to where Jane had parked the tilbury when they'd arrived. They clambered onto the seat.

"What are you hoping to learn at the Institute though, Celia?" asked Jane, releasing the brake. "Mr. Greaves will interrogate the women involved and unearth the truth."

"None of them have divulged the truth so far," Celia replied, arranging her skirts and securing her hat. "And they may continue to refuse to be honest. So I seek evidence there, Jane. Evidence that might force an admission of guilt out of one—or all—of them, should Mr. Greaves fail to be persuasive."

Jane steered the tilbury toward Sutter. "I do hope Miss Campbell isn't involved."

"So do I, Jane. But I've hoped and been wrong before."

⌀ Chapter 19 ⌀

"Have you found Mrs. Wynn's murderer, Detective?" The landlady had opened the front door with a harried look on her face. This made the third time Nick had been to her boardinghouse, and he was coming to believe the expression was permanent.

"We've got a man awaiting indictment," he replied.

"Thank goodness," she exclaimed, her expression briefly rearranging into relief. "My ladies have been scared out of their wits."

"I need to speak to Miss DiPaolo," he said.

"She went out right after breakfast—to Calvary Cemetery, she claimed—and hasn't been back since," the woman answered.

"You won't mind if I look around her room while she's gone, then."

"Having poor Mrs. Wynn brutally struck down in my backyard has been hard on my lodgers, Detective. The ladies won't like police rummaging around in the house again," she said. "Besides, if you've arrested the brute who killed her, what else do you need from us?"

"Just a few minutes, ma'am," said Nick, his level of irritation rising.

"Are you implying Miss DiPaolo is somehow involved in poor Mrs. Wynn's death?" she asked. "One of my girls? In this very house?"

Yes. "If Miss DiPaolo has got something to hide, ma'am, don't you think you'd like to know?"

That got her attention. "Come with me."

She climbed the stairs. A few of the female lodgers congregated in the ground-floor hallway. Two more looked on from the doorway to the parlor.

The landlady turned right at the first landing. "She's there. The room at the end."

A room that faced the yard in back. Where Giulia DiPaolo had either noticed Mr. Platt and his distinctive red hair, or she'd spotted Mrs. Wynn slinking across the yard and intercepted her with a broken chunk of cobblestone.

The landlady unlocked the door. "I'm standing right here to make sure you don't take anything."

She stepped aside, making way for him to enter. About ten by six, the room had two windows, their curtains pulled back to let in the midday sun. Brighter and airier than the ones overlooking the cramped light well. He peered out at the yard, yesterday's lines of laundry gone. The shed did block the view of where Mrs. Wynn's body had been dumped. But the fence between the yard and the alley . . . how tall was Platt for Giulia DiPaolo to have been able to see him over its top?

"We scraped up the gravel," said the landlady. "Hope that's okay."

Any reminders of yesterday's tragedy removed with it. "That's okay."

The bed linens were rumpled, a cotton dressing gown tossed on top as if she'd been in a hurry to dress and leave. The washing basin on the dressing table hadn't been emptied, her hairbrush and pins scattered next to it.

Nick pulled open drawers in the chest against the wall. There were clothes inside, which meant she hadn't packed to bolt from town like Mrs. Wynn had attempted. He felt around, through each of the drawers. No tucked-away messages. No store receipts for chloroform. Only stockings, underclothes, a spare petticoat. No evidence of blood on any of them. If she'd murdered Mrs. Wynn and stained her clothing in the process, she must have gotten rid of the proof.

He closed all the drawers and squatted next to the wastepaper basket alongside the dressing table. Nick pulled out the few scraps of paper in the waste bin. A shopping list like the one he'd found at Bauman's. A section of the *Dramatic Review* newspaper, read by a young woman who might have aspirations beyond warbling in a Barbary saloon. A handbill from the Hygienic Institute.

"What's that you've found?" asked the landlady, leaning through the doorway.

Nick held the paper aloft. "Was Miss DiPaolo ever a patient at the Hygienic Institute?"

"Where that politician fellah died?"

"The same."

"Don't think so." She squinted at the pamphlet in Nick's hand. "Mighta gotten that from Althea."

He folded the handbill and shoved it into his coat pocket. At the very bottom of the waste bin was a crumpled paper wrapper printed with the name Roesler's.

"That came from her beau, I expect," said the landlady.

"Ambrose Shaw?" he asked, tucking the wrapper alongside the handbill.

"Ambrose? No, his name's Leo," she said. "He should be asking her to marry him any day now."

Well, well, Miss DiPaolo. The inappropriate woman worth spoiling dinner at the Shaws' to argue about. The unnamed female who was Leo Shaw's alibi for an early departure from a boring Wednesday night meeting of the San Francisco Club. And possibly the reason he'd stopped in Bauman's last evening.

The building's front door closed, prompting a fury of whispering among the women standing in the ground-floor hallway. Nick jumped to his feet, sprinted to the head of the stairs, and leaned over the banister.

"Don't even think of running off, Miss DiPaolo," he shouted down to the woman, her hand on the doorknob, preparing to do just that.

She lowered her hand and looked up at him. The eyes of the other lodgers clustered around her did likewise. "Good afternoon, Detective," she said. "Are you here to take me to the station?"

• • •

Jane brought the tilbury to a halt outside the Hygienic Institute, its windows shuttered against the world. Their arrival attracted the attention of the gawkers collected outside on the pavement, who pointed their direction and murmured. One yelled out for them to be careful.

"After we spoke yesterday, I came here and left a note saying to expect us, but it doesn't look open," said Jane.

No one from the Institute came to take charge of the carriage, forcing them to leave it and the horse in the hands of the most trustworthy-appearing of the boys who scrambled forward to do the job.

"This will be a short trip if the facility is closed," said Celia. "What excuse did you offer for why we desired an appointment this after-noon?"

"A vague comment about feeling under the weather," said Jane, tidying her skirts as she stepped onto the pavement alongside Celia.

"Adequate." Celia looked over at her friend. "Shall we?"

Jane nodded, and Celia pushed open the door. A bell rang in the depths of the building. Within seconds, Mr. Ross darted from the hallway at the rear of the entry hall.

"Ladies, welcome! Were we expecting you?" he asked, striding across the marble entry hall with a wide smile, his hands outstretched toward Celia and Jane.

"I left a note yesterday," replied Jane.

He glanced around the entryway, seeking out the displaced missive. "I don't know why I didn't receive it. Well, no matter. I bid you welcome!"

He had changed out of the clothes he'd worn to Mr. Shaw's burial service, the hems of his trousers dirtied by the dusty paths of the cemetery, and into a clean gray suit with matching silk waistcoat. Why go to the effort, Celia wondered, when the likelihood of patients arriving under the current circumstances was so remote. Perhaps a superstitious faith that dressing for guests meant guests would appear.

And, ta-da, we had.

"I am Mrs. Davies and this is Mrs. Hutchinson," said Celia. "I must say, your facility is more impressive than I had heard."

To their right, a parlor, supplied with a healthy quantity of tables and overstuffed chairs, opened off the vestibule. *The parlor also possesses a clear view of the entry hall and main staircase.* Which made it difficult for

Miss Shaw to have climbed those steps without being noticed. Unless the parlor had been empty or she'd found another way to get to her father's room. Or she'd not needed to sneak upstairs, because someone else had supplied her with his key.

On their left and further along was the door to the dining room, the end of a long table just visible. At the end, the hallway from which Mr. Ross had emerged cut a right angle, the muffled clink of crockery indicating the location of the kitchen. The building's central staircase rose straight ahead, its brightly patterned carpet worn but clean, the wood banister polished, the air scented by the fading flowers of a large bouquet. A Frederick Butman landscape of a majestic mountain towering above a pristine lake graced the wall.

"Very comfortable," Celia added.

He was not paying attention. Instead, he'd been eyeing her over the rim of his spectacles. "Haven't I seen you someplace recently, Mrs. Davies?"

A hasty glance took in Celia's unconventional attire. Thank goodness she'd exchanged her dark blue dress for her brown skirt and Garibaldi; he'd have been more likely to remember her from the cemetery, standing alongside the police detective investigating Mr. Shaw's murder, if she'd not. The less Mr. Ross knew about her connection to the case, the better her chances of examining the premises without interference.

"I do not believe we have ever met, Mr. Ross," she said, feigning bewilderment. "Unless you recently attended a charity function hosted by the Ladies' Society of Christian Aid?"

"No, I haven't."

"Perhaps you have seen my doppelgänger, then. I have heard so much about your establishment," she said, moving to a safer topic. "And my friend here is eager to partake of its offerings."

"I was not intending to open the Institute today." His pleasant demeanor slipped. "We've suffered some dreadful news lately."

"The crowds outside are distressing," Celia tutted sympathetically.

"They're back again?" He shot a look at the closed front door before turning back to her. "Are you here to discover if what the newspapers are saying is true? That my establishment is a danger to the citizens of San Francisco?"

Jane was quick to comment. "No, certainly not, Mr. Ross. We don't believe what they're saying at all."

"You are one of the few, Mrs. Hutchinson," he said, his affable manner restored. "So, how might I assist you two ladies?"

"Do you have electrothermal baths? I've heard about those," said Jane.

"Yes, we do, in addition to our cold- and hot-water bathing therapies," he replied. "I am shorthanded, but I could summon my day-nurse, should you desire an invigorating Swedish movement treatment. I assure you that your muscles and body will feel refreshed and reinvigorated afterward. We also offer a course of medical gymnastics, or perhaps a lengthy wrap in cold bandages."

"On a chilly day like today, a cold-water treatment sounds freezing," said Jane, appearing startled by the concept of being encased in bandages like an Egyptian mummy. "Just a hot-water bath, I think, Mr. Ross."

"And what about you, Mrs. Davies?"

"My dear young friend, Miss Campbell, has informed me that the vegetarian diet you offer here is first-class," she said. "Miss Campbell was here to receive treatment for her paralytic arm, which pains her so. You may recall her."

He tilted his head to one side. "Miss Campbell . . . I might recollect her. Paralytic pains, you say? No doubt she made use of one of our many treatments designed for attending to such conditions."

Frustratingly, his reply did not reveal if Libby Campbell had actually ever been a patient there.

"No doubt she did," said Celia. "Is it too late for a light meal, Mr. Ross? I have heard nothing but praise for your food, and that is what I've come for. I do realize it is past the lunch hour, and your cook may not be available, however . . ."

"Mary Ann is here today. She's been taking advantage of this . . . this slow period to engage in a most thorough cleaning of the kitchen," said Mr. Ross. "She would be more than happy to provide a light meal, Mrs. Davies."

"How fortunate, Celia," said Jane.

"Indeed," said Celia. "I will be happy to wait in the parlor. I see there are books and magazines available."

"Only the most improving of reading materials." He extended his arm toward the staircase descending behind him. "Mrs. Hutchinson, if you would follow me to our treatment rooms on the lower floor. I'll have Mary Ann come and assist, so you've no need to worry. Everything is done with the greatest decorum and privacy."

A multitalented cook, apparently.

Jane handed off her reticule, bonnet, and shawl to Celia and accompanied him. In case he looked back, Celia strolled into the parlor as though she meant to read his "improving materials." He called for Mary Ann, his voice echoing off the hard stone floor, and another set of footsteps scurried to join those of Mr. Ross and Jane.

Celia deposited Jane's belongings, along with her own items, onto the nearest chair. Returning to the entry hall, she searched for a visitors' logbook. But the gate-legged table it probably had occupied stood empty against the wall. Had Mr. Greaves or Mr. Taylor taken it? *Blast.* Without the book and its entries, she still lacked proof that Miss Campbell had been a patient.

"Now what, then?"

Time to research alternative ways to arrive at Mr. Shaw's first-floor suite. She did not have to worry about Mr. Platt interrupting her investigation this time. She tiptoed up the staircase, alert to a telltale creak of the treads that might bring the cook or Mr. Ross running. The treads remained silent, though, and she arrived at the first floor without drawing attention to herself. A small private dining parlor, its table and chairs covered by a holland dustcloth, was located to the left of the stairwell. The closed doors of guest rooms stretched ahead, the air in the hallway stuffy. At the far end was a door—the private entrance, no doubt—where Mrs. Wynn had detected an intruder.

The room assigned to Mr. Shaw was marked with a small plaque labeled *Blue Suite*. Unsurprisingly, the door was locked, as were the others. It was dreadfully dark in the hallway, the only light the meager amount the stairwell windows provided. Without guests, Mr. Ross had no need to set alight the gas fixtures suspended high upon the walls. The knob of the door leading onto the private staircase turned easily in her hand, however. The stairwell windows, opening onto the alleyway Celia had snuck down to test that key, were far smaller and gave even less light than the main stairwell's.

She descended the steps. At the bottom was the door that probably led onto the alley. Opposite it, another door stood partly open. She peered around the edge. Beyond was a hallway leading to the kitchen, passing other service rooms on its way. The exterior door was private, so long as one had a key to open it with. Otherwise, there appeared no other ready means to gain access to the side stairwell.

Celia retreated upstairs again, back into the first-floor hallway. She stared at Mr. Shaw's secured room. The only way an outsider could arrive at this spot was by climbing the main staircase or by utilizing the private entrance, which required that bloody key. The one the killer had planted on Mina, unconscious in the alley, after they'd finished incapacitating Mr. Shaw with chloroform. Killing him, a man with a weak heart . . .

"Who'd had difficulty sleeping," Celia murmured aloud.

Rebecca Shaw had told her as much, that first day at the studio. A comment she would not have made if she'd planned to murder her father that same night. What better remedy for poor sleep than an application of anesthetic, though? Despite Mr. Ross's assertion to the police that he did not use the substance, perhaps he'd purchased some for the needs of his wealthy client, who'd also been allowed to indulge his fondness for alcohol. Perhaps he'd dosed Mr. Shaw with a chemical that had not proved helpful but deadly.

"Excuse me, ma'am?"

The voice startled her. It belonged to a pleasant-looking young woman, an apron tied over her checked drab dress. "Ma'am?"

Celia's cheeks heated. "I do apologize for being overly inquisitive, but I have heard so much about the Institute's accommodations that I simply had to see them for myself."

"None of the rooms are open," she said. "You must be the lady hoping to have a meal."

"I am."

"I'm the cook. My name's Mary Ann," she said. "Do you want to eat in the dining room or the small parlor?"

"The dining room would be fine," said Celia, joining her at the head of the stairs. "This is indeed a very fine establishment."

"If it survives," said Mary Ann, descending the steps.

"Oh, I do hope it shall," said Celia. "My friend Miss Campbell has nothing but praise about the time she spent here. Do you recall her? She has a paralytic arm that causes her much pain, but such a winning manner."

"I do remember her, but it's been months since she was a patient of ours. Sweet young thing. I did feel sorry for her."

So Libby *had* been a resident, which she'd denied. But who was Celia's main suspect now?

"Miss Campbell feels terrible about forgetting to return the key she had been provided," she said.

"Oh? She can just bring it back whenever." Mary Ann rounded the newel post at the bottom of the stairs and indicated the dining room. "You can wait in there, ma'am, but it'll be another twenty minutes or so before I have your food ready, since I have to help Mr. Ross downstairs with your friend."

"Not a problem in the least."

"A nice leek soup and simple dressed salad is what I'll be preparing."

"Sounds delicious. Thank you," said Celia, turning into the dining room. It was surprisingly large and outfitted with a sizable walnut table and shield-back chairs. A marble-top sideboard held silver-plated serving dishes, which gleamed in the midday sunshine. Mr. Ross had spared no expense. "I hope Miss Campbell has the opportunity to return. Her good friend, Miss DiPaolo—do you know her, also?—is gathering the funds necessary to pay for another treatment."

"Don't think we've had a Miss DiPaolo here, ma'am. That's kind of her, though."

Ah.

"I was surprised to hear from Mr. Ross that this establishment once made use of chloroform liniments to treat the sort of condition Miss Campbell suffers from," she said, slanting the cook a sideways glance to observe her reaction to Celia's lie. "I am pleased, though, that he has now converted to the truth of the purity of the water treatment."

Mary Ann looked shocked. No, more than shocked. Horrified. "He admitted to having used chloroform?"

Look how many of them have killed their patients . . . A prescient comment by Celia's patient, the one with the nettle rash. *A comment I should have more closely heeded.*

"Should he not have done, Miss Newcomb?" she asked.

"I'm just . . . I need to get to the kitchen, ma'am, and get your meal prepared. So if you'll excuse me," she said, rushing from the room.

• • •

"I'm sorry about Mina, Detective." Head down, Giulia DiPaolo perched on the chair in front of Nick's desk. She stared at the floor, maybe noticing how filthy it was. Maybe spotting an ant or two. "I didn't mean to hurt her."

Nick shut the door to the detectives' office and went to sit across from her. "Well, you did."

She clutched a plain cotton handkerchief in her lap, squeezed it nervously. "I was scared and not thinking straight."

He settled onto his chair. Taylor hadn't returned to the station with

Miss Campbell; hopefully he would soon, because Nick needed him to take notes.

"Scared because you'd just killed a man," he said.

"But I didn't kill anyone!" She leaned forward, stretching her hand toward him. "You've got to believe me, Detective. Mr. Shaw was already dead."

He retrieved the advertisement for the Hygienic Institute and spread it flat on his desk. "I found this in your room, Miss DiPaolo, along with a paper used to wrap candies. A gift from Leonard Shaw?"

"Yes," she replied, sitting back again.

"What about the box that was delivered to Bauman's this week?"

She frowned. "Those were from Ambrose. A bit of a bad joke to get under my skin."

And just how much did they irritate you? "Did you and Leonard work together to get rid of his father, Miss DiPaolo? Ambrose had to have opposed your relationship. Stood in the way of getting married."

"We did not work together to kill Mr. Shaw," she said. "I went to the Institute to find a document Ambrose had shown to Leo."

"A document," said Nick, resting his elbows on the chair arms and tenting his fingers.

"It supposedly proved I couldn't marry Leo because I'd been in a common-law marriage," she explained. "With a man down in Los Angeles. I'd told Leo about the fellow, but—"

"But not that you and this man had been married."

"It was a lie!" she insisted. "I'd lived with him—I was desperately poor, then—but we'd never pretended to be a married couple. It wasn't like that at all."

Funny how folks might believe otherwise, when a man and a woman shared a home.

Knuckles rapped on the door and it opened, Taylor slipping inside the room. He shook his head. "Couldn't locate her, sir. Want me to . . ." He tapped his coat pocket where he usually stored his notebook.

"Yes, Taylor." Nick waited for his assistant to get prepared before continuing with the woman across from him. "Did Leonard believe you, Miss DiPaolo? About the common-law marriage never happening."

She chewed her bottom lip. Nope, he hadn't believed her.

"Leo said he couldn't marry me, not with that sort of report out there," she said, her voice not as forceful as it had been. "So I thought I'd take care of matters myself."

"By killing Ambrose Shaw and stealing the incriminating document," said Nick. "It wasn't in his room at the Institute, Miss DiPaolo. One of my men would've found it, if it had been."

"I didn't kill anyone," she repeated. "And I don't know why you didn't find that paper. It should have been in that room, because I didn't take it."

Nick tapped his fingertips together. "How did you get inside the Institute?"

"Libby gave me a key."

"Olivia Campbell, you mean," he said. "You met her through Rebecca Shaw."

"I did. At her studio during one of her portrait sessions. Rebecca is an amazing woman." Her eyes gleamed with respect. "I find her so inspiring."

"And how did Miss Campbell come by that key?"

"From Rebecca," she said. "She got ahold of it somehow."

You were right, Mrs. Davies, about these women.

"They are both so awfully clever, and desperately wanted to help me, once I told them about that document." Miss DiPaolo flashed a smile. Brief and out of place, given the gravity of her situation. "Libby had once been a patient at the Institute and knew its routine, when dinner was served and Mr. Shaw wouldn't be in his room. Told me how to find the private door and get to his suite without anybody noticing. Our plan was going to work beautifully. I'd grab that piece of paper, and Leo and I would be free to wed."

"You'd grab that document when dinner was being served . . . seven thirty?" he asked.

"No, I was at Bauman's before then," she said. "I arrived at the Institute around quarter 'til seven."

"That's a pretty precise recollection, Miss DiPaolo," he said.

"I'm sure of the time because there's a bank on the corner with a big clock," she replied. "It was chiming forty-five minutes after the hour when I hurried past it."

Bauman *had* told him she'd shown up for work by seven. "However, you brought chloroform along to knock out Mr. Shaw in case things didn't go as smoothly as Libby Campbell claimed it should," said Nick. "Were you surprised when the substance caused his heart to fail?"

"I didn't bring any chloroform with me. Why would I? Mr. Shaw was supposed to be out of his suite, having dinner." She shuddered. "God, it was awful. The room smelled of coal gas, and he was so unnaturally white . . ."

Nick studied her. Out in the main room, the booking officer clanged his keys against the holding cells door, the harsh sound making Giulia DiPaolo wince. "What happened after you—supposedly—found Mr. Shaw deceased and fled his room?"

"I was sobbing, so frightened I could hardly see, stumbled back down the steps and out the side door," she said, gathering her strength. "I ran into Mina in the alley. She'd followed me, I think. She must have overheard me telling Leo I meant to get ahold of that document. He tried to stop me, Detective. He said Libby's and my plan wouldn't work."

Nick questioned if there ever *had* been a document reporting her common-law marriage. Maybe Leonard Shaw had made up the story about his father showing it to him, looking for an excuse to break off his relationship with a tavern girl after an argument with his parents.

"You went ahead anyway," he said. "And Mina Cascarino came to the wrong conclusion about your intentions."

"She misunderstood what I meant to do," she said. "She was worried about me. That was stupid. Mina shouldn't bother to worry about someone like me."

Taylor scribbled furiously, snapping the tip of his pencil. Nick tossed him a replacement so he could continue.

"Mina Cascarino tends to care about the wrong people." People like Giulia DiPaolo. People like him. "So you ran out and saw her . . ."

"Out in the alley. She shouted—*what have you done?* She must've thought I'd killed him." She pressed her lips together. "I panicked—I mean, Mr. Shaw was dead and here I'd come screaming out of the building like I was guilty—and shoved her. Really hard. She fell and smacked her head on the ground, knocked her cold. I was scared half to death you'd figure out what had happened. Or she would tell you. I thought it was a stroke of luck that she'd forgotten everything."

How long had Mina lain in that alleyway, drifting in and out of consciousness? Finally rousing herself, but leaving her blue shawl behind. "The luck was that her fall didn't kill her, Miss DiPaolo."

She took to staring at the floor again.

"Did you leave the key to the private entrance in Mina's pocket?" Nick asked. Mrs. Davies's solution to the question.

She nodded. She'd supposedly been half-crazed with fear after finding Shaw dead, but clearheaded enough to leave an incriminating piece of evidence with the woman whose biggest mistake had been to worry about Giulia DiPaolo.

"Leonard Shaw came to Bauman's last night. To talk to you?"

"I'd sent a message, asking him to stop in," she said. "He hadn't been by the saloon in days, and I wanted to explain what had happened Wednesday night. He wouldn't listen. He told me we were finished."

"Mighty coldhearted, miss," said Taylor, sympathizing. Clearly, he believed her story; Nick wasn't convinced.

"Rebecca believed me, though," she said. "That I hadn't killer her father."

She had been the woman Mrs. Davies had spotted with Rebecca Shaw. "You spoke with her early yesterday morning?"

"I did. We spoke for a long while, and it was her idea to try to talk to Leo again. At the cemetery today. But he wouldn't even look at me. I may as well have been one of the statues." The tears she'd been holding back welled in her eyes and she began to cry. "I may as well have been dead."

"Now, miss, it's gonna be okay," soothed Taylor.

Nick exhaled and waited for Miss DiPaolo to regain her composure.

"If you didn't kill Ambrose Shaw, Miss DiPaolo, who did?" he asked. "Leonard? He stood to inherit a lot of money, plus his alibi isn't holding up. He left his meeting of the San Francisco Club early. Really early."

"He wasn't at the Parker House Wednesday night?"

"He's told me he left early because he had a meeting with a lady friend, Miss DiPaolo," said Nick. "I take it that lady friend wasn't you."

"He lied to me, lied to my face when he stopped in the saloon last night. Said he still cared, even with that document, but it was going to be impossible for us to ever be together." She let out a mirthless chuckle. "Impossible to be together because he's fallen in love with someone else."

Probably so, thought Nick. "Miss Campbell gave you that key, but could she have made a copy for herself? She despised Shaw," he said. "Maybe *she* got to him before you showed up in Shaw's room. Knew you'd be arriving there soon and might take the fall for the crime."

"No." She shook her head, maybe hoping the rapid motion would dislodge the thought he'd put there. "Libby hated Ambrose, but she'd never kill somebody."

"She's told an associate she was with Elliot Blanchard Wednesday evening." All of their suspects tangled together like coiled barbed wire. Or a writhing mass of snakes.

"That's where she'd gone . . ." Her eyes met his. "I didn't kill Mr. Shaw, Detective, and I didn't kill Althea. She was a friend, one of the few I have. I'd never hurt her."

"Did she spot you running out of Shaw's room?"

"She couldn't have seen me, Detective. She was downstairs when I snuck in through the side door. I heard her voice, echoing along the ground-floor passageway, and that's the truth," she said. "But I did lie to you about spying that redheaded fellow in the alley yesterday morning. I'd seen him at the Institute when Libby took me there to show me the side entrance. Why not blame him?"

"Because he's locked up right now, accused of murder based on your false claim, but might actually be innocent?" asked Nick, getting hot with anger. He didn't much like Platt, but he didn't want the man to hang for a crime he hadn't committed.

"I shouldn't have. I know," she said. "I did hear noises around the time Mrs. Wynn was murdered, but I didn't get up and look out the window like I said."

"You wanted us to believe you'd heard a man's voice because you were actually afraid one of your friends was responsible, weren't you, Miss DiPaolo?"

She covered her mouth with her hand; it was shaking, hard. "For a moment I was."

Nick studied Giulia DiPaolo, her ashen complexion, her anxious trembling. Damn, but her story made sense. Unfortunately, it brought them no closer to figuring out who had killed Shaw.

He pushed back from his desk. "Taylor, escort Miss DiPaolo home."

She didn't move, bewilderment at her unexpected release leaving her glued to her chair. "I'm free to go?"

"I could arrest you for assault, but I have a feeling Mina Cascarino won't press charges."

Miss DiPaolo slowly rose to her feet. "I don't know who killed Ambrose Shaw, Detective. I wish I did."

"I'm going to trust you for now, Miss DiPaolo, but don't make any plans to leave town. We'll be keeping an eye on you, in case you get any ideas along those lines," said Nick, standing. "And you might want to watch your back, miss. Because if you're innocent, that means a murderer is still on the loose. And if that person knew where to find Mrs. Wynn, they know where to find you."

ᗌ Chapter 20 ᗌ

"Did Miss DiPaolo say anything else to you, Taylor?" Nick asked his assistant, returned from escorting the young woman to her boarding-house.

"No, sir," he replied, settling in next to Nick, who leaned against the iron fence surrounding Portsmouth Square. "Other than to ask me why you let her go free."

"I did because of what she told us. She admitted to causing Mina's concussion and planting the key on her. She also admitted to lying about seeing Platt yesterday morning," he said. "In my experience, Taylor, that's not what folks guilty of murder do. They don't admit anything."

"Suppose so, sir."

Nick resumed his contemplation of the square. It was quiet, aside from the whinny of horses tethered to the line of cabs waiting for passengers, the tap of a gentleman's walking stick on the sidewalk passing in front of City Hall at Nick's back, a steamer whistle echoing up from the bay. The corner barker's cries had halted, the fellow either having given up on luring customers into the store or gone off to lunch. Nick liked to come out here and stare at the patch of dusty grass and shrubs. Enough green to help him think.

"Well, Miss DiPaolo couldn't have been the intruder Mrs. Wynn saw at seven thirty," said his assistant, scanning the entrances of the neighboring saloons, on the alert for any evidence of midday rowdies. The Bella Union Melodeon wouldn't open for another few hours, giving Taylor one less business to scrutinize. "So who did she see?"

"Maybe nobody."

"Mrs. Wynn lied to us?"

Nick didn't have to look at Taylor's face to know he was wrinkling his forehead; he could hear the confusion in his assistant's voice.

"All right, Taylor, let's reconstruct events, based on what we've been told." He drew in a breath, catching a whiff of fish frying at a nearby restaurant, and thought back on what they knew. Or had been told. "At ten before six, Mary Ann Newcomb takes a tray of food to Shaw, who's having his meal upstairs. She returns to the kitchen to finish preparing dinner, where she encounters Mrs. Wynn, enquiring about the evening's menu. The patients begin gathering a few minutes after six and Miss Newcomb serves dinner."

"Around six fifteen, right?"

"Correct," he said. "Mrs. Wynn gets into a fight with one of the male patients and storms upstairs about fifteen minutes later, claiming to notice Shaw—alive—in the small parlor on the way to her room. Here's our first problem, Taylor—how long does it take *you* to eat a meal by yourself? Forty minutes?"

"Fifteen, twenty, maybe?" Taylor answered. "Although I do eat fast. Just ask Miss Ferg . . . ahem, friends of mine."

"Taylor, you can say Addie Ferguson's name around me, you know."

"I just presume you don't want to be reminded of Mrs. Davies and all, sir."

"Don't worry about that, Taylor," said Nick. He always thought about the war; he'd always think about Celia Davies, too. "So, where was I? Ah, Mrs. Wynn's claim that she'd seen Shaw loitering in the parlor at six thirty should've been my first clue that she wasn't being fully honest."

"Why lie, sir?" asked Taylor.

"Because he wasn't alive then, but she wanted us to think he was?" proposed Nick. He was trusting his instincts on this case, hoping they wouldn't fail him.

"If she'd lied about Mr. Shaw still being alive, sir, then there might not have been an intruder at seven thirty, either."

"Precisely," agreed Nick. "Back to our timeline. Mina Cascarino departs Bauman's, around six thirty, worried about what Giulia DiPaolo is up to."

"If Miss Mina went straight to the Hygienic Institute, she would've gotten there in about ten minutes," said Taylor.

"Or fifteen," said Nick. "Miss DiPaolo is bound for the Institute with a key Miss Campbell has supplied. She enters the building around six forty-five, hears Mrs. Wynn's voice from the kitchen. The woman had returned there after a few minutes spent upstairs."

"Miss Newcomb did also say that Mrs. Wynn was in the kitchen from around then until about seven thirty," said Taylor, bending down to scrape a match across the ground in order to light a cigar.

"Therefore, that part of Miss DiPaolo's story is corroborated by another witness," said Nick. "She makes her way to Shaw's suite only to find him dead."

"She claims."

Nick looked over. "I thought you were rather sweet on her, Taylor, and believed her story."

He blushed. "Me? Sweet on Miss Giulia? I just like her singing, that's all, sir."

"Anyway, let's presume she's telling the truth." Nick glanced over at the gentlemen's clothing store. A different fellow had come to stand outside it, proceeding to sing praises about their supply of satinet pants and pilot cloth jackets. "Miss DiPaolo's not in the building long, running outside and bumping into Mina, who's tracked her down. In thanks for worrying about Giulia, the woman attacks Mina, who hits her head. Miss DiPaolo plants the key on her and rushes to the saloon, arriving around seven, according to Bauman."

"I'm glad Miss Mina's not guilty, sir," said Taylor, cigar smoke drifting on the air, sweet and pungent.

So was he. "Oblivious to the assault out in the side alley, the Institute's male guests finish their dinner and retire to the parlor," said Nick. "Meanwhile, Platt arrives at work around seven and meets with Ross to discuss their overnight guests. Their meeting concludes and Ross heads home. In the parlor, the male patients proceed to break a crystal pitcher, causing Mary Ann and Platt to chase them off in order to clean up the mess. Platt tells Mary Ann he has matters under control and she's free to go. Not long after, Mrs. Wynn comes shrieking back downstairs claiming to have spotted an intruder. It's now just past seven thirty."

"An intruder who might never have actually existed, because she'd wanted to blame stealing that watch on somebody else."

"Right," said Nick. "Platt sends for Ross, who summons the police. Mina, suffering from a concussion, manages to stumble home between seven thirty and eight." *Where I then accused her of killing Ambrose Shaw.*

"Sir, don't you think it's possible Mrs. Wynn did spot Miss DiPaolo sneaking in—or out—of the building and gave us a false time in order to protect her friend?" asked his assistant. "When Mrs. Wynn went into Mr. Shaw's room to steal his watch and saw he was dead, she about had to conclude Miss DiPaolo had killed him."

"Maybe she did, Taylor," he said.

"Hmm." Taylor puffed on his cigar for a few seconds before plucking it from his mouth. "What should we do about Mr. Platt?"

"Leave him in his cell for now," said Nick. Across the way, a fellow slowed and halted in front of the gentlemen's clothing store, the barker taking advantage of the man's potential interest to snag his coat sleeve and drag him inside. *Glad one of us is having good luck today.* "None of this is resolved yet. None of it."

"So who *was* it who'd soaked that handkerchief with chloroform and tossed out that bottle?" His assistant resumed smoking his cigar and talked around it. "If Giulia DiPaolo's not responsible."

Nick shifted on his hip to face his assistant. "You know, Taylor, the handkerchief Miss DiPaolo brought with her to the station wasn't like the one Harris found. Hers was simple cotton. The handkerchief underneath Shaw was a good-quality, embroidered linen." A fancy gray pattern decorating the edges. "Harris and I assumed it was one he'd brought with him, as nice as it was. But what if it wasn't?"

"Miss DiPaolo wouldn't have doused an expensive handkerchief in chloroform if she had cheaper ones on hand," said Taylor. "Meaning she really is telling the truth about finding Mr. Shaw dead."

His comment spurred a memory. *Damn.* "I've seen stacks of fine linen handkerchiefs elsewhere, Taylor."

"Like the one in Mr. Shaw's room?"

"Not an exact match, but if we search again, maybe we'll come across one just like it."

"Where at, sir?" asked Taylor, stubbing out his cigar.

"At the Hygienic Institute," he said. "In a supply closet."

• • •

*T*wenty minutes.

Not much time to discover where a supply of chloroform might be stored.

She should have more seriously considered Mr. Ross's culpability, rather than imagine a man with so much to lose by having a guest perish at his water-cure establishment meant he was an unlikely candidate. Mrs. Wynn must have discerned he was the intruder—except he hadn't been intruding at all—lied about not recognizing the person, and sought to escape the city in hopes of saving her life. Except he had uncovered her plans and prevented her.

"In a very cruel fashion," whispered Celia, leaning through the dining room doorway and casting a glance in the direction of the kitchen. A heavy utensil tapped against the edge of a pot, and Mary Ann muttered to herself. The cook had returned from the basement where Jane was receiving her treatment. At the hands of the fellow who may be a murderer.

Jane will be safe. Mr. Ross had no reason to suspect she was involved in the case and would not harm her. *I must not worry.*

Where, though, would the final proof required to convict the man be located? A storage cupboard, likely downstairs near the treatment area. Which would take Celia perilously close to the room where Jane would be soaking in a hot-water bath. Mr. Ross would not stay with her, though, and could be wandering about anywhere.

Celia tiptoed from the dining room, her heart beating a rat-a-tat against her ribs for fear her heels might strike the checkerboard marble floor. She reached the staircase without incident, however, and stole down. The air turned damper, smelled faintly dank. But the hallway was bright, the walls whitewashed and lit by gas lamps. To her left were the treatment rooms, every door closed but clearly labeled in large, florid black lettering. *Steam Bath, Electro Thermal Bath, Vapor Bath*, read the nearest. Jane must be farther along the hall. Celia listened for voices and heard only the faraway drip of water. Perhaps Mr. Ross had returned to the main floor. Giving Celia the only opportunity she'd have to locate the storage cupboard.

"Which needs to be unlocked and containing incriminating bottles of chloroform," she whispered to herself.

She turned right, hugging the wall as she passed more doors, these unmarked. She sped along the passageway, searching for the cupboard that had to exist, feeling sweat rise along her hairline. At last, she came upon a narrow door at the very end, its sign reading *Supplies–Private.*

Here goes nothing.

To her utter astonishment, the door was unlocked. Celia stepped inside and shut the door behind her. The room was dark, the blinds on the cupboard's small window closed tight, and she took a precious few moments to allow her eyes to adjust. She hadn't much time at all; within minutes, the soup would be ready and the cook would be delivering it to the dining room. Expecting to find Celia waiting.

As quickly as she could, she rummaged through the items stacked upon the shelving that lined both walls. Towels, rags and scrubbing brushes, spare necessities for guests who may have forgotten to bring the items from home—hair nets and horn combs, packages of tooth powders, an open box of linen handkerchiefs interspersed with bits of camphor to ward off moths. No bottles of chloroform, however.

She turned to the other shelves, holding more of the same. Putty powder for cleaning grates. A quantity of hearthstones for whitening doorsteps and windowsills. Candles and colorful paper boxes of washing soaps and starch. She bent down, hastily moving aside a short pile of blankets on a lower shelf. They collided with an object, which tipped off the shelf. A tin of pulverized sand for scouring floors that clanged to the ground.

"Blast!" she hissed and rushed over to the door. She pressed her ear against the wood, straining to hear the footsteps she anticipated would be running down the hall. Nothing.

Letting herself breathe again, she resumed searching through the shelves. Each passing second was forcing her to accept she might not find the evidence she hunted for. She knelt and reached between a set of coverlets, each one carefully wrapped in sheets of paper sprinkled with spirits of turpentine. The smell made her eyes water, but the effort was worth it.

"Aha!" she exclaimed, withdrawing the clear glass bottle she'd found at the very back, its caoutchouc stopper sealed with a glued strip of unbroken paper, the label on its front proclaiming the contents to be *Chloroform*.

She clambered to her feet, the bottle clutched in her fist. Not definite proof that Mr. Ross had used the substance on Mr. Shaw, but it *was* evidence he'd misled the police about storing chloroform on the premises. Why lie if he was not guilty?

The door flung open. "What are you doing in here?"

Celia swung to face the voice and its owner, who was hefting a thick-handled and very dangerous-looking scrub brush overhead.

Gad.

• • •

"We've been questioning if Mrs. Wynn had concocted a story with a fake timeline in order to protect Giulia DiPaolo," said Nick, he and Taylor dodging a buggy steered by a kid who looked no older than Owen Cassidy. A boy laughing over his reckless driving until he realized he'd almost run down a policeman. "But what if she'd been protecting somebody else?"

"Miss Campbell?" asked Taylor. "Or maybe Miss Shaw."

"I'm not sure she knew either of those ladies."

"Well, it wouldn't have been Mr. Platt she'd been trying to protect," said Taylor, leaping across a puddle of filthy water tossed onto the road. "She'd probably have been plenty happy to turn him in."

"I'm thinking of somebody else," said Nick. "A man who'd referred to her as a faithful client. A woman he'd trusted . . ."

"Mr. Ross?" Taylor whistled. "But wait. His wife vouched for him."

"Maybe she was scared of her husband," he said. "Too scared to tell the truth."

"Why kill Ambrose Shaw, though?" asked Taylor. "The fellow's death will likely destroy Mr. Ross's business."

"He'd wanted me to believe Shaw had committed suicide, and I might've, if it hadn't been for that handkerchief and Harris's suspicion the fellow hadn't died from coal gas exposure," Nick replied. "Maybe Ross didn't mean to kill Shaw. Maybe it was a horrible accident."

A boy in oversized, hand-me-down pants and jacket had noticed their headlong race along the street and taken to scurrying after them. "Hey, whatcha doin'? Somebody dead?"

"Police business," declared Taylor. "It's best you hightail it outta here."

"Police business? Wow!" the boy whooped, his excited yell alerting other scruffy kids with too much time on their hands and even more curiosity.

The gaggle of boys chased after Nick and Taylor like an excited pack of puppies. *Great.* Nick rounded the corner just as the bank clock—the one Giulia DiPaolo had mentioned—chimed the hour.

"What in hell is the Hutchinsons' tilbury doing parked in front of the Institute?" Nick snapped. "Don't bother to answer, Taylor. I have a good hunch whose idea it was to come here."

And just how much danger she was in.

He ran, hell-bent for leather.

• • •

The light in the hallway was brighter than inside the storage cupboard, casting the person wielding the brush in shadow. They wore a dress, however, so it wasn't Mr. Ross Celia was dealing with.

"What are you doing in here?" the woman repeated.

"You may put down the brush, Mary Ann," Celia replied, slowly moving the hand holding the chloroform behind her back.

But the cook had the advantage of the lighting, which shed its glow over Celia. "What's that you got there?"

"Nothing." Her voice was trembling. Nearly as much as her legs, which had turned the consistency of aspic. She was alone with Mary Ann Newcomb, and who might come to her rescue, should she scream? Jane, peacefully enjoying a hot-water bath at the far end of the hallway? Mr. Ross, on another floor of the building entirely and conceivably not all that inclined to come to her aid?

"You do have something. In your hand behind your back," said the other woman, inching forward.

There was little sideways space to swing the heavy brush, which she'd turned so that the wood head and not the bristles faced Celia, but plenty of expanse to swing downward. And though Celia was taller than most women, she only had a scant inch on Mary Ann.

"Oh, this." Celia brought out the bottle of chloroform and held it up. "It is most curious that I discovered it stashed behind the coverlets. Did you not remember it was back there? The bottle is a trifle dusty."

"What do you want?"

Someone to distract you. "It was an accident, was it not, that led to Mr. Shaw's death. I am positive you did not mean to hurt him."

The cook was breathing hard, the rasp of air wheezing between her parted lips the only sound Celia could hear. *Can I get past her? Take her by surprise by lunging into her and knocking her to the ground?*

"It *was* an accident." Mary Ann's breath caught in her throat, the brush she wielded quivering. "I was trying to help him. He tried to push away the handkerchief, struggled a bit, but I was only trying to help him."

Oh my heavens. She had confessed. "I am sure you were, Mary Ann. How awful, though, that he perished from the chloroform meant to help him sleep."

"It *was* awful." She'd shifted and a portion of her face was lit by the hallway lamps. Her eyes glittered with an emotion Celia endeavored to read—fear? Regret? Confusion? "Mr. Ross wouldn't use the chloroform. Called it a poison. But I knew where we kept the old bottles."

"And when you heard that the police had discovered the one you'd discarded, you attempted to get rid of the rest."

"That's not when I cleared them out. It was because of Mr. Greaves questioning Mr. Ross about using chloroform in his treatments." The arm holding her improvised weapon drooped. "I realized then that the police had figured out how Mr. Shaw had died. That he hadn't suffocated from coal gas, even though I'd opened the jet. Soon they'd be poking around, hunting for chloroform bottles. I thought I'd found them all down here. Didn't matter, because I'd missed that broken-off piece the officer found in the alley."

Celia's pulse ticked away like a frantic timepiece. "Althea saw you when you ran out of Mr. Shaw's room."

"She'd come back from dinner, earlier than she should've, because of that argument she'd had," said Mary Ann. "I was panicked over what had happened, that Mr. Shaw had died. But Althea said she'd help me. That she'd tell the police and Mr. Ross there'd been an intruder who'd come to steal Mr. Shaw's watch. That it would be okay. I thought she believed me when I said I didn't mean to hurt him."

"When you went outside to discard the chloroform bottle, you must have been startled to encounter a young woman in the alley." Mina Cascarino, trailing after Giulia DiPaolo. "A momentary panic that caused you to strike her down. You left that key in her pocket, did you not, to make it appear she'd been the trespasser."

"There wasn't a young woman in the alley when I tossed out that bottle."

What *had* happened that night?

"But why think Althea Wynn was a threat?" asked Celia. "And why leave me that note?"

"I didn't leave you any note. I don't know what you're talking about."

No? "I do not believe Mrs. Wynn meant to inform Mr. Greaves about you, Mary Ann."

"But she did! That's why she was heading to Crescent City so soon," she said. "I went to see her, Thursday night. The police had asked me to come into the station, and I got scared. I needed to be sure she still believed me. But one of her fellow lodgers said she'd gone to get a boat ticket to leave town the next morning." Mary Ann's voice broke. "She was going to inform the police that I'd killed Mr. Shaw and run off. My friend. I'd thought she was my friend."

Mary Ann began to cry, sobs that shook her body. *Now, Celia, now . . .*

Celia lurched toward her. Mary Ann startled and flourished the thick scrub brush again.

"Don't. Don't make me hurt you, too," she warned.

"You will not get away with it, Mary Ann. My friend is here." *Please, Jane. Please still be all right.* "And Mr. Ross. There will be no one else to blame if I'm struck down."

"I can't go to jail. I can't!"

She lunged, and Celia hurled the chloroform bottle, striking Mary Ann's shoulder before crashing to the floor. Mary Ann recoiled, and Celia sprang at her. Just as a scream echoed along the hall and someone dove through the doorway, tackling Mary Ann from behind, knocking her down and landing on top of her with a wheezing thud.

Celia stumbled backward. "My goodness, Jane. Well done."

A man shouted, and he skidded to a halt in the doorway. "Damn it, Celia," cursed Nicholas Greaves. "Mrs. Hutchinson!"

"Good afternoon, Mr. Greaves," Jane replied calmly, shoving wet hair out of her eyes, the towels and dressing gown she wore tangling around her legs. Mary Ann Newcomb struggled to get out from beneath her. "Don't tell Frank about this. Please."

Mr. Taylor hurtled into the room, halting alongside the detective. "What . . . sir?"

"Help Mrs. Hutchinson up, will you? And take Miss Newcomb away before we all collapse due to chloroform gas." He glowered at Celia. He was not truly angry with her, though; he was scared. "As for you, Mrs. Davies—"

"I am going to help Jane dress," she replied, taking her friend's hand and helping her stand. "I shall meet you at the station to discuss matters once she and I are finished here."

Mr. Taylor hoisted Mary Ann Newcomb to her feet. Jane, as dignified as was possible in bath sheets and a loose gown, accompanied Celia into the hallway.

Mr. Ross slumped against the wall, his spectacles dangling from his hand. "Mary Ann, Mr. Greaves . . . what is the meaning of this?"

What answer might he receive, wondered Celia, that would be satisfactory? *The evil that men do . . .*

Or women in this case, Mr. Shakespeare.

℘ CHAPTER 21 ℞

"Mr. Ross had recommended a quick cold bath after the hot-water bathing session, which I agreed to, and Mary Ann was going to help me move between rooms," said Jane, her hair and clothing in place, her dignity fully restored.

She climbed onto the seat of the tilbury and took the reins from the lad who'd patiently held the horse while mayhem had erupted in the basement of the Institute. Celia climbed aboard, the carriage swaying beneath her weight, and settled onto the seat next to her friend. The crowd that had been standing outside the Hygienic Institute when they'd arrived—she consulted the watch pinned at her waist—forty-five minutes ago had swelled in size. The arrival of policemen followed by Mary Ann Newcomb being loaded onto a police van had sent tremors through those who'd gathered. The notoriety of the Hygienic Institute was guaranteed, unfortunately for Mr. Ross.

"But just when Mary Ann showed up to help me, she heard a noise down the hallway and went to investigate," Jane continued, flicking the reins across the horse's back, setting the animal to a slow walk. Celia expected that neither of them would move or think or breathe with any urgency for the remainder of the day; they'd both endured too much excitement already.

"That was me, Jane, being clumsy," she said. "I knocked a tin of scouring sand onto the floor in my haste to unearth a stash of chloroform, which would prove that Mr. Ross had lied to Mr. Greaves about not having a supply. Incriminating, obviously, but if he'd been honest from the start, Mary Ann Newcomb might have been arrested before she dispatched Mrs. Wynn."

Jane turned the carriage toward the police station. "Do you think she planned in cold blood to kill her friend, Celia?"

"Perhaps she acted purely out of panic," she answered. "She must persuade a judge and jury that her actions occurred in the heat of the moment, though, in order to save herself from the noose."

The horse's hooves clopped on at a steady tempo as they ascended Kearny toward City Hall and the police station, the noises of the city a comforting blanket of normalcy.

"Mary Ann was absolutely skittish when she was assisting me. Dropping things," said Jane. "I didn't pay much attention, though. I was too worried about you."

"I was not in any serious danger until she charged into the storage cupboard with that excessively large scrubbing brush," Celia replied with a wry smile.

"That was when I became alarmed. When she walked off to investigate the noise with that heavy brush," said Jane. "It took me a while to get out of the bath, find something proper to wrap myself in, and figure out where she'd gone. I'm sorry."

"What are you apologizing for?" Celia squeezed her friend's arm. "You may have saved my life. Or at least, saved my skull."

"I should've gotten to you earlier."

"It all worked out. That is what matters most." She gave Jane's arm another squeeze and folded her hands in her lap. She was not as steady and calm as she'd like Jane to imagine; her fingers were trembling.

They passed through the Barbary, blandly innocent on a Saturday afternoon. Not far from where they drove was Bauman's, another busy evening ahead for the saloon. Perhaps Giulia DiPaolo would be there, Mina still recovering at home. Celia needed to visit her as soon as she could in order to inform her she was free of suspicion in any of the crimes. How ready they'd been, though, to consider her guilty.

Celia sighed and cast a look at the passing alleyways, which stretched into the shadows cast by towering buildings and balconies. What mysteries and perils did those dark spaces contain? Ones as terrible as what a desperate young cook had visited upon an equally desperate widow? *Had nearly visited upon me?*

But there was no darkness quite like death, and those who now crept in shadows might one day find themselves emerging into the light, into hope.

"At least we know Rebecca Shaw and Elliot Blanchard are innocent," Jane was saying, unaware of Celia's gloomy thoughts. "And Libby Campbell too, although what a tale she concocted in order to protect Mr. Blanchard."

"I do wonder, Jane, if we can be positive that she lied about being with him that evening," said Celia.

"Oh, dear. Maybe we can't be."

They arrived at City Hall and Jane steered the carriage to the curb.

"What should I tell Frank?" she asked. "He'll read about Miss Newcomb's arrest in the newspapers soon enough and figure out I was at the Institute at the same time."

"Feign innocence, or simply blame me."

"He'll stop allowing me to associate with you if I blame you."

"Since when, Jane, do we permit gentlemen—even if they are husbands—to dictate all that we do?" she asked. She leaned over and kissed her friend upon the cheek. "Thank you and go home and rest. You look positively spent."

"I am tired." She glanced at the police station. "Good luck."

"With Mr. Greaves? I can handle him," said Celia, stepping down from the carriage and straightening her skirts.

Jane sobered. "I wish . . ." Her expression brightened again. "It doesn't matter what I wish. I'll talk to you later. Geeyup," she called to the horse and drove away with a hasty wave of her hand.

Celia waited on the curb until the carriage disappeared from view. *I wish that too, Jane. I wish I could be with him.*

. . .

"Leonard Shaw hired you to snoop on Giulia DiPaolo," said Nick, leaning over Briggs's desk. "To find incriminating information in order to get out of a liaison with the young woman."

Briggs brushed crumbs off his vest and smirked. "I wouldn't exactly say 'hired.'"

"You'd better believe, Briggs, that I'd tell Captain Eagan if you were taking money on the side."

"I turned Shaw down, Greaves, so get off your high horse," he said. "Even though he offered me a pretty sum, and I've been wanting to buy a new rosewood chamber set for the missus."

There was a *Mrs.* Briggs? "Are you responsible for that cock-and-bull story about a document Ambrose Shaw had detailing Miss DiPaolo's supposed common-law marriage?"

"I was sorta proud of that idea."

"Didn't you ever think Miss DiPaolo might do something reckless as a result of that fabricated story?" asked Nick. Problem was, Briggs didn't do enough thinking. "A young woman has a concussion as a result. She could've died."

Briggs puffed out his chest. "Well, she didn't, did she?"

Nick clenched his fist and was about to throw it when a knock interrupted him.

"A Mrs. Davies is here to see you, Mr. Greaves," said one of the station cops, leaning through the doorway, his gaze darting between the two men.

"Your timing's perfect, Officer." Fortunately for Briggs's face. And Nick's job. "Do you mind, Briggs? I'd like to speak with Mrs. Davies alone."

"I'll bet you would." Briggs stomped out of the office, brushing against the officer on his way out.

"Is there something else?" Nick asked the officer.

"A fellow was in about an hour ago, Mr. Greaves, confessing to breaking into Elliot Blanchard's house," he said. "He'd been paid by that politician, Ambrose Shaw, to upset Mr. Blanchard and his wife, apparently. Thought he'd come clean, though, what with Mr. Shaw being murdered. Didn't want to be implicated in that crime. Guess his conscience was bothering him."

"Well, well."

"Then, according to this fellow, one of Mr. Blanchard's supporters decided to retaliate by stalking Mr. Shaw," he continued. "Trying to put a scare into him."

And succeeding.

"Inform Taylor about this once he's finished getting his statement from Miss Newcomb." She'd shuffled into the holding cells with her head down, tears dripping onto the dirty floor, and had crossed paths with Platt, heading the other direction. The man had cackled in disbelief all the way out of the station. "And thank you, Officer."

The cop nodded, stepping aside so Celia Davies could enter the room.

Her smile was warm and lovely. "Forgive me for eavesdropping, but the officer's information was quite interesting, Mr. Greaves."

"Wraps up that part of our investigation." He gestured for her to take a chair and closed the door behind her. "Have to say, Mrs. Davies, you once again beat me to the solution."

He took his chair and leaned back, happy the room was empty except for the two of them. Which meant it didn't feel empty at all.

"You were only a few minutes behind me, Mr. Greaves," she said. "You'd reasoned as I had that the Hygienic Institute held the answer to who'd caused Mr. Shaw's death and murdered Mrs. Wynn."

"I'd searched that supply closet for chloroform bottles yesterday—not as thoroughly as you did, apparently—and noticed the stack of handkerchiefs kept there. Did you see them?"

She inclined her head. "I did."

"A couple are identical to the one Harris discovered wedged beneath Shaw's body. I'd been interrupted while examining the contents of that room—by Mary Ann Newcomb, as it turns out—and didn't pay enough attention to those handkerchiefs. Almost forgot about them entirely until I saw the handkerchief Miss DiPaolo had on her when we brought her into the station," he said. "By the way, she's admitted that she went to Shaw's room Wednesday. Got inside the building with the key Rebecca Shaw had taken and Miss Campbell, acting as intermediary, had handed over. And she *was* the woman you saw with Rebecca Shaw."

"What were their intentions?" she asked. "Murder?"

"No." He explained about the document supposedly proving Giulia DiPaolo had been part of a common-law marriage. "There wasn't any document, though. A story fabricated by Leonard Shaw and Briggs to shake off an undesirable dalliance. She went to search for it, only to find Shaw dead."

"She must have panicked," said Mrs. Davies. "And then to encounter Mina out in the alleyway . . ."

"A brief altercation that got out of hand," he said. "I apologize for ever thinking Mina killed Shaw."

"You should tell *her* that, not me, Mr. Greaves."

"The less Mina Cascarino sees me, Mrs. Davies, the better." But he should apologize to her. Again.

"I admit that I was upset with you for insisting Mina was guilty," she said. "But the evidence *was* damning."

She smiled, offering her forgiveness, which he readily accepted. Maybe even hungrily accepted. He'd take anyone's forgiveness of his weaknesses, his mistakes, since he never forgave himself.

"Thank you, ma'am."

"Yet you trusted Miss DiPaolo's story. Why?"

"She admitted that she'd lied about seeing Platt," he said. "I've never met a criminal who willingly retracted the alibi they'd conceived. She wanted to fess up. I did trust her, and my instincts."

"Luckily for her," she replied, shifting in her chair to get more comfortable, the scent of lavender—ever-present on her clothes and in her hair—wafting over. He might be imagining the aroma, given the stink all around, but he inhaled deeply anyway. "And when you realized the handkerchief found by Dr. Harris had come from the supplies at the Institute, you reasoned that Mr. Ross had actually been the perpetrator."

"Yes, I did. Even though I was wrong, as it turned out."

"I wonder if Mr. Shaw had demanded that Miss Newcomb administer the chloroform," she said. "His daughter told me of his difficulty sleeping. Mr. Ross had refused to help, but Mary Ann was clearly persuaded."

"She decided on her own to murder Althea Wynn," he said. "No wonder she was shaking like a leaf yesterday morning when I interviewed her here. She'd just come from killing her friend."

"She'd acted out of fear, Mr. Greaves."

"A common excuse, ma'am." Not one a judge would be all that sympathetic to.

She sighed. "I suppose I should send Mr. Blanchard a contrite note, begging his pardon for nosing around in his house in search of chloroform."

Nick lifted an eyebrow. "Contrite, Mrs. Davies?"

"Apologetic, Mr. Greaves," she corrected. "For reading too much into the offhand comments of a young woman who is inadvisedly in love with the man."

"Both Miss Campbell and Miss Shaw," he said. "Even though Blanchard is married."

"Love does not always choose the wisest path, Mr. Greaves," she replied softly.

Her gaze locked on his, lingered. He clenched his jaw against the desire to jump up and gather her in his arms, forget that her husband had come back to haunt them, show her that he would never cease loving her. Instead, he resisted, and her gaze flickered away, a wistful smile on her lips. *Damn.*

"I hope Giulia DiPaolo gives up on pursuing Leonard Shaw," he said, escaping into the details of the case. Where he too often found himself. Cold comfort. "He's not worth her while. Plus, his family won't let her win. Even more so, now that he's taken charge of the bank."

"Will she be punished for her part in the crime?" asked Mrs. Davies.

"Only if Mina presses charges," he said. "And it seems unlikely Ross will be interested in accusing Miss DiPaolo of trespassing. I'm sure he wants to put all of this behind him as quickly as possible."

"No doubt," she said. "Oh, I have forgotten to tell you that I promised Owen you'd speak to his employer, who has dismissed him from his position. Please inform Mr. Roesler that Owen was acting on police business when he provided me with the list of people who'd received gifts of candy from Mr. Shaw."

"You told him I'd do that?"

She grinned wickedly. "I trust you shall be persuasive."

He laughed. "All right, I will," he said. "And you tell that Irish kid to keep away from Caleb Griffin before he finds himself in genuine trouble with the law."

"All right, I will." She stood and extended her hand. "It has been a pleasure, Mr. Greaves. Another case concluded, though I pray it is my final case. As do Barbara and Addie, I am sure."

He got to his feet and took her gloved hand, the warmth of her skin filtering through the thin crocheted cotton. He wanted to hold on forever. "I expect it won't be your final case, ma'am."

"It must be." She withdrew her hand from his grip. "I told you last time when we said goodbye that it would not be forever, Nicholas, but I was wrong to wish for an impossibility. You and I both know it is hopeless."

His head ached. His chest ached. His heart . . . ached. "What are we to do, Celia?"

"Remain friends." Her lovely pale eyes examined his face as if memorizing every line. "Good friends."

"I do suspect, ma'am, we'll see each other again."

"Take care of yourself, Nicholas," she replied sadly, sweeping from the room, leaving nothing but a whisper of the fragrance she wore behind.

• • •

"I'm sorry, Mrs. Davies." Libby Campbell held tight to her weak arm, her shoulders slumping. The wind coming up Vallejo whipped a loose strand of her hair across her cheek. "I should've told you that I gave Mr. Shaw's key to Giulia, the key Rebecca had taken from his room at the Institute. That I knew what Giulia intended to do."

"It was a dangerous plan, Miss Campbell," Celia replied, studying the other woman's face to gauge the sincerity of her apology. "A young woman I care about suffered a serious concussion because of Miss DiPaolo."

"That wasn't supposed to happen, but Giulia was in such a state after finding Mr. Shaw dead . . ." She stared out at the street. "She stopped by my place Thursday, questioning if Rebecca could have done it. I had to wonder, too, especially after Rebecca told me you'd been asking questions. I was afraid for her, for all of us, but I shouldn't have left that note."

"It came from you."

She nodded. "That was stupid of me. I hope you didn't get too scared."

"The note did alarm Addie." So many acts of subterfuge by so many people. "*Were* you with Mr. Blanchard Wednesday evening, Libby?"

She paused before answering. "I went to his house on a whim. But I saw Rebecca coming out, running down the front steps," she said. "She begged me to forget I'd seen her. So I came up with a story that might protect them both."

"Oh, Libby." Another young woman desperate for love, and searching in the wrong place. She could hardly condemn Libby's poor judgment when she herself, a married woman, had fallen in love with another man.

Miss Campbell's eyes met hers. "I've come to a decision about my employment here, Mrs. Davies," she said. "I've decided it's best I no longer continue. Given all that's happened."

"Perhaps that is the right decision," Celia replied.

Tears shimmered in her eyes. "Give Barbara my regards. She was going to be the most wonderful student."

"I shall, Miss Campbell. Best of luck to you," she said and held out her hand.

Miss Campbell briefly took it before retreating down the front steps and walking off. Inside, Addie was waiting in the entry hall, a tray with a teapot and cup in her hands.

"What has Miss Campbell to say for herself?" she asked, trailing Celia into her examination room.

"She withdrew from her position here, sadly, but not before apologizing for her role in assisting Miss DiPaolo's scheme and for being the author of that note I found. She seemed sincere," she answered. "I do not believe, though, that she feels sorry for having claimed to be with Mr. Blanchard. She loves him."

Addie tutted and set the tray on the desk. "*Weel*, that's done for, at least. And I trust you and Mrs. Hutchinson are finished with interfering in police business, ma'am."

"Addie, you are beginning to sound like Mr. Greaves," she replied, smiling. Chasing away the fleeting recollection of the look on his face when she'd bid him goodbye. "I've no further intentions of becoming involved in police business. I need to concentrate on my clinic. I have been neglecting it and my patients, of late."

"I am glad to hear you say so," said her housekeeper, pouring out some tea, its smoky aroma drifting over. Freshly brewed souchong. "I've an apple pudding planned to go with dinner tonight."

"Sounds delicious. I am famished."

Addie retreated to the kitchen, leaving Celia to enjoy the tick of the entry hall case clock, children laughing as they played on the street, Barbara calling out that she was headed to the back garden to read. *Take it all in, Celia. This is your life and it is a good one.* She must not wallow in thoughts of how it could be better.

She dragged over her stack of patients' records and began to review them. The clang of the front doorbell interrupted her.

"I'm up to my elbows in flour, ma'am," called Addie from the kitchen. "Do you need me to answer?"

"No, I shall go, Addie." Celia got up from her desk. She was not expecting a patient, but women often arrived without an appointment and she was always prepared to assist. "Finish what you are doing."

"Aye, ma'am."

Celia fixed a welcoming smile on her face and pulled open the door.

"How can I—"

The man who stood on the threshold stopped her cold.

"Hello, Celia," he said, his Irish lilt deceptively warm, his blue eyes as bright as she remembered, his broad grin, teasing. "Glad to see your old husband?"

Author's Note

I have always had a fascination with the forms of medicine practiced in history, and have often written alternate medical therapies into my books. Among all the various methods I've touched on, the water cure was relatively innocuous and its emphasis on pure water bathing and a simple diet may have even promoted healing. In 1867, there were four individuals offering the water cure in San Francisco, but by the 1880s the fad had died out in the city. By the 1890s, it had faded away in the rest of the country as well.

In this series, I have also occasionally alluded to the fallout from the Civil War, not just as it affects Nick. The September 1867 state elections saw unexpected losses for Lincoln's Republican party in several races, not just California's. The fight to ratify the 14th Amendment, which would provide citizenship to anyone born in the U.S., had stirred animosity among Americans who felt threatened by the prospect of former slaves becoming equals. Californians dreaded the possibility that Chinese people born in America might also become citizens, and folks rallied to vote and show their opposition. Despite their success in 1867, the 14th Amendment would be passed in 1868 and the national election for president would see Republican U. S. Grant elected that same year. In 1870, the 15th Amendment would grant every citizen the right to vote, including former slaves. But not women. That right would be another fifty years in the making.

ABOUT THE AUTHOR

Nancy Herriman left an engineering career to take up the pen and has never looked back. She is the author of the Mysteries of Old San Francisco, the Bess Ellyott Mysteries, and several stand-alone novels. A winner of the Daphne du Maurier Award, when she's not writing, she enjoys singing, gabbing about writing, and eating dark chocolate. After two decades in Arizona, she now lives in her home state of Ohio with her family.